Baby Farm

DEBBIE TERRANOVA

Published by Terranova Publications 2014
Revised 2018
PO Box 4144, St Lucia South, Queensland 4067 Australia
Email: terranovapublications@gmail.com

ISBN-13: 978-0-9941700-0-2

Cover design by Rosetta Lake Mills
www.rosettalakemills.com

For Sam, Elise and Adam

1

Tuesday, 18ᵗʰ February

He was back. Steptoe. The rag and bone man whose life story was a question mark. Unmistakable in the same khaki greatcoat, scarlet beanie, and football shorts that he wore summer and winter alike. The coat was unbuttoned, the only concession to the heat of the morning. It flapped about his hairy legs like flying fox wings.

From the front seat of the taxi, Vann watched him lumber up the hill.

Today he carried a grubby green shopping bag, the reusable type you'd get for a dollar from the supermarket to save the planet. Steptoe wouldn't use it to take the groceries home. For him it would be a blanket, or a rain hat, or a groundsheet, or a container for an arsenal of scrap metal. Everything had a vast array of uses. Today's effort must have been heavy, for he held the bulging bundle with both arms against his chest.

His progress through the morning crowd was erratic. In the crush around the railway station everyone conformed to unspoken laws. Like sheep, they followed the leader down the ramp to the platform. They kept to the left—always to the left—the same side as the traffic on the road.

But not Steptoe.

Whatever was on his mind—*if* there was anything on his mind—blinded him to the customs of the flock. People flowed around him as if he was a tree stump in a stream. Except he pushed against them, bumping them away without the usual muttered *sorry* that was part of the etiquette.

Just as the taxi found a space to turn from the driveway onto the road, Steptoe reached the external stairs of the electorate office.

Vann Willis MP Member for Riverdale, the sign read. Beneath in smaller letters, *Minister for Communities*.

As he laboured up the steps, Vann caught a glimpse of his determined expression. His eyes were focussed on the glass door at the top as if nothing would get in his way. What did he want this time? A tremor of foreboding rippled through her mind. For a moment she considered telling the taxi driver to stop so that she could nip whatever it was in the bud. But she was already cutting it fine for an important meeting in town.

She sighed and turned her attention to the papers she'd prepared. In half an hour she would be centre stage for ten precious minutes. In that short time, she would have to sell her proposal to the Premier and her Party colleagues. Compensation for the victims of forced adoptions. She had been chipping away at the 'elephant in the room' ever since she'd gone into politics long ago. Recently she had made progress on the tail of a senate enquiry and a royal commission into other unmentionables such as the treatment of children in orphanages and paedophilia by clergymen.

There was also a down side. Her worthy cause came with a price tag. Sadly, there were no hidden buckets of money in government coffers. Seven years after a global financial crisis triggered a spree of altruistic spending, a dark cloud of austerity had settled over the state budget. It would have been easier to let matters slide, but an election promise was still a promise. For many reasons she was determined to keep it.

The line of traffic outside her office had not moved. Cars were honking a P-plate driver who'd broken down at the lights. With the papers for the meeting on her lap, Vann reached into her satchel for reading glasses. Then she remembered they were sitting on her desk. Holding the page at arm's length did nothing to stop the print from going blurry. Her presentation would be impossible without them.

She glanced at the screen on her phone. Big bold numerals showed it was 9:07 a.m. The traffic was gridlocked. Over the course of five minutes the taxi had gone exactly nowhere. She touched the number for her office.

Freya's bright voice answered, professional as always.

Vann said, 'Can you get my glasses? I'm outside, stuck in traffic.'

'James already noticed them. He's bringing them down.'

'There he is!' Vann waved to her young policy advisor as he trotted toward the taxi. He was smiling, teeth impeccably white, eyes so blue you could swim in them. At twenty-seven he oozed confidence and ambition. If only she were his age again!

Freya's voice dropped to a whisper. 'By the way, Steptoe is here.'

Vann sighed. Of course he was there. Again.

'Oh, and a package just came. Marked to you. Personal,' said Freya.

'It's probably sales stuff. I'll get it later. What does Steptoe want?'

James and the reading glasses had almost reached the taxi.

Freya breathed into the phone. 'I don't know. He's behaving kind of strange. It's as if——'

KA-BOOM!

The explosion rocked the taxi, banging Vann's head against the door.

'Holy crap!' yelled James as he dived for cover.

Glass shards pelted the bonnet like hail. Down the concrete staircase rolled a thunderous cloud of smoke.

Vann's jaw dropped, her eyes glued to the awful spectacle. One minute her office was there; the next it was a raging ball of fire. Surreal, fascinating, incredible. Like seeing footage of the planes slamming into the World Trade Centre all over again. Over the years she must have seen it a hundred times and still it was impossible to believe.

Suddenly she remembered the half-finished conversation with Freya. She lifted the phone to her ear. 'Freya?'

No reply.

'Freya. Can you hear me? Freya!'

The connection was dead. Bile rose up Vann's throat. For a moment she thought she might be sick. Then, swallowing hard, she managed to muster her courage.

Flinging open the cab door, she raced toward the churning smoke. Somewhere inside that mess was Freya, her friend and confidante. This could not be happening! It must be a terrible dream.

Flames licked the entrance to the building. Smoke stung her eyes, burnt her nostrils, filled her lungs. Unable to get within fifteen metres of the place, she retreated to the taxi. Powerless, she could do nothing but hope and pray.

Standing beside her, James was on the phone to the emergency services. In an even voice, he described what had happened and gave the address in Riverdale.

How could he be so calm? His life had been saved by a pair of spectacles. One minute later and he might have been dead. Just like ...

The cacophony of car horns, alarms, sirens, the crackle and crash of fire converged into one chaotic roar. The upper floor of the two-story office block was now alight. Flames lapped the adjoining structure. People scattered like crazy ants. Some who had been struck by glass or debris lay moaning on the ground. Everywhere there was blood.

Numb and sickened, Vann leant against the vehicle. The driver was pacing around the cab, examining the damage to the paintwork. He shook his head and made tutting noises, as if a few dents were the major catastrophe of the day.

A high scream snapped Vann out of her stupor.

The clouds of smoke momentarily parted. Writhing on the staircase was a woman of about forty. Her blouse and skirt were covered in blood. A yellow handbag lay close by, its contents scattered like confetti across the pavement.

Her face was glistening with shards of glass. She began to convulse.

Vann baulked at the sight of all that blood. Then adrenalin kicked in. Swallowing her revulsion, she forced herself on.

The woman reached out her hand.

Vann held it, cold and slimy as a fish.

The woman's breathing became shallow. She was slipping in and out of consciousness.

Vann squatted beside her. 'You're okay, honey.' Her stomach was knotted but her voice was calm.

On the pocket of the blouse was a nametag. *Lara.*

'Lara,' said Vann. 'Can you hear me?'

The eyelids lifted slightly then closed.

'Lara, stay with me.'

The air was thick with a metallic stench. Another wave of nausea rolled over and away. Vann focussed on holding Lara's slimy red hand. The nails were neat and natural; there were no rings. It was the hand of an office worker or a teacher or a librarian. A lover of books, like herself.

'You're okay. You're okay.' Vann repeated the mantra again and again. But in her mind she was screaming *where the hell's the ambulance?* Hot flushes shot up her neck. Her heart was racing.

Only last week the Minister for Health had bragged in Parliament about *his* world-standard emergency callout times. She had a good mind to ring the idiot and tell him exactly what he could do with *his* statistics.

After what seemed like an eternity, the howl of sirens cut through the confusion. Two fire appliances roared onto the footpath. Men in helmets and protective clothing unrolled and fitted hoses. Jets of water gushed into the core of the blaze.

Meanwhile the grip on Vann's hand was loosening. She shook Lara's arms in an effort to keep her awake. That's what they did on TV medical dramas. With no first aid training, it was all Vann had to work with.

An ambulance siren. Finally! She waved to get their attention.

Paramedics came and eased the limp form onto a stretcher. Vann scooped up cosmetics, cards, keys, coins from the footpath, replaced them in the yellow leather handbag. It was an expensive brand. Mimco.

She zipped it shut and put it in the back of the ambulance near the stretcher. 'See you soon, honey.'

'Are you a relative?' asked the paramedic.

'Just a friend. Where will you take her?'

'The Royal if we can get in.'

'Please look after her.'

The paramedic gave her a reassuring smile. 'Of course we will.'

Lights flashing and sirens wailing, the ambulance sped away.

Vann glanced at the screen of her phone. Less than an hour had passed since the world turned upside down. A smoking ruin was where her office used to be. And Freya ... she blocked the thought before it could fully form.

Blue-and-white police tape criss-crossed the footpath, marking the boundary between the crime scene and the zoo. Calamities always attracted a motley audience of stickybeaks and do-gooders.

A two-man team from Channel Six News had set up. The reporter, in standard attire of faded jeans and smart navy jacket, was positioned so that the smouldering building was the background. He was interviewing an eyewitness, a young man with short blond hair and a slim black suit.

Vann gazed beyond them at the shell of steel and concrete. It could have been her who'd taken the brunt of a madman's plot. No, it *should* have been her. Something she had said or done must have made Steptoe snap. She rolled back her memory.

Several months ago, before he last disappeared, Steptoe had gone to her for help. He was facing eviction from the ramshackle boarding house he called home, so she'd gone to see the landlord on his behalf.

What she'd found had shocked her. In the backyard was a collection of junk that dwarfed the Willawong dump. Tyres, bicycle frames, ancient fridges, rusty paint tins, machine parts, roofing iron, cracked TV screens, garden gnomes, curls of chicken wire, a wooden ladder with three missing rungs, PVC pipes. Black plastic bags that oozed foul juices. God only knew what they contained and Vann had no inclination to find out.

Somehow she had convinced him to clean it up. He wasn't happy and he told her so. Despite his protests, she arranged for a man to cart it away and paid for it from her own wallet. It was a wonder the Council hadn't condemned the place. Reluctantly the landlord agreed to let Steptoe stay, on the proviso that he stopped bringing home other people's rubbish.

For all her trouble, he did a disappearing act soon afterwards and hadn't resurfaced until this morning.

She should have followed him up, kept a better eye on him. She had no idea where he had gone or why. Perhaps he bore her a grudge for taking away his hoard. For, just like his namesake in the vintage British comedy series, the items he acquired were treasured like family heirlooms.

Whatever his movements had been, she should have been more alert. In hindsight, he had been a ticking time bomb. And now, along with his own troubled self, he'd wiped out at least one other soul.

Vann's attention returned to the TV reporter who was babbling on. Actually, he was grilling the interviewee about the upcoming election. Since when did an eyewitness to a catastrophe become an expert in politics? It was all a bit bizarre. The blond man answering the questions had his back was towards her, but his voice was oddly familiar.

Then it came to her. He was Jake Stone, political rival and endorsed candidate for the People's Progressive Party (PPP). The young upstart was criticising her for ignoring the plight of a homeless man and neglecting her constituents in the pursuit of power.

The very hide of him! Point-scoring at a terrible time like this!

Seething, she balled her fists and took a step in his direction. She was smart enough to know that retaliation would make her look foolish but was too rattled to care.

Before she could open her mouth, a deep voice as smooth as chocolate floated across the crowd.

'Ms Willis, can I have a word?'

She spun around. It was *him* again. Her heart skipped a beat.

'Seth VerBeek, what are you doing here?' she said a little too sharply.

He was a senior reporter from *The Morning Post*. New to this city but not to the media, he'd established his career covering war zones in Europe and the Middle East for a Sydney newspaper. His craggy appearance suggested a man who enjoyed a drink. His reputation as a ladies' man was the worst-kept secret in town. Despite this, his articles were well researched, insightful and even-handed. Besides, he was so easy going it was hard to not like him.

He sidled towards her. 'Good Lord,' he said frowning. 'Look at the state you're in!'

She looked down at her shoes, her skirt, her blouse. She could have passed as an axe murderer. The crisis had passed but the bloody evidence remained. In fact, it was all over her. Until now she'd managed to keep herself more or less in check. She began to shiver. Unexpected tears rolled down her cheeks.

He took her arm, guided her to a quiet corner by the garden wall. Like a gentleman he offered her a clean hanky.

Gratefully she accepted it, cleaned her fingers and blew her nose. 'Thanks, I'll wash it and send it back.'

'Keep it. I'm just glad you're okay.' He sounded genuine. After dipping into his pocket, he rattled a tin of Eclipse mints. 'Can I tempt you?'

The corners of her lips lifted. 'Perhaps another time.' Her mouth was as dry as the Simpson Desert. What she really needed was a good stiff Scotch. On the rocks. Double shot.

He tossed two mint pellets into his mouth. 'You want to tell me about it?' Casually he leant against the wall. 'Off the record of course.'

Vann gnawed her lip, trying to stop trembling. 'I was on my way to town.' With renewed disbelief she stared at the dismal scene and wracked her brain for answers. 'That bomb … it was meant for me.'

'Whoever would do such a thing?' Seth stroked his chin and followed her line of sight to the skeleton of the building.

She looked down at her palms. The creases—the life line, the heart line, the head line—were marked out in dried blood. She rubbed them together and brushed off the sticky red rolls. 'I have no idea.'

In her mind there was only one suspect. But before she exposed him, she had to make sure. Dead, as he most certainly was, he was no longer a threat to anyone.

People never ceased to amaze her, even those she knew and trusted. That was why she loved her work. Her community programs tapped into the vagaries of human nature and sought to mend broken lives. Sometimes they worked, which gave her joy. When they didn't, she rationalised them as *learning opportunities* and moved on. Steptoe was one big learning opportunity. One day he'd be as lucid as a professor, the next he'd be a mumbling idiot. Yet despite his mood swings and curious behaviour, she'd never picked him as a violent type.

One burning question haunted her. Why?

'Thanks for the moral support,' she said to Seth. 'And for the hanky.' Her self-control returned. Without it she'd never have survived a lifetime in the dirty game of politics.

The TV spotlight swept over the crowd and found her hidey hole. The reporter in the jacket was metres away, the cameraman close behind.

'Minister, was this a terrorist attack?' The reporter shoved the microphone under her nose. The scent of cheap aftershave tickled her nose.

With a stern expression, she held up her hands to stop. 'Not a word unless you show respect. I don't want this to look like a bloodbath.'

The reporter nodded his assent. The cameraman repositioned himself to get headshots only. The question about terrorism was repeated.

She looked directly into the camera. 'We'll have to see what the investigators come up with. In the meantime, I appeal to anyone with information to contact the police. My deepest sympathy goes to the victims and their families.' Her voice was steady, unemotional.

'Was your office specifically targeted?'

'Aren't you jumping to conclusions? For all we know, the explosion might have been caused by a gas leak.'

'Is it true you've received death threats?'

'People threaten me all the time. It comes with the job.'

'Witnesses say they saw a man in an overcoat just before the blast.'

'Perhaps they should tell that to the investigators. Now, you must excuse me.'

Outside Café Nero on the other side of Station Road, James was talking to a sergeant of police. Vann threaded her way between vehicles that jammed the roadway. An ambulance was parked across the footpath. At the foot of the stairs, paramedics waited for casualties who might come out alive. The building released a final puff of smoke. Fire fighters began to hack their way in.

'Any news about Freya Ekeberg?' Vann asked the police sergeant. She tried to sound upbeat but in her heart she knew.

'It doesn't look good, I'm afraid.'

Vann nodded. 'Has anyone called her family?' Her lips pressed into a narrow line.

James answered. 'Yeah, worst thing I've ever had to do.'

Against her will, tears again filled her eyes.

Usually James was as unemotional as a hit man in Tomb Raider. To her utter amazement, he opened his arms and drew her into his broad chest. She allowed herself the luxury of one giant sob, then she realised that he too was weeping.

As quickly as he had lost it, he pulled himself together. 'Leave this to me. You should clean up and go to that meeting in town. If you don't, you'll probably regret it.'

Before she could protest, he was on his phone for another taxi.

He was right. She needed to go. If she stayed, she'd only wallow in grief and self-pity and that would achieve nothing. The cabinet session would have long begun and it was a meeting she could ill afford to miss. If she was ever to get support for her proposed *Compensation for the Victims of Forced Adoptions Bill*, it was now. This would be the Holy Grail, the most important achievement of her career. The time was right, the mood was right. All the excruciating evidence had been unearthed, raked over, scrutinised *ad nauseam*. Money for the victims might help wash away their pain.

The taxi arrived. As was her habit, she sat in the front. Egalitarian society, she liked to argue. As the cab turned onto the road, she wound down the window and called out to James. 'I want to visit everyone who was hurt. Get their names and details.'

Again, the shockwaves ripped through her. She was glad of Seth's hanky, which she used to daub her eyes.

'Tough day, luv?' said the cab driver.

'The worst!' The finality of her statement shut down any further conversation. She was free to process her thoughts.

Today's events happened in other countries. International news was full of violence and bloodshed: the Bali bombings, 9/11 in New York, a passenger jet shot down over the Ukraine. No-one did those things in sleepy suburban Riverdale. Who was Steptoe really? The label *suicide bomber* didn't sit comfortably on his shoulders.

At her apartment, Vann quickly showered and changed into a cream suit. In the taxi again, her mobile phone showed two missed calls and three text messages. All were from Lance, her partner. She pictured him in the restaurant he owned with his brother in Paddington. He'd be wearing a white chef's cap, hounds-tooth trousers and black shirt. This time of day he'd be prepping for lunch. She pressed the recall button.

He answered at the first rang. 'Are you hurt, baby? I heard about it on the radio.' There was a quiver in his voice. In the background was the sizzle of a frying pan.

'I'm fine. Can't say the same for Freya though.' Tears again. If she wasn't careful she'd ruin her makeup. There'd be plenty of time for grief tonight, when she was alone in the apartment and Lance was on dinner shift at the restaurant.

At the end of their brief exchange he said, 'Why don't you give this away? We could get that farm at Maleny and enjoy life instead.'

She snapped back, 'I can't. There's a big job to do, and no-one to do it but me.'

'Then you're a misguided egotist!' he shouted and ended the call.

That didn't go as expected. Feeling peeved, she slouched in the seat. The line of jacaranda trees along Coro Drive blurred together as the taxi kept pace with a downstream ferry, laden with students and tourists. On the front deck, a man was taking snaps of his wife and kids against the jagged silhouette of city high-rises. Happy and carefree they seemed, unaware of the horrors of this smouldering summer's morning.

The road spilled into North Quay and the traffic lights lined up green. Vann had five minutes to concentrate on her pitch before entering the dog-eat-dog arena. No doubt the Premier and her colleagues would have heard the shocking news. For a few minutes they'd express support and sympathy. Then they'd debate their policy platform and strategies for the election soon to be announced. The Australian Conservative Party (ACP) needed to get it right, for the balance of power in government rested on the votes of two unlikely independents. The latest public opinion polls showed increased support for the dreaded PPP. If that young upstart Jake Stone were to be elected instead of her, she would never live it down.

At six o'clock in the evening, after many exhausting hours of debate and lengthy briefings, Vann headed to the Royal Hospital to fulfil a promise of a non-political kind. The air was thick with humidity, the twilight clouds glowed bilious yellow, the sign of a brewing storm. Her energy reserve was bordering on empty.

At the desk she asked about the three bombing casualties by name. As usual James had done a thorough job of research. Not only had he emailed her their names but also their home addresses and phone numbers.

'Lara Dainford is in ward 5F. Her condition is stable,' said the receptionist.

From the gift shop Vann bought three bunches of colourful gerberas, put on a bright face and navigated the labyrinth of polished lino and stark fluorescent lights to Ward 5F. The nurses' station was unoccupied, so she sat in the drab grey waiting area for someone to come.

Her only experience of institutions like this had been more than forty years ago, when she'd spent five miserable months in a dorm with nineteen girls. Often she'd wake in the night to the sound of her own weeping. Sensible shoes would click on the floorboards, a hard shadow would fall across her bed.

'Why aren't you asleep like the others?' the old bitch would snarl.

'I can't sleep in this place.'

'It's your own fault you are here. So shut up and don't be a cry-baby.'

Vann shuddered at the memory.

With no nurses in sight, she picked her way along the length of the corridor, checking bed numbers as she went, until she reached the cubicle at the end.

The shoebox was shared by six patients, separated by lime-milkshake coloured curtains, suspended from the ceiling. In the bed closest to the door was Lara, sound asleep on her back with her hands folded across her chest. She wore a primrose hospital-issue nightie. Her chestnut hair was tied back from her face, revealing a line of salt-and-pepper regrowth. Her face was a patchwork of dressings. Tubes and drip-lines attached her to the medical hardware on the wall. On the bedside table was a magnificent bouquet of pink roses and carnations.

For a few minutes Vann stood at the end of the bed and watched the rise and fall of Lara's chest. She was obviously knocked out with strong painkillers. Vann arranged the gerberas in a jar of water and scribbled 'get well soon' on the back of her business card.

The card on the big bouquet was tantalisingly under her nose. Like a thief she glanced around. The coast clear, she lifted it from the plastic holder and turned it over.

Dear Lara,

Hope you make a quick recovery. Best wishes always.

Jake Stone, your next Member for Riverdale.

Vann's mouth fell open. Over her dead body! Bring it on. This was war.

The thought crossed her mind to swap the cards. Against the starburst of delicate pinks, her straggly gerberas looked limp and garish. No-one was looking and Lara was off on another planet. Did she dare?

After making the rounds of the other casualties, who also had spectacular floral tributes from Jake Stone, she hailed a cab outside the hospital. Lightning cracked over the western ranges, the air was crisp with the scent of coming hail.

Her last appointment at the Ekeberg residence was going to be tough. The inner strength that had powered her through the day was spent. The thought of the usual taxi-driver chat about the state of the economy or the cricket scores was enough to make her brain snap, so she slid into the back seat where she could quietly lick her wounds and think.

On any other morning Freya would have been at Café Nero for the office coffee order. Skinny flat whites all round. James would have been answering emails at his desk. Vann would have been on a teleconference in her private office instead of *en route* to a Party meeting in town. The tables would have been turned.

That bomb was meant for her. Of that, she was sure.

Why would Steptoe want to kill her? Granted he was as unpredictable as a cut snake but he wasn't a psychopath. Was he acting as someone's puppet? Someone who wanted her dead.

The taxi wove along Gympie Road, dodging buses and road works that never seemed to end. Lightning flashed like strobe lights, rendering the neon signs of the shopping strip dim. Her head throbbed, her eyes stung. Her handbag was stuffed with dozens of soggy tissues and one blood-stained hanky.

Maybe she should take Lance's advice and called it quits before the election. Retirement might have its benefits. For one, long nights of carefree sleep.

The cab dropped her at a modest weatherboard house with striped metal awnings. A coach lamp on the wall lit up the foliage of a blossoming Murraya bush. Its cloying sweet perfume triggered a rush of sneezes.

An icy gust propelled her through the gate. Hard rain smashed onto the path. Holding her handbag like an umbrella, she raced to the porch. The sounds of grief spilled through the doorway. Inside, human shadows moved about slowly.

She knocked.

A middle-aged woman came. Big breasts, fair hair, upturned nose. An exact replica of Freya, only older.

'Mrs Ekeberg?' said Vann.

'No. I'm Hanna, her cousin. Poor Hilda's in a bad way. Losing an only daughter like that. So horribly utterly dreadful …'

She howled for a moment, then mopped her face with a tea towel. 'Please excuse me, Ms Willis. I'm a bit upset. Do come in.'

Vann followed her into an old-fashioned living room where she met

Freya's parents, two elderly aunts, and one dog. She sat in a floral armchair and listened through three cups of tea to stories about their beautiful girl. Inside, her heart was breaking, but she remained calm and strong for the sake of the family.

From its perch above the TV, a cuckoo clock announced the passage of an hour. Her head was as light as a balloon and her bladder was full of tea. When the taxi tooted, she hugged them all goodbye (even the dog) and promised to see them at the funeral.

The thunder storm had cleared, leaving the rich scent of moist earth. The city was washed clean. She inhaled, held the fresh air in her lungs like a drug, felt in its restorative powers a new sense of wellbeing. The cab rolled around the bends of Route 20 to Riverdale in the west.

Her tenth-floor apartment was exactly as she'd left it. Breakfast dishes in the sink, ironing in the basket, piles of papers on her desk. So cosy, so familiar. Yet, in that short space of time since this morning, her entire life had changed.

Vann poured herself a long-awaited Scotch and soda, turned off the lights, and sank into an easychair on the balcony. The first hit of alcohol took away her breath. She swallowed it like medicine, felt its warmth flow through her veins. As she nestled into the cushions, her eyes drifted across the nightscape. To the east was a forest of lights, sprinkled here and there with patches of dark foliage. To the west the suburbs petered out at the humped backbone of the ranges. Somewhere, in that vast twinkling curve, there must be an answer.

As she dozed in the chair, the kitchen light came on. She jumped up, the whisky glass rolled off her lap and broke on the tiles.

With her heart in her mouth she hissed, 'Who is it?'

'Only me.' Lance.

'You scared the shit out of me.'

'Thought you'd be in bed.'

She squatted and picked up the pieces of glass. The aftertaste of the Scotch was rough in her mouth.

He bent over as if to help but kissed her forehead instead.

'Ooow, that hurts.' She felt about the hairline and found a plum-sized lump where she'd hit her head on the taxi door. She leant in to him and breathed the heady scents of pasta sauce, garlic, and red wine that had seeped into his clothes.

'Sorry I didn't get home sooner. We were busy tonight.' He ambled to the kitchen and opened the pantry. 'A supremely shitty day all round.'

She wrapped the broken glass in newspaper and dumped it in the bin beneath the sink. The stink of last night's cabbage and pork bones reminded her to take the garbage out to the chute. By the time she came back, he'd made two cups of camomile tea with honey and lemon, and a toasted cheese sandwich.

'You want to talk?' he said.

Before she could stop herself, every sordid detail came tumbling out. 'I can't believe what happened. I saw it with my own eyes and I still can't believe it.'

'You were good on TV. Came across calm and sensible.'

'You know me. Always in control.' She gave a tight smile. 'Nevertheless, it should have been me in the morgue today.'

Lance squeezed her hand. 'I'm glad it isn't.'

Across the kitchen bench they embraced. Over the ten years they'd been together, their lives had become as comfy and sexless as old slippers.

Vann pulled away. 'I saw him from the taxi. I know who he was.'

'Did you tell the cops?'

She raked her fingers through her hair. 'What good would it do? Poor bastard's dead.'

'He tried to kill you and you're sorry for him?'

'Normally the man wouldn't hurt a fly.'

'So, who is this *harmless* murderer?'

'We knew him as Steptoe. You know, from the sixties TV comedy.'

'I lived out west, remember? No TV.'

'He collected old junk and castoffs but never sold a thing.'

'Why would this Steptoe fellow want to blow you up?'

She shook her head. 'I don't know but I intend to find out. He surely wouldn't have acted on his own. There must be another person behind it.'

'Then go to the police.'

'I will when I've worked it out. It could be some sort of political protest against our policies, or the budget cuts, or the job losses. Some people will stop at nothing to prove a point.'

Lance grasped her wrists and pulled her to him. He looked her straight in the eye. 'Are you sure you want to go through with this election? You don't have to. We have enough money. I don't want you to get hurt.'

'We've been over this many times. One more term. I can't let it go. There's too much to be done. The report from the Commission of Inquiry is due in a week.'

She gasped. 'Oh my God. That's it! Who's going to be exposed?'

Her mind was in overdrive, churning through the events and the individuals who'd come forward since the adoption inquiry first began. Nothing stood out, nothing made sense.

'What if you're wrong? What if it's a terrorist cell?' he said.

'You've been reading Jeffrey Archer novels again.' She flashed a wan smile.

He kneaded her shoulders. 'Your muscles are as tight as steel cables.'

Starting to relax, she turned to him.

He kissed her mouth, lifted her blouse, unclipped her bra, cupped her breasts in his warm hands.

It felt so good. She melted into him, sighed. It'd been a long time.

Then, like a lover in a trashy paperback novel, he scooped her into his arms and carried her to their bed.

2

Tuesday 18 February

The midmorning news was packed with stories about the Riverdale bombing, including pictures by Seth VerBeek of *The Morning Post,* who was first on the crime scene. At three o'clock the police released CCTV footage of the man in the overcoat to the media and appealed to the public for information.

In his cubicle at Newspaper House, Seth examined the grainy images on his computer screen. He was searching for a hook on which to hang an investigation of his own. Good journalists always looked for ways to beat the police at their own game, to find the one piece of overlooked evidence that would make an explosive story. Already he'd been to the hospital to interview the casualties, and he had tasked his researcher with obtaining whatever background information she could find.

At this stage Seth had little to go on, apart from an interesting observation made when he had spoken to Vann Willis at the scene. Despite having seen the alleged assassin from a relatively short distance, she *claimed* she had no idea of who he was. Yet the way she had said it planted a seed of doubt. Was she hiding something?

He sucked the end of his biro and replayed the events in his head. It was possible the bombing was a protest. Vann Willis was a political leader, a Minister with responsibility for a string of agencies and programs focused on people whose lives were damaged. Her department dealt with issues of mental illness and homelessness, helped people in crisis or who were disconnected from their families. Something had pushed the wrong buttons and the overcoat man had snapped.

The evening deadline was an hour away and Seth had to work fast. He phoned his police contact—Dave Frame of the Criminal Investigations Branch—ostensibly about using a still shot from the CCTV that showed the bomber as he turned at the top of the steps. His face was partly shadowed, but the picture was clear enough for a friend or relative to recognise.

'Any developments on the Riverdale bombing?' he said. 'Any nice titbits that will bring me fame and fortune?'

'When there are, you'll be the first to know. And I expect likewise.' The detective's emphasis was on the last sentence.

'Davo, you drive a hard bargain.'

Dave Frame laughed. 'And you, my friend, are a hard case.'

Seth wrote a graphic piece about the chaos of the scene and focussed on the vignette of the woman with horrific glass injuries being comforted by the Minister for Communities. The candid image of the pair that he caught on his phone wouldn't win any prizes for photojournalism, but it showed the agony of the moment when mild suburban Riverdale became as racy as New York City.

He signed off the article with his contact details at the newspaper and asked readers to phone or email him with information. In the past this had worked. Witnesses often talked to journalists in preference to the cops.

The article appeared on page three of Wednesday's edition. By mid-afternoon, when Seth returned to the office after a callout to an ugly incident between a chicken farmer and a group of RSPCA activists, he had fifty-three emails. He boiled the jug for coffee and settled into the faux-leather office chair to read his inbox.

Half the messages were about the bombing article. As he'd found in a lifetime of newspaper work, those who write to the editor generally have extreme and passionate views. Today's haul was no exception. There was a mix of snappy two-liners and tirades that rolled on and on like the end credits of a disaster movie. Most offered their sympathy to the victims; one blamed Minister Willis for her 'short-sighted penny-pinching attitude to child protection'; one pointed the finger at Al-Qaeda but gave no evidence in support. One, signed Older and Wiser, put the blame squarely on 'drug-addicted dole bludgers'.

Not one useful lead. What a waste of time!

As he finished, another email pinged into the inbox. It was from The Prophet, founder of The Miraculous Flock of Christ.

According to the Holy Scriptures, this heralds the Second Coming of our Lord. He is risen! He will unleash His wrath on our land and our people so that we might pay for the decadence and inequalities spawned by the corrupt capitalist state.

Seth whistled and rolled back the chair. Where did these people come from? He pressed his shoulder blade at the achy spot, a war wound sustained from long hours battling a computer. His tendons felt like knotted rope. He kneaded the place until the spasm released, then cracked his neck for good measure. Investigative journalism was never easy. Acts of extreme violence brought out the loonies as surely as the full moon.

He closed the inbox and began writing the story about the chicken farmer. It didn't come easily, for his mind wasn't on the job. He stood up, stretched, looked about the office at his colleagues who were banging their keyboards with purpose and intent. The collective din sounded like a skirmish of machine guns.

Everyone was on edge. The deadline for tomorrow's edition loomed.

His editor, who was usually a patient man, relieved his angst by yelling at the new grad. 'You've totally fucked this up! Don't they teach you anything at uni?'

Under his breath Seth swore. The curser winked accusingly at him. The screen was white and blank. He rested his fingertips on the keyboard, closed his eyes and began to touch-type. Words became sentences, sentences became paragraphs. He didn't stop until it was done.

Before he packed up for the night, he reopened his inbox and found yet another string of messages. He prepared a standard thankyou response which he sent to all the sympathy-givers, chest-beaters, and religious zealots. As he shut down the computer, the phone on his desk began to ring.

'Are you the bloke that wrote about the bomb at Riverdale?' Although strong and clear, it was not the voice of a young man.

'Sure am.' Seth automatically flipped his notebook to a fresh page and poised the biro. *Get it down, get it all down. In black and white. Don't rely on memory.* That was the drill all those years ago, and that's how he'd operated since.

'That picture in the paper, I might know who it is. I'm not one hundred percent sure, an' I don't want to cause strife if I'm not.'

'Have you spoken to the police?'

'Not in yer life. I want to talk to *you*.'

'Can you give me any names?'

'I will if I can see you face to face. You can't be too careful these days. Someone might've tapped the phones. They could be listenin' in right now.'

'Do you want to come here or would you rather meet somewhere else?'

'What about the Brekkie Creek Hotel. Ten tomorrow?'

'How will I recognise you?'

'I'll wear me red shirt. See you in the public bar. Come alone.'

Before Seth could ask more questions, the line went dead. He checked the received-calls log and was not surprised it showed *private number*. No call-backs possible.

What was there to lose? Good information sometimes came from unlikely sources. An ageing bar-fly just might recognise a madman who liked to wear an army coat in the scorching heat. He scribbled the appointment time in his diary before heading to the car and the crawl home through peak-hour traffic.

Thursday morning at ten sharp Seth pulled into the parking area at the rear of the Breakfast Creek Hotel. He'd been there once before in the late nineteen eighties when he was a young reporter for the *Sydney Sun*.

He and his boss were in town to cover the Fitzgerald Inquiry into police corruption. They'd gone to the Brekkie Creek for one of their world-famous steaks and a several pots of XXXX beer, served ice-cold and straight off the wood. In an alcohol haze he'd dozed through the entire afternoon's proceedings and not taken a single note. His boss was not impressed, and he'd very nearly lost his job.

In all those years the quaint red brick pub hadn't changed at all. He made his way to the beer garden, hunkered under a white sail that overlooked the car park, and then wove between the empty tables and chairs to the central corridor. Inside the old building, shafts of morning sunlight slanted through the front windows, bathing the vast public bar in golden light. The glossy tiles and painted tongue-in-groove walls sparkled.

Slouched on a stool at the island bar was a weather-worn man in a red checked shirt. The foam on his beer brimmed over the top of the glass and oozed down the side onto a yellow bar towel.

Seth raised his eyebrows.

The man said, 'You that reporter bloke?'

'Seth VerBeek. Pleased to meet you, Mister …?' He extended his hand.

'Porter. Call me Charlie.' The skin of his hand was as rough as a bag of oyster shells. He raised his beer and downed three quarters of it in one swallow. 'First one o' the day doesn't touch the sides.'

Seth ordered a schooner for Charlie and a pot for himself. He wished him *bottoms up* and gingerly took a sip, knowing his stomach would convert it straight to acid. What he yearned for was a coffee, black and strong. But he dared not risk losing a potential informant who was obviously wedded to the grog. Experience had given him the nose of a bloodhound for a story.

'I suppose I better tell you what I know,' said Charlie.

'That's why I came.'

'Promise you'll tell the story right? No cock-ups or nothin'. I don't want me name in it neither.'

'It's a deal.'

'Okay, here goes. That bloke in the picture is me son.' Charlie paused to down the rest of the beer and to check the effect of this revelation on Seth. 'I should say, he *was* me son.' Moisture misted his rheumy eyes.

Seth glanced away, studied the chorus line of red-and-gold Xs doing a can-can across the bar towel. The day had scarcely started and the old man was already 'tired and emotional'.

'Yeah, his name was Bertram … we called 'im Bertie. Lovely kid but as thick as two short planks. Couldn't help it. He was born like that I expect. Wasn't his fault his mother was a whore.'

Seth took a sip of beer and sighed. He could tell this would be the start of an awkward family saga and he'd have to stay until the end. 'Are you sure it's him?'

'Of course I'm sure! I've known 'im all his life.'

'Why would he go to see the Minister for Communities?'

'I'll get to that if you give me a chance.'

'Okay. No more interruptions. You want another beer?'

Charlie nodded vigorously. Two frothy glasses appeared on the counter. Charlie made a lunge for the larger one.

'Now, where was I? Truth to tell, I'm not Bertie's real father. I dunno who he was. I dunno that his real mother knew neither.

'You see, me missus—bless her soul—wanted a kid right from the start. We tried for a couple of years but for whatever reason nothin' happened. She went into this funk. Cried and cried. So we put ourselves on the waiting list to adopt. She was that excited she wanted to go straight out and buy baby clothes. Just as well I stopped her.

'A year went by. Then out of the blue came this phone call. "Your little boy's here, ready and waiting. Come and get him tomorrow at three."

'He was two and a half and a lively little chap. Even though he had that dark look about him, we took 'im in and loved 'im like our own. At school he wasn't the brightest spark in the bonfire. But what good's an education when you gotta earn a living? As soon as he turned fifteen, I got 'im a job with a builder bloke I knew. He picked that up real quick. Before I knew it, he was earning more than me. He had that much money, he didn't know what to do with it.

'Then, out of thin air, came 'is real mother. Turned up on the doorstep one Friday afternoon. Bonita, she called herself. I never found out her last name.

'That woman was trouble. You could tell just by lookin' at 'er. She would have been late thirties and her hair was this sucked mango seed colour. Big boobs too, all pushed up like they was melons.

'She said she wanted to see her son. She told him who she was and that she needed money. And, like an idiot, he gave 'er everything he had. Of course she shot through without so much as a *kiss my arse*. That's when Bertie first went all weird-like.'

Charlie slurped a long draught from his glass and glumly traced the scum on the side with his finger. 'It was probably my fault he went strange.

You see, I never got around to telling him he was adopted.'

Seth bit his lip. What an appalling story! He'd never much thought about adoption or the damage it might have caused. 'So, you think the shock of finding out sent Bertie over the edge?'

'Too right. After that he moved out and wouldn't talk to us. He disappeared for maybe four or five years. One time the missus was that upset I called the cops. They put 'is picture in the paper and 'is mate wrote to tell us he was alive. After that the missus was a bit brighter but she never recovered. Passed away soon after, poor old chook.'

'Did he ever contact you himself?'

'Yeah, about two year ago he phoned. Said he wanted to see me. I told him I'd moved to a pensioner flat, but he must've forgot and went to our old house instead. When he tried to get in through the back door all hell broke loose. The new owners were screaming and shouting, and he was screaming and shouting.

'I heard about this from me old neighbour. Bertie never did come to see me. The cops arrested him and had him certified. He went to the loony bin for a spell, then he vanished again.'

'So, you haven't actually seen him since he was about nineteen?'

'Nope. I haven't laid eyes on him for more than thirty years.'

Seth scratched his head. 'Then how do you know it's him in the photo?'

Charlie's eyes were swimming in beer and grief. 'I just know.'

As Seth steered the Jeep towards the office at Bowen Hills he switched on the radio. A Coldplay song about Paradise was on, his favourite of the moment, so he turned up the volume and sang along at the top of his lungs. The lyrics could have been written especially. Bertie might have expected the world, but it couldn't have turned out more differently. Whether or not he was the Riverdale bomber would be revealed in time.

If nothing else came from the meeting, Charlie had agreed for the paper to run his story—with no names and *no cock-ups*—about an adoption gone wrong. It would make a fine feature article for a weekend edition and would likely snare plenty of reader interest. Just what was needed to sell papers to a readership tired of pre-election posturing and dirty politics.

In the office he gave the task of research into adoptions to Cate Bradshaw, a journalism student who worked part-time for practically free. An exuberant twenty-something, she had lots of drive and absolutely no fear. With dark mermaid hair and teeth like pearls, she was easy on the eye as well.

She jotted down the names and details in a notepad. 'When do you need it?'

'Get whatever you can about Bertram Porter today. I want to be ready in case Charlie is right about his son. For the feature article, you have a week.'

'No probs, boss.' She smiled wickedly.

'Don't call me *boss*.' It was a game. He knew it was a game. And it got up his nose. He already felt ancient enough without being spoken to like a tribal elder.

3

Saturday 12 June 1971

The sneezing fit struck as Miffy Jones arrived at the front gate of Michelle's house. If she wasn't careful, the dreaded allergy to wattle would ruin her entrance to the party. From every bough of the massive wattle bush, thousands of yellow pompoms puffed out pollen that stank of overripe honey. Even the birthday balloons bobbing on the chain-wire fence were coated in yellow sneeze dust.

Her eyes were already red raw, but for a reason unrelated to her allergy. She held her hanky to her nose, opened the gate and raised her hand in acknowledgement of her mother who'd begrudgingly driven her there. Merle gave a curt nod and hauled on the steering wheel. The Austin crawled from the gravel shoulder of the road onto the bitumen strip.

Earlier they'd argued.

As usual, Miffy had left it until the last minute to ask permission to go the party, Michelle's sixteenth. Her folks didn't approve of parties. They didn't approve of rock music or short skirts or boys or, for that matter, anything else associated with fun. She'd put off asking the question in the hope a miracle would happen and they'd see it her way. On past occasions she'd managed to sweet-talk her father. But not Merle.

At four o'clock the now-or-never moment arrived. Miffy waited until the afternoon tea was brewed and her parents were comfortable with steaming mugs and choc-nut cookies before she summoned the courage to broach the subject.

The result was predictable.

'I don't approve of night-time parties for young girls,' Merle snapped.

'I'm not a *young girl*. I'm nearly sixteen. And all my friends are going.'

'You know I can't drive in the dark. My eyes …'

'… *aren't what they used to be*. You've told me a hundred times. I didn't ask you to drive. I'll catch the bus.'

'You're not going anywhere alone at night,' Merle said.

'Then I'll call Gaye and get a lift.'

'Who'd be the driver? Not that lead-footed brother of hers.'

'Probably. He's the only one with a car.'

'Hrmmph!' Merle slammed her orange mug down so hard on the kitchen table that the tea splashed over her nice clean tablecloth.

The thrill of possible victory surged through Miffy's body. She dared not smirk or raise her eyes for fear it would flow right over her and out the kitchen door.

Merle scrubbed the spill with the dishcloth. 'If this stains it's your fault, my girl.' She threw barbed looks at Arthur, slouched in his favourite armchair. The football was on the telly, the tea mug was in one hand and a cigarette was in the other.

'If you got off your bum and renewed your driver's licence, *you* could take her,' Merle said. 'There's enough for me to do without being a taxi driver as well.'

He turned up the volume and puffed out a few defiant smoke rings.

'How were you planning to get home afterwards, Myfanwy?' said Merle.

At the sound of the name she hated, Miffy cringed. Why hadn't they chosen something *normal* like Julie or Susan or Christine?

'It's a sleep-over. One of the mums will bring me back tomorrow.'

'Let her go, love.' Arthur's voice cut through the rambling football commentary. 'Where's the harm? Sooner or later you'll have to cut the apron strings.'

She could have leapt over the couch and kissed him. Not often did he take her side, and rarely did he oppose his wife. He'd probably expect something in return too, like mowing the lawn or cleaning his precious silverware (trophies he'd won decades ago when he was the footy hero).

It wasn't fair. Miffy's life was as chaste as a nun's while everyone else could do whatever they liked. Gaye's folks didn't care if she stayed out until dawn. Michelle's parents were fine when she hooked up with a senior boy from St Gregory's College. He was two years older, rode a motor bike and played in a garage band.

Outside Michelle's place, Miffy shouldered her overnight bag, flicked back her auburn hair, and straightened her cheesecloth blouse. On the door was a handwritten sign. *Go round the back*. She picked her way to the path at the side of the house and walked toward the rabble of voices and the catchy beat of the Beach Boys.

Her school friend, Gaye, beckoned her over with a can of forbidden rum and cola. A cigarette smouldered on her lip. She was putting on a show for two good-looking guys who wore the latest in denim flairs. One had a wiry blond afro and the other had a dark ponytail and moustache.

Miffy hadn't seen either of them before. Obviously they were far more mature than the boys in her class. They could have been as old as nineteen. She wondered if they were friends of Gaye's brother.

Gaye introduced them. 'This is Pedro and this is Dirk.' She put her mouth to Miffy's ear and lowered her voice. 'Aren't they cute?'

'Hi.' Shyly Miffy looked down at her sneakers.

'Hey doll, we don't bite,' said the one called Dirk. His voice was as smooth as chocolate. The moustache parted to reveal a set of broad even teeth.

'Did you bring anything to drink?' said Gaye.

Miffy patted the overnight bag. 'Yeah. It wasn't easy.'

'What've you got? Southern Comfort? Bacardi?' Pedro with the billowing hair casually slipped his arm around Gaye's shoulder. She grabbed his hand as if he were about to run away.

'I should say hello to Shelley.' Miffy backed out of the tight-knit group and meandered between the clusters of teenagers to the bright lights under the house. Balloons and streamers framed the entrance of the concrete grotto. Inside were two saggy couches and several chrome and vinyl kitchen chairs. Beside the washing machine a table groaned beneath bowls of Cheezels, potato chips, French onion dip, and porcupine oranges stuck with toothpicks of cheese, kabana and pickled onions. In the laundry tub, soft-drink cans drifted between floes of ice.

At the record player, Michelle was loading LPs onto the drop-feeder.

Miffy sneaked up behind and blindfolded her. 'Guess who?'

'Yay! You got here after all!' Michelle jumped up and flung open her arms. She smelt as fragrant as winter lemons. A combination of *4711 eau de cologne*, and the Southern Comfort on her breath.

'Happy birthday!' Miffy produced a small box wrapped in silver paper.

Michelle peeled off the sticky tape and lifted the lid. Inside, was a wad of cotton wool followed by a layer of tissue paper.

'I made it myself.'

'You clever thing!' Michelle put on the apple-seed necklace and pirouetted. Her pink maxi-dress filled out like a tulip. 'How do I look?'

A masculine voice answered from across the room. 'Sexy, babe.'

'Mac!' Michelle leapt onto him and kissed him full on the mouth.

Fascinated and a little embarrassed, Miffy looked away. She'd heard all about him, for Michelle shared her secrets with everyone. But this was the first time she'd seen them together. His collar-length hair was as dark as the night. He had a strong body, thick eyebrows and smouldering brown eyes. In an odd way, she felt jealous to have lost her best friend to this good-looking boy.

'This is Miffy,' said Michelle when she came up for air.

'That can't be your real name.'

'It's short for Myfanwy.' She drew an arc with the toe of her sneaker.

'Remember when we used to call you *My Fanny*?' said Michelle, laughing.

The sting of the nickname still hurt. 'It's Welsh,' she said as if to apologise.

Mac's face lit up like a carnival. 'Can't hold your name against you. I'm Patrick McConaghie. At school I got *Paddy Whack* and I was in trouble often enough to earn it. Now it's plain old Mac.'

'Not exactly plain,' Michelle chuckled. 'Or old.'

The compliments bypassed him completely. His eye was on the shelf behind the record player. 'Babe, who gave you *that*?'

'My folks. They're are amazing. It's exactly what I wanted.' Michelle lifted the Polaroid camera from its box. 'Wait till the place gets pumping. I'm gunna get pictures of *everyone* so I'll remember this birthday forever.'

She aimed the camera at him and he pulled a face. When the card popped out, she counted to sixty and peeled off the strip.

'You spoiled it!' Playfully she slapped him.

An excited commotion started outside and Michelle was off. The camera flashed. One minute later came squeals of delight. The instant photo was passed around.

Meanwhile Mac fizzed open a can of Coke and swallowed a mouthful. He took a silver flask from his back pocket and poured dark liquid into the can. It smelt like Christmas. 'Want a drink?'

'Yeah, thanks. Lemonade.'

He waggled the hip-flask. 'Want to make it more interesting?'

'I've brought my own.' Miffy fingered the shapely bump of the liqueur bottle through the forest-green vinyl of the overnight bag. How she'd acquired it was pure genius. Two weeks before, on the way home from school, she'd had found the empty bottle by the roadside. She'd taken it home and washed it. Later, when her parents were out, she'd rifled through the cocktail cabinet. Cherry brandy sounded delicious so she'd poured the lot in and refilled her parents' bottle with red cordial.

Inexpertly she followed Mac's lead. The result was sweet and easy to drink.

'Come outside and meet my band.' He led the way through a maze of shrubbery to the Hills clothes hoist, where a huddle had formed around the brazier. The two boys she'd met earlier cut dark silhouettes against the glow.

'You mean Dirk and Pedro?' she said.

'You know each other already? Radical! Any fireworks? Any stirrings of lust?'

She didn't know how to respond, so she gulped cherry brandy and lemonade until the comfortable warmth of the alcohol flowed into the veins of her legs.

The coals in the iron cradle cracked and hissed. Shining faces were flecked in orange and black. Bottles of rum, bourbon, and vodka littered the ground. Cigarette smoke curled into the gathering mist. The boys told off-colour jokes she didn't fully understand, but she chuckled as if she did and hoped no-one noticed when she blushed with embarrassment.

Dirk ducked in beside her, nudged her with his hip. 'Babe, you loosened up yet?'

She looked into the dark pits of his eyes.

'You looked real tense when you got here, like you needed a massage.' His deep silken tone made her go weak at the knees.

'I'm fine.' Her voice was as scratchy as fingernails on glass.

His face loomed close. 'Are you a *good* friend of Michelle's?' His breath was syrupy with rum.

'Shelley? We've known each other since Grade Eight.'

He edged even closer. She leant back and took a swallow from the can.

'Me and Mac too. Except I got myself an apprenticeship. Mac's gunna finish Senior and go to uni. While he's hitting the books, I'll be raking in the bread. Unless the band takes off, that is. Then we'll be set.'

While he was talking she studied his face. Beneath all that dark hair, he was rather good-looking. And his voice was to die for.

'What's your band called?'

'Phoenix. It's sort of a tribute.'

'What to?'

Before he could reply, there was a flash as stark as lightning.

'Smi-ile,' sang Michelle behind the Polaroid. 'Okay, people. Food's on.'

They trotted between the citrus trees and the vegie patch to the under-house cave, which was now bathed in candlelight and oozing with the velvet voice of Roberta Flack. Platters of Kentucky Fried Chicken, hot chips, sausage rolls, and cheerios steamed on the table.

'Now that's what I call a spread!' Dirk stuffed a drumstick in his mouth and reached across for a second.

The smell of the greasy food turned Miffy's stomach. She sat on a vinyl chair near the washing-machine and nibbled on a bread stick.

With an overflowing plate, Dirk came and sat beside her. 'Want some?'

Feeling a little dizzy from the brandy, she shook her head. She wanted to say something cool or witty so he wouldn't lose interest and walk off. Her big chance, but no words would come. She was too shy and stupid to ever get a real boyfriend.

Mac took control of the record player, replacing Michelle's top-of-the-pops with an LP of his own. He swung the needle into position, cranked up the volume and sat back on his heels as a heavy metal riff blasted the room.

The music was like nothing Miffy had heard before. It was primal, visceral. The pulsating beat stirred in her a passion. No, a craving. The tempo pumped harder and harder. Faster and faster. It built to an impossible crescendo. Split-second pause. Then a free-fall into the depths of ecstasy.

Dirk abandoned his plate for an air guitar. The expression of his face was pure rapture. 'Oh man! Black Sabbath rocks!'

Flash!

'You two look great together.' Michelle was gone before the photo had time to whir out of the camera. 'Everybody into the yard! Spin the bottle!'

They sat in a circle on the dew-moistened lawn. Mac gave an empty Bacardi bottle a spin and the neck conveniently pointed at Michelle.

He stood up, pulled her into his arms, and pashed her long and slow. Ten upturned faces hungered on their every move. Miffy squirmed with embarrassment.

When they parted, everyone cheered as if love were a spectator sport.

Michelle's spin stopped at Pedro. His frizzy hair screened the kiss but his hands lusted around her slim body. Mac clapped encouragement and laughed while his mate molested his girlfriend.

Miffy shrank from the circle. What had she let herself in for? She could never do that with a stranger, but to exit would paint her as a prude. She crossed her fingers and hoped the bottle wouldn't find her.

Pedro spun a girl Miffy scarcely knew. She spun Dirk. He spun Gaye. The game continued. Each time the bottle passed her by. The tension had reached a climax when Michelle's little sister trotted into the circle.

'Mum says to come and cut the cake now.'

Saved by a seven-year-old.

Around eleven o'clock, Michelle's folks came downstairs to greet parents who'd come for their kids. Of the thirty-odd guests, only the two best friends—Gaye and Miffy—were to stay overnight in the granny flat beneath the house.

The bottle of cherry brandy was almost empty and Miffy's head was in a foggy state of bliss. Mac packed up his records and stowed his rum bottle in the downstairs bedroom. He and the boys made a great show of thanking the folks for a wonderful night. They even shook hands with Michelle's old man.

'How're you getting home, fellas?'

'Train.'

'They stop at eleven-thirty. I'll drive you to the station.'

'No thanks, we'll walk. Need the exercise.'

'Suit yourselves.' The old man began to toss the empty cans, paper plates, chicken bones, serviettes into a plastic garbage bin.

'Leave the cleaning-up, Dad. The girls and I will do it in the morning.'

With that, Michelle and Mac disappeared up the path alongside the house, followed by Gaye and Pedro. Miffy was left alone with Dirk.

'Better get going or you'll miss your train.' She started up the pathway.

Dirk was close on her heels. 'Not so fast, babe.' He grabbed her hand and guided her into the shadows beneath big wattle tree. The golden pompoms bobbed and gyrated like dainty dancers in the breeze. Although it wasn't cold, she was shivering. Her nose began to itch. A wisp of soft hair brushed her cheek. His hungry lips nibbled her neck, her jaw. Found her mouth and pressed hard against it.

She was locked in a tussle of emotions. Never before had she been kissed like that. It was what she'd wanted, yet the musky odour of his body and the taste of his mouth unleashed a sensation that terrified her. She pushed him away.

'What's wrong, babe? Don't you like me?'

She sneezed five times in quick succession. 'Not you, it's the wattle.'

The others were sitting together on the kerb. Cigarette ends flared like fireflies.

She stumbled across the footpath and sat at the end of the row. Dirk followed.

'Now what?' said Gaye.

'We say goodnight and the boys leave.' Michelle sounded smug and mysterious, as if she were talking in code.

The six exchanged goodbye hugs and the boys ambled noisily down the road in the direction of the station.

'C'mon, we need to thank the oldies for the party.' Michelle trotted ahead to the house.

'What's going on?' whispered Miffy.

Gaye gave her a knowing wink and ran up the stairs behind Michelle.

In the light of a solitary candle the three girls lounged on the old couch under the house and sipped hot chocolate. Tartan blankets were wrapped around them like saris against the chill of the incoming fog.

Michelle checked her wrist watch. 'Not long now.'

With the stoneware mug cradled to her chest, Miffy yawned. 'Until what?'

Gaye sniggered. 'You really don't have a clue!'

'Then *please* tell me.' Miffy hated it when they purposely left her out of secrets. And she was feeling too queasy for silly guessing games. She shouldn't have drunk that fifth can of lemonade and cherry brandy.

'Shhhh! You'll wake the oldies,' hissed Gaye.

'Mac and the boys will be back at midnight.' Michelle spoke as if explaining a simple concept to a dull child.

'What for?'

'Oh for God's sake!' snorted Michelle. 'You're such a … *virgin*!'

The rebuff was like a slap to the face. Of course it was true, but lately she'd bragged at school about her many lovers. Her tales were romantic and complicated. She could have sold the storylines to *Days of our Lives*. Better to lie than admit the sad truth that she couldn't attract one single boy.

Perhaps it was her frightful red hair or the freckles, or the frumpy clothes Merle made from paper patterns of the 1950s and insisted that she wear. While her friends exposed their beautiful long legs, her skirts were barely three inches above the knee. She was a refugee from a past era. She might as well join a convent.

She put the mug on the ground and walked to the edge of the concrete. Dew frosted the lawn. The call of a curlew reverberated through the mist.

Her mouth had a sour taste and her stomach felt gross. If she stayed, she had an inkling of what might happen. Although she yearned to cast off the veil of innocence, she hadn't imagined it would be like this.

In her fantasy, her first lover would be handsome and fair with sparkling blue eyes and a kind smile. There'd be moonlight and rose petals, a crackling fire and a seduction scene straight out of a Mills and Boon romance.

This was a concrete cave draped in cobwebs. It stank of musty furniture, cold chook carcasses and tomato sauce. She pictured Dirk, dark and brooding, whom she'd just met. Ultra-cool and attractive in a Mick Jagger sort of way, he'd made it plain he what he was after. She didn't even know his last name.

Leave now, before you make a fool of yourself. On foot, she'd be home in an hour. She could sleep in the downstairs laundry and tell her parents she been given a ride home in the early morning.

Through the rolling fog came the ribald shriek of flying foxes in the banana trees, the flap of leathery wings. Then she heard their voices, muted and masculine.

'They're here,' Miffy breathed.

Three human shapes stepped out of the whiteout. Michelle and Gaye dropped their blankets and ran into their heroes' arms. The two couples disappeared into the granny-flat and shut the door behind them.

Abandoned to a boy she barely knew, Miffy pulled the blanket close around her.

Dirk smiled. 'Looks like it's you 'n me, babe.'

She forced a nervous smile. Why did he make her feel so insecure? She'd grown up around boys and knew their ways. Some were her closest friends. At school they'd talk for hours about football, physics, music, TV. They called her *mate*.

He took her hand, led her towards the couch, kissed her lightly on the cheeks. He undid her tartan sari and let it drop to the ground. Beneath was the outfit she'd bought with her hard-earned pocket money. White cheesecloth top, love-beads, Levis and sneakers. Although fully-dressed, she felt completely naked. His eyes caressed her and she went to jelly.

Abruptly she retrieved the blanket and pulled it around her like armour.

'Would you rather talk?' he said, sitting down on the couch.

'What about?'

'You.'

'I'm not very interesting.' She picked at the woollen tassels of the blanket. A thread came away. She held it out to the candle. The smell of burning reminded her of Merle's mutton chops.

'What do you like? What do you hate? Do you have a boyfriend?'

'In order of questioning: my friends, my mother, and no.'

'Are you always so … um … forthright?'

'Mostly. You talk instead.'

'Whatever. I'm eighteen, live with my mum. My brother's in Sydney and my dad is dead. I play bass guitar for Phoenix, the coolest band in town. There, is that enough?' He pulled her toward him, nuzzled her neck, breathed into her ear. Soft lips worked their way along the line of her jaw.

'Babe, I'm aching for you.' His hand explored the pillow of her breast.

She brushed it away. 'Not yet. Not yet.'

'Take your time. You 'n me have got all night.'

All night! Her heart dropped like a stone.

Straightening, he took a pouch and cigarette papers from his pocket, rolled a smoke, leant in to the candle to light it. The tobacco popped and fizzed. It didn't smell at all like her father's cigarettes.

Dirk passed it to her.

Holding it between her fingers like Gaye, she took a puff. The smoke came out in a herbal cloud and sent her into a coughing fit.

'You're wasting it! Hold it in. Like this …'

Miffy took a drag and held her breath. It burnt her throat and made the room spin. Soon she softened and felt light enough to float. She was a bubble in a rainbow, floating on the breeze.

In a sensuous dream, soothing hands slipped through a chink in her armour. Like the strings of a bass guitar, every fibre of her body hummed.

Piece by piece he removed her clothing. His hands were silk against her skin. When he pulled the blanket over them, he too was naked. He moved against her, exploring her curves. He fumbled with what sounded like a lolly wrapper, positioned himself above her and moaned as he pushed into that forbidden spot between her legs.

Instead of rapture, she felt shredded. It wasn't at all as she imagined. Certainly not what she'd read in Mills and Boon. If this was love, she could do without it.

Thankfully it was over within minutes.

'Sorry I came so fast but you were that tight I couldn't wait.' He peeled off the condom and groaned. 'Oh man, just my luck!'

'What's happened?'

'Oh, nothin' ... I guess.' His answer was vague enough to make her frown. 'Let's have another joint and do it again.'

Later, Miffy woke with a start. Sunday's dawn arrived in a shroud of silence. Not a bird or an insect stirred. Beside her was her lover. His slumbering breath came and went in a slow peaceful rhythm.

She put on her clothes and crept to the toilet. Behind the shut door, she snapped on the light and sat on the bowl with her legs apart. She was sore and bleeding.

Her mother would ask (as she always did) *was it a good party?*

What would she say?

What would she tell her friends?

What do midnight lovers say in the harsh light of day?

Without further thought, she made her decision. Before the others woke, she'd leave. The two-mile walk home would give her time to get her story straight. She wouldn't have to face her friends in her current state of remorse, and she'd avoid the awkwardness of swapping of phone numbers with Dirk and making insincere promises to see each other again.

She tiptoed back to the den of debauchery. He was still asleep, one foot on the ground and the other entangled in the blanket. A lock of dark hair wisped across his cheek, caught on his moustache.

For a moment Miffy wavered. What if she simply crawled back on the couch?

She shook her head, picked up her bag and padded across the concrete to the yard. Without a backward glance, she dissolved into the mist.

On Monday, Miffy arrived at school exactly as the first bell sounded. After her sudden departure the morning before, she was dreading her first encounter with Michelle.

In the mirror inside her locker door she examined her reflection. Her newfound knowledge about the mysteries of life hadn't changed a thing. Same carrot-top hair and freckles. What she'd lost and what she'd gained had not made an iota of difference. She was still plain boring Miffy Jones.

She shrugged, dumped her homework books in the locker and took out her *Geometry for Year 11* and an exercise book. As she snapped the lock, she sensed someone behind her.

'Why did you leave?' Michelle snarled.

Miffy's answer was a reflex response. She'd practised it a dozen times. 'I felt sick so I went home.'

'How come you didn't tell me?'

'You were … um … busy with Mac.'

'You could've left a note or told Dirk or phoned me in the morning.'

'I wanted to go home and that's all there was to it.' She could have bitten off her tongue. She sounded exactly like Merle.

'You have no idea the trouble you caused.' Michelle's neck flushed with rage. 'I put my alarm on for six so the boys could leave safely. You were nowhere. How bloody inconsiderate! Dirk was ropable. My oldies gave Gaye and me a really hard time. They got it in their heads you'd been kidnapped.'

'Why didn't they just phone my folks?'

'What? And admit they'd lost a kid at a sleepover?'

'Guess I didn't think of that.'

'No. You didn't think about us at all. We had to search the neighbourhood. I had this massive hangover and we had to go out and hunt for you. And all the while you were snug asleep in your own bed.'

'I'm sorry. If it makes you feel better, I copped it from my folks too.'

'What for?'

'Merle cleaned out my bag and found the cherry brandy bottle.'

Michelle started to smile. 'I didn't think there was any left.'

'There wasn't. I forgot to throw out the empty. She went straight to the cocktail cabinet and checked her Vok bottle. Then it was on.'

'You wanna know something really funny?' Michelle's eyes narrowed. 'You know that bottle of Dimple whisky Dad keeps on the sideboard?'

'Yeah, he told me he won it for being *Salesman of the Year*.' Miffy pressed her hand to her mouth. 'Shelley, you didn't!'

Michelle burst into a fit of giggles. 'He'll kill me if he finds out it's tea.'

The second bell clanged in the corridor.

'We'd better go.' The two linked arms and walked to class together.

Forgiven but not forgotten, a hairline crack had opened which would change their friendship forever.

4

Wednesday 19 February

Morning sunlight chinked through a gap in the block-out curtains and filled Vann Willis's bedroom with optimism. The sounds of a waking city percolated through the hum of the electric fan. The chortle of kookaburras, screech of lorikeets, whirr of the six o'clock express as it accelerated from the station. Through the thin wall of the apartment came the voice of the *G'day Australia* newsreader and the ripple of a sliding glass door. Somewhere a baby was crying.

Vann lay on her back beneath the sheet and listened to Lance's snuffle. The sleeping sound he made wasn't loud enough to qualify as a snore. The rhythm—the deep inhale, the pause, the long outward rush—was the soundtrack to her dreams. Without it, she'd hear every creak, groan, click and rattle that an apartment building this age could make.

She rolled to her side, pushed herself up, padded to the bathroom where she rinsed her mouth and drank water from the cup of her hand. In the mirror her short auburn hair looked as tangled as a magpie's nest. But her eyes! Bloodshot across the whites and dark smudges below.

'Are you sure you're up for this?' she whispered to the glass.

You'd better be, said her reflection.

She jutted out her jaw and set the shower to cool and strong.

Cool and strong was how she had to appear to the world. The voting public, her supporters, the media, her Party colleagues, the Opposition, her department, her staff. And now the police, the bombing victims, their families. To succeed she'd have to wear her cool and strong mask every day. She'd worn it for so long already it had bonded to her skin. Sometimes she worried she'd never get it off again.

After the shower she made herself toast, a boiled egg, and a cup of tea.

The sum total of her culinary skills. She checked the emails on her phone while she ate. There were three times more than usual, mostly about the tragedy. Some she answered, some she forwarded to James to deal with. As she finished up, the phone began to buzz. The caller's number was blocked.

She answered formally. 'Hello, this is Vann Willis.'

'Detective Sergeant Dave Frame, Criminal Investigations Branch. Do you have a minute?'

'Sure. What can I do for you?'

'We've got security camera footage of the suspect, some of which has been released to the media. I have a few questions. Can you come down to the Riverdale police station this morning?' His voice was clear and deep, bordering on gruff, the tone of a seasoned cop.

'Can't we do this by phone?'

'Sorry, ma'am. What's the earliest you can come?'

Vann checked her electronic diary and sucked her teeth. There was scarcely a spare time slot. 'What about now? See you in half an hour.'

She called a cab and left a note for Lance. He wouldn't be up for another two hours at least. Six nights a week he worked late at the Paddington eatery he owned with his brother. Aptly named *Due Fratelli*—Two Brothers— it had won the Best Ethnic Restaurant award three years running. Business was brisk despite the gloomy economy.

Detective Sergeant Dave Frame was a tall man. He was so tall that his body had taken on the shape of a permanent S from trying to contain its extreme height. Although Vann was in high heels, her head came level to his shirt pocket. He smiled coyly and extended his hand. He had extremely long fingers.

'Sorry to call you so early, but the quicker we do this the better.'

'No problem. My life is frantic any time of day.'

The detective took her to an interview room, where a laptop purred on the desk. 'These are the CCTV images in question. What do you see?'

Vann focused on the screen. The first run of black-and-white pictures showed the footpath and the driveway outside her office. Pedestrians walked up the hill from the station. Some wore school uniforms, others were in business wear. A white taxi rolled up the driveway and stopped.

He paused the video.

Vann peered at grainy image. Two indistinct shadows were inside. 'That's me in the front seat nearest the camera.'

'When you were in the car, what did you see?'

'There were a lot of people about. I guess a train must have come in. One in particular caught my attention. A vagrant we called Steptoe. An odd-bod but harmless.'

'What do you know about him?'

'He drifted in and out with the seasons, lived in a shambles of a boarding house that should have been condemned twenty years ago, collected stuff out of garbage bins.'

'Know his real name or where he came from?'

'Nope, that's all I've got.'

The video rolled. The white car was now on the road. Dozens of people pushed along the footpath. In the right-hand corner was a blur that was James as he ran out with Vann's reading glasses. A dark blob was close behind him.

'Stop! There's Steptoe,' she said pointing at the screen.

Dave Frame slowed the feed. The blob moved jerkily up the stairs where the image resolved. Steptoe was easily recognisable by the overcoat and beanie. A woman in a dark skirt and light blouse was climbing the stairs behind him. On her shoulder was a large handbag with big-buttoned pockets.

Vann gasped. 'Oh my God, that's Lara!'

'Lara?'

'Lara Dainford. She was hit by flying glass. I saw her at the Royal last night.'

'How well do you know her?'

'Not at all. I found her covered in blood. I felt sort of responsible, so I stayed with her until the ambulance came.'

'But you went to see her in hospital?'

'I went to see everyone who was hurt. You might think I'm a cold-hearted politician, Detective Sergeant, but I do care about people.'

The edge of Dave Frame's lip gave an upward twitch, but he kept right on talking. 'What did she say?'

'Nothing. She was asleep.'

'From the footage it seems she intended to visit your office. Do you know why?'

Vann shook her head. 'We share the building with three other tenancies: a financial planner, a solicitor, and an accountant. She could have been going to see any one of them. As I said, I don't know her at all.'

Images from a different CCTV camera streamed onto the screen. From the angle, the camera was located on the shop opposite the electorate office. At the start of the sequence, people in business clothes entered and left her building. Tom White, the financial planner, hurried out in the direction of Café Nero. Vann could set her watch by him. Every morning he'd feed his addiction. Yesterday, caffeine might have saved his life.

At the top of the stairs Steptoe turned his head from side to side in an agitated manner. At the office door he stopped. Despite the poor quality of the recording, the shot of his face was clear. Age around forty, unshaven, big nose, fleshy lips. As he reached for the handle, he turned his back to the camera. His overcoat was oddly bunched between the shoulders.

Dave Frame paused the video and zoomed in. There was a definite bulge beneath the fabric. 'Now what do you make of that?'

'Explosives?'

'Maybe. I'll get the boys to take a look.'

The video streamed on and Vann's mind was racing. With a routine dictated by tight timeslots, she'd developed an inner minute-counter as accurate as a Swiss watch. Half an hour had elapsed and she needed to leave before her entire schedule was shot.

'Is there anything else I can help you with?' she said to wrap up the interview. She was good at that too, had a real skill for ending a discussion that threatened to blow into a timewaster without offending the other party. 'If we're done, I should be getting along.'

'Sure, Ms Willis. Thanks for coming. I'll be in touch.' Dave Frame opened the door of the interview room and stood aside to let her pass. The S-bend of his spine compressed as he reached down to shake her hand.

Almost as an afterthought he took a business card from his pocket and scrawled on the back. 'This is my mobile number. If you receive any threats or see anything suspicious, call me immediately.'

At the end of another long day of public appearances, press conferences and meetings, Vann was running on nervous energy. But before she could retreat from the world and unwind with a frothy novel and a good bottle of red, there was one last visit she'd promised to make.

Tonight she had no difficulty locating Ward 5F. Swathed in bandages, Lara was propped up on pillows, aiming the remote control at a small TV screen on the wall. She operated it with both thumbs like a game controller. Her face showed the same intense concentration as Lance, a late starter to channel-surfing, who was now a world-champion of the sport.

The intravenous drip and monitoring devices were gone. A machine at the foot of the bed wheezed air into the mattress.

'How are you tonight?' Vann said.

Lara's eyes were swollen and purple. The exposed skin on her face looked like a patchwork quilt. 'Do I know you?'

'You probably don't remember yesterday. I'm Vann Willis.'

'Sorry, Ms Willis. I can't see too well at the moment.' She patted the dressings on her cheeks. 'I must look a mess.'

'You'll heal up in no time.'

Lara shook her head. 'They pulled out enough glass to make a leadlight window. I look like Frankenstein's monster.'

Vann positioned a visitor's chair close to the bed. 'I dropped by last night but you were asleep.'

'Thanks for the beautiful gerberas. They're my favourite flowers.'

'Glad you liked them. We should have met sooner. It seems you intended to visit my office but a bomb got in the way.'

'How did you know?'

'Security footage. You were on the stairs when it happened.'

'What I wanted isn't important anymore.'

'Try me. It's the least I can do.'

'Just family stuff. I was going to ask for help because I couldn't get any sense out of your department. It can't be fixed anyway. I'm done with the past. From now on I'm going to live for today.'

'That's the spirit!'

'I'm going to quit my job and go overseas. South America or Central Europe. Somewhere exotic where I can take lots of lovely photos. Twenty-three years and seven months with the one employer is far too long.'

'Where do you work?'

'Promise you won't say anything? I don't want to get the sack.'

'A minute ago you were going to quit.'

'Yeah, but I've still got a mortgage to pay.'

'Okay, my lips are sealed.'

'Centrelink. I'm so over it. Every day is the same as the one before. Same old people, same old problems. At the start I thought I'd be able to … I don't know … change lives for the better. But now I know it's hopeless. Generation after generation, the system keeps churning them out like cheap sliced bread.'

'Don't be hard on yourself. Sometimes we do make a difference, we just can't see it at the time. We can give a person hope when they've hit rock bottom. We've all been there. I was there once myself.'

'Perhaps you're right. But it sure as hell didn't help Bert Bagley.' As soon as Lara said the name she clamped her lips. 'Forget I said that.'

'Who's Bert Bagley?'

'The overcoat man. Everyone calls him Steptoe.'

'You know him?'

'I wouldn't say *know* him. I shouldn't be telling you this.'

'Was he a client?'

'It's against regulations to talk about clients to anyone outside the service. I don't want to get in trouble.'

'Have the police seen you yet?'

'Yeah. I made a witness statement this morning.'

'And you didn't mention Bert Bagley?'

'They didn't ask, so I didn't say.'

Vann leaned in close. 'Lara, if you want to make a difference to a whole lot of lives, you need to tell me what you know.'

Lara twisted a tissue into a knot and unwound it again. Tears spilled over the rims of her eyes. 'I didn't think of it like that.' She patted the tissue between the dressings and sighed. 'He was a bit of a nutter. On and off Disability Support for as long as I can remember. All year round he wore that overcoat like a security blanket.'

'And?'

'Couple of years ago he went to jail. Nothing serious. Break and enter or possession or something like that. He'd stay in Riverdale a few months and then go walkabout. And now he's gone for good.'

'You really *ought* to go to the police.' Her haughty tone slipped out by accident.

Lara folded her arms across her chest. 'You go. It's not so easy for me right now.'

Vann chewed her lip, annoyed with herself.

Lara said, 'Sorry, I didn't mean to snap. They're discharging me tomorrow and I'm on edge. How can I look after myself with all these bandages and dressings? Public hospitals! I knew I should've taken out health insurance.'

'What can I do to help?'

'You stayed when I thought I would die. You've done heaps.'

Vann squeezed Lara's hand. 'I'll call later. See how you're doing.'

On her way out, she glanced over her shoulder. The TV was on and Lara's thumbs were again busy with the remote-control buttons.

Home at last, Vann dumped her handbag on the table and kicked off her shoes. Her feet had swollen and the straps had made furrows across the toes.

On the sideboard was a handwritten envelope addressed to her. Usually Lance opened and managed their mail. He was secretary, accountant and cook all in one. For some reason, he'd left it unopened.

The writing was neat and round. Originally postmarked in Sydney a month ago, the address didn't include the postcode. Consequently, it had done the rounds of four other locations that went by the name Riverdale.

She ripped it open. Inside was a white and gold card, an invitation to a reunion of her Senior year at Riverdale High. Unbelievable! The event was a sit-down dinner at the Ballymore rugby union club in two weeks' time.

Her school days had been like her mother's all-in stew. A mixture of nice bits, juicy bits and tough bits. The worst she'd tucked away in the darkest corner of her mind. Sometimes, when she was feeling low, she'd get flashbacks that would replay over and over like a black-and-white horror film on a continuous loop.

On such short notice, it would be almost impossible to squeeze in a formal dinner on a Saturday night. Doubtfully she opened her electronic diary.

She was scheduled to present prizes at a talent quest for the homeless and there was no way she could get out of that. Wait, it was due to finish at eight. Perhaps she could make it after all.

Feeling a little apprehensive, she entered the appointment in her diary. She'd lost contact with her closest friends from school. Things had happened that couldn't be mended. Terrible things, secret things. But life was short and they were now mature women. Perhaps she should be the one to rebuild the bridge.

The night of the reunion Lance would be busy at the restaurant and wouldn't notice if she came in late. She slipped the invitation beneath a fridge magnet and opened the fridge door to rummage for leftovers.

On the balcony she settled in the easychair with plate of cheese and crackers, and a large glass of chilled red wine. Under the cover of low cloud, the city lights were muted as if glowing through a gauze of silk. Later it would rain. She could smell it in the air. She wiped sweat from her neck and rolled the cold glass against her forehead.

Soon there would be a change, when the putrid heat of summer would switch into balmy autumn. Perhaps the reunion would help her move forward. She was tired of keeping all that emotional baggage hidden away.

5

Friday 21 February

Nine o'clock in the morning and Cate Bradshaw looked decidedly ragged.

'Big night?' Seth dumped his bag on the desk and plugged the phone into the charger. 'Want my spare coffee? I got a two-for-one deal on the way in.'

'You're a life-saver.' She yawned and reached for the cardboard cup. 'It *was* a big night, and I guarantee you'll be delighted with the outcome.'

Seth raised his eyebrows. 'Really?' The girl was full of surprises.

She passed him a manila folder entitled *Forced Adoptions: 1950s to 1970s*. Inside was an executive summary, a table of contents, and scores of A4 printouts. She perched on the corner of his desk, quietly sipped the coffee and watched him leaf through the wad of documents.

'You're right. I *am* impressed. Talk me through your findings.'

She explained how there'd been a Senate inquiry into forced adoptions. On the website were heart-wrenching stories about babies forcibly removed from mothers whom the government had deemed unfit. Typically, the excuses were that the mother was unmarried, or the family was poor, or there were too many other mouths to feed.

'In the olden days,' she said, 'there was no welfare for single mothers and no child care so they could work.'

Seth smiled, aware he was about to reveal his vintage. 'Ah yes, Women's Lib changed all that. When I was at uni, the female students made a bonfire with their bras.'

Cate's bow-shaped mouth fell open. 'Why would they do that?'

'Symbolic protest about the constraints of womanhood. A lot has changed for the better, but a lot has stayed the same.'

'Sounds like you were a Feminist.'

'Men weren't allowed but I supported their cause. What else did you find?'

Cate flipped through her notes. 'Girls who got pregnant were often disowned by their families and put into unmarried mothers' homes. They were mainly run by the state government or religious organisations like the Sisters of Mercy or the Salvation Army. When the girl went into labour, the hospital almoner—a sort of unqualified social worker—would pressure her into adoption. Almoners would say anything to make the girl sign the papers. She'd be a hopeless mother, or she'd end up as a prostitute and the child would become a delinquent. The only alternative was for the baby to be given up and raised in a loving Christian home.'

'Sounds like a no-brainer. What happened?'

'The inquiry found that adoptive parents weren't necessarily good parents after all. Sometimes the children were treated like slaves, or the marriage failed and the kids ended up in an orphanage. That's a whole other story. Lots of people discovered they were adopted only after their 'parents' died. It's a secret that's wrecked lives.'

'Great stuff. Did you get anything on Bertram Porter?' asked Seth.

'Sorry, boss. There's a privacy issue. The Department won't talk unless the file is about you personally.'

'Hmmm, thought as much. You've done a great job. I'll write it up later.' He swivelled his chair and clicked the computer mouse. Dozens of new emails scrolled down the screen.

Cate gathered the papers and put them back in the folder. She lingered longer than necessary, as if stalling for an opportunity to talk.

Seth turned to face her. 'What's on your mind, Cate?'

She lowered her eyelids and cleared her throat. Her voice was soft yet assertive. 'Would you let me write it? I was up most of the night on the research and it's all there in my head.'

'What year are you in at uni?'

'Third. I'll do it justice. Give me a break?'

He leant back in the chair and made a show of deliberating on the matter, but there was no doubt in his mind she'd do a thorough and competent job. 'Okay Cate, it's all yours. Have a draft ready first thing Monday morning.'

'I won't let you down, boss.' She hugged the folder to her chest and scuttled to the other side of the divider.

'And don't call me *boss*.'

Wish I had her commitment, he thought. The passion Cate showed for journalism was how he once was. In the early days of his career, he believed he could change the world by exposing corruption and evil. It took him years to realise changing societal attitudes would be harder than the plugging all the leaks in a giant sieve. Real life had no grand design and no divine intervention. The leaders of countries were neither wise nor infallible and much of the bad stuff that happened was due to greed, alcohol, or plain rotten luck.

He stretched his lower back. His sciatica was playing up. Although he'd never admit it, Cate made him feel ancient. In all his years in the profession he'd heard so many lies and seen so much pain and brutality that his appetite for exposing villains had all but faded away. Now he was just another cantankerous old news hound who'd snarl if he didn't get what he wanted.

He returned to the screen full of emails. There was one from Detective Sergeant Dave Frame. He clicked on the message.

Preliminary forensics are back. If you're interested drop around to The Usual at lunch time and I'll shout you a beer.

Was he interested? Nothing would interest him more than lunch and a beer on a Friday. He checked the time: eleven o'clock. If he swung by Vann Willis's wreck of an office and talked to the neighbouring business-owners, he'd easily kill an hour. With any luck he'd also get information about what happened in the lead-up to the bombing.

To find a car park on the busy strip of shops, Seth had to drive two laps around the block. Even then he had to reverse the Jeep into a space that was better suited to a Hyundai Getz. He slid out of the driver's seat and checked the parking signs.

Twenty minutes was all he had until they called in the tow truck. This was a not an idle threat. The Council officers who patrolled the precinct had a reputation for military precision and efficiency. Too bad if you were caught in the queue at Medicare or kept waiting at D'lish Deli while they toasted your *focaccia*. Excuses fell on deaf ears. There were only two choices. Pay up or face the courts.

He hurried along the footpath in the shade of bull-nosed shop awnings from the 1920s. At the end of the row was Café Nero, the coffee bar opposite Vann Willis's old office. The toasted-bean aroma seized his attention and enticed him to stop. The long queue outside was proof that they made the best espresso in town.

Seth knew coffee. He was weaned onto the stuff. His boyhood home in Paddington was three blocks from Caffe Arrosto, an Italian joint that roasted their own. Six days a week the earthy fragrance pervaded the suburb. He tasted coffee in the air, it permeated his skin, it was infused in the fabric of his uniform. At school the girls gave him hugs just to breathe the smell. Not that he ever complained.

He joined the coffee queue. Directly across the road, shreds of blue-and-white police tape fluttered from the posts like Tibetan prayer-flags. Vann's blackened office was a sad reminder of the transience of life. Bad things sometimes happened to good people. He made a mental note to phone his younger brother and patch it up before it was too late.

The woman beside him followed his gaze. 'Dreadful business,' she commented. She would have been fifty, trying to look thirty in a leopard-print blouse and black tights. Her hair was styled in a short platinum bob that looked a bit like a pith helmet.

'Yes, dreadful,' he echoed.

'I saw the whole catastrophe from my salon next door.' Her black varnished nails tapped out a rhythm against the mesh of her coin purse.

'The papers say it was a crazy guy in an overcoat.'

'That's what they *say*, but that's not what I *saw*.' She gave him a knowing wink. 'But who'd want to talk to a *hairdresser* about the wicked ways of the world? No-one's thought to ask me.'

The line inched closer to the counter. Seth glanced at his watch. Ten minutes had passed, ten to go. An inner voice screamed about the fate of his Jeep, but this was too good an opportunity to miss.

'Would you like to join me?' he said. 'My treat.'

She arched a perfectly-drawn eyebrow and smiled. 'Sure, why not? There's a courtyard out the back. I could do with a sit-down. I've been run off my feet. High school formal tonight. Last customer's at six. By the way, I'm Maureen.'

'Seth.' They shook hands.

With a cappuccino in one hand and a raspberry muffin in the other, Maureen led the way through the rear door into a walled courtyard of potted palms, ornamental gingers and bougainvillea. Of the three vacant tables, she chose the one beneath a market umbrella.

Seth stirred the *crema* and filled his lungs with heavenly scent. 'That's what I call good coffee,' he said. 'So, what happened the other day?'

'Are you a detective?' Maureen spooned froth into her mouth.

He shook his head. 'I'm a reporter trying to find the truth.'

'Good. I don't trust cops. That man in the coat wouldn't hurt a fly.'

'What was his name?'

'I don't know his proper name. We all called him Steptoe. He used to collect other people's rubbish. He'd have a field day every time the Council ran a footpath clean-up. You'd see him pushing a handcart full of pipes and wires and pieces of broken furniture. I don't know what he did with it all.'

'Sounds like he had the right components to make a bomb.'

'He wouldn't know how.'

'What makes you say that?'

'Look, this guy wasn't the full quid but he didn't have a bad bone in his body. He was a phantom that most people didn't notice, yet he'd lived around here for years.'

'Do you know where?'

'There's a rambling old place at the end of the road. Timber, with a wide veranda all round. It's run as a boarding house. I don't think it's legal. You'll know it by the junk pile in the backyard. But you're wasting your time with Steptoe. What I saw happened two minutes before he walked up those stairs.' With a dramatic pause she poured in two sachets of sugar and stirred.

She licked the spoon and continued. 'A courier took a package into that office. He was out again and down the street before you could bat an eyelid.'

'Can you describe him? Was there a logo on the van?'

'It was a motor bike. I couldn't see his face because of the helmet.'

'What sort of bike? Did you get the number plate?'

'Whoa! If I knew all that I'd have tracked him down myself. Freya Ekeberg—the woman who died—was a client of mine. Not only that, she was a nice lady.' For a moment Maureen seemed close to tears, but she quickly recovered and attacked the muffin with a fork. 'This is really tasty. Would you like a bit?'

'I'm having lunch with a friend.' He checked the time. 'Speaking of which, I'd better get going.'

Maureen patted her mouth with a napkin. 'Me too. No rest for the wicked, so they say.' She flashed a smile. 'Thanks for the coffee and cake.'

'My pleasure. Give me a call sometime if you like.'

They swapped business cards and he followed her down the lane to Station Road, where she turned left to the salon and he turned right. He sprinted up the hill to the where the Jeep was parked, arriving in time to witness a Council inspector slide the ticket beneath the wipers.

'Officer, can we talk this over?'

The man in the uniform scowled. 'The vehicle overstayed the twenty-minute parking limit. You're lucky not to have been towed.'

Seth offered his press pass and explained why he was late.

The inspector wasn't swayed. 'It's out of my hands. If you want to appeal the penalty, you can write to the address on the back.'

Seth snatched the ticket and climbed into the driver's seat. The amount of the fine was one hundred and ten bucks. 'What a fucking joke!'

There was no-one to hear him. The parking officer had moved away, leaving a paper trail on every windscreen along the road.

A short time later and still seething from the weight of the fine, Seth entered the Sports Bar of the Riverdale Tavern. The timber-lined bar room, decorated with heavy nineteen-eighties furniture, was homely and comfortable. An enormous plasma screen showed a replay of last season's AFL footy final.

A group of old blokes, who seemed to be buddies from the local retirement village, sat side-by-side at the bar. The tables were occupied by young business people who showed their mental dexterity by conversing and texting at the same time. Texting was Seth's newest-found skill. He could bash out a brief message in five minutes flat.

In the corner, beneath a pile of dirty plates and empty beer bottles was a free table. Seth claimed it just as Detective Sergeant Dave Frame loped into the bar.

'What do you know, Davo?' said Seth. His standard greeting sometimes brought surprising results. People liked to show off their insider knowledge. He'd heard confessions, received tipoffs, and picked up breakthrough leads. All from that clever one-liner.

'You can't catch me with that old trick.' Dave Frame smiled.

They ordered schooners and fisherman's baskets and bantered about the price of petrol and the cricket. It was just like old times when they were pals.

After the second beer Seth again asked, 'So, what *do* you know?'

Dave Frame leaned close and whispered. 'The preliminary forensics are back.'

'You told me that in the email. And …?'

'And … nothing. They found absolutely nothing of interest.'

'Then why did you want to meet me for lunch?'

'I thought it'd do us both good to get out of the office.'

'David Michael Frame, you're a shameless bastard.'

'You and I have been mates for … how many years?'

'Fifty, give or take.'

'… fifty years, so you ought to understand what I can and can't talk about.'

'Never mind, it was worth a try. Can you give me any information at all?' Seth took a long swallow of beer.

'The bomb was on the reception counter. Yep, the epicentre was right in the middle of the office. Not near the entrance, as we first thought.'

'Does that change anything?'

'It's too soon to know. We won't get the full report for weeks and we haven't even started on the autopsies. Huge backlog. Not enough staff. Did you do any good with your article and the CCTV photo?'

'Got a couple of leads, but mostly stupid comments and sympathy mail. One claimed he was a long-lost son, another said he was a dimwit neighbour.'

'Steptoe?'

'That's the one.'

'Do you know his real name?'

Seth shook his head.

'He'd been going by the name Albert Steptoe but we know it's an alias. Remember *Steptoe and Son*, the TV series in the 60s? Albert was the father, a conniving old man. Anyway, one week ago our Steptoe was in the psychiatric unit at the Prince Charles after a one-man rampage at the Riverdale Mall. He's as cunning as a sewer rat, that one. He convinced them he was sane and so they let him out.'

'Now the poor bastard's dead. Was he the bomber?' said Seth.

'Hard to say until the coroner's done. Tell me about the long-lost son scenario.'

'I promised to keep it quiet. Truth is I don't think he's a reliable source.' Seth tipped his hand to his mouth, indicating his informant's fondness for the drink.

'Whoever Albert Steptoe really was, he had not a friend in the world. No-one's been reported missing all week.'

'Remember when we knew all our neighbours by name? It wasn't that long ago. Our parents lived in the one house for a lifetime. We kids roamed from backyard to backyard. We climbed trees, made cubby houses, ate mulberries straight off the bush. We knew who came and who went. No-one went missing without being noticed.'

'Mate, you sound just like my old man,' said Dave Frame.

Seth finished his beer. 'I *am* an old man.'

'Ha! Not by a long shot.'

'I should get back. You know how it is. Deadlines to meet.'

The detective's unmarked police car was parked in the shade of a blossoming grevillea alive with lorikeets. The flock flew off screeching, leaving the bonnet splattered with red tendrils and bird shit. They shook hands and promised to keep each other 'up to speed' about developments, although neither really expected it to happen.

Seth slid into the driver's seat of the Jeep. The black leather was as hot as a barbeque plate. To return to the office he chose a circuitous route. East along the barren scar of the Western Freeway; left at the busiest roundabout in the city; left again into Frederick Street and past the gothic spires of the old Toowong Cemetery. He rode the roller-coaster road around the hills to Rosalie, where he turned off near the primary school. After navigating the familiar back streets to Paddington, he stopped outside a century-old workers' cottage.

The giant camphor laurel under which he parked was even bigger than he remembered. The house where he'd grown up was typical of the cottages of the early twentieth century. A box of timber and tin. It was all the average family man could afford on a single income. And his father, who was a tram driver, was the epitome of the average family man.

A set of stairs led to a wide veranda with vertical bannisters like prison bars. The door was centred between the two double-hung windows of the front bedrooms.

His room was on the left, his younger brother was on the right. Their parents' room was at the back near the kitchen. When Pa worked late, as he often did, he'd enter by the back door so as not to disturb the boys. Whether Mum was home or not that door stayed open day and night. It was the quickest exit to the dunny in the backyard. Burglaries were rare. There wasn't much to steal.

Seth reached for a cigarette, thought better of it, settled for an Eclipse mint instead. He didn't see the house as it actually was—dilapidated, over-run with creepers and badly in need of paint—but as it was when he was eleven, the year of the fire.

In 1962 the cottage was duck-egg blue and the bannisters along the veranda were white. Pa devoted all his spare time to painting the place. Never did a year pass without the trestles marching along the side of the house like wading birds joined at the hip. Amongst paint-rag bunting, sandpaper squares and the acrid smell of turps, Pa would whistle soulful ballads while he smoothed the paint over the chamfer boards.

Poor old Pa.

The night of the fire Seth was reading a *Phantom* comic in bed. The clang of the bell at Ithaca Fire Station cut through the sounds of the night. He looked out the window as the fire truck laboured up the steep stretch of Given Terrace. People called to each other from house to house. The *bush telegraph* they called it, even though Paddington wasn't in the bush. With unlined timber walls you could hear every conversation anyway. Their neighbour's house, belonging to Mr and Mrs Frame, was so close that Seth and Davo could sneak into each other's rooms by means of a ladder, strategically placed between their bedroom windows.

News of the fire rolled down the hill. 'It's the Tram Depot!'

Seth raced down the hall onto the back veranda. The sky was brighter than all the bonfires of cracker night. Flying embers flashed in the choking cloud. He held his pyjama shirt like a gasmask over his nose to stop himself coughing.

Mum came onto the veranda behind him and placed her hands on his shoulders. A teardrop fell onto his skin. It wasn't like her to turn on the waterworks and it made him feel scared.

'Why are you sad?' he asked.

Before she could answer, an explosion rocked the foundations of the cottage. From beyond the treetops came a terrific roar. Mum gnawed on her lip and dug in her fingernails.

'Where's Pa?' he said.

'Stay here and look after your brother.' Her voice was unsteady. She pulled her shawl close, her scuffs flip-flopped down the stairs and she vanished into darkness.

At dawn Seth ventured up the winding road to see for himself what had happened to the Tram Depot. Its blackened carcass, eerie against a pink sky, looked like the skeleton of a dinosaur. Curlicues of smoke spiralled into the crisp air. Entombed inside the beast were most of the city's trams. Sixty-five in all. Some had crashed right through the burnt floorboards into the bowels of the wrecked building.

Workers in tramways uniforms—navy trousers, blue shirt, legionnaire's cap—paced around the ruins, shaking their heads and surmising about the fate of their jobs.

In the midst of it was Pa. Seth trotted to him and slipped his hand into his father's comforting paw.

Pa looked old and worn out. He and his mates had kept a vigil throughout the night. They were covered in soot. Cigarettes hung despondently from the corners of their lips.

Seth left them to mourn their loss. It was hard to believe the place was gone. Part and parcel of his childhood, his father had worked there more than twenty years. Their tramway mates were like family. School holidays there'd be excursions to the seaside at Sandgate or Manly, a trip to the Ekka in August, and at Christmas a gala picnic with presents and ice-cream.

If the day of the fire was bad, there was worse was to come. Because so many trams were lost, the workers were expected to retrain as bus drivers.

Pa was furious. 'I've only ever driven a tram. I'm fifty-three years old. How can I drive a bus when I haven't even got a proper driver's licence?'

The choice was simple. Learn or be sacked. The latter was not an option for a proud man with a wife and two sons to support. So, he tried being a bus driver. For six weeks he tried. Then one rainy day in October he misjudged a curve outside the Toowong Cemetery. The bus skidded off the road and hit a post. No passengers were injured but Pa suffered two fractured kneecaps. When he got better he couldn't drive anymore because the foot pedals were stiff and hurt his knees. The compo ran out, so did his health. By year's end he lay in that very cemetery, not fifty yards from the site of the accident.

After that, life in Paddington was a struggle. To make ends meet, Seth delivered newspapers before school and pumped petrol at the Shell service station in the afternoons. At seventeen he escaped to Sydney, where he matriculated through night school and won a cadetship to become a journalist with the *Sun*.

In the Jeep outside that dilapidated worker's cottage, Seth sucked thoughtfully on an Eclipse mint. For all his family's troubles, he wouldn't have swapped his life for another. He knew who he was and where he'd come from. He'd loved the parents who'd raised him, and they'd loved him in return.

How tough it would've been to not have had that. To be a Bertram Porter or an Albert Steptoe. Alone and drifting without the anchor of a family who cared.

6

Wednesday 11 August 1971

That year the August westerlies arrived right on schedule. The blustering gales that marked the end of winter sent small children and furry pets stark raving crazy. Tiny leaves rained like golden confetti from the deciduous jacarandas. Houses whistled like kettles and fingers of icy air poked through cracks in the timber. Crisp sheets of eucalypt bark skittered along concrete paths and banked up against doorways.

In the kitchen Merle blew her nose on a man-sized hanky. 'O my poor sinuses! I hate this wind.' She took a pill from a brown bottle. 'With that racket going on I haven't slept a wink. Today of all days!'

What her mother said, scarcely registered. Miffy was halfway through the latest James Michener tome, *Hawaii*. It was exotic, erotic, and nothing like Mills and Boon. Where the saucy bits were, she'd turned down the page corners for quick reference later. Snuggled in the armchair, she'd grazed through an entire box of Nutri-Grain and was feeling a bit sick. Since the night of Michelle's party, her social life had become a wasteland and her friendships had practically dissolved.

Michelle had become a wannabe celebrity and did backup vocals for Mac's band. Phoenix had scored a regular gig at a tavern on the north side. Although Michelle was five years short of the legal drinking age of twenty-one, when she trowelled on the makeup and squeezed her breasts into a low-cut dress, she easily passed. To get the contract at the pub, Mac had lied about all their ages, for not one of the members was a day over nineteen. Friday and Saturday nights, they played turn-about with a group of stage veterans, and afterwards they drank themselves stupid.

Gaye latched onto the sluts from Eleven E who wore Pink Zinc as lipstick, hid combs inside their ties, and hitched up their skirts so high you could see the bare skin above their stockings.

From Dirk, she'd not heard a peep. He was probably still angry with her for taking off, but she didn't care. She had no interest in being a groupie and trailing around after a bunch of self-centred musicians. Her plans were for a career and money and travel, none of which involved a boyfriend or (heaven forbid) marriage.

Her path to fame and fortune wouldn't be easy. Most of the girls in her Year Ten class had left at fifteen and now worked as typists, shop assistants and nurses' aides. Only after winning a scholarship had she convinced her parents to let her stay at school two more years. Now she needed extra-high grades in the state Senior exam to win a university scholarship. On a bright note, having no friends meant lots of time to study.

This windy day was the second Wednesday in August, a public holiday to celebrate the Royal Exhibition. The Ekka, as it was known, was the annual agricultural show. This year, Merle insisted they go together as a family, the prospect of which thrilled neither Arthur nor Miffy.

'You're looking quite anaemic, Myfanwy. Getting out in the sun will do you the world of good.'

'If you want to drag someone through all those boring displays, you should ask Auntie Elsa. She loves flowers and chooks and cows.'

'What about the animal nursery? You always like that,' insisted Merle.

'Yeah, when I was six.'

'You're coming with us, and that's THAT!' Merle sniffed and wiped her nose. It was useless to argue once her mind was set.

Miffy snapped the book shut, thundered into the bathroom and slammed the door. She left her pyjamas in a heap on the floor and wrenched on the shower taps. The pipes gurgled and spat while naked she shivered. It took an age before the hot water came through. She shampooed her hair, shaved her underarms, scratched a small scab from her knee and began to soap her body. When she came to her breasts, they felt swollen and tender. Her hand slid to her stomach, taut and flat, and rested there a moment while she gnawed on her lip. She hadn't bled in two months.

He'd told her not to worry. He'd ripped open the wrapper with his teeth and fumbled it on in the dark. But later he said it broke.

She rinsed off, towelled dry, dressed in faded jeans and a purple shirt.

Her parents were waiting in the lounge room. Arthur wore his best brown trousers, a speckled sports jacket, and a woollen tie. Merle looked as dowdy as usual in a navy coat-dress (which had to be ten years old), stockings and low-heeled shoes. They could have been going to church.

'You can't go to the Ekka like that!' Merle eyed a grass stain on Miffy's jeans. 'What will people say?'

'They won't say anything, Mother. No-one will know who we are.'

'Wear your nice pink pullover, the one I made for your birthday.'

'It'll be too hot.'

'Bring it here. If we stay for the fireworks you'll thank me.' Merle muttered about *insolent teenagers* as she stuffed the jumper into her voluminous bag alongside cheese sandwiches, apples, and a Tupperware container of home-baked peanut crispies. It was a wonder she didn't pack the thermos as well.

The train station was packed with mums and dads and little kids. As the Exhibition Special eased into the platform, four teenagers scrambled down the stairs from the overhead bridge.

Michelle and Mac were hand in hand. Dirk trailed a half-step behind. The fourth was a girl. Long hair, orange mini-dress, cork platform shoes. As they reached the carriage, Dirk grabbed the girl's hand. It was a casual gesture, as if they'd been going together for months.

Miffy ducked, hoping her distinctive red hair wouldn't give her away.

They'd probably head for Sideshow Alley and the rides. The Wild Mouse, the Chair-o-plane, the Octopus, the Paratrooper. With the sort of money the band raked in, they could afford to stay until the place shut down for the night.

On the other side of the vast showgrounds were the pavilions where Miffy and her folks would spend the day. Better to be bored rigid than to bump into Dirk and the new girlfriend. The thought of his rummy breath made her want to puke.

At the Exhibition station, noisy passengers spilled out of the corrals and crushed into the pedestrian tunnel. To the north was Sideshow Alley, to the south the main ring and the pavilions. The tunnel was the main link between the two sections. There was always a traffic jam, which roving photographers turned into a business opportunity. As planned, the Jones family turned south. Merle, who'd pored over *The Morning Post* at breakfast, had the day all mapped out.

First, was the judging of pampered pooches. Miffy yawned as fluff-balls that had no right to be classified as dogs paraded before an adoring crowd. Whether this one's jaw was overshot or that one was bandy made no difference to the entertainment value. There was absolutely nil.

The thrill-seekers moved on to the chook pavilion, raucous with crows of arrogant roosters. Then the flower show where Merle had to spend fully fifteen minutes reading the tags on every plant of every exhibit.

'You don't even like gardening,' Miffy complained.

'Don't try my patience, Myfanwy. I've had quite enough of your whinging.'

The fashion parade in the Wool Pavilion was tolerable, but the so-called *fashion* had not a mini-skirt in sight and was obviously aimed at old ladies like her mother.

For lunch, much to Merle's disgust, Arthur bought hot chips from the Tasmanian potato stand.

'I've brought perfectly good sandwiches and you're wasting money on rubbish.'

'Lighten up, luv.' Arthur handed Miffy a tub of the delicious fare. Crispy on the outside, squishy on the inside and so hot they burnt the roof of her mouth.

Afterwards he dragged them through the machinery pavilion to see one-tonners, off-roaders and tractors. Like a small boy with a new Tonka truck, he was riding on a high of diesel. He could be a boring old fart and they often clashed, but secretly she adored her only ally in this tough teenage world.

At sunset, they made their way to the main ring to sit it out until the seven o'clock fireworks. The sheepdog trials were in full swing. A black-and-white Border collie called Scamp was doing his best, but the dumb sheep kept breaking away.

Arthur was immediately enthralled. He pushed through the bottleneck at the gate and led the way between rows jammed with kids and showbags to the plank seats at the far side.

Merle produced a rubber ring that looked like a flat tyre tube and proceeded to blow it up. It took some doing, her face was red. She positioned it beneath her ample buttocks. 'Can't be too careful,' she said. 'Hard seats give me piles.'

'Must you be so *gross?*' Miffy buried her head in her hands.

'Bodily functions aren't gross.' Merle voice was as loud as a foghorn.

Captivated by the trials and tribulations in the arena, Arthur munched on a piece of dried apple he'd found in his pocket. Scamp the sheepdog had his work cut out. The woolly lumps of mutton defied all attempts to make them walk between two white posts. The entire performance was pointless.

Merle peeled a mandarin, broke it in half and gave one to Arthur. 'Eat this, dear. It'll help with your constipation.'

Miffy rolled her eyes and stood up. 'I'm off to get sample bags. See you in half an hour.' She was gone before either could say a word.

The showbag pavilion was a short walk up the hill from the main ring. To get in was like squeezing through a crack in a concrete wall. You needed protective equipment and a battering ram to get through all the people. Babies screamed, mothers baulked at being squashed in the crush. Some families sat on the lawn outside and sent their strongest to run the gauntlet with the shopping list.

Sixteen years of navigating the pavilion made Miffy an expert. The showbags themselves held little interest. She was too old for *Phantom* comics and cheap plastic toys. Although she loved chocolate (and there was always plenty of that), she could buy six Violet Crumble bars at Coles for the price of one showbag.

What she loved was the pavilion itself. Its soaring roofline, the colourful stalls, the Silhouette Man who cut paper portraits with tiny scissors, the aroma of fresh-cooked popcorn, the atmosphere of delight. The showbag pavilion was part of her childhood. It was fairyland and Santa's workshop and a pirate treasure cave all in one.

Once inside, her spirits lifted. She ambled from stall to stall—Allens, MacRobertson, Cadbury, Nestle—to the far side of the vast shed.

The Beekeepers Association had a live display. Between two glass panes the little insects worked away, oblivious to their audience. She watched one with a blue dot on its thorax stumble clumsily across the honeycomb.

Through the glass, a set of human eyes was watching her. Suddenly a hand snapped around her wrist and she was dragged to the other side of the display.

'Why'd you run out on me?' Dirk's eyes bored into her.

She wrestled her arm free. There was a mark like a Chinese burn around her wrist. 'Where's your new girlfriend?' she countered.

'I asked you first.'

She lowered her eyes.

'If I don't deserve an apology, at least I deserve an explanation.'

The last thing she wanted was an ugly confrontation in the best place on Earth. She saw that he had no intention of backing off, so she said what had been tormenting her ever since the night of the party. 'What we did … it wasn't right.'

'If you didn't want it, why didn't you stop me?'

'I … I … didn't … know …' Tears prickled her eyes.

'Yeah, you didn't know anything. That's the trouble. You made me look like a complete dickhead in front of my mates. I may never live it down.'

'It's all about you! I've got more to lose than you have.'

His face hardened. 'You're not up the duff, are you?'

'Shhhh! Not so loud.'

He looked her slender body up and down. 'Nah, you couldn't be.'

'What if I was?'

He dug his fists into his pockets. 'Look, I gotta go.'

'Thanks for your concern.'

'You're a weird chick, Miffy. You need to lighten up.'

'Piss off and die!' She stuck out her chin and stalked off, half-expecting him to follow. He didn't.

The vast space closed in on her. The colours became garish and the noise was deafening. She put her fingers in her ears and struggled through the crowd. The sea of heaving odours—greasy fries, armpits, rancid ice-cream, hot butter—became a tidal wave of nausea. She had to get out of there.

Ahead were the brick arches that would lead to fresh air. All she had to do was hold her breath and run. She got as far as the Silhouette Man, five paces from the exit. In a forty-four gallon rubbish drum she emptied her stomach. Afterwards she clung to the filthy rim like a drunk. The Silhouette Man, eighty if he was a day, asked if she wanted him to call the St John's Ambulance.

She shook her head, wiped her mouth and managed to stagger outside. When she'd recovered, she picked her way back to her parents' ringside seat.

'Where are the sample bags?' said Arthur.

'Didn't go in. Too many people.' She shivered in her thin cotton shirt. 'Mind if we don't stay for the fireworks?'

'Are you cold?' said Merle. With a look of *I told you so,* she handed over the pink jumper from her bag.

Gratefully Miffy pulled it on. 'I think I must be getting the flu.'

*

Six weeks later, Miffy could no longer deny what was happening to her body. Secretly she made an appointment with the Women's Health Clinic and told Merle she had to stay back after school for a rehearsal of the school musical.

This was not a complete lie. She'd been appointed props manager and Michelle had won the lead female singing role. Miffy's own vocal talents started and ended in the shower and were howled at by the neighbour's dog. Props suited her bowerbird tendencies and gave her an excuse to cruise the op shops. For a few dollars she'd bought a set of faux-Gothic windows, porcelain beer steins (slightly chipped), a trestle table, and an acre of red velvet curtain fabric for the production.

Straight after Biology, the last lesson for the day, she caught the Number 24 bus to the Valley. While she waited to cross the road, she gnawed on a fingernail and prayed that her constant puking was a real illness like a food poisoning or gastroenteritis. Something she could explain to her folks.

The entrance to the clinic was low key. An unmarked doorway led to a steep flight of stairs. On another occasion she might have walked right past and not noticed it was there.

She entered a small waiting room sparsely-furnished with plastic chairs. There were two other patients, both as young as she. The receptionist gave her a form to complete and told her to take a seat.

Shortly after, the surgery door opened and a youngish woman in a white lab coat called out. 'Mrs Jones?'

Miffy sighed and stood up. Time to face the truth.

'I'm Dr Adele Gibb. Come in.'

The consultation room was plain and practical. Desk, filing cabinet, two chairs, examination table, wall clock.

Dr Gibb scanned the details on Miffy's form. 'Now Mrs Jones, how can I help?'

'Why do you call me *Missus* when you know I'm not married?'

'Force of habit. At med school we're trained to call the gynaecological patients *Missus*. Less awkward, they say.'

'I'd rather you called me Miffy.'

'Okay, Miffy. Can you tell me why you're here?' Her face was gentle and kind. She didn't look or behave like a real doctor.

Their family physician, Dr Blake, was a crusty old man in his fifties. He never spoke to her directly and filtered all his questions through Merle, who insisted on coming into the surgery every visit. While her mother and Dr Blake discussed her symptoms and shortcomings, Miffy would sit there silent and useless, like a broken appliance at the repair shop. And no matter what the ailment—stomach cramps, an ingrown toenail, or a rash on her chest— she'd be prescribed a course of penicillin.

Miffy picked at her fingernails and couldn't think of how to begin.

'Would you like a jelly bean?' Dr Gibb smiled and offered the jar.

She took a red one and the doctor took one too.

'Why don't we pretend we're friends and just have a chat,' said Dr Gibb.

'I've never seen a doctor on my own before. My mother usually does the talking.'

'Do you want her here today?'

'No way!'

'That sounded definite.'

'I don't want her to know ...'

'Know what, Miffy?'

'That I might be pregnant.' There, it was out. Hanging in the room like a fart. It felt good to say it out loud to someone who wouldn't judge her.

'What makes you think you might be?'

'I haven't had a period in three months and my boobs are really sore.'

'Have you had sex?'

'Can you get pregnant from doing it just once?'

'I'm afraid so.'

'But he said not to worry. He put something on ...'

'Let's not jump to conclusions. Up on the bed with you.'

Throughout the ordeal Miffy kept her eyes shut, yet tears managed to squeeze out and trickle into her ears. This was it, the dreaded moment. Her fingers were crossed but she knew, long before Dr Gibb pulled off the examination gloves, what the verdict would be.

'You're right, Miffy. About three months.'

'Are you absolutely certain?'

'I'm afraid so.'

She sank onto the bed and covered her face. 'My mother will *kill* me.'

Dr Gibb offered tissues. 'It mightn't be as bad as you think. Sometimes mothers surprise you. If you give her a chance, she might understand.'

'You don't know Merle.' Miffy swung her legs over the bed and sat up. The tissues were soaked through. 'All I wanted to do was finish Senior and go to uni.'

'There's a lot to consider. You'll need to make adjustments and compromises but if uni is what you want, you'll find a way to get there.'

Miffy shook her head and wailed. 'My life is over.'

'What about the child's father. Can he help?'

'I hardly know him. You see, there was this party.' She sounded like a total slut.

'There's no need to say.' Dr Gibb slid a business card across the desk. It was for a counselling service. 'Under the circumstances I strongly recommend you call this number. You must do what's best for yourself and your child.'

'I don't want to have the baby. Isn't there something you can do?'

'I'm afraid termination is out of the question. For one thing, it's illegal in Queensland. Even if it weren't, you're too far advanced to do it safely. You *could* look at adoption. The baby would go to a good home and you'd be free to go to uni.'

The suggestion had appeal. Her mind was racing. With only four weeks until the end of term, she could hide her thickening waistline. Next year she'd arrange to stay with a school friend who'd moved to Victoria. The big exams were in November. She'd have seven whole months to catch up. She might get away with it. But Merle would be sure to find out, a prospect that again brought her to tears.

'I know this is a lot to take in. Would you like me to make an appointment with the counsellor?'

Miffy put the card in her purse. 'No, I'll do it straight after school tomorrow.'

With doom hanging over her head like a guillotine, she left the doctor's surgery. Before the rehearsal, she'd have to pull herself together and put on an Academy Award winning performance. She wandered aimlessly down Brunswick Street, looking vacantly in the shop windows and worrying.

Outside the Lucky Duck Restaurant, she stopped and looked at the menu. For the first time in weeks she felt hungry. She checked her finances and went in. The meal, which arrived five minutes later, was a pile of glossy noodles with chicken, cashews and shallots. It smelt divine and she wolfed down the entire plateful.

As she crossed Wickham Street, her bus swung around the corner. The stop was fifty yards away and the next one wasn't due for an hour. She started to run, waving her arms for the driver to wait. She lunged onto the step and collided with an old bloke who was arguing about the fare. His pockets were turned out. He was ten cents short.

She gave him the money. Then she bought a ticket for herself and dived for the back seat as the bus swerved onto the road.

Tomorrow she'd phone the counsellor. And then … maybe … she might drum up the courage to tackle what she most dreaded. Merle. What would happen afterwards was anyone's guess.

7

Monday 3 March

Two weeks after the bombing Vann Willis moved into new premises in Station Road, a block away from the old. James had arranged everything through a friend of a friend who worked in the accounting firm that was vacating. Space along the strip had been at a premium for years and would continue to be scarce until the commercial tower under construction at the top of the hill was finished. That would take another six months. In addition, he'd hired a temporary staffer to get through the busy period leading up to the election. He was training her in protocols—the who's who of the political world—as well as attending to his own workload. There was nothing that young man couldn't achieve when he put his mind to it.

Vann had given him complete control over the electorate office while she'd been caught up in a vortex of community duties and parliamentary process, and the grief of Freya's passing.

As if all the planets had lined up against her, the PPP had chosen to mount a dirty smear campaign. That pip-squeak, Jake Stone, accused her of orchestrating the whole bombing catastrophe to get publicity and support for her reform agenda. 'Dubious grandstand tactics to get the sympathy vote' he was quoted in *The Morning Post*.

The police investigation was going nowhere. There'd been no positive identification of the alleged bomber and no mention of a possible motive. If Detective Sergeant Dave Frame knew anything, he was keeping it to himself.

In frustration, Vann asked James to find what he could about Steptoe, whose real name (according to Lara) was Bert Bagley. Acting on little more than a hunch and a lifetime of dealing with damaged people, Vann thought better of divulging her line of inquiry to Dave Frame. In any case, he'd probably laugh her out the door for relying on women's intuition.

Vann's new office was smaller than the old one but the fit-out was modern and sleek. Polished wood floors, black granite reception desk, a small but functional kitchenette at the rear, and a door that led directly down to the basement car park. What pleased Vann most was the plate-glass shopfront which was highly visible from the street. There'd be no furtive comings and goings and no place to hide. What you saw was what you got.

On the morning of the move she spent precious time sorting through boxes of material brought from home and organising her goldfish-bowl office. Finished at last, she spun around and admired the pristine orderliness of the place, a state that likely wouldn't endure the passage of the day.

At reception, James was run off his feet coaching the new girl and simultaneously dealing with a queue of constituents and phones that were constantly ringing. Total chaos and no-one to help. She checked the time: half an hour until the next appointment.

Vann hated answering the office phone, especially this close to an election. You never knew what sort of caller you'd get. She gritted her teeth and picked up, taking care not to identify herself. A state minister answering the phone was not good for the image.

The first caller complained about rude service from the Department. Easily handled with an email to the Director General. The second was an elderly woman who wanted protection for her granddaughter, a pawn in an ugly custody battle. That one she could manage as well. The third wanted to sell her a new telephone system. Yeah, right.

Then came the voice, smooth as chocolate. Even before he said his name, she knew who it was. She was a sucker for a voice. That was the reason she listened to Radio National; that was why she went to Gerard Depardieu films (certainly not for his looks); that was what attracted her to her first beau all those years ago.

Seth began with his usual greeting. 'Hey Ms Willis, what do you know?'

'How did you know it was me?'

'It sure as hell isn't James. How come you're answering the phone?'

'In exactly three minutes I have an appointment elsewhere. What do you want?'

'I've dug up something very interesting. Can we meet?'

'You've got to be joking!' She clamped the phone receiver between her shoulder and neck while she stuffed papers into the attaché case.

'Whoa. I want to help, not start World War Three.'

Her voice softened. 'What's it about?'

'The bomber. I've got a couple of leads.'

'Shouldn't you talk to Detective Sergeant Frame instead?'

'I happen to know you're doing some investigations of your own.'

He was right of course, but she wasn't about to let on. She scarcely knew the man. And he was a reporter who'd just as likely write outlandish lies about her withholding evidence from the cops. Yes, that was it. A trick so she'd spill the beans and he'd get a story.

'I don't know where you got such a notion. Sorry Mr VerBeek, you're out of time.' Before he could protest, she hung up. Not the most professional way of ending a call but effective.

All the same, she couldn't help but feel curious about what he'd said. She'd read his article about the bombing and the request for public assistance. What if someone had come forward? She was convinced Steptoe was not the man, which meant she wasn't safe from another attack. The thought sent a shiver down her spine.

She looked out through the broad plates of green-tinted glass to the footpath. A straggle of kids from Riverdale High wandered up the hill; a young mother with a pram waited at the crossing; the bitumen sparkled outside her old place on the next block. She imagined the thousands of glass slivers, caught in cracks or mashed into the tar. She pictured Lara's face, lacerated beyond repair. How lucky they both were to be alive!

A flash of colour caught the corner of her eye. On awning opposite her office was an enormous green-and-orange banner. Glittery, it shimmered in the sunlight.

Jake Stone rocks! On election day vote 1 for the PPP.

The size and brilliance of the colours made her modest blue-and-white effort look drab and old fashioned. His message—*Jake Stone rocks*—summed him up. Shamelessly he was pursuing the youth vote with unfunded promises, bluster and pizazz. Anyone over the age of twenty-five would see right through him.

In a flashbulb moment, Vann again cast her eye over the people in the street. Students, young professionals, new mothers, fresh-faced trainees of the Violet Beauty Academy. Not one of them would have been a day over twenty-five.

She was a dinosaur in her own electorate. What had happened to the middle-aged parents and the old dears on walking frames who used to live in Riverdale? When did they leave? Were they dead? Her election promises were stuck in the past. Compensation for victims of forced adoptions in the 1970s, housing programs for the elderly, employment programs for mature-aged workers. If her observations were right, she'd better get with the times or she might not even see another term.

Perhaps she should call Seth back. He was an excellent journalist who'd be good to have on side. But would he support her?

The day of the bombing they'd made a connection that went beyond being polite. Her guard was down. She'd said things she later regretted, yet he'd not taken advantage.

Her hand hovered over the phone.

'Vann, don't forget your eleven o'clock appointment in town.' James, efficient as always, was standing at her office door. 'I've called a cab.'

Seth would have to wait.

The meeting was a private briefing with the Commissioner of the *Inquiry into Possible Corruption and Illegal Activities Relating to Forced Adoption*. Vann had been looking forward to it with a touch of trepidation. She expected the Commissioner, a retired magistrates court judge, would go through the recommendations and confirm whether her proposed reforms to the legislation would address the issues raised. Throughout the weeks of public hearings, the Inquiry had received around two hundred submissions from people and organisations all over the state. While she had a good idea of the likely issues—maltreatment within institutions, physical and emotional abuse, coercion of the birth mothers—she hadn't yet been privy to the entire content.

Not that she was ignorant of the raw deal dished up to young women in the nineteen seventies and earlier. Before Women's Lib and the civil rights movement spurred grassroots opposition to the paternalistic attitudes of the government. In those days she was at university, a raging rebel who agitated for abortion on demand and equality for women. She protested against domestic violence and demanded safe houses for the victims of abuse. Once in 1974, she'd been arrested in a street demonstration against the police state of right-wing Premier Joh Bjelke-Petersen.

She'd suffered personally too, through the death of a friend and someone very precious, because of the social stigma surrounding women who fell pregnant out of wedlock. Her life's purpose was to stamp out that sort of injustice forever.

At Parliament House, she met the five members of the commission in a wood-panelled meeting room off the central courtyard. The Commissioner did the talking. She explained that, in addition to written submissions, they'd accepted verbal contributions made anonymously under oath. On several occasions they'd had to adjourn because of the contributor's distress.

'One account epitomises the whole sorry system,' said the Commissioner. 'At sixteen and pregnant, Miss X was admitted to an institution where the girls earned their keep laundering hospital linen. *Slave labour* was the way she described it. During her confinement, she was kept under lock and key, was allowed no contact with her family or friends and was sworn to secrecy. At the birth there was no medical help. Sadly, the baby was stillborn. One can only wonder how differently it might have been with proper care.'

To Vann the story sounded familiar. She was tempted to ask names and dates but this was not the time to side-track discussion.

The Commissioner continued. 'The odd part was, when we compared Miss X's description of the institution to departmental records, there was no match. We were unsure how to treat this because it was outside the terms of reference, so we included it in this separate confidential report for further investigation.'

The Commissioner opened the confidential report at the appendices.

Vann tried to read it upside down. Where the contributor's details should have been, was a single word. *Withheld.* An official government apology had opened the door to investigations of wrongdoing and victim compensation. When she'd ordered this Commission of Inquiry, she'd had an inkling of what might be revealed. Now it was all there in black and white, in two spiral-bound books—one public, the other confidential—containing the details of the wreckage and perhaps the names of people who were responsible. Her palms were itching.

Vann left the meeting with a copy of the two reports. She had a week to absorb the official report before tabling it in Parliament, and four weeks to obtain her department's response. That would likely coincide with the pre-election ban on new legislation. If the recommendations were contentious, she'd need a political mandate. Her proposal to compensate girls who had been in state-run institutions was one promise she was determined to keep. She had modest support from her colleagues, but would it be enough?

With the reports heavy in her briefcase, she hastened to the car. Her next face-to-face appointment was late in the afternoon. She had two hours to herself. Two precious hours to peruse the submissions and recommendations. From the outset she'd suspected some institutions had operated outside the law, yet she'd never had enough evidence to refer matters to the police.

She directed the driver to Riverdale, not to her office where she was exposed like a store mannequin to the street, but to her apartment high on the ridge. There she'd have a quiet place to read and digest the information and decide what she must do next.

With time ticking she flew into the lift and hit the tenth-floor button. Her key was out ready to slot into the lock. She flung open the door, kicked off her shoes and trotted down the hall.

Voices floated from the lounge room. For a moment she froze, replayed the brief conversation she'd had with Lance the night before. He'd said he was on lunch shift at the restaurant and his brother was on for dinner. Or was it the other way around? Lately her days and nights had all run into one. After the election she'd promised herself time off. She was so exhausted she'd sleep an entire week.

Lance was on the couch, watching an American sit-com on TV. His feet were on the coffee table beside an empty plate. In his hand was a half-drunk glass of red wine.

As she came in, he jumped in fright. 'Geez Vann, you nearly gave me a heart attack.'

'I thought you were at work.'

'Change of plan. My stupid brother's broken his wrist. He's trialling a temporary chef for the lunches. Hey, I didn't expect to see you until late. Everything okay?'

'Yeah, fine. I've got a report to read and wanted somewhere quiet.' She took a banana from the bowl in the kitchen, perched on the stool and peeled it. The report lay unopened on the bench.

Lance was watching her, his head tilted to the side. 'What's up? You *never* come home in the middle of the day.'

'It's the report from the adoption inquiry. I need to concentrate. Simple as that.' She finished the banana and switched on the electric kettle for tea.

'You look dreadful.'

'Thanks for the compliment,' she snapped, realising he wouldn't let her get off lightly. Her two precious hours of peace were about to evaporate like steam from the kettle.

'You don't sleep, you scarcely eat. You drink more than you should. Vann, you're a train wreck waiting to happen. Why are you *really* doing all this?'

'One more term,' she said firmly. 'What I've started, I must finish. There's a lot riding on it for a lot of people.'

He'd obviously had way more than half a glass of wine, enough to make him morose and belligerent.

'You might have your nice fat report, but it'll open up terrible wounds. The fallout will take years to clean up.'

'Let me be the judge of that. This has been a long time in the making. The skeletons *must* come out of the closet before we can move on.' Against her better judgement she poured herself a Scotch. She seldom had alcohol at lunchtime. But between the document burning a hole in the bench and Lance's hostility, a cup of green tea and ginger wasn't going to cut it.

She tossed the Scotch down neat. Instantly her body relaxed and her mind sharpened. If she had to, she'd debate him all afternoon.

'What's the good of stirring up old muck? What's past is past,' he said.

'People have suffered because of bad policies and lack of control. I want to expose the culprits and bring them to justice.'

'If you ask me, it's nothing but a power-hungry witch-hunt.'

'I didn't ask you,' she snarled.

'Maybe you should. In case you haven't noticed, there are two people in this relationship. Or there used to be. At the moment I'm not so sure.'

'Give me a break, Lance. You know it's tense before an election.'

He pressed the remote control and turned up the volume. Canned laughter from a fake audience drowned her out.

She ate another banana and poured another Scotch. On the balcony, she shut the glass door, settled in her favourite easychair and opened the report.

8

Saturday 2 October 1971

Saturday morning after the final dress rehearsal, Miffy lay in bed until late. Miraculously she'd survived two weeks since her appointment at the clinic without telling anyone her secret. At school she'd played the clown, which was totally out of character. She was surprisingly good at it. A natural in fact. Her antics had everyone in stitches and the drama teacher promised her a part in the next comedy production.

Of course, Merle wouldn't stand for any such nonsense. You're there to study, not waste your time playing silly buggers.

Sunlight streamed through the diamond-cut louvres, casting rainbow patterns onto the wall. Miffy examined the egg-and-dart mouldings on the cornice of her room. Soon her condition would begin to show and she still hadn't phoned the counsellor.

Those two little words—I'm pregnant—would hit her parents like a brick. She'd practiced saying it aloud. It was as subtle as the punchline to a dirty joke.

No, she couldn't bring herself to tell them. Not today. Maybe next week.

She thought about the alibi of her friend in Victoria. What if she really went? Not to her actual friend's place, because the girl's mother would be sure to tell Merle. Perhaps she'd go to Sydney or Perth, get a job and a cheap room in a boarding house. Some girls went to New Zealand for a 'working holiday' and no-one was any the wiser.

But who'd employ a pregnant teenager with no experience? The paltry amount she'd saved from her pocket money would barely cover the fare.

A knock on the bedroom door brought her back to reality.

Merle said, 'Myfanwy, are you awake? Telephone call.'

'Coming.' She slid out of bed and wrapped herself in a brunch coat to hide the slight bulge in her middle.

It was Michelle. She was practically hysterical. Between sobs she managed to say, 'Mac ... dumped ... me ... can't ... live ... without him.'

'I'll be over straight away.' Miffy hung up the phone and asked Merle for a lift. The city's centralised public transport system was pathetic. On Saturdays cross-suburban buses were non-existent. A trip that took ten minutes by car would take an hour by the time she caught one bus into the city and another out again.

'A friend in need is a friend indeed,' quoted Merle, 'but don't neglect your study.'

'No, Mum.'

'We've made great sacrifices to give you an education, your father and I.' Merle was winding up for her usual lecture.

Miffy could quote it word for word. Her mother never gave credit for her hard work and determination that won the senior high-school scholarship and saved her from a lifetime of working in Coles' cafeteria.

She pulled on her stretchiest shorts and a loose t-shirt. Fifteen minutes later she was at Michelle's front door.

Shelley's hair was as messy as a crow's nest, her eyes were red and her breath stank like a hangover. She grabbed Miffy's wrist and pulled her along the hallway to her bedroom at the rear.

Although the house was empty, she shut the door behind them. 'I don't know what to do. Everything was fine. Last night he picked me up after rehearsals, then in the car he told me it was over.' She flopped onto the bed and hugged her knees. Tears cascaded down her cheeks.

'You poor thing.' Miffy reached out her hand, but the other girl pushed it away.

'He used to say ... he loved me ... I thought ... we'd be together ... forever.'

'I'm sure he'll be back.' The well-meant remark sounded fake and hollow.

'It's my fault ...' For several minutes Michelle bawled uncontrollably. Recovering, she said, 'Remember I took two days off school last month?'

Miffy nodded in the affirmative. In truth she hadn't noticed. Ever since Michelle started going with Mac, she'd kept her distance. Lunchtimes she snubbed her friends and listened to rock music with the weirdo bunch called the *metal-heads*.

'Mac took me to Sydney.'

'You *wagged* school? But you never wag school.'

'Just shut up and listen.'

'Okay. Okay.'

'We saw this woman in the Cross. The place was filthy. Her tools were like torture instruments. I couldn't go through with it. Mac got angry and said I'd cost him a fortune. But I was scared. I know what can go wrong. He promised to take care of me, and now he's gone.'

'Oh my God, you're ...'

'I wish I was dead!' Michelle's body trembled with grief.

'Shelley, we're in this together.'

'Don't patronise me. This is the worst thing that could ever happen.'

'You don't understand. I've got a secret as well.' Miffy patted her stomach.

Michelle's mouth opened in surprise. 'Are you kidding?'

'Due in March.'

'Have you told your oldies?'

'Not yet. You?'

Michelle picked at lint on the bedcover. 'Maybe we should run away and have our babies together.'

'Have you got any money?'

'Hmm. Not much.'

'Oh, I almost forgot.' Miffy took the counsellor's card from her purse.

Michelle read it aloud. 'Julia Grice and Associates. Confidential pregnancy and adoption help. *Confidential*, I like the sound of that. Should we give her a call?' She sounded more like her old self.

'I was going to ring one day after school. I've been kind of putting it off.'

Laughing and crying at the same time, they hugged each other. To not be alone was what Miffy had prayed for, but to share the burden with her best friend was almost too good to be true.

Footsteps were coming up the back stairs. The lock rattled. The floorboards of the old timber house creaked, grocery bags rustled in the kitchen.

'Yoo-hoo! We're home,' sang Michelle's mum.

'Be out in a sec.'

She whispered to Miffy, 'How do I look?'

'Gross. Give me your brush and I'll fix your hair. Do you have any mouthwash?'

Michelle breathed into the cup of her hand. 'Phew! Sorry about the dogs-breath. After what happened I had a few shots of Scotch. Then I had to puke. I do that a lot.'

'Yeah, me too.' Miffy dragged the brush through the tangled mess and braided it neatly. Her tears ran freely at last. 'Promise you won't tell another soul?'

'Our secret forever,' said Michelle.

They spat on their palms and pressed them together.

School on Monday was longer than one of Merle's bad moods. It culminated in a torturous double period of Physics. Miffy's wave experiment wouldn't work and her teacher roused on her for using the wrong formulae. When the three o'clock bell finally sounded, she threw her books in the locker and raced to meet Michelle at the gate.

They walked a short distance to the phone booth outside the post office. Miffy unhooked the receiver and dialled the number on the business card.

After two rings a kindly voice answered.

Miffy swallowed. It felt like a game of truth or dare. 'Um … I wanted to ask … um … what happens if … um … you're in the family way and … you aren't married?'

Michelle leant in to listen. Her breath was warm on Miffy's cheek.

'Do you have a place to stay?' said the woman at the counselling service.

Michelle cut in. 'It's not like we've been kicked out of home.'

'Sshhhh! You want me to do this?' Miffy elbowed her out of the way.

Michelle put up her nose and flounced out of the booth.

'Can we see the counsellor please?'

After a brief discussion she made an appointment for four o'clock the next day.

Outside, Michelle was sitting cross-legged on a low brick wall, petulantly sifting her mane for split ends. 'I don't want to see this counsellor person,' she announced. 'We agreed to go someplace until the babies come but I don't want to give mine up. It's all I have left of Mac.'

'Are you crazy? Let's hear what she says. We don't have to take her advice.'

'Have it your way.' Michelle flapped her arms. 'Look kid, I've got to go. See you tomorrow.'

The next afternoon at four, the two girls stood outside a white stucco house in a quiet suburban street in New Farm. With a green concrete path flanked by rose beds and two giant palm trees guarding the gate, it looked like an ordinary family home.

'You sure this is the right place?' said Michelle.

Miffy checked the business card. 'Yep, this is it.'

An old woman with a grey bun opened the door. 'You must be the lass who phoned yesterday. Come in and take a seat. Julia will be with you shortly.'

The waiting room was long and narrow with four padded armchairs at the end. Sunshine filtered through the leadlights. Spots of colour tiptoed across the polished floorboards. A parlour palm in a brass pot nodded in the musty heat.

Within minutes their names were called. Julia Grice was an exact replica of the woman who'd greeted them, except her hair was light brown and she looked much younger. She led them to an airy room and closed the French doors behind them.

It was unlike any other office or doctor's surgery. There were no desks, no examination tables and no medical instruments. Instead of antiseptic, the room was scented with lavender. Bookshelves lined the walls. Miffy ran her eye along the titles, which ranged from *Treating Anxiety*, to *Sons and Lovers*, to *The Female Eunuch*. At the centre of the room were four matching armchairs, one on each corner of a Persian rug.

They all sat down.

Julia poured glasses of water, offered Minties, and made small talk about the latest movies. 'I'm pleased you decided to come. When you spoke to my mother yesterday, you sounded unsure. Would you like to fill me in?'

Her face was open, her mouth was soft. Her hands lay quietly in her lap. She had a look of empathy that Merle totally lacked.

Haltingly Miffy sketched out what had happened.

Michelle chipped in from time to time but omitted the part about Sydney.

Julia listened without interruption. 'So, what are your plans now?'

Miffy shrugged. 'That's why we came to see you.'

'Do you have the support of your parents?' Julia looked directly at Miffy.

She shook her head. 'I haven't told them yet. We were going to leave town together and stay away until after … you know.'

Julia sucked air through her teeth. 'You think that's a good idea? You think your folks might *care* about what happens to you?'

'Yeah, I suppose.'

'And you want to go where nobody cares.'

'I suppose it's not a great idea. But I can't bring myself to tell Merle.'

'You told *me*, didn't you?' said Julia.

'Yeah, with Shelley's help.'

Julia raised her eyebrows. 'Maybe she'll help you again. One way or another you've got to tell them. In the eyes of the law, you are a minor until the age of twenty-one. Until then, your father is legally responsible for you. How do you think he'll react?'

'Arthur will get mad at me, but he'll probably take my side.'

Michelle piped up. 'Your dad's a sweetie compared to mine.'

Julia said, 'Okay here are the options. One, you stay at home and your family wears the cost and the shame of what you've done. Two, you go to a state-run institution where you'll be treated like slave labour. Three, I can refer you to a lovely homestead in the country that's set up for girls in your condition. You'll get accommodation and meals and you'll be well looked after. There's a midwife for the birth and your child will be matched to a loving couple. Discretion absolutely guaranteed.'

'Wow!' breathed Miffy. 'Sounds perfect. What do you think, Shelley?'

'What if I want to keep the baby?'

'That's your decision. Caring for a young child is a fulltime responsibility. It would mean the end of your education and no prospect of a job. It would put a huge financial burden on your parents who'd have to support you until you found a husband prepared to raise another man's child.'

Michelle puffed out her cheeks. 'Then could I go to this place and decide what to do with the baby later?'

'I'm afraid not. All the babies are put up for adoption. The child gets a good home and you can get on with your life.'

'I'm going to tell the oldies before I chicken out. Will you come with me, Shelley?'

Michelle sighed. 'How did we get ourselves into this shitty mess?'

Julia said, 'Talk to your folks, both of you. If they're interested in the country homestead, they should phone immediately. Vacancies are scarce.'

Outside, the late afternoon sun cast long shadows of banana trees and ripple-iron rooves across the bitumen. On the bus they scarcely spoke.

Miffy mulled over how to deliver the information to her folks and came up blank. She knew it would go down like a sledgehammer. There was no way to soften the blow.

At the door Michelle squeezed her hand. 'Okay kid, let's do it.'

The cinnamon aroma of stewed apples wafted down the hall. Merle was clattering pots in the kitchen. In the lounge the TV showed grainy black-and-white images of the war in Vietnam. A still shot of a chopper crash flashed onto the screen.

Arthur was in his yard shorts, a beer stubby halfway to his mouth. 'Poor bastards. We should let 'em sort it out for themselves. We've got no right to be there.'

Miffy marched to the TV set and switched it off.

'Hey, I was watching that!'

'Mum and Dad, I have something important to tell you.'

Michelle perched on the arm of the settee and nodded her encouragement. It was good to have her there for support.

Wiping her hands on a red tea towel Merle ambled into the room. 'Can't it wait until after the news?'

Fear threatened to strangle her. What she must say began to unravel into a tangle of woolly thoughts. She cleared her throat, took a breath and launched. 'I'm going to have a baby in March. Before you get mad, this was a big shock for me too.'

Merle looked like she'd faint.

Arthur slammed the stubby onto the coffee table. 'Who's the father?'

'No-one you'd know.'

'Give me his name! I'll make him live up to his responsibilities.'

'Dad, I hardly know him.'

'If he forced you into this, I'll have his hide.'

'He didn't rape me. It sort of just happened.'

'You don't even know his name?' Merle gasped. 'What were you thinking, girl? I didn't raise you to be a slut!' She slapped Miffy hard across the cheek. 'How dare you drag this family's reputation through the mud!'

Miffy's eyes filled with tears but she stood her ground. 'I didn't mean to get pregnant and I don't want to cause trouble.'

'Of all the stupid things you've ever done! You can pack your bags and get out!'

'Now, Merle. Don't lose your head,' said Arthur.

'You're a wicked, wicked girl! You're not fit to be my daughter.' Merle flapped the tea towel up and down, a red rag to a bull.

'Kicking her out won't solve the problem.' Arthur came to the rescue.

Merle threw herself into a chair. 'Why this! I'll never be able to show my face in public again. God help me. God help us all!'

Michelle offered to make *a nice cup of tea* and promptly fled to the kitchen.

Miffy sat on the settee opposite while her folks worked through their anger. There was a strange sense of unreality. She felt detached, as if watching characters in a soap opera, not the people in her own life.

From the kitchen came the sounds of the jug bubbling, the clink of china, the sigh of the fridge door. Michelle reappeared with four mugs which she put on the coffee table between the newspaper and Arthur's abandoned stubby.

Michelle whispered in Miffy's ear. 'Keep going, you're doing fine.'

'I went to see a counsellor today. She said she could help.'

'Myfanwy! You consulted a perfect stranger before you told your own parents!' Merle's face was puce with rage.

'Mrs Jones, she wanted to get proper information.' Michelle was like a rock in a wild tumultuous sea. She smoothed her school uniform and took a sip of tea.

'What did this counsellor person say?' said Arthur.

'Julia said I should talk to you and do what's best for the child.' Miffy gave him the business card and told them about the country homestead.

Arthur put on his reading glasses and studied the card like the Saturday form guide. He passed it to Merle, stomped to the cocktail cabinet and poured himself a large glass of Scotch.

Merle put the card in her lap. 'I can't think about this now. I'm too angry. Michelle, you should be going home.

'I'll call Mum to pick me up.'

Outside, Miffy and Michelle sat on the kerb and breathed the stench of over-ripe mangoes. Flying foxes—rats of the sky—screeched and squabbled in a neighbour's tree, adding to the layer of rotting fruit already on the ground.

'That went okay, don't you think?' said Michelle.

'Are you kidding? It hasn't even started. It'll be like the Cold War until the middle of next year. When will you tell yours?'

'Tonight. I want to do it alone.'

Miffy gave her a hug. 'Thanks for coming. I'm sort of excited about a long holiday in the country with my best friend.'

Headlights swept around the bend. A red Toyota stopped opposite. Michelle waved and trotted to the car.

'Good luck,' Miffy called.

'Piece of cake.' Michelle eased into the passenger's seat and the car sped away.

On Friday, Michelle wasn't at school. It was the opening of the musical and final preparations were being made. The drama teacher asked about Michelle but Miffy had no answer. The understudy, a Grade Nine girl with a voice like an angel and a face full of pimples, was called for a last-minute rehearsal. She was so excited she could barely remember her lines.

The teacher frowned and clicked a string of worry beads that were her constant companion. 'Come on, kids. Get your act together. Showtime's at six.'

After the three o'clock bell, Miffy sprinted to the phone booth at the post office and dialled Michelle's number.

The phone rang out. Should she go around? She'd have to be back at the hall by five and she didn't relish calling Merle for a lift. She couldn't risk being grounded now. The entire production depended on her to manage the props and set changes. Unlike the performers, she had no understudy.

She paced a lap of the shops, bought an Icy-pole from the store, tried Michelle's number again. Still no answer.

It was unlike Michelle to miss school. Miffy chewed on her nails and stared in the shop window worrying about what to do next. Her inner voice told her something was wrong, or perhaps it was telepathy between friends with shared secrets. Her chest hurt as if it were being squeezed between the jaws of a giant bench vise.

She wandered past the laneway where the Senior boys gathered after school.

'Hey, Miffy!' Gaye bounded up the laneway. Cigarette smoke trailed behind her like a streamer. The skirt of her uniform was rolled way above the line of her stockings. 'Whatcha doin', chicky babe?'

'Killing time. Have you heard from Shelley?'

'Not for a couple of weeks. She's gone a bit weird if you ask me.'

'You heard Mac broke it off?'

'Yeah. Shame, he was such a spunk.'

'She's really cut up about it. She wasn't at school and she's meant to be on stage in a couple of hours.'

A Senior boy called Mark emerged from the cloud of smoke and bawdy laughter and swaggered towards them. 'Who's the goss about?'

'No-one,' Miffy snapped.

'You can't fool me. You girls are always talking about someone.'

Gaye flashed him a sexy smile and struck a pose that displayed every curve to perfection. 'Have you seen Michelle lately?'

'Hmmm.' He stroked the fuzz on his chin. 'Actually, I saw her this morning.'

'Where?' Miffy piped.

'In a car with her mum. They were stopped at the lights in Brunswick Street near the Story Bridge turnoff. I gave her a wave but she ignored me.'

'What time did you see her?'

'What is this … the Spanish Inquisition?'

'Please, it's important.'

'Would've been about ten. I forgot to put on my alarm. Holy shit, I copped it from the Principal when I got to school.' He turned his palms over. Three pink welts cut across them.

'Poor baby.' Gaye kissed the wounds. 'Come down the lane with us, Miffy. Someone wants to meet you.'

Miffy checked her watch. 'I'm off. People to see, things to do.'

'Sure,' said Gaye. 'Good luck tonight.'

'You're meant to say *break a leg*,' said Mark.

'That's only if you're an actor. I don't want her to break her leg.'

Miffy left them to squabble about theatrical terms of endearment, trudged five hundred yards to the school hall and sat on the brick fence overlooking the car park. Perhaps Michelle would still turn up, all smiles and apologies, and everything would return to normal. Half an hour before the performance was due to start, she gave up and went backstage with the others. Michelle wasn't at Saturday's performance either. On Sunday, Miffy tried to phone her several times throughout the day but couldn't raise an answer.

Meanwhile the climate at the Jones's residence had become a frigid zone. In a double-whammy move that was as sudden as it was out of character, Arthur regained his driver's licence and took up golf. Weekend mornings at six he took the Austin to the course at Victoria Park for lessons from the pro Charlie Erp, followed by eighteen holes which lasted the rest of the day.

Merle buried herself in mountains of flour, butter, and raisins. Every year she baked fruit-mince pies for the church Christmas stall. The pastry was crisp and the centres were rich with spices. Of all the goodies she made, these were the best.

But this year Miffy had sinned and she was forbidden even the smallest morsel. The whine of the mixmaster blotted out any hope of peace talks and provided Merle with camouflage while she planned her next attack.

With the exams fast approaching, Miffy shut herself in her room and spread her text books over the bed. Her motivation to study was zero.

Eenie, meenie, minie, moe.

Biology. Reluctantly she opened the weighty book. *Chapter Ten: Vertebrates*. Her eyes skimmed over the sentences like skates over ice. At this rate she'd never pass.

Sunday night, everyone in the household was in bed by nine, a timeworn tradition summed up by Merle's favourite maxim, *a good night's sleep brings a good next week.*

Miffy had just turned off her bedside lamp when the phone began to ring. She rushed to the living room and eagerly snatched it up.

At first she didn't recognise the voice, for it was distant and as incoherent as a granny without dentures. She was about to hang up, when she caught the sound of her own name.

'Shelley? Is that you?'

The line crackled and whined. Amidst the static were two clear words. *It's gone.*

'I can't hear you. Can I call you back?'

Several sharp thuds vibrated down the line. 'Is that better?' said Michelle.

'Yeah. Where are you?'

'Phone booth. Byron Bay. I've only got forty cents. Can't talk long. I wanted tell you ... '

A shiver ripped down Miffy's spine as if she already knew.

'The baby ... it's gone ... Mum made me.'

'Oh my God, Shelley. What—'

Out of coins, the line cut out.

She cradled the receiver and replayed those last words. *Mum made me.* Of all her friends' mothers, Michelle's was the kindest and most understanding. Surely Shelley would have let her know she wanted to keep the baby. Why didn't anyone listen? First she'd had lost Mac and now she'd lost his child.

Miffy laid her hand on the curve of her belly. Her clothes were tight. Soon she'd no longer be able to hide her shame. It was clear that Merle would do whatever it took to safeguard the family's reputation. The course of her future was yet to be set. But whatever her fate, she'd now have to face it alone.

Monday morning, Miffy woke to the sound of knocking on her door.

'Get up, Myfanwy,' Merle shouted. 'You've got a big day ahead.'

These, the only words her mother had spoken to her since last week.

'Be out in a minute.'

She rolled over and lifted the curtain. Overnight, rain had come in. The sky was the colour of lead. She yawned and stretched. Her mood was as miserable as the weather. All night she'd had disturbing dreams about Michelle.

In the kitchen, the kettle whistled. Merle buttered slices of toast. Arthur, dressed in his overalls and work boots, attacked a bowl of Corn Flakes with a soupspoon. *The Courier Mail* was spread over the table like a black-and-white tablecloth. Absently, he slurped while he scanned the headlines.

'Eat properly,' Merle snapped in disgust.

He said nothing but kept on slurping and reading and slurping.

Miffy poured herself a glass of milk and sat opposite her father. Merle brought the teapot and the plate of toast, which she dumped in front of Arthur.

He didn't lift an eyelid.

Merle plumped into her usual chair and poured herself tea. It was then that she broke the news.

'Your father and I have considered our position and we've decided you should go to that home for naughty girls recommended by Julia Grice. We think it will be best all round, don't we Arthur?'

No response from Arthur, not even a grunt.

'Anyway, we've already made the arrangements. Straight after breakfast, you'll pack your bags. Your father will drop you off in New Farm on his way to work.'

'But the exams start in two weeks!'

'I can't see any point in sitting those. You'll never get into university. In fact, if you ever amount to anything in life it'll be a miracle. Now get a move on. Your father hasn't got all day.'

Miffy ran from the table and slammed the door of her room. She flung herself onto the bed and punched the pillow until her fists hurt. Red-faced and puffing she hauled her school bag onto the bed and turned out its contents. She packed t-shirts, jeans, stretchy shorts, underwear, and a notebook she'd used once as a diary. In the back were phone numbers for Michelle, Gaye, and the other girls from school. Abandoned in a *home for naughty girls*, the notebook might be her only friend.

Arthur carried the bag down the stairs and put it in the boot of the car. Miffy trailed behind him. Merle was nowhere to be seen.

'Hop in, luv. We don't want to be late.'

Barely a word was spoken the entire way. In New Farm he pulled up outside the white stucco house. He left the engine idling while he opened the lid of the boot and lifted the bag onto the rain-soaked pavement.

'Be good, luv.' He gave her a quick peck on the forehead and bolted.

On the footpath beneath a red umbrella she watched the Austin accelerate toward the crossroads. In less than a minute it was gone.

She lugged her bag to the door and pressed the buzzer. Instead of showing her to the waiting room, the older Grice woman led her through the house to a glass-enclosed room that was a jungle of palms, wax-leafed tropical plants, and curly-whirly ferns. With the rain pattering outside, it had the steamy atmosphere of a grotto behind a waterfall. Beneath the foliage lay a dappled grey cat. On a white cane chair sat another girl, long-limbed and fair. She wore a vacant expression and held her body as rigid as a statue.

'I'll leave you to introduce yourselves,' said Mrs Grice in a birdlike voice. 'The van will be here at nine.'

Miffy sat by the door. The other girl didn't seem to be in the mood to talk, so she turned her attention to the cat.

'Puss, puss,' she cooed. The animal yawned, arched its back and padded across the mosaic tile floor. Purring, it rubbed its face against her chair. Suddenly it dived to the floor and rolled on its spine, flicking its tail from side to side. She leant down and stretched out her hand toward the cotton-wool fur of its belly.

The fair girl said, 'It's a trap. If you touch him, he'll strike.'

Miffy pulled back her hand. 'Thanks for the warning.'

'No probs. I know cats. I've got five at home.'

'We haven't got any pets, not even a goldfish.'

'I'm Fiona.' said the fair one. 'Are you going to the farm?'

Miffy nodded and gave her name. She untied her hair ribbon and jiggled it out of reach of the cat. Its white-tipped paws were padded with pink, an irresistibly cute animal. It batted the ribbon which soon became entangled in its needle-sharp claws.

Fiona waddled across the room and squatted. 'There, puss.' She unhooked the ribbon and stroked the sleek fur. She looked around six months gone, maybe more. 'I'll miss my cats,' she said wistfully.

From outside came the chug of an engine. Miffy jumped up in time to see a blue-and-white Kombi van reversing down the driveway. The driver, a woman in a large floppy hat, got out.

Without a word, she strode to the passenger's side and wrenched open the sliding door. The girls followed her out, bundled their bags into the rear of a vehicle bursting with sacks and boxes and squeezed into the back seat.

The driver slammed the door, fired the ignition and let out the clutch. As the van rolled onto the bitumen, she took off the hat. Her face was clearly visible in the rear-vision mirror. To Miffy's surprise, it was Julia Grice herself.

9

Monday 3 March

After an anticlimax of an afternoon and the Mexican standoff with Lance, Vann returned to her electorate office around five. James was packing up to leave.

'How was the meeting?' He indicated the satchel under her arm.

'All good,' she said. 'Got the documents but haven't finished reading them.'

'Mind if I go early?' He stuffed the *Financial News* into his computer bag. 'Family matter I can't get out of,' he added by way of explanation.

'Okay, we'll catch up tomorrow.'

'By the way, a very insistent woman came to see you. Three times.'

'Did you get her name?'

'She wouldn't give it, but I'm sure she'll be back.'

'Thanks for the warning.'

She locked the door after him, walked into her goldfish-bowl office and dropped the satchel on her desk. Inside were the adoptions reports and other documents that needed her attention. For now, they'd have to wait. After the argument with Lance, a couple of glasses of Scotch, and a wasted afternoon at a kids' swimming carnival, she wasn't up for it. A hit of caffeine was what she craved. Optimistically she peered through the window at Café Nero down the road. Damn, it was shut. A coffee bag from the kitchenette would be a poor substitute but it'd be better than nothing.

Halfway down the hall she stopped. Someone was tapping on the front door. The body shape obscured by the frosted glass looked to be female. The head and upper body were swathed in black like an Islamic veil. At her side was a bright yellow bag, instantly recognisable.

Without hesitation, Vann opened the door.

79

'At last, you're here!' Lara was jumping out of her skin with excitement. She grabbed Vann by the forearm and looked as if she might kiss her.

'Nice to see you too. Come in.'

'Sorry to bother you when you're so busy, but you did say to call any time. I really need your help.' From the yellow Mimco handbag, she extracted a plastic folder.

'Can I get you a coffee? I'm making one for myself.'

'That'd be great. White, no sugar.'

'Same as me.'

By the time she returned with the coffees, Lara had laid out photographs like playing cards on the desk.

Vann picked one up. A middle-aged woman was nursing a young baby. She was standing outside a white house with barley-twist columns. The shadow of the photographer, a man in a broad-brimmed hat, crinkled across the path.

The house looked familiar, but Vann couldn't put a finger on where it could be.

'How much time do we have?' said Lara. 'This is going to be a long story.'

Vann said, 'I'm all ears.'

Lara took a swallow of coffee. 'Okay, here goes.'

'When I left home the day of the bombing, I had everything planned out. Half an hour to see you, then get to work before the morning rush. The night before I'd packed the documents in my bag in the hope you'd help me solve my life's mystery.

'We both know what happened next. I could have regarded it as an omen and given up, but I'm a very determined person, Ms Willis.' She drained the coffee, put down the cup and emptied the contents of the folder onto the desk.

'Go on,' said Vann.

'I found these papers at my mother's place in an old biscuit tin. She'd already been dead six months when I went to clean out the house. We'd had a falling out, you see. I hadn't been there in years and didn't have the heart to do it sooner. By then the accident reports and the post-mortems were in. My mother was at fault. She'd fallen asleep at the wheel and caused the head-on crash that killed her. The blood sample showed a cocktail of drugs. Prescription drugs. What a shock that was!

'She used to brag, *I'm seventy-four and never taken a pill in my life*. The bitch was lying through her teeth and I never suspected a thing.

'Walking into that house was like re-entering my childhood. Green shag-pile carpet, foil wallpaper, mirror tiles. Nothing had changed. I didn't know where to start. The cupboards were jammed with stuff I didn't know what to do with. My place was already bursting at the seams. But of course, *I'm* not a hoarder like Mum.

'I wandered around and around the house, opening doors and shutting them again. All Dad's clothes were still hanging in the closet. His shoes were under the bed, his notebooks were in the desk. He died ten years ago, not that you'd know it.

'By then I had this massive headache so I went to the medicine cabinet, not really expecting to find painkillers. In my day it was all Band-Aids and Dettol. But it was full of prescription drugs. I took them out one by one. *Prozac*, laxatives, antacids, *Valium*, asthma sprays, pills to make you sleep, pills to keep you awake.

'Every one was for my mother. All that crowing about her health! What other lies she told me?

'Then I remembered her secret tin. Blue with roses. I knew exactly what it looked like. I was six when I'd found it, hidden beneath her petticoats in the bedside chest.

What a pretty tin, I'd said opening it.

'Mum's face went purple and she ripped it out of my hands. *Don't you ever go through my things again!* She gave me a hiding and locked me in my room.

'Later when she was outside, I sneaked back in for another look. The tin was gone.

'That was thirty-six years ago and I've never forgotten. Whatever that tin held must have been important. I tore Mum's bedroom apart but it was nowhere to be found. The only place I hadn't looked was on top of the wardrobe. I stood on a stool and felt about. There it was at the very back, amongst the cobwebs and dead cockroaches.

'I held it in my hands. It was sky blue with red roses, exactly as I remembered.'

'So?' Vann was sitting on the edge of her chair. 'What was inside?'

'These.' Lara unfolded two age-spotted documents.

The first was an original birth certificate for Lara Rachel Dainford, born fifteenth of March 1972.

At the date, Vann did a double-take.

The parents' names were listed as George Henry Dainford and Pamela Jane Dainford. George's occupation was garage manager and Pam's was home duties. The witness to the birth was Mrs K. O'Brien (Midwife).

The second document was a receipt, handwritten in pen-and-ink, for five thousand dollars. It was made out to G. H. Dainford on the sixteenth of March 1972.

Vann whistled. 'That was a lot of money. More than a year's salary.' She put on her reading glasses for a closer look at the receipt. The signature at the bottom started with a D and ended in a series of loops.

Lara said, 'I've always felt different, ever since I was a child. I didn't fit in with my family. When I was in hospital the other day, they did a blood test. My blood type is O positive.'

Puzzled at the direction the story was taking Vann said, 'That's the commonest type. Around forty percent of the population, me included.'

'Yes, but my father was type AB. He used to say his blood was so rare it was worth bottling.'

'Hmm,' said Vann. 'So that means …?'

'It means my father wasn't my real father. It also casts a cloud over Pam. Either she was playing around (which I doubt) or she wasn't a genetic parent either. That's why I came to see you. I think I was adopted but there's no actual proof. Can you help?'

'I'll see what I can do. Can I take photocopies of these?'

'Sure. I'll give you my mobile number. Did I tell you I work for Centrelink?' Lara wrote her number on the back of an Australian Government business card.

'I seem to recall you were on the verge of quitting,' said Vann.

'What gave you that idea?'

'You told me in hospital. You were high on morphine at the time.'

'I wasn't happy at work, but now we've got a new manager. She's a breath of fresh air. I'm working half-days in the back office until this ugly face of mine heals.'

'Pleased to hear it … and your face *isn't* ugly.'

Vann made the photocopies and then saw Lara to the door. Outside, a smudge of orange ignited the western sky. A steady flow of people trudged home from the station.

She relocked the door and dashed back to her desk. She opened the adoption report, skimmed down the index. There he was. *Doyle, Dr Rowland.*

Her fingers were on fire as she flew through the report to the nominated place in the appendices. The related submission from *Name Withheld* was just two pages long. As she read it tears sprang to her eyes. It told the story of a couple who'd mortgaged their home to adopt a child. The baby was supplied by a private agency run by the doctor and his wife. The amount of money that had changed hands was obscene.

Baby trafficking, it could not be described in any other way. But was there enough evidence? At present, there were only inconclusive stories—one from Lara with the enigmatic receipt, and one from *Name Withheld* about Dr Doyle.

But, as they say, *where there's smoke there's fire*. If illegal activities had been going on at a home for unwed mothers, others might come forward once the media got hold of the information.

10

Monday 3 March

The minute Seth set foot in his cubicle Monday morning, Cate ambushed him.

'Hey boss, I've finished that article. I went through the snail-mail from your report, and got heaps of responses about the adoption stuff on Facebook and Twitter. And I found some amazing information on the internet.'

'Whoa. Let me catch my breath.' He dumped the canvas bag with his laptop on the desk and unpacked the charger and mouse.

She lowered her eyes. 'Sorry, I didn't mean to rush you. Only I thought you'd want to edit the copy before the deadline.'

'Leave it on my desk. I'll get to it soon enough.'

She deposited the paper in his in-tray. 'I know you're going to love it.'

He pushed the start button on his computer and left it to boot up while he made himself a strong cup of coffee. Monday mornings were never good, especially after a weekend on the turps with a journo mate who'd arrived unexpectedly from New York. He should never have opened the third bottle of shiraz at eleven last night, but they were thirsty from chewing the fat about religion, war, politics, and women. *What the hell*, he'd said as he opened the lid.

Live hard, die young.

Yep, Monday mornings were never much good. He scanned the list of unopened emails, saw nothing of interest. His electronic diary listed the tasks for the day. Number one, *make appointment with Vann Willis re adoption inquiry*. It was in red, which meant it had been carried forward from last week. He wrote himself a note to call after the caffeine cleared away the brain-fog. That would happen late morning if his estimation of residual alcohol in the bloodstream was accurate.

He drank the coffee. His head hurt. There wasn't much point in attempting to write, so he picked up Cate's report.

Baby Scandal

How much is a baby worth?

That was the question thousands of childless couples must have asked before the invention of IVF. In the 1960s and 70s these couples relied on adoption to get the babies they longed for.

At that time the contraceptive pill was not widely available, society frowned on pre-marital sex, and there was no welfare or income support for single mothers. Young women who accidentally fell pregnant had few choices.

While some babies were voluntarily surrendered for adoption, our research shows a substantial number were taken involuntarily or under duress. In some cases, exorbitant fees may have been involved.

Last week we revealed it was likely that the bombing of Minister Vann Willis's office was linked to the Commission of Inquiry into corruption and illegal activities relating to forced adoptions. Since then, hundreds of readers have come forward with their stories.

Mrs J, 68 of Palmwoods, wrote, 'The almoner said I should stop being selfish. I should give him to a decent family who'd raise him properly.'

Ms B, 57 of Darra, wrote, 'Two years ago my daughter tracked me down. I was seventeen when my parents sent me to the girls' home. I made it clear I wanted to keep my baby but they tricked me into signing the papers when I was groggy after the birth.'

Mrs W of Mitchelton, wrote, 'For ten years we tried without luck to have a child of our own. When we applied to the State to adopt, we were rejected on account of our ages. We'd heard of a private adoption agency in New Farm. There was a sizable fee but we didn't care, we paid in instalments. Six months later, we went to pick up our newborn son. I held him in my arms. He was gorgeous. Then they said the fee had gone up and if we wanted to take him, we'd have to pay the extra money then and there. They had us over a barrel but we couldn't refuse.'

We can only wonder how many people were affected by the forced removal of babies and the deceptive or illegal means by which it was done. The victims of forced adoptions need more than an apology from the government. They need support, counselling and compensation for lifetimes of unresolved grief. Furthermore, those who took advantage of the mothers deserve nothing less than prison sentences.

Seth reread the third vignette about the private adoption agency. It had the distinctive odour of a rat. To the best of his knowledge, the adoption process had been controlled by the State. This could be the start of something big.

He called to Cate over the divider. 'Do you have those readers' letters? I want the one from Mrs W.'

'I'll bring them around.' She bounded into his cubicle and deposited the folder on his desk. Her long hair rolled off her shoulder like luscious coils of liquorice.

The letter was written in fountain pen in an old fashioned style—thick down-strokes, abundant loops and flourishes—the way his mother had written. He scanned the page. The return address was an aged care facility in the northern suburbs. The writer, whose name was Mrs Vera Wilson, was probably in her eighties. If he didn't act soon, her story might be lost forever.

'Are you up for an interview?' he said to Cate.

Her face lit up. 'Absolutely!'

'Your article is a great start, but if you dig beneath the surface I'm sure you'll find much more. Give this lady a call and ask if we can see her tomorrow. We'll go together but you can do the talking. Later, you might like to call the Minister for Communities for her comments.'

That'll make Vann's day, he chuckled to himself.

From the outside, the old people's home looked like a fortress on a hill. Red-brick walls soared four storeys above clipped lawns and manicured gardens. On the ground floor was a colonnade of white gothic arches. Two life-sized statues of the Madonna—one praying and the other cradling the Baby Jesus— overlooked the comings and goings of the car park.

Seth and Cate walked through an entrance archway where they found a reception counter and asked directions to Mrs Wilson's room. A trolley piled with bed linen and towels was parked in the hall.

They climbed a grand timber staircase that wound up to the second floor. The treads were covered in carpet, grey with pink flowers, which muffled their footsteps. It was as quiet as a cathedral on a weekday morning.

The room numbers counted down as they walked from the staircase to the dining room. The tables were set with pink placemats and white crockery. Multi-coloured sunlight from stained-glass windows cast rainbows on the vinyl floor. Beyond the tables was a shared lounge area with winged armchairs, a huge TV screen, and a bookcase that ran the length of one wall. The place was neat and clean but entirely devoid of vitality. Seth had seen more life at the morgue.

Outside Room One, Cate cocked an eyebrow.

Seth nodded encouragement. She knocked.

Straight away the door opened. The wizened woman in the doorway looked as if her body had shrivelled onto a skeleton the size of a child's.

'Good afternoon, Mrs Wilson. I'm Cate Bradshaw from *The Morning Post* and this is my boss, Seth VerBeek. We're here about your letter.'

'Do come in, my dears.' When she smiled, her teeth were far too white to be real.

Her room was large, simply furnished and lush with potted orchids. Boogie-woogie music of the 1940s belted from the radio, a canary trilled in the breaks. They followed her shuffling slippers past the single bed and into a sitting area with three armchairs and a desk on which sat a small laptop open like a scallop shell.

'Would you like a chocolate?' She snapped off the music and offered a half-empty box of Cadbury Roses.

On behalf of them both, Cate declined.

'Don't mind if I have one myself.' She picked through the foil-wrapped sweets for a Turkish delight, then settled in the chair next to the cage with the canary. 'His name's Sylvester,' she said with a wicked grin. 'Who's a pretty boy?' she cooed to the bird.

Seth stood at the window and looked out. The view was spectacular, west over the treetops to the purple hills of the D'Agular Range. White clouds striped the sky. Magpies strutted across the bowling-green lawn. Peace and serenity incarnate.

'Sit, sit. Make yourselves comfortable.' Mrs Wilson produced an album of black-and-white photos. Proudly she pointed to herself as a younger woman, seated in a cane chair holding a tiny baby. The date beneath the photo was 1963.

'You must promise not to publish my name,' she said. 'What happened would bring terrible shame on my family.'

'Then why did you write to us?' said Seth. 'Why not take the secret to your ...' Embarrassed he stopped.

'To my grave?' Mrs Wilson cackled. 'Don't worry, dear, I know I haven't much longer in this world. Sometimes I wish it'd be over. People make such a fuss.'

Now that the interview had started, Seth found it impossible to keep his mouth shut. He backed up the question with a more professional attempt. 'In your letter, you mentioned a private adoption agency. Can you tell us about it?'

Cate glared at him. He'd promised to let her do the talking.

'As I recall, the government didn't want to know us. I was forty-three when we got Jack. It was our last chance to have a family and I haven't regretted a single minute.'

Mrs Wilson picked up on the look of puzzlement on his face. 'I can see maths isn't your strong point, dear. To save you the trouble, I'm ninety-four.' She might have been old but her mind was as sharp as a dagger.

Cate took the put-down as an opportunity to jump in. 'Where did you find such an adorable child?'

The elderly face softened. 'We used to call the place the *baby farm*. That wasn't its real name and I'm not exactly sure where it was located. It was a home for teenage girls who'd gotten themselves in trouble, if you know what I mean. They'd match you up with a child that you could pass off as your own.'

Cate said, 'So, they took customers' orders to suit the girls who stayed there?'

'I can't say for certain, but I think that's how it worked. They asked for photos of my husband and me. Later we saw a picture of the girl who was the mother. She was petite and fair-haired, just like me when I was seventeen. Good honest face she had too, not at all slutty or common.'

Seth said, 'Do you still have her photo?'

'Good heavens, no! They only showed us so we'd sign up.'

Cate said patiently, 'What happened then, Mrs Wilson?'

'We waited. Several months later I got a phone call to say our son had been born. We collected him from New Farm.'

Seth asked, 'Do you remember the address?'

'Merthyr Road. It was a lovely house. Lowset, white stucco, two big palm trees out front, and nicely furnished inside.'

Seth said, 'You said in your letter that you were practically held to ransom. Exactly how much …' He stopped short, aware that he'd said the wrong thing.

'In my day a gentleman never asked about money.'

Cate pushed the point. 'Would you say the fee covered their expenses, or was it more?'

The old lady's eyes misted over and she picked at a loose thread on the armchair. 'At the time, we thought it was probably wrong. But that little boy was so gorgeous we would have paid with our souls.'

'Do you remember the names of the people involved?' said Seth.

'The woman called herself Mrs Grice. At the time she looked as fragile as a stick. I'd expect she'd be long gone.'

Cate interrupted, 'Are you sure you want us to go ahead with this story?'

Tears ran into the canyons of the old lady's cheeks. 'Soon my life will be over. We weren't the only ones. It's time the sorry story came out. I'm ashamed to say I haven't had the courage to tell Jack. I've written him a letter to be opened when I'm dead. I suppose it's the coward's way, but it'd break my heart to lose him now. Promise me you'll not to publish my name?'

'You have my word, Mrs Wilson,' said Seth.

'Thank you, young man.' She grasped his forearm and gave it a little squeeze. Her hands were like claws, a squiggle of blue veins showed through her transparent skin. 'Now, my dears, you must excuse me. I'm tuckered out.'

Seth gave her a business card. Cate gave her a kiss on the cheek.

He pulled the door closed behind them and they hastened along the hallway toward the stairs. Although spotless, the place exuded the musty odour of old age. Outside Room Five a lonely alarm beeped and flashed. A male nurse with blue-gloved hands bustled down the hall and disappeared inside. Muffled voices filtered through the shut door.

They galloped down the staircase and out into dazzling light. Seth filled his lungs with sweet fresh air. Then he patted his pockets for the lighter and a packet of smokes and checked the cover for the pic of the day. It was his second-favourite, an eyeball popped open with fish-hooks. *Smoking causes blindness.*

Audibly and shamelessly he puffed away until the filter was at singe-point.

He'd hate to end up in a place like this, counting the hours until the next feed or next handful of pills. Nothing to look forward to but his own funeral. His mother lived in such a place on the other side of town. He hadn't been to see her in months. Guilt weighed on his conscience. It was heartbreaking to watch her totter about on walking sticks like a decrepit praying mantis, to hear her repeat the same stories six times in the space of an hour. She was no longer the mother he knew, but a miserable geriatric who happened to have the same name as the vibrant, funny, clever person she'd once been.

He lit a second cigarette and glanced sideways at Cate. Leaning against the bonnet of the Jeep, she calmly jotted down notes of the interview. Her gentle manner had elicited important information without the old lady realising. Skills like that made a good journalist.

His phone pinged with emails. The editor wanted someone to cover a story about two women who'd chained themselves to a Moreton Bay fig tree to prevent it being bulldozed for a new development. He emailed back that he might have a scoop.

'Fancy a drive to New Farm?' he said to Cate. 'I want to check out that house.'

Merthyr Road was wide and lined on both sides with trees. Poinciana, camphor laurel, Cocos palm, crepe myrtle, mango. The old houses—chamferboard, iron roof and neat picket fence—were from a simpler era, when the suburb was home to ordinary workers. Interspersed between the relics were expensive new townhouses, six-packs of pale brick flats from the seventies, and an occasional boarding house for single men.

Halfway along on the right was a dwelling that approximated Mrs Wilson's description. It was single-storied, Spanish mission style, yellow render, terracotta roof, barley-twist columns, towering Phoenix palms on either side of the gate.

He pulled up opposite. 'You reckon that's it?'

Cate craned to see out the driver's window. 'Do a lap of the street and see if there are any others.'

To be sure, he did two. In the fifty years since Mrs Wilson's baby purchase, the place could have been demolished or renovated beyond recognition. Maybe she'd confused the street names. All the same, there seemed to be no other prospects, so he parked outside the yellow house.

'I'll give it a shot,' he said. 'Wait here.'

He ambled up the path. The door was open but the entrance to the house was barred by an iron security gate. Classical music—bold and orchestral—echoed down the corridor. Beethoven, if he was not mistaken. He pushed the doorbell. No-one came. This was not surprising, for the boom of the symphony drowned out any competition.

At the third attempt, the music stopped and a slender woman in a red sarong came to the door. Her eyes were sharp, her hair was white, her skin was too tight for her face. She could have been any age between fifty and seventy-five.

Seth said, 'Sorry to bother you, I'm trying to locate a woman by the name Grice.'

The woman narrowed her eyes. 'Who wants her?'

He presented her with his business card and said he was researching a feature article. 'Is this the right house?'

'I suppose. Depends on which Grice you're looking for. This has been my family's home for more than eighty years.'

'You're Mrs Grice?'

'*Doctor* Grice,' she corrected him stiffly. 'My mother passed away years ago. Can I ask what your article is about?'

'Adoption.'

The woman froze. 'I'm sorry, you have the wrong place.' Without another word, she slammed the door in his face.

He pressed the buzzer and called out her name. His voice was drowned out by whirls of woodwinds and strings and percussion.

In the Jeep, he wavered between another cigarette and the tin of mints.

'No luck?' said Cate.

He popped a mint, shifted the gearstick and planted his foot on the accelerator. 'Right place, right woman, wrong approach.'

'Want me to try?'

'Let me think it through. There's more than one way to crack a hard-boiled egg.'

11

Monday 11 October 1971

Julia Grice's Kombi van bounced across the Story Bridge and turned west onto Ipswich Road. The morning rainclouds had cleared. Before them was a vast wide sky of deepest blue, striated with white cotton wool.

Out of the city traffic, Julia seemed more relaxed. She turned up the radio. 4IP, the station with the coolest music. *Wild World* by Cat Stevens was playing. Of all his hits, this was Miffy's favourite. Although she knew every word, she'd rather die than share her tone-deaf voice with strangers, so she sang along inside her head. In her upside-down world, she had an inkling it would be hard to get by on a smile.

With the suburbs far behind, they travelled for an hour or more through farmlands as flat as a billiard table. The Kombi took a right turn off the highway onto an unsealed track barely wide enough for a wheelbarrow. Dust plumed behind as the vehicle bounced from pothole to pothole.

Miffy shut her window but the fine red talcum powder still managed to seep into the cabin. With it came the scents of the countryside. Eucalypts and millet grass. Cattle and manure and hay.

She sneezed, a monumental effort that began in her toes and worked its way through her entire body to her nose. Fiona passed her a tissue from her pocket.

Ah-choo! Ah-choo! Ah-choo!

Wattle allergy without the wattle. Her eyes were itchy and streaming.

'It'll be better up at the house,' suggested Julia.

Ahead was a flat-topped hill that jutted above the tree-line. Between two spreading camphor laurels she could see about an acre of silver roof, several chimneys and a turret like a fairy castle.

As the Kombi climbed, the trees thinned and the mansion came into full view. Julia pulled on the brake. 'That's *Maidenhead*. Beautiful, isn't she?'

They craned their necks for a glimpse. The homestead was indeed beautiful. Two-storied brick with broad verandas, white columns and wrought-iron lace. In her heyday she would have been the belle of the west, hostess of tea parties and hunting weekends. Now, she looked a bit like grandma in an antique wedding dress.

The Kombi revved up the hill. The wheels skidded on gravel and tiptoed around washouts until they reached a wire farm gate.

'Get that, someone,' said Julia.

Miffy scrambled out, lifted the chain and started to open the gate. Without warning three vicious-looking dogs sprinted out, snarling and baring their teeth. With a scream, she raced to the van and barely shut the door before they flung themselves against it.

'That's odd,' said Julia Grice. 'The Dobermans are usually kept under control.' She beeped the horn, but it did nothing to stop the commotion. The dogs were out for blood and nothing less.

A grey-haired woman in a tailored dress and sensible shoes strode across the lawn. With every step she switched a riding crop against her skirt. One whistle and the dogs dropped to their haunches. Another whistle and they skulked back to the house.

The woman marched to the gate and held it open. Once the Kombi was through, she rethreaded the chain and fastened the padlock, then followed the trail of dust to a gravel driveway.

Once the van was parked, she greeted Julia with a handshake, calling her *Doctor* Grice. Despite their age difference, they seemed quite chummy. While they exchanged pleasantries, the girls got out and collected their baggage. The gravel was as hot as burning coals, and there was not a square inch of relief from the brutal sun. Within minutes, Miffy's feet were singed through the soles of her shoes and her skin was turning pink.

Four girls with big bellies unloaded the cargo. Cartons of tinned baked beans, strawberry jam and beetroot, sacks of flour and sugar. Working in pairs, they walked crabwise, sharing the weight of the provisions between them.

Julia said, 'Mrs Doyle, I'd like you to meet my *special* girls, Fiona and Myfanwy.'

Expressionless, Mrs Doyle gave them both the once-over. 'Myfanwy!' she sniffed. 'What a dreadful name! While you're here, you'll be known as Mary.'

Although she too hated the sound of her name, she wasn't thrilled about *Mary* either. 'You could call me Miffy,' she ventured.

'Don't back-answer me, girlie! You might get away with murder at home, but here you'd best mind your manners.' Mrs Doyle's scowl could have stopped a herd of stampeding water buffalo. Without doubt this was a woman no-one dared to cross.

Without batting an eyelid, the she turned to Julia and spoke as if butter wouldn't melt in her mouth. 'Now, Dr Grice, would you like a cuppa before you go?'

'Love one.'

Mrs Doyle snapped her fingers at a girl who'd unloaded the van. 'Daphne, bring us tea in the parlour. A nice strong pot, not that dishwater you usually make. Bring us a plate of fresh scones and jam too.'

The girls picked up their bags and followed the clip-clip of sensible lace-up shoes up the stairs and across the veranda. Through the French doors was a stately room with crystal chandeliers and honey-coloured polished floorboards. Maroon velvet armchairs were arranged around an Oriental carpet square. On the wall an enormous gilt-framed mirror hung over the marble fireplace.

Daphne brought the tea things on a trolley. She glowered as she hoisted the oversized aluminium pot and poured tea the colour of molasses. Miffy added her usual slurp of milk and one sugar, but the tea was strong enough to melt the spoon. She dug into the sugar bowl two, three times. Hawklike, Mrs Doyle watched the movement of the spoon from bowl to cup, her lips pursed as a reprimand for taking more than her quota.

While the girls devoured the scones, which were warm from the oven, the women debated the weather and the state of *that dreadful war in Vietnam.*

At length Mrs Doyle put aside her cup and cleared her throat. 'Girls, before you meet the other guests, you must know the rules of the house. *Maidenhead* prides itself on absolute confidentiality. We don't use surnames here. We don't talk about our homes, or our families, or our backgrounds. We obey orders and we do not question. When your babies arrive, they will be placed into loving homes and you must not attempt to contact them. Not ever. You must give your solemn oath—on pain of death—that you will never speak to anyone about *Maidenhead* or what goes on here.'

Obediently they raised their right hands and swore an oath of silence.

Julia, who'd obviously heard the speech before, flipped through a notebook she'd taken from her handbag, pausing here and there to scribble.

'And lastly while you are here, there will be no mail or telephone calls to or from parents or friends. Especially not boyfriends. No-one must know where you are, and you will *not* make your whereabouts known. Is that clear?'

Miffy said, 'But what if—'

'I said, *we do not question.* You need to listen, girl. Or are your ears full of wax?'

Miffy shrank back into the chair. 'No, ma'am.'

'I think we're done, Dr Grice.' Mrs Doyle tinkled a bell on the table.

Daphne reappeared and began to stack the dishes.

'Leave that. I want you to show these girls to their dorm and keep an eye on them. Put them in adjoining beds in the south wing. I don't care who you have to move, just make them comfortable.'

Daphne pulled a sour face and stomped outside without saying a word. Miffy and Fiona gathered their things and followed. Ahead was an ageing barnlike structure, two-storied with walls of silvered timber and a corrugated iron roof. Around fifty yards to the right was its twin. Same size, same shape, same vintage.

'Leave your bags here and follow me,' said Daphne. She was a wild-looking girl with eyes as dark as coal. Her eyebrows were thick—masculine almost—and her black shoulder-length hair was tied in a messy ponytail.

They descended a short flight of stairs to a path on the lower level, passing two open doorways. One led to a six-pack of toilet cubicles and the other to an all-in-together shower room. Both were reminiscent of the stark concrete bomb shelters left over from World War Two that still adorned the streets of the inner city.

Further along the path was a third doorway, from which floated a babble of young voices and the tick-tick-tick of sewing machines. As they stood at the entrance, the conversations stopped and every head turned.

Daphne stood with her hands on her hips and glared at the girls inside. 'What're you gawking at, bitches?'

No-one smiled or said hello. Apparently, no introduction was needed. The chatter resumed as quickly as it had stopped.

'What are they making?' said Fiona.

'Go in and see for yourself,' was Daphne's curt reply. She leant against the door frame and lit a cigarette.

In the workroom were a dozen or so benches, set up with treadle sewing machines. The girls who operated them looked no older than seventeen. In the centre of the room was a massive pine table, swathed in white cloth. One girl wielded scissors the size of hedge shears. She was slim and tanned. A thick braid of chestnut hair traced the full length of her spine. To cut the broad-loomed fabric, she had to lean right across the table. The edge pressed into her neat round belly.

By means of explanation the girl said, 'Hospital sheets.'

'What are you doing with them?' said Fiona.

'Mending. They're from hospitals in Ipswich and Toowoomba.' The girl put down the scissors and stretched her fingers. 'I'm Isabelle.'

'I don't know how to sew,' Miffy said.

'You'll learn quick enough.'

'Is that what you do … all day?' Fiona's face went as white as the sheets.

'Just in the mornings. We have to finish by one o'clock when the truck comes, otherwise we get in trouble. See those bags?' Isabelle pointed to several bulging bales at the entrance. 'They're ready to go. The washing's done in the north wing and the mending comes to us.'

'Do we have to work in the laundry too?' said Miffy, dismayed. Merle had only recently acquired a washing machine after a lifetime of boiling the linen in a gas-fired copper. Ever since she was a toddler, Miffy had been expected to help. The laundry room was a torture chamber of flames and choking vapours. The copper was a witch's cauldron that spat and hissed as she fished out the heavy clothes with a special stick and dropped them into the concrete washtub.

'Nah,' said Isabelle. 'We're smarter than that lot. That's why we're here.' She picked up the scissors and expertly manoeuvred them around a tear in the sheet. Snip. The ragged bits were gone. Snip, snip. A neat patch was ready to fit. She pinned the pieces together and slid them across the table to a waiting machinist.

Looking bored, Daphne swaggered into the workroom. 'This place stinks. Let's get outta here.' They retraced their steps past the ablutions block and climbed an internal staircase to the first floor.

The dorm was the size of a basketball court and as hot as a sauna. The structural joists of the building were exposed. There was no lining and no ceiling to soften the room or give protection from the heat. Two rows of beds, set head-to-head, ran down the middle. The only separation was a central spine of open timber boxes that were stuffed full of clothing and other possessions. Apart from that, nothing gave a vestige of privacy between neighbouring beds.

Daphne took them to the last two beds in the row. She pulled the sheets from the mattresses, the clothing from the storage cubes and bundled them up together. 'C'mon, give us a hand.'

'Where do we put it?' said Fiona.

'Dump it on a spare bed.'

'Won't the girls who own it be mad?' said Miffy.

'Puss-arse has spoken. *We do not question.*' Daphne flashed a wicked grin.

Moving the swags from one end to the other was easier said than done. The loads were surprisingly heavy and awkward. Dust motes swirled in sunlight that speared through cracks in the wall. Miffy began to sneeze.

Fiona took the bed at the end. Miffy was next and then came Daphne herself. They made up their beds and stowed their gear in the storage cubes. As they finished, a bell at the homestead rang twice.

'Lunchtime at last! I'm starved.' Daphne bolted out the door before either could ask where to go.

Outside, groups of girls waddled up the hill to the big house. The refectory on the ground floor was a spacious wood-panelled room that might have once been a ballroom. Long trestle benches were covered with white tablecloths that looked suspiciously like hospital sheets. Near the entrance was a servery; the kitchen was behind. Pillars of sandwiches and bowls of green apples were laid out ready for a swarm of teenage locusts. Lunch girls doled out the ration of two sandwiches and one apple each. No choice, you got what you got.

At the table, Miffy bit into the thick-cut bread, filled with peanut paste and strawberry jam. The water from the jug on the table tasted of tin.

Fiona opened her sandwich and pushed it to the edge of the plate. 'Eew, Vegemite.'

'You want that?' said Daphne.

Fiona shook her head.

Daphne reached across the table, grabbed the sandwich and stuffed it into her mouth.

Miffy yawned. 'What do we do after lunch?'

'Muck out the chook-pens, tie the grapevines, weed the vegies, milk the cows. Sometimes we do stuff you wouldn't want to hear about.'

The blood drained from Fiona's face. 'I thought this was a *rest* home. You know, where we'd be looked after until we have our babies.'

Daphne guffawed. 'What moron told you that?'

'Julia Grice, the lady who drove us here.'

'Well she's fed youse a heap of bullshit. Only time you're looked after here is when the pains start.'

The bell rang three times. *En masse*, the girls scraped back the seats and returned their plates to the servery.

'Half an hour 'til the afternoon slog. Youse can do whatever you want. I'm off for a smoke.' Daphne loped down the hill past the dorm, beyond which was a stretch of bushland punctuated by clusters of lofty eucalypt trees.

Miffy and Fiona wandered towards the giant camphor laurels, whose bark smelt like mothballs, and sat on a rustic bench beneath. In the shade the temperature must have been ninety degrees. Sticky-footed black flies that refused to be shooed crawled up their nostrils and sipped moisture from their skin.

Fiona's eyes filled with tears. 'We can't stay here. They'll work us to death.'

'I'll probably die of hay fever,' said Miffy, sneezing.

For several minutes they sat in silence, the only sounds were the calls of birds and the rustle of camphor laurel leaves in the breeze. From the knoll was an unbroken vista across a patchwork of fields to the purple wall of the Great Dividing Range. The sky stretched from horizon to horizon, unspoiled by the mark of man. Kookaburras settled on the fence, a family of black-and-white currawongs strutted across the grass, a skink lizard darted around their feet.

Miffy was lost in thought. Apart from those initial crazy ideas she'd discussed with Michelle, she'd really had no choice but *Maidenhead*. She couldn't stay home (not with Merle) and there was nowhere else to go. Five months, that was all. Then her life would return to normal and she'd be back at school with Gaye and Michelle as if none of this had happened.

The house bell rang twice.

From the direction of the barn came the hum of voices. Girls wearing old jeans and overalls thundered down the stairs. Armed with brooms and rakes and secateurs, they made their way down the slope to the fields below.

With her riding crop under her arm, Mrs Doyle stormed out. 'Why aren't you girls working?' She pursed her lips, exaggerating the wrinkles around her mouth, a perfect impression of a cat's arse. 'Where's that layabout, Daphne?'

Fiona waved vaguely in the direction of the eucalypt forest.

Mrs Doyle snorted. 'She's supposed to be showing you the ropes. You——Mary—go and get her. Look lively now!'

Miffy trotted past the south dorm to where the long grass began. To the chirp of cicadas, she marched along a goat track that traced the line of the ridge. The sound of a human catfight stopped her.

Isabelle, the scissor-girl from the workshop, stormed past. 'Bitch!' she spat.

Daphne lumbered up the track, nursing her left cheek.

'Mrs Doyle's looking for you,' said Miffy.

'Shit, that's all I need.' Daphne wiped her nose and lit a cigarette.

'You okay?'

'Yeah.' She lifted her hand. Three red stripes raked from cheekbone to jaw. 'Stupid cow thought it was my idea to give youse the end beds. Now she's got it in for me.' Smoke snorted out of her nose. She took two quick drags, picked out the embers and put the remainder of the cigarette in her pocket. 'Better see what the old bag wants.'

'Daphne!' The word shrilled across the lawn.

Ma Doyle took one look and wrenched Daphne's hand from the battle wound. 'Goodness gracious, girl, what happened?'

'Nothing, ma'am. I ran into a branch.'

'I want you to take the new girls down to the vineyard and show them what to do. No shortcuts, we don't want to lose any vines. And Daphne …'

'Yes, ma'am?'

'Do stop that filthy habit. Smoking is no good for the baby.'

After changing into shorts, t-shirts and sandshoes, they went to the shed for tools. Daphne collected secateurs, wire, tin snips, and spaghetti of white fabric strips.

In the vineyard she showed how to train the shoots. Every plant had hundreds of arms that needed to be snipped or tied to the trellises. In the flush of summer, the tendrils were growing as fast as they could tie them up.

The broad brim of Miffy's hat shaded her face but her arms were sizzling. She cursed her ancestors for her red hair and white skin, and their decision to leave the mild climate of Wales for the shimmering heat of Australia.

At three o'clock the bell rang twice, the girls downed tools for a break. Miffy sat on a mound in the shade of the foliage. Persistent flies crawled all over her. It was too hot to swat them, too hot to breathe.

She lay back and gazed through the sap-green leaves at the sapphire-blue sky, unspoiled by a single cloud. The strength and contrast of the colours was sublime. All of a sudden, she was engulfed in a whirlpool of emotions. Joy, despair, love, grief. She began to weep. It was at that moment she first felt the flutter, deep inside. She pressed her hand near the base of her belly, down low near the pubic bone. Beneath her fingers was a small movement, quiet like a sparrow in a dust bath. She sat up and gasped.

'What's wrong?' said Fiona.

'I don't know.' She placed Fiona's hand on the spot. 'Can you feel that?'

'It's only the baby.'

'You mean … it moves?'

'Yeah, all the time. Sometimes in the middle of the night, I hold her through my skin and feel her wriggling inside me. It helps to know I'm not alone. I've named her Hope, because that's what she gives me.'

Miffy put both hands on her bulge. Until then she'd thought of *the thing* inside her as an inert lump. A benign pain-in-the-arse growth she was better off without.

But those little flutters meant it had a life of its own. In a few months it would have a mind and a personality and a name. There was no going back. Inside her was a tiny replica of herself. And despite the lamentable deed that produced it, this child was undeniably hers.

Three bells.

Daphne stubbed her cigarette in the dirt. 'Back to work before Puss-arse comes down on us like a ton o' bricks.'

They continued to tie vines until the bells rang at five o'clock and they trundled up the path to the dorms. A delicious aroma wafted from the kitchen. Comforting and homely, like Merle's oven-baked casserole of mince, rice and chicken noodle soup mix.

Daphne said, 'The food's only as good as the cook. Everyone gets a turn.'

Fiona examined at her hands, cracked and stained with sap. 'I'd rather cook than tie vines. Look at my poor nails.'

In the dorm everyone scrambled to clean up and be first in the dinner queue. Miffy grabbed her toiletries bag and headed for the stairs but an angry shriek stopped her in her tracks.

Daphne stormed along the row of beds. 'You bunch of bitches, where's my bloody stuff?' She tore off the covers and looked beneath each bed. 'Fuckin' thieves!'

From the other side of the storage boxes came the sound of sniggering.

'That'll teach you to mess with the Ipswich mob.' This was Isabelle's distinctive nasal twang. Rubber thongs slap-slapped down the stairs.

Daphne launched herself onto her mattress and hammered it with her fists. After several minutes of uncontrolled rage, she curled up and began to sob. 'Those snooty sluts always pick on me. I hate the lot of 'em!' Her face was puce. Strands of black hair stuck to her cheeks.

'Maybe we shouldn't have taken their beds,' said Miffy.

'What, and get a taste of Puss-arse's whip? No thanks.'

'I've got spare clothes you can borrow until we find your stuff,' said Miffy.

With a look of surprise and gratitude, Daphne accepted the offer.

By the time they entered the refectory, the queue was as long as it was impatient. They stood behind a girl who'd been mending sheets earlier, one of the Ipswich mob. On purpose she kept her back to them, gave them no acknowledgment, said nothing. Her blonde hair flowed freely about her shoulders. Her sleeveless top showed off a hazelnut tan that was to die for.

The heat of the dining room made Miffy's sunburn prickle and sting. She'd be in for a sleepless night for sure. Tomorrow, blisters would come and later a thousand more freckles would be added to her collection. One day the spots would all join together and she too would have a glorious all-over tan. *In your dreams*, Merle would have said.

Stainless steel trays of food steamed in the servery. Hugging a plate to her chest, Miffy shuffled along at the tail end of the line. She received two slices of white bread, a ladle of savoury mince and a dollop of mashed potato.

Juggling cutlery, a mug of water, and a plate that was mostly gravy, she picked her way along the refectory tables to where they'd sat at lunchtime. The room was quiet apart from the clink of metal on china. Everyone was gobbling as if their last meal had been a week ago. With the best table manners she could muster, Miffy ate with knife and fork. If nothing else, she was determined to retain her self-respect amongst the dirty herd. She glanced sideways. Fiona was doing the same. Their eyes met and she smiled.

When she'd mopped up the last of the gravy with a square of bread on her fork, Miffy pushed back the seat. 'I'm knackered. Where's the TV room?'

'That'd be the day,' said Daphne. 'Lights-out at eight. We'll be up again at dawn.'

Miffy groaned. 'Why so early?'
'Because that's how people live on a farm.'

That night she barely slept. Sunburn aside, she wasn't used to sharing a room with nineteen others. Every cough, snore, and fart woke her. As she tossed from side to side the wire base of her bed creaked like a rusty gate. The mattress springs dug in her ribs, her pillow was like a sack of potatoes.

Through the windows shone a wan half-moon. Shadows of the eucalypt trees danced across the walls. A haunting symphony of night noises floated in. An owl's hoot, a dog's howl, the eerie *coo-eeee* of the storm-birds, the axe-murderer guffaw of the kookaburras. In a roomful of slumbering strangers, Miffy felt completely alone. She lay on her back with her hands folded across her belly, hoping to feel the fluttering. Nothing moved. Her little sparrow was asleep.

Yellow torchlight flitted across the beds. Wide awake, she pushed herself up on one elbow. The light was coming from the stairwell but the holder of the torch was concealed by shadow. The dazzling beam fell on her face. She shaded her eyes and dropped back to the pillow.

Sensible shoes clipped across the floorboards.

'What's wrong, girl? Are you sick?' hissed Ma Doyle. Even when whispering, her voice hacked the air like a machete.

'I can't sleep in this place,' Miffy whined.

'Lie down and shut your eyes. Perhaps you should count your blessings.' The torch turned around. The shoes clicked toward the door.

Darkness returned.

No matter how hard she tried, Miffy couldn't think of a single blessing to count.

12

Thursday 6 March

Two days was all it took for Seth to hatch a plan to crack Dr Grice. He'd been pondering the information he'd accumulated about the bombing and adoptions and baby-trading when it came to him.

Maureen, the hairdresser.

In their brief conversation at the coffee shop, she'd given him more information than the rest of his leads combined. But it was one comment that was the catalyst.

Who'd want to talk to a hairdresser about the wicked ways of the world?

The answer was obvious. Everyone. That's what people did while they got their hair cut. A captive audience for hours at a time, they talked about themselves, what they did, who they knew, where they'd been. Seth's barber in Sydney, whom he'd patronised for decades, could have written his biography without asking a single question.

He opened his wallet, took out the business card she'd given him and dialled the number. Maureen answered the phone.

'If you're free after work, would you like to have a drink?' he said.

'Business or pleasure?'

'A bit of both. What time do you finish?'

'Thursday night shopping. Nine o'clock too late for you?'

'It's not past my bedtime, if that's what you mean.'

She laughed. 'You're a bit of a wag, Mr Newspaper Man.'

'Then we should get on like a house on fire. I'll meet you at the salon.'

Smiling, he hung up the phone. He might be pushing sixty but he hadn't lost his touch with the ladies. He booked at table at an intimate late-night café in Milton. His conscience pricked him briefly about how far he ought to push an informant before the line between professionalism and taking advantage was crossed. Luckily he'd never been brought to task, though there'd been many instances when he'd received privileged information whispered over the pillow after plying his target with wine. Where did it say not to combine business with pleasure? Over the course of his career, he'd become a master.

At nine he entered Maureen's salon. She'd already changed from her work attire into a black top tied at the waist and skinny jeans. Her platinum hair was done in a style reminiscent of the sixties: a topknot with the ends flicked up. She greeted him with a kiss on the cheek as if he were family.

At the café, they ordered pasta and a bottle of chianti. Without a doubt Maureen was easy to talk to. Too easy. If Seth wasn't careful, he'd end up spilling the beans about himself and getting nothing in return.

Consciously he began to answer questions with questions. Typical politician's trick. Vann Willis would have been proud.

He accidentally hit the jackpot by asking how long she'd had the salon.

'Only eight years in Riverdale. After twenty years of managing the Beauty Spot in New Farm, I put my money where my mouth was and went out on my own. Some of my old clients make the trek across town to see me.'

'You must be good.'

Her face lit up. 'I can truly say I love my job. Of course there's more to hairdressing than scissors and dye. You've got to be a social worker as well.'

The woman had a healthy appetite. Between anecdotes, she polished off the pasta—a mountainous serve—and several glasses of chianti. She settled into the topic and all Seth had to do was nod and listen.

'One of my long-time clients is counsellor herself. A well-known professional in her field. I swear she comes to me every week just to debrief. The problems she's dealt with! All the stories are anonymous of course. It wouldn't do to spread rumours about the influential half of town.'

She began to ramble and her words were slightly slurred.

Seth took the leap. 'So, how long have you known Julia Grice?'

Without picking up on his name-drop, she answered without hesitation. 'Ever since we were young things. I used to do her mother's hair in the early days. Mrs Grice was a marvellous woman. She ran a support service for teenage girls who'd fallen by the wayside. You'd see the poor things going to see her after school. Some were from well-to-do families. Just shows you never know what happens behind closed doors.'

It was all the stuff of Australian of the Year, with not one ounce of dirt. Perhaps the old lady, Mrs Wilson, had high functioning dementia and had mixed up the names and places.

By eleven they were the only two customers in the café. The waiter was resetting the tables for breakfast. Seth paid the bill.

As they walked to the Jeep Maureen said, 'Fancy a nightcap?'

Seth glanced at his watch. The night was young. 'Your place or mine?'

She arched a neatly-pencilled eyebrow and said in an offended tone, 'Do you think I'm *that* sort of girl?'

He started to back off but she laughed at her own joke. 'Well, you're absolutely *right*, Mr Newspaper Man. My apartment's not far. Let's go there.'

Her place was not what Seth expected. It was a museum of the nineteen sixties, from the sleek box design of the building, right down to the green-and-white lino inside. Pure unadulterated vintage. Porcelain ducks flew up the wall. Melamine canisters lined the kitchen bench and a red onion-dome hung over the dining table.

She made him a martini in a V-shaped glass, complete with two olives on a stick. Frank Sinatra crooned from the stereo. They sat close on the sofa. Her skin was soft and warm and fragrant. She drained her glass, set it on the side table and began to unbutton her blouse. Those voluptuous breasts spilled over the top of her bra.

He didn't need a written invitation. Within minutes they were naked on her queen-sized bed. He stroked her curves with well-practiced hands, making broad slow sweeps down her spine and over the mounds of her rump. She pressed herself against him, arched her body and purred like a cat in heat.

When he touched her buttons, she turned voracious. She rolled him onto his back and lay on top. With her luscious pink tongue, she tasted his body, moving down from his neck to his nipples to the aching rod between his legs. It'd been months since he'd had a woman. He worried that he'd rupture before giving or taking pleasure.

She seemed to sense the change in him and eased off. For an hour or more they tickled and teased and played out the game of passion.

Exhausted, they slept.

In the morning, he drove her to the salon. She showed him where to park, in the back lot of the neighbouring cinema where there was a connecting laneway alongside Café Nero. There he gave her a lingering kiss.

'Thank you for a wonderful night,' he said. 'We must do it again.'

'Sure, but I'll be out of action for a while. My old man gets back from Hong Kong tonight. He can be a bit of a tyrant.'

'You didn't tell me you were married.'

'Would it have made any difference?'

He kissed her again. 'Forbidden fruit is always sweeter.'

'Our secret then. Promise?'

'On my father's grave.'

13

February 1972

One by one, the girls from Miffy's dorm went into labour and were taken up to the big house. There, she supposed, the babies were born and the girls returned home shortly afterwards. There was no way of knowing exactly, for going to the big house was a one-way street.

Sometimes in the middle of the night, Miffy would hear the screaming. Her knowledge of the mechanics of birth was zero and none of her fellow inmates appeared any wiser. The nights of the screaming she'd wrap the pillow around her ears and pretend it was the howling of the wind. But the awful sound would filter through. Whatever they did there, it must have hurt like hell.

One day Daphne told her about the birth of a calf on her uncle's farm. 'It was totally gross. Uncle Nick stuck his arm up the cow's arse, right up to his shoulder. Out came this pink watery muck and two hooves. The cow was bellowing but the calf was stuck. Uncle Nick tied a rope around it and pulled so hard I thought it'd break in half. Then all of a sudden, the calf slid out onto the grass.'

Miffy shuddered and unconsciously crossed her legs. 'They wouldn't do that to a *person*, would they?'

'I'll be first to find out.' Daphne rubbed her bulge in a rotary motion. Her navel had popped. It looked like the plug of a blow-up beach ball.

'That's no help to us,' said Miffy. 'We won't get to see you again.'

'Perhaps it's best not to know,' said Fiona quietly.

As her belly expanded toward bursting point, Miffy found the physical work of the farm exhausting. Even the mornings hunched over a sewing machine made her ache. By bedtime she'd be practically numb but sleep eluded her.

Whereas the year before she'd slept like a hibernating bear, now her body punished her day and night. There was indeed *no rest for the wicked* (another of Merle's favourites).

The space where her organs should have been was full of baby. It squashed her stomach and pressed on her bladder. Although ravenous, she could eat just a few mouthfuls at a time. To ease the nightly heartburn, she packed bundles of clothes beneath her pillow and dozed while sitting upright.

After three weeks of insomnia, she finally fell into a blissful sleep. In her dream she was drifting in the crystal-clear flow of Eli Creek on Fraser Island where her family once went on holiday. The cool water eddied around her, easing her aches, calming her mind.

Beneath the water, something soft brushed against her.

The hairs of her neck stood on end.

The thing gripped her arm in a toothless bite, shook it like a rag.

'Miffeee …' it moaned. 'Miffeee …'

In a panic she jerked her arm free.

'Miffeee ...'

She spiralled back to reality. Her bed was hard and the dorm was stinking hot. It was dark and deathly quiet. Something was close. She could feel its warm breath on her cheek.

'Miffy ... are you awake?' It was Fiona.

'Wassa madder?'

'I've had an accident. Help me?'

Miffy groaned. 'Can't it wait 'til morning?'

Fiona made a whimper like an abandoned pup.

Wearily Miffy sat up. 'What?'

Fiona's hair was across her face, but it was plain she was crying. 'I've … um … this is so *embarrassing* … I've … um … wet the bed.' Her tears fell onto Miffy's arm.

'C'mon, let's get you cleaned up.'

As quietly as they could, they removed the bottom sheet. Miffy folded a towel over the mattress and they tucked the top sheet over it.

'Put the dirty one under the bed and we'll wash it in the morning.'

'Shit! It's happening again!' Fiona bundled her nightdress between her legs and raced down the stairs to the toilet block.

Miffy lay down on the bed and shut her eyes. She must have drifted off.

Sometime later she woke with a start. Her heart was racing and her body was moist with sweat. Outside, the bantam rooster had started his predawn reveille. Inside the dorm, the light was soupy and dim. She glanced across the three-foot gap to Fiona's bed. It was empty.

She tiptoed down the stairs. The toilet block was a concrete cavern that tinkled with running water. Every sound was amplified. Heavy drops hammered the stainless-steel wash-trough. The whine of a mosquito was as loud as a siren. Toilet paper crackled like dry leaves in a westerly.

'Fiona?' The name rebounded off the walls.

'Yeah.' She was in the end cubicle.

'You okay?' Miffy took a step towards the shut door.

Fiona sniffed and blew her nose. 'I can't stop peeing.'

'Do you want me to get Mrs Doyle?'

'I'll be all right … I suppose.' The door creaked open. Fiona's nightie was hitched up around her chest. 'Miffy … I'm really scared.'

'About the birth?'

'Sort of. I don't want them to take away my baby. Hope belongs to *me*.'

'Then you must tell them.'

'But I *know* they won't let me keep her.' Fiona thumped her fists on her knees.

'Let's run away before it's too late. We could go now, before anyone gets up. What do you say?'

Suddenly Fiona's face contorted with pain and she made a low primordial cry.

Shivers of terror ran down Miffy's legs. She took two steps closer to the toilet cubicle when she saw blood all over the night-dress, on Fiona's hands, on the floor.

Miffy's head began to whirl. She'd never been good with blood. Even changing her own sanitary pads made her go weak at the knees.

Fiona's spasm was over as fast as it began. She blew out pent-up breath and her face relaxed. 'Phew that was bad! Must have been the mystery stew from last night.'

'Clean yourself up and I'll help you back to bed.'

Fiona stuffed a wad of toilet paper into her panties and made a pathetic attempt to push herself off the toilet seat. It was too much, she sank back down. 'I can't. You'd better get Mrs Doyle after all.'

'Stay right where you are.'

'I'm not going anywhere. Make it quick.'

With the pale stars illuminating the path, Miffy sprinted to the big house. A single light shone from an upstairs room, which she hoped and prayed was Ma Doyle's. At the back door she and jiggled the knob. To her surprise it wasn't locked.

She entered the dining room, normally buzzing with chatter. But now it was a stranger, gloomy and still. She felt her way along the wood-panelled wall to the bottom of the staircase. From there she called out to Ma Doyle.

The floorboards squeaked. At the top of the stairs was an apparition in a long flowing garment. 'Who's there?' The unmistakable rasp of the old witch.

'It's Mary. Fiona's sick. Can you come?'

Down the stairs came the clip-clip of hard leather soles and the rustle of cotton cloth. Ma Doyle snapped on the hall light, took the torch from the shelf and marched into the darkness without a word. With scarecrow hair, white nightie and work-boots, she could have passed as an extra in a B-grade horror movie.

'She's in the loo,' Miffy shouted as she trotted behind.

The cubicle door was open. Fiona sat on the pedestal, rocking to and fro.

Ma Doyle put her hands on her hips and examined the patient from a distance. 'How often do you get the pain?'

'Every few minutes.'

'Mary, help us up to the house.'

With Fiona propped between them, they slowly crossed the lawn towards the lights of the homestead. At the foot of the stairs, Fiona clutched the bannisters, bent double and let out an anguished groan.

Ma Doyle rubbed her back. 'It'll be over soon. Be strong, my girl.'

Words of encouragement? Perhaps Puss-arse was human after all.

When the pain wave passed, the threesome started up the stairs. Slowly, one step at a time. All thirty-two of them. At the top, Ma Doyle opened a solid oak door and snapped on the light. The room was large and airy, furnished with a single bed, a wash-basin, commode chair, and shelves of neatly-folded linen. By the window was a tray, set with what looked to be instruments of torture. Syringes, iron pokers, big curly tongs, and an item that resembled a bicycle pump. The bed was fitted with metal posts, slung with stirrups. The astringent scent of Pine-O-Clean mingled with the breath-wrenching pungency of chlorine bleach and medical dressings.

Ma Doyle fitted a rubber cover to the mattress while Fiona changed into a plain cotton nightie. She crawled onto the bed and curled up in the foetal position.

'Mary, stay here while I call the midwife.'

Before she could protest, Ma Doyle scuttled out of the room. Miffy's body began to tremble with apprehension. Would they use a rope to pull the baby out?

'Oww, my back hurts.' Fiona said. 'Oww. Owww! Don't stand there. Rub it!'

Miffy stroked her lightly, as if she were a kitten.

'Not like that! Here!' She shoved Miffy's hand to the spot. 'Harder. Harder! Oh God it hurts! It hurts!' She panted and snarled like a wild beast.

Completely out of her depth and scared to the core, Miffy pressed her hands against her friend's body and prayed like she hadn't prayed in years.

After what seemed like an hour Ma Doyle hurried back in the room.

Her hair was tied back and she was dressed for business in a pinafore frock and apron. 'The midwife's coming … and so is this child.'

Between contractions Fiona wailed, 'Don't take my baby!'

'Yoo-hoo!' A female voice reverberated up the stairwell. 'I've let myself in.'

'There's Mrs O'Brien. Now run along, Mary. Get some sleep.'

Tears blurred Miffy's eyes as she realised she may never see Fiona again. Despite the warnings to keep their identities a secret, she'd always intended to swap addresses or phone numbers. Now it was too late.

'Everyone out who's not havin' a baby today.' The Irish accent belonged to a stout middle-aged woman whom she hadn't seen before.

Miffy gripped Fiona's hand and forced a smile. 'Good luck.'

'God bless.' Fiona's forehead was pearled with sweat. 'When all this is over, I'll find you somehow.'

Miffy kissed Fiona's cheek. 'See you then.'

A second later the Irish midwife bustled her out of the room.

As expected, Fiona did not return to the dorm. Without her, *Maidenhead* was unbearable. The dust, the heat, the isolation. Topping it off was Daphne's rage against everyone, the latest target being Miffy herself.

And there was the baby. Her baby. The little bundle she'd secretly named Claire. After Fiona's departure, Miffy came to depend on the child as much as it depended on her. When she was alone, she'd stroke her belly and hum. When panic threatened to suffocate her, the drone of her own voice— tone-deaf though she was—was like a lullaby.

In the summer twilights she went on solo rambles, exploring the goat tracks that crisscrossed the property. Sometimes she'd wander through stands of eucalypt, remainders of the heavy bushland that would have once cloaked the land.

Sometimes she'd visit the cow paddock where she'd lie on the crisp grass and talk to the child growing inside her. She'd close her eyes, breathe the honest scent of the earth and listen to the methodical chewing of the cows. Their contentment was contagious. She was not alone in this harsh and convoluted world.

On one of her expeditions into the eucalypt forest, she discovered a clearing with a circle of granite boulders. Inside the ring, which was about ten yards in diameter, the ground had been cleared of leaf litter and the grass grew flat like lawn.

She stepped between the boulders, from deep shadow into the golden spotlight of the setting sun. It was then that she noticed the grid of simple wooden crosses. She counted. Twenty-two. Each bore a handwritten inscription, weather-worn and faint.

She knelt before one. On the crosspiece was a single word. *Katy.*
No rhyme, no explanation, no date to mark Katy's passing.
She moved to the next cross. *Bozo.*
It was unlike any other cemetery she'd seen. Whoever heard of grave markers with only Christian names? What connection did all those dead people have to *Maidenhead?*
She walked between the rows to the far side of the circle. One cross stood a little apart from the rest. Its fresh white paint glistened like a channel buoy in the sea of silvered wood. She squatted before it. The name was printed in black marker pen.
Her hand shot to her mouth.
The sun retreated behind a cloud and a chill wind swept up the valley. Fallen leaves skittered across the clearing. The sickening-sweet scent of the eucalypt flowers threatened to overwhelm her. She sneezed. From a distance came the rumble of thunder.
For a long time Miffy sat beside Hope's grave, wondering how many others apart from Ma Doyle knew of the cemetery's existence. A person could stay out here and not be found for days.
The pre-storm tension was palpable. Birds that raged at the setting of the sun fell silent. Gum leaves clattered, branches creaked. A storm-bird across the valley wailed an eerie chorus. *Coo-oo-eee ... coo-oo-eee.*
It was starting to give her the creeps. Hastily she picked a posy of fluff-ball flowers and laid it on the little mound of earth.
A greenish bruise darkened the sky. Strobe lights pulsed above the canopy, thunder rolled. Great globules of rain pelted into the clearing.
Never shelter under a gum tree was another of Merle's maxims. It was not without its truth. At random and without warning, a eucalypt could drop a massive limb quicker than the crack of a whip. Merle called them *widow-makers.* Out here in the circular graveyard, Miffy was surrounded by them. As fast as her pendulous body allowed, she sprinted along the goat track to the safety of the dorm.
She didn't breathe a word about the lonely cemetery. But she made a vow to her baby Claire that she'd not end up there. The only way to keep that promise was to escape before it was too late. She'd hitch-hike to the nearest town, find a real hospital with qualified doctors and proper care. That much she owed her child.

14

Saturday 8 March

The night of the high school reunion dinner, Vann was in a panic. Rain pelted sideways, driven by a gusty sou'wester that promised colder weather to come.

Half an hour before, she'd called a cab to take her from the charity talent quest in New Farm to the Ballymore rugby club for the dinner. In the cold and wet, she'd waited beneath a flat slab of reinforced concrete on stilts for a taxi that never arrived. After two heated phone calls to the company, a cab finally came. The driver barely understood English and had no idea of how to get there. She sat in the front passenger seat and directed him with combination of signals and sign language through the maze of suburban streets.

In a monsoonal downpour the cab pulled up beneath the porte-cochere. She paddled through a lake of rainwater to the entrance. Her hair was dripping, her suit was ruined, and her new leather shoes squelched all the way up the stairs.

The dining room was packed with middle-aged men and women pretending to be schoolkids for one night. The din was like rainy days under B Block when there was never enough space and everyone yelled over the top of everyone else. The heavier the rain, the louder they got, until Principal Trewin would storm downstairs and yell at them to shut up.

Waiters wielding massive silver trays dealt entrée dishes onto the starched white tablecloths. There were few spare seats. Vann eased along the wall, stepping over chair legs and handbags, until she was halfway down the room. She scanned the crowd for familiar faces. At the far end a buxom woman in a hot-pink dress was waving to get her attention. Her hair was bottle blonde, done in the style of Marilyn Monroe.

'Spare seat over here!' shouted Gaye.

109

Vann sidled around a table of grey-haired men who greeted her like a long-lost mate. She responded with her widest smile but didn't recognise one.

Gaye flung her arms around her neck and smooched her with bee-stung lips. 'You look absolutely fabulous, honey! You haven't changed a bit.'

'Neither have you,' said Vann diplomatically. Gaye's wrinkle-free complexion and pumped-up cleavage would have made a substantial contribution to some cosmetic surgeon's lifestyle.

Vann slid the chair beneath the stiff folds of the tablecloth and took in the others at the circular table. Although strangers to her, everyone behaved as if she were their best buddy. But then again, her picture was everywhere in the media. In a small city like this she was practically a celebrity. Without a doubt they knew who she was. There were rounds of *What are you doing now? How many kids? Remember when ...?*

Between the entrée and the main, Gaye brought out an envelope from her gargantuan studded handbag. Dozens of Polaroid photos flowed onto the table.

Vann picked some up. It was a party sometime in the seventies, judging by the wide denim flares and cheesecloth. Apart from school photos she had almost no pictures of that period of her life. With the passing of the years, she'd forgotten half their names. Not that it mattered, everyone in the obligatory three-line school formation—sitting, standing, perched on a bench at the rear—looked the same.

'Where did you get these?' said Vann.

'I have my sources,' Gaye said enigmatically.

With curious fingers Vann sifted through the pictures. One showed a group of teenagers, drink cans in hand, standing around a backyard fire. She could almost smell the crackling coals and taste the sickly sweetness of liqueur mixed with soft-drink.

She rummaged in her handbag for reading glasses and held the photo close. It was faded and the colours had bled, but it was clear enough to see the brooding eyes, long dark hair and moustache. Next to him was Michelle, the girl who'd had it all.

Although she'd never admit it, she'd envied Michelle. She wore the latest fashion and had the coolest boyfriend. As well as that she had brains, wit, humour, drop-dead gorgeous looks. Who would have guessed that ...?

'Here's dinner.' Gaye began sweeping the photos back into the envelope.

Vann picked out a shot of herself, posing with the members of the band. 'Can I take this one? I'll make a copy and post it back.'

'Keep it. There are heaps more of you in there.'

'Actually, I'd like a nice one of Michelle. All I have are class photos.'

'Sure. We'll go through them properly after we eat.'

Alternate plates of chicken and beef were placed around the table. Neither meal looked particularly appetising. A slab of protein sat in a puddle of sauce, green rafts of broccoli floated around an island of mash.

'Do you remember that party?' Vann poked dubiously at her chicken. It could have passed for a silicon breast implant. Luckily the flavour was better than the appearance.

'Like it was yesterday,' said Gaye, giggling. 'And I *especially* remember what we got up to *afterwards*.' She gave a sly wink and skolled a glass of white wine.

Brazen as ever, Gaye really hadn't changed at all.

'I don't know what you mean.'

'Don't play the innocent with me. You were tonguing for it. So *did* you?'

'As I recall, you were rather preoccupied yourself.'

'Typical pollie. Can't give a straight answer.' She laughed and poured herself another wine. 'Want a top-up?' The bottle seesawed above Vann's empty glass.

'Just a splash. I'm at a junior netball match tomorrow. Mustn't be hung-over.'

The bottle was empty. 'Hey, sweetie,' Gaye called to a passing waiter, 'can you get us another sav blanc?'

Gaye turned to Vann. 'Well?' There was an expectant lift to the word. 'I'm not going to let you off until you tell me if *Miss Goody Two Shoes* lost her *virginity* that night.' Slurring her words, she sounded brash and trashy.

Suddenly the entire table was staring at her. A hot flush rose up her throat and crawled across her cheeks. She attempted a smile. It felt more like she'd bared her teeth.

'A *lady* would never tell.'

'She's a hard case, that Gaye,' said a woman on the right. Little dimples creased the corners of her mouth.

'I'll say.' Vann trawled her memory for the woman's name. Anne? Carol? Gayle?

'You don't remember me, do you?'

'Of course I do …' Desperately, Vann was running through the alphabet when the name suddenly materialised. 'Julie. You played the part of Kathie in the 1971 musical.'

Julie nodded and chatted away. Her dimples crinkled in such an animated manner that it was hard to concentrate on what she was actually saying.

The place to her left had become uncharacteristically quiet.

Vann glanced around and discovered an empty chair. On the prowl at the next table, Gaye's cleavage was gloriously revealed by the low-cut V of her dress. Her arm was draped around a bald man with the gaunt body of an ageing athlete. Once, he'd been their school captain. The girls swooned every time he walked by.

Too much testosterone, Michelle used to say with her fingers pinching her nose.

Julie and two other women at the table, whom Vann scarcely knew, claimed her. All three were teachers from the same school district. They told outrageous stories, gulped down wine like it was water, and cackled at in-jokes only they understood.

A woman with cotton-ball hair tinkled a glass with a spoon. 'Ladies and gentleman, your attention please.'

'Oh my God,' whispered Julie. 'It's Miss Bourke. She must be a hundred and twenty by now.'

They laughed. At the time they'd all thought she had one foot in the grave.

Miss Bourke spoke in her usual robust voice. 'I was surprised and honoured to receive an invitation to this anniversary reunion. Please join me in thanking the organisers for their marvellous work.'

Hoots and whistles.

'What a pleasure it is, after all these years, to see such a fine group of men and women.' She raised her hands and applauded the assembly. The years fell from her face.

'I'm not going to spoil your night with a long boring speech –'

'Thank Christ for that!' A ripple of laughter.

Like a true professional she ignored it. 'All rise for the school anthem. Tim Roberts,' she pointed to the one who'd made the smart-arse comment, 'will lead.'

'She's still got it,' whispered Julie. 'She never missed a trick.'

Unsteady on his feet, Tim Roberts rose and warbled the opening bars. Others picked up the tune. The lyrics were printed on the back of the menu, but no-one needed them. The song was emblazoned on their memories. Earnestness lit their faces, a sense of pride and belonging. But it was maudlin too, to see a roomful of fifty-somethings sing their school anthem with such gusto.

Dessert arrived. Alternate plates of apple crumble and raspberry pavlova.

Gaye sidled into her chair and looked longingly at Vann's. 'I simply *adore* pav. Want to swap?'

They exchanged plates. Vann dug the spoon into the crunchy crumble topping. Luscious apples oozed from beneath. 'This is delicious and I *know* desserts. Did I tell you Lance is a chef?'

'You must be spoilt,' said Gaye through a mouthful of cream. 'Dean can't even make a bowl of cornflakes.'

'Dean? Not the fellow you were going with after Senior.'

Gaye nodded. Her eyes had a devilish look.

'How long have you been together?'

'Six months. Both of us are twice divorced. Third time lucky, so they say.'

'You always had a lust for life.'

The last forkful of pav was washed down with wine. 'Plenty of lust, any rate.'

At eleven o'clock the crowd was starting to dwindle. Julie with the dimples phoned for a cab to the northern suburbs and the three teachers left together.

Gaye fidgeted with the tassels on her handbag. She looked tired and a bit ragged.

They were standing in the foyer. Vann asked if she wanted to share a taxi.

Gaye shook her head. 'I might go out for a drink with one of the boys.'

'Still living dangerously?'

'What's the good of living if you don't have fun?' Gaye opened her handbag and took out the envelope of Polaroid prints.

'Here, you can borrow this.' She pushed it into Vann's hands, along with a business card. 'When you're done, give me a call and we'll get together.'

Vann kissed her cheek and walked down the staircase. At the bottom she turned to wave, but Gaye had already gone.

Outside, it was still raining but not as heavily as before. The noisy throng milled around a snaking line of vehicles driven by spouses or adult offspring. Seventeen years young again, the revellers cheered as engines revved and tyres spun in the mud.

In the taxi and impatient to get home, Vann clutched the envelope of photos. The big question in her mind was whether to show Lance. He'd probably quiz her about the reunion. Were there any incriminating shots that might give her away?

For once, Lance had beaten her home. When she opened the front door, he greeted her with a glass of champagne. His was three quarters empty. They kissed politely and clinked glasses.

'What's the occasion?' she said.

'We finished early. Wedding party. They'd booked out the entire restaurant. That new chef, Myra, is fantastic. So switched on and organised. It would have been a disaster without her. You know, watching that love-struck pair got me thinking.'

Vann arched an eyebrow. 'And?'

'How many years have we been together?'

Vann sighed. She had a premonition of what might be coming and she wasn't sure how she should react. 'Ten years, I guess.'

He took her hand and led her to the living room. Without preamble or fanfare, he went down on one knee. 'Vann Willis, will you marry me?'

She looked down at his pleading expression, his blue eyes as wide as a child's. They'd never discussed marriage, a taboo topic since he'd been through it once before and had declared it an unparalleled disaster for two people to be locked into a promise of lifelong fidelity that neither would be likely to keep.

He lifted his eyebrows a little by way of encouraging a response.

Yes, she did love him. Yet she had an underlying suspicion that there was more to this sudden change of heart. Was it a ruse to get her to give up politics?

Still without an answer, he softly kissed her hand. 'I've loved you all of those ten years, Vann. You and you alone. Please don't make me beg.'

A look of anguish and doubt crossed his face and Vann took pity. What a selfish heartless bitch she must be to doubt a man who'd never wronged her. Tears rolled down her cheeks and fell onto her blouse, one big splosh after another. She sobbed from joy and from relief and from love.

Lance dived into his pocket and took out a handkerchief. It was white, neatly folded and ironed into a square. He shook it open and held it out for her. In one corner was a monogram in blue thread. It caught his eye and he took the hanky back.

Vann knew at once what the initials were and bit her lip. She'd laundered it herself and had meant to put it in her handbag to give back to its owner. It must have become mixed up with other things and landed in Lance's drawer by mistake.

'Who's SVB?' he demanded. He was no longer on his knees. He was standing over her, dangling the offending article in front of her nose.

'No-one important,' she said offhandedly. If she tried to explain, he'd only say *typical politician bullshit* and not believe a word.

'Then why is his handkerchief in our apartment?'

'Don't get yourself in a state.'

'What's *really* going on here, Vann?' he snorted. 'I want the truth!'

She hesitated, and in that moment she saw that she'd lost him. Whatever she said now, he'd twist to suit himself. The anger and hurt that had ended his first marriage never seemed to abate. Whatever his ex- had done to him, he projected onto her. It seemed he *expected* her to be unfaithful and found it impossible to believe she wasn't. Besides, they were tired and it was late. Hardly the time to settle an ugly debate.

'I'll tell you when you've calmed down.' She pushed past him with her glass of champagne and went onto the balcony. In the kitchen she could hear the clink of a bottle and the strike of a match. Cigarette smoke drifted out through the open sliding door. Another time she'd have told him to quit filling her living space with filthy carcinogens. But tonight she let it go.

On Monday, Vann was early into the office. With the election expected to be called any day, her campaign was about to hot up. She'd managed to avoid Lance for much of the weekend. Saturday night he'd slept on the couch and Sunday morning he'd left her a note to say he was going fishing with a mate. Whether or not he actually *did* go fishing was never established, but he returned to the apartment near midnight, reeking of garlic and rum. This morning she'd left him to sleep it off. Perhaps the storm would blow over by the time she got home.

There were still a million tasks to do before the election campaign proper began. Speeches to edit (James did the writing), appearances to make, and her ultimate triumph, the announcement of the government's response to her adoption inquiry that she'd tabled in Parliament the week before. She'd begun campaigning in her electorate, attending kids' sporting events, barbecues at the local mega-hardware store, opening the rowing regatta sponsored by the Chamber of Commerce. She'd been busy jotting *notes to self* in the little notebook she carried everywhere.

That notebook was what she was searching for in her deep oversized handbag. When her fingernails scraped the bottom, she discovered the manila envelope of Polaroids from the reunion. After the altercation with Lance, she'd almost forgotten about it. She took it out and tipped out the photos on her desk.

As a photographer, Michelle had done her job well. That night she'd promised to take at least one snap of everyone who'd attended. That she'd done. Of the thirty-odd pictures, five were of Michelle herself. In each she was with at least one other person (mostly Mac). Several were of Gaye and the boys from the band. What was it called again? The year after the party they'd released two singles, heavy-metal head-bangers. The Independent Underground radio station had given them airplay for a while, but when they stopped performing live, the band slipped into oblivion.

Vann pored over the youthful face and that wispy moustache that felt like feathers. Suddenly the memories flowed as if not forty years had passed, nor even forty days. It could have been last Saturday night. Gaye was right, that night she'd hungered for him.

In preparation for making scanned copies she sorted the photos into three lots. Yes, no, and maybe. The *no* pile went straight back in the envelope, leaving half on the desk.

She checked her watch. Nearly eight-thirty. James would be in soon. Then they'd be open for business and she'd be off on her endless rounds of meetings and interviews and photo opportunities. The phone in reception began to ring. Three more times and the call would go to message bank. She might as well pick it up and save the trouble.

The voice of the female caller was polished and well-modulated, with an accent that might belong to a Shakespearean actress or a barrister at court. She asked to speak to Ms Willis about a personal matter.

Vann hesitated. 'This is she.'

The woman said, 'Before I make a complete fool of myself, could I ask if you were once known as Miffy?'

Vann almost fell off the chair. Only her school friends knew her by that name. The voice on the phone most certainly didn't belong to one of them. Recovering, she cleared her throat. 'Who *is* this?'

'Fiona.'

For a moment, Vann was dumbstruck. That segment of her life had been erased from her memory. That was the way she'd coped, and her strategy had almost worked.

Cautiously Vann said, 'Where do I know you from?'

'Once we were friends.'

A dozen scenarios flashed through her mind. It could be a set-up, a ruse to attack where it would hurt her most. Many a political career had been destroyed by events dredged up from the past. Although times had changed, she was too close to achieving her ultimate political goal to be caught out by a wily rival.

Fiona said, 'Do you remember me?'

Deciding the phone call was genuine Vann said, 'Of course. How did you find me?'

'*The Sunday Post*. School reunion photo in the social pages. The caption named you as *Miffy Jones*. I've been following your inquiry into forced adoptions. I have news that'll knock your socks off. I've been sitting on it because I didn't know what to do.'

'Do you want to talk face to face?'

'Yes. Can we meet after work for a drink?'

If Vann juggled a couple of meetings, she could make it. She had to fit in a meal sometime and she might as well eat with Fiona. 'Meet you at six. There's a cafe at Southbank called *The Grotto*.'

'I know it. See you then.'

In a daze Vann replaced the handset. There was no time to think now. She snatched her handbag and sunglasses and threw instructions to James— who'd rushed in late again—to rejig her afternoon schedule.

As she dashed out, she collided with Seth VerBeek.

'Hey Minister, what's the hurry?' he said in his silken drawl. 'I was in the neighbourhood. Thought I'd drop by on the chance of arranging a *liaison*.'

A joke, she realised. He smiled in the most charming way that she fleetingly wished *liaison* were the correct word.

Vann waved her hand. 'Sorry, Seth. I'm flat out today.'

'This is really important.'

'I need to talk to you too. What about first thing tomorrow?'

'What time do you call first thing?' He sounded doubtful.

'Six-thirty.'

He blew through his lips. 'Yeah, sure. Why not?'

15

March 1972

A thick band of cloud, the remains of a tropical cyclone that had drifted too far south, finally brought relief from the soaring temperatures of an exceptionally hot autumn at *Maidenhead*. Since that day in the eucalypt forest, Miffy had not been well. Her body was bursting with knobby limbs that constantly poked and prodded. The weighty bubble upset her balance and she was as clumsy as an old drunk. Her belly was covered in bruises from bumping the corners of things.

Twice more she'd visited Hope's grave and twice she'd reaffirmed her conviction to leave. But, short of hiking fifty miles on derelict bush tracks, she'd not been able to think up a workable plan. At night the Dobermans patrolled the grounds. Ma Doyle insisted this was necessary to keep the girls safe from rapists and murderers. They might have afforded protection but they also made escape impossible. Without their mistress to control them, the dogs would eat her for supper.

All afternoon, Miffy had been in the vineyard with several other girls, picking the crop of black grapes. While they worked they took the opportunity to stuff themselves with sweet juicy fruit until the house bell rang to mark the end of the day. Tired and bloated, they waddled to the bathroom to wash up.

On the unforgiving concrete floor, Miffy stood on one foot then the other. Lately her legs had begun to ache. She'd put it down to her increased size and the oppressive heat. To ease the pain, she'd invented a dance she called her *disco cramp routine*. Left foot, stretch. Right foot, stretch. Shake your booty round and round.

Isabelle, the scissor-girl, watched her and frowned. 'Have you checked your ankles lately?'

'Haven't seen them in weeks.'

'They look like elephant legs. You should tell *Puss-arse*.'

Miffy couldn't help but grin. Despite the animosity between Isabelle and Daphne, the latter's unflattering nickname for their sour-faced warden had stuck. In the midst of the heatwave two weeks before, Daphne's time had come. Despite her bluster about being tough, when the pains struck she'd meekly allowed herself to taken to the big house and had not been seen since. No-one knew what became of her or the baby, and no-one bothered to ask. In fact, most seemed glad to see her go. There were no new crosses in the forest, so it was likely they'd both made it through the ordeal alive.

Miffy sat on the bathroom bench and tried to see past the rise in her middle. She twisted and turned, but without a mirror it was useless. 'How bad are they?'

'Humongous. Go now before dinner.'

In the stuffy office behind the staircase, Ma Doyle's nose was buried in a ledger book. Hundreds of dockets were placed in neat piles around a wooden desk that was far too big for the room. As she made each spidery mark in the ledger, she crossed out the docket, turned it over and put it in a basket to her left. There was a rhythm about the process, as if she'd been at it for hours and wouldn't stop until she'd finished.

Miffy stood in the doorway, quiet as a ghost, waiting for the ugly beak to come up for air. Suddenly a cramp gripped her calf in a painful spasm. She started her stretch routine and her joints made noises like popcorn.

Over the rim of her glasses Ma Doyle glared at her.

'Sorry to bother you …' Miffy squeaked.

'What is it, girl?'

'My ankles, ma'am.' She lifted the hem of her maxi-dress.

The chair scraped back and Ma Doyle edged around the desk. 'They're up like balloons, girl. Come outside in the light.'

They sat on concrete stairs at the entrance to the house.

'How long have they been like this?'

'Isabelle noticed this afternoon. I've been getting cramps for weeks.'

Ma Doyle placed her hands around one ankle and squeezed. 'That hurt?'

'No, ma'am.'

She pressed the other ankle then worked her way up each leg from the toes to the thigh. She pursed her lips and rubbed her chin.

Although all the girls at *Maidenhead* were well into their pregnancies, no doctor ever came. Ma Doyle was both facility manager and physician. She made the diagnoses, meted out the medicines, dressed wounds, and enforced quarantines when she determined that an illness was contagious. On rare occasions she'd driven a girl to the ambulance centre in town, but only if her life depended on it.

'Do you have pain anywhere else?'

'Yeah, sometimes. It goes through my ribs into my shoulder.'

'Bed rest for you, girl. Go get your things.'

In the dorm Miffy packed underwear, two nighties, a toothbrush, and a change of clothes. She shouldered her bag and trudged to the big house. The babble of fifty young voices drifted in from the refectory where they'd gathered to eat. Through the doorway she glimpsed Isabelle with two of the new girls who'd come in during the week. Judging from their expressions of horror, she must have told them Daphne's calf story. It had become an initiation of sorts, which gave the old hands no end of delight.

Miffy climbed the staircase to the bedroom where she'd last seen Fiona. On the bedside table was a tray of steaming food. Beef casserole with mashed potatoes, peas, and carrots. All had been grown on the farm. For dessert, rice pudding. The one tolerable aspect of *Maidenhead* was the food. That, she'd miss. Although Merle made the best cakes in town, her idea of an evening meal was greasy lamb chops with two veg, usually sloppy pumpkin and watery choko from the vines that overran the backyard.

Ma Doyle bustled in with a blood pressure machine and stethoscope. When she finished the test, her eyebrows knitted.

'What does it say?' said Miffy.

'Never you mind. Keep your feet up and don't move unless I say so.'

'Can I go to the toilet?'

Ma Doyle pointed to the commode chair in the corner. 'Now, get some sleep.' She took the tray, snapped off the light, and pulled the door behind her. It groaned under its weight. Solid oak and three inches thick, it must have weighed half a ton.

Keys clinked.

Miffy leapt out of bed and rattled the knob. It was locked. She ran to the double-hung window and turned the latch. The window wouldn't budge. She slid her hand along the timber frame and found nails that held it shut.

That's when she realised she was a prisoner.

A full moon drifted through the clouds, casting enough light to see the outline of the furniture. She tiptoed about, opening drawers and closets. Set out on a metal tray was an assortment of medical instruments (thankfully no rope). She picked up a set of forceps and fitted them together. They were like oversized salad tongs. Surely not ...

She replaced them on the tray and scuttled back to bed. Wide awake, she propped herself up on the pillows and gazed through the glass at the shimmering stars. Earlier she'd dared to hope that this unexpected change in circumstances might give her a means of escape. But her room was like a fortress and her elephantine legs were in no shape to trek through the countryside. She must think of a different plan.

For the first time in four months she had a bedroom to herself. The silence was deafening. Not a sound suggested there was a living breathing world outside.

All night the timbers of the old house creaked and groaned like a sailing ship. She scarcely slept a wink. How many other girls had lain awake on that same hard mattress with the blanket pulled up to their chin? At dawn, instead of the jubilant screech of lorikeets, insidious shafts of sunlight prodded her eyes until they opened. As she lay there, waiting for her warden to come, she heard the faint mewling of a kitten. She held her breath and sharpened her ears.

There it was again.

Kneeling on the bed, she pressed her ear to the wall. For several minutes she listened, but all she could hear was the gush and rumble of her stomach.

The lock scraped, the door opened.

Isabelle brought in her breakfast tray. 'How's the elephant this morning?'

'Banished to the garret by Puss-arse.' Miffy pursed her lips, a perfect impersonation of Ma Doyle.

Isabelle laughed. 'That's funny. You know, if it wasn't for that bitch Daphne, you and I might've had a better start.'

Miffy shrugged. 'My mother would have called her a *rough diamond.*'

'She was rough all right. Did she tell you who the father was?'

'We never talked about it.'

Isabelle smirked knowingly. 'She took on an entire American basketball team.'

Miffy's eyes widened. 'You're joking!'

'There's more.' She paused for dramatic effect. 'They were *black.*'

'Wow!' Miffy breathed. 'Did she tell you that herself?'

'No. But I have it on good authority.'

Isabelle's expression was hard to decipher. Was she telling the truth or repeating nasty gossip? Certainly Daphne was no angel. Did it matter who she'd slept with?

'Anyway, just thought you'd like to know. Better eat up while it's hot.' Isabelle dumped the tray on Miffy's lap. 'Oh yeah, another batch of new girls arrived.'

'Who brought them?'

'A bloke I haven't seen before. They're all in the parlour.'

'Are the dogs tied up?'

'Yeah, thank God. I'm shit-scared of those mongrels.'

Miffy eyed the porridge. It was dotted with black bits. She tested a morsel off the spoon. 'Yuk! It's burnt.'

Isabelle perched on the bed end and toyed with the hem of her t-shirt. 'I know about the cemetery.'

Miffy raised her eyebrows. 'And …?'

'I also know you don't want to give up your baby. I'm having second thoughts myself.' She twisted the t-shirt into a knot. 'If you stay here, you won't have a chance.'

'I know.'

Isabelle threw her a sympathetic look. 'I hope it turns out okay.' She took the tray into the corridor and said in an overly-loud voice, 'I'll lock the door now, Mary.'

If Miffy's blood pressure was already high, being locked up again in the chamber of horrors shot it right off the scale. 'What's *with* this place?' She shouted and slammed her fists down on the pillow.

With nothing else to do, she dozed on and off until Ma Doyle came in midmorning to take her blood pressure. She read the gauge and seemed pleased.

'How long until I go back to the dorm?' said Miffy.

'A couple more days. You'll have new room-mates.'

It was the most information she'd ever winkled out of the old bat.

When Isabelle brought the tray for lunch, she wore a wicked grin. 'Here you are, just what you ordered.' On the plate were two boring jam sandwiches and a glass of milk.

'What?'

Isabelle dipped her hand between her breasts. 'I'm giving you your freedom.' She produced an old black key with a long shank and filigree bow.

'Where did you get it?'

'A drawer in the devil's lair.'

'You went into her study?'

'She told me to. Well, not exactly. I was supposed to be mopping the floor.'

Miffy flung her arms around her neck. 'Thanks a million times over. I'll never forget you for this.'

'Leave it under the back doormat when you go.' Isabelle gave her a squeeze. 'Good luck.' She took the tray and made a commotion about relocking the door.

Miffy scanned the room for a place to hide the precious key. Not in the bedside chest, nor under the pillow. Her bag was likely to be searched. In the end she chose a well-worn sandshoe and stuffed in a smelly sock for good measure.

With no TV and no books to read, the window was both her amusement and observation post. If she knelt on the commode chair, she could see the entire curve of the driveway. What she was looking for, she didn't know, so she studied the rhythms of the house. The cars that came and went, the daily routine of Ma Doyle and her Dobermans. She noted the times when they were fed, when they were tied up and when they were free to roam.

In the afternoon she again heard the mewling noise through the wall. This time she was certain. It was no kitten, it was a baby. But whose? She knew that *Maidenhead* babies were taken by their adoptive parents immediately after birth, but she'd never contemplated the process of the transaction.

She held an empty glass to the wall and put her ear to it. She'd seen this technique in old spy movies and it had worked a treat. For ten minutes she focused her attention on the vibrations of the glass, but she heard not another sound.

She was about to give up and go back to bed when something outside flashed. She leant on the windowsill and squinted at the shimmering haze. A plume of red dust rose from the track to the house. Intermittently the western sun reflected off the windscreen glass, shooting spots of brilliance through her window.

The vehicle was a white panel van with blue lettering on the side. A ladder was on the roof-rack. Probably an electrician to fix the dodgy switches. The van rumbled to the back entrance and stopped directly beneath her window. Quickly she drew herself back into shadow.

The Dobermans raced out to snap and snarl at the newcomer. Ma Doyle was hot on their paws. She whistled. Obediently they dropped. She clipped chains to their collars and tethered them to a fencepost.

The driver's door opened and a man got out. His dark suit and tie proclaimed that he was no tradesman. Judging by his greying hair, he'd have been around fifty.

What happened next was totally astonishing. The man opened his arms and Ma Doyle flew into them. For a brief moment they hugged. Then they became amorous and started pashing like movie-star lovers. It was disgustingly gross but Miffy couldn't tear her eyes away.

The pair broke apart laughing. From the van he collected an overnight bag and briefcase. Hand-in-hand they walked to the house.

Miffy put her ear to the keyhole. Silence.

She scrabbled under the bed for her sandshoe with the secret key. She slid it into the lock. Her hand trembled. Did she dare?

Before she could stop herself, she was on the landing. She tiptoed to the head of the staircase. Voices echoed from below. From halfway down the stairs, she spied them in the parlour. They were sitting together on the chaise. Papers were spread across the coffee table. The stairwell had the acoustics of an amphitheatre so she could hear their every word.

'He's upstairs,' said Ma Doyle. 'Kathleen's been looking after him. He's a fussy little mite, hard to settle. We can't keep him here much longer.'

Miffy looked up the stairs to the landing. At the end of the corridor was a door she'd not noticed before. So, there *was* a baby. The last girl to be moved to the big house was Daphne. That was two weeks ago.

The scent of tobacco smoke curled up the stairwell. The man's voice was apologetic. 'I'm telling you Iris, I've tried every contact and they've all come to naught.'

'I knew there'd be problems the minute I set eyes on that trollop. And, as you know, I'm an excellent judge of character.'

'Of course you are, sweetheart.'

Iris? Sweetheart? Who *was* this man?

'Problem is, no-one's prepared to fork out for a kid like that,' he said.

Miffy's mind was spinning. *Like what?* What was wrong with the baby?

Iris Doyle said, 'We're not running a charity here, Rowland, our reputation mustn't be tarnished. We need a *permanent solution.*'

Miffy pictured the cemetery in the eucalypt grove. It was then that she made up her mind. There'd be no *permanent solution* for her child. She'd save Claire's life at any cost.

The scuffle of shoes warned they were about to leave the room.

She flew up the stairs, relocked her door and slipped the key into her knickers. In bed under the covers, she pretended to be asleep.

The squeak of a hinge, a puff of fresh air. Icy eyes bored through the sheet. Though her heart was running like a rabbit, she forced herself to breathe in a deep regular rhythm. If they realised she'd overheard, she might find herself in the cemetery.

'She's out to it,' whispered Rowland.

'Quick then. We've got half an hour.'

The lock clicked.

Half an hour was all she needed too.

She pulled on shorts and t-shirt, laced her sandshoes, stuffed her possessions into her bag and used the turret key for the last time.

To her left was Ma Doyle's room. The door was shut, muffled laughter filtered through. She blocked all thoughts of what they might be up to. It was too revolting to contemplate.

In the kitchen she took whatever food was left on the bench. Bread, apples, a tin of baked beans. At the back door, she lifted the mat and slipped the key beneath.

Taking care to avoid the dogs, she skirted around the house. She found a goat track that dived into the scrub along the barbed wire fence. Where the track veered away, she located a gap in the wire large enough to climb through. Her sketchy plan was to make her way to the highway. Then she'd hitch a ride to … wherever. She didn't care. Anywhere was better than *Maidenhead.*

Half an hour later she hadn't covered much distance. The Gothic spires and chimneys of the big house were still visible on the rise. She pictured Iris Doyle and her lover slinking out of the bedroom. Would they check Miffy's room before going downstairs? Perhaps not, it was nearly tea time and the kitchen girls would be peeling vegetables and reheating the stew-pot.

To be safe, Miffy had fashioned a bolster to look like a girl asleep.

Puffing and sweaty, she sat on a fallen log in the shade. The grass was tender-dry and buzzing with cicadas. The air was as hot as a furnace. Smoke from a bushfire triggered a sneezing fit. Geez, that was all she needed. To be given away by her stupid nose.

Her balloon-belly made it hard to navigate the uneven ground. Twice, her foot caught in a bandicoot hole and she almost fell. Her ankles were sore and her pace was no faster than a hobble. The sun was on its western descent. If she didn't get a move on she'd have to spend a night alone in the bush. Fear spurred her on.

In the valley below were the treed banks of a meandering creek. If she couldn't reach the road before dark, the creek might provide water and shelter until morning.

She began her descent. Long shadows rippled across the track, crisp air gathered in the dips and pockets. Blue-tinged mist promised a frosty night.

When her ankles finally forced her to stop, she perched on a boulder and ate an apple. Soldier ants trailed nose-to-bum across a barren patch of earth. Behind her, the dry leaves rustled ominously. She spun around but whatever it was had vanished. To be sure, she tucked up her legs beneath her.

Seconds later the rustle came again. With her heart in her mouth, she scanned the ground around the boulder. A snake's tail, scaly and brown, slid beneath the litter. Was it a death adder or a harmless python?

The light was fading, she dared not move. Her eyes were fixed to the spot. The barking of a dog resounded through the valley. Mosquitoes picked the back of her neck. Minutes passed. The snake didn't move.

Tendrils of heavenly fire splayed across a purple sky. Soon it would be too dark to find her way to the creek. The creatures of the night were beginning to reveal themselves. A tawny frogmouth swooped onto a branch and eyed her with disinterest. Hundreds of flying foxes, screeching like demons, glided above the treetops. From the base of the rock came the dreaded rustle. With every ounce of courage, she leapt from the boulder and bolted down the track.

The moon cast wan shadows that moved suddenly and unpredictably like spooks. Shivering, not from the cold, she followed the tinkle of running water. Although it sounded close, she couldn't yet see the creek bank. The moon disappeared behind a cloud. Darkness folded around her like a blanket.

Coming towards her was a pair of dazzling lights. Up and down they juddered as the vehicle hit the corrugations. Caught like a roo in a spotlight, she was temporarily blinded. She stopped in the middle of the track and folded her arms across her face. Tyres skidded, the dogs in the back bayed for blood. The engine cut, a door squeaked open.

In the glare she couldn't see the faceless driver. Friend, foe or serial killer? It was unlikely to be *friend*. No-one knew where she was and her parents had disowned her. That left *foe* and *serial killer*. Stories of hitchhikers murdered on lonely roads streamed through her mind. Paralysed with fear, she had to make a split-second decision.

She chose self-preservation and took off into the bush.

Too heavy and awkward to run fast, the dogs soon caught her up. Working as a pack, three black brutes surrounded her. With gut-ripping snarls and treacherous teeth, they closed in. No match for their size or strength, she shut her eyes and prepared to be eaten alive.

A whistle.

Instantly the dogs fell quiet. A wet nose touched her leg.

'Mary! Get in the ute!'

Her heart sank. Out of luck and out of energy, she'd have to suffer whatever punishment the devil-woman meted out.

'You wicked, wicked girl! You could have lost the baby.'

Ma Doyle chained the dogs in the tray back. Miffy climbed into the cabin. The ute bungled along the steep winding track to the towering fortress.

Upstairs in her prison chamber, Miffy washed her face at the basin, put on a clean nightdress and curled up exhausted on the bed. Through the window the moon slipped between strips of cloud. It was late and getting cold. In the last hour a cramp of sorts had been playing at the base of her bulge. Sharp, yet not exactly painful, like the first day of her long-lost periods.

She cradled the baby inside her and whispered, 'Not long now, my darling Claire, and we'll be together.'

16

Monday 10 March

Along with hundreds of residents, workers and tourists, Vann strolled through the Southbank parklands, enjoying a time of peace just before sunset. She was glad she'd allowed enough time to walk from the Parliamentary Annex across the Goodwill Bridge, for she hadn't taken any exercise in months.

The autumn weather was warm. The brown river was awash with golden light. Although it was Monday (quietest day of the week), the place was alive with young families, lovers hand-in-hand, workers de-stressing with a cold beer before embarking on the long commute home. Mouth-watering aromas wafted from a host of ethnic restaurants. Indian vindaloo, Thai tom yum, Greek souvlaki, Italian cacciatore. A melting pot of cultures and nationalities and ages, Southbank had the atmosphere of a never-ending festival.

At *The Grotto* bar and restaurant, Fiona had claimed a table outside. Legs crossed, she was flicking through the menu and nibbling on a grissini. As soon as she spotted Vann, she rushed towards her with open arms.

For a full minute they clung together, lost for words.

'You look fabulous!' said Fiona at last. 'Better than on TV.'

'Thanks. You haven't changed either.' It was true. Age hadn't touched Fiona's fresh-faced complexion.

They ordered salt-and-pepper calamari and a bottle of mineral water to share.

'I know about your loss and I'm truly sorry,' said Vann.

'Are you *sure*?' It sounded like a challenge.

'I found the cross with her name in the babies' cemetery.'

'It's not her.'

'I saw it with my own eyes. I wept for you both.'

'Miffy, she's not dead.'

'What!'

'Two years ago she found me. She's very much alive. The people she went to called her Margot after a great-aunt who'd left them her estate.'

'I'm totally and utterly speechless!'

'That's a lot, coming from a politician.' Fiona smiled.

Vann shrugged. 'How do you feel about it?'

'Like it was the end of a nightmare. All I ever wanted was to have a choice in the matter. You know how much I wanted to keep her. I wept about her all those years.'

Vann's gut was doing cartwheels. 'I'm so glad she found you. Now she must know how hard it was—'

'It was hard all right. Do you remember the morning she was born?'

'How could I forget? No-one prepared us. I thought you were dying.'

'All that morning I fought with them. The midwife gave me an injection to calm me down. When I woke up, they told me it had been a difficult birth and my little girl had died.' Fiona's eyes glistened with tears.

'They said she'd died?' Vann's mind was galloping away.

'Yes. I was shattered. The doctor made me sign papers. The death certificate and permission to release the body. I was inconsolable and begged for her to have a proper burial. They gave me a white cross and I wrote her name—*Hope*—on it in Texta pen.'

The waiter brought the mineral water. Vann waved it away and ordered a double Scotch instead. Fiona asked for a gin and tonic.

'Was it a funeral with a priest and all?'

'They'd already sealed her in a little coffin. It was rough pine and looked home-made. Mrs Doyle and I said prayers over it in the upstairs bedroom. I never visited her grave. I was packed off home the next day.'

'So, forty years later Hope turns up out of the blue?'

'That's right. She said she'd had the devil's time tracking me down.'

'Are you certain it's her?'

'A mother knows her own flesh and blood. She's exactly like me, down to the same pattern of moles on her back.'

Vann took a mouthful of Scotch and slowly shook her head. It was like being in a thick fog. Nothing was quite what it seemed.

The meal arrived. The calamari, crisp and spicy, came with a mountain of chips. It smelt divine. The last time she'd eaten was breakfast.

'Did Margot know she was adopted?'

'Her parents told her the day she turned twenty-one.'

'Wow! That must have been *some* birthday present!'

'That's not all. They said they'd paid a king's ransom for the privilege, and not to look for her real mother because she'd died in childbirth. She's never forgiven them.'

Vann ordered another Scotch. 'So, to be clear, you were told your baby had died, but in reality she was stolen and sold. The adoptive parents were told *you'd* died while giving birth.'

'That pretty much sums it up.'

'Do you have any proof?'

'Only Margot's say-so.'

'How did she find you?'

A cloud crossed Fiona's face. 'I've never asked.'

'Hope was buried in the babies' cemetery at *Maidenhead*, right?'

'I guess so.'

Vann tapped the edge of the Scotch glass. 'But if she's alive, who—or what—is buried there instead?'

'I'm not going to the cops. I don't want to lose Margot again.'

'What are you afraid of?'

'She's done it tough, poor pet. She was just out of drug rehab when she called me. It was either that or jail. I've helped her back on her feet.'

'If I'm re-elected, the victims of this whole sorry saga will get the compensation they deserve. I know money isn't everything, but it helps.'

Fiona sighed. 'Throwing money at pain doesn't make it better. I don't want money. What's needed is the truth about what went on there. This has been swept under the carpet for too long. Remember those oaths of silence we had to make? What utter twaddle! Yet until now, I've not said anything. If my child is alive, how many other mothers were swindled out of their babies the same way? People like the Doyles must be punished. This must never happen again.'

Vann gazed at the river walkway. Young children frolicked along the garden edges, holding hands with their mothers. Fiona was right, no amount of money would compensate for what they'd missed. She needed time to process this new piece of information, time to rethink her response.

'I hear what you say, Fiona. I'll give it my best shot.' The alarm on Vann's phone beeped, reminding her of her next appointment. 'Sorry, got to fly. I'm delighted about your news, and thanks for being frank.'

They embraced. Fiona held onto her wrist. 'Promise you'll be careful. There's more to this than meets the eye.'

'Take care yourself.' Vann downed the remainder of the Scotch in one mouthful, left eighty dollars for the bill, and bolted to the taxi rank.

17

Tuesday 11 March

At six-thirty a.m. Seth stood outside Vann's office and peered through the glass door to an unlit interior. He rattled the handle, found it was locked and swore beneath his breath for agreeing to see her at such a ridiculous hour. He was never fully awake until ten, and then only after several shots of caffeine. Café Nero was down the road. He patted his pockets for coins and darted through the queue of early-shift traffic waiting at the lights.

The aroma of the coffee was the kiss of life. He ordered a double espresso and downed it on the spot. It hit him like a power surge. For breakfast he ordered a take-away latte—strong and easy on the milk—and as an afterthought a second cup for Vann. When he walked back with the hot cardboard cups, he was primed and ready to fire.

They reached the door of the office at the same time.

She was pink-faced and puffing. 'Sorry I'm late.' She rattled the keys, opened the door and rushed inside to deactivate the alarm. 'Phew, it's hot in here. Take a seat while I turn on the aircon.'

He swaggered past the sleek granite reception counter into Vann's office. On her desk were two piles of photographs. Polaroids. He hadn't seen a Polaroid in years. He put the cups on the desk and picked one up.

A teenage girl and a youth at a party. The girl had pale skin, auburn hair and a smile that was unmistakeably Vann's. Fresh-faced and wide-eyed, she would have been about fifteen. Cute.

He looked at the boy whose arm was tight around her waist. Shoulder-length hair, wispy moustache, Black Sabbath t-shirt.

Seth's jaw dropped.

'Would you like tea?' Vann's voice floated through the doorway. 'I'll make a pot.'

'I brought us coffees.'

'Coffee's good. I'll be out in a mo.'

He sifted through the photos. The youth was in several, performing an unimaginative repertoire of silly faces. Tongue out, finger up the nose, rolling the whites of his eyes. Obviously pissed.

High heels clicked on the polished wood floor. In less than a second she'd catch him snooping. He shuffled the photos into two piles the way he'd found them.

All but one.

'So, Mr VerBeek, to what do I owe the pleasure?' Vann positioned herself behind the blond timber desk. Briskly she swept the photos into a manila envelope which she locked in the bottom drawer. Did he detect a hint of embarrassment?

'Remember the article I wrote about the bombing when I asked the public for help? There were rather a lot of responses. As you'd expect, most were complete rubbish. But a couple were worth following up. I thought you'd be able to help.'

'I assumed you had answers, not questions.' She uncapped the take-away cup and took a sip. 'By the way, thanks for the coffee.'

He grinned and inclined his head. 'It's my job to ask questions.'

Vann gave him a come-hither flash of teeth. The same sexy smile that had been captured on Polaroid decades ago. She was still an attractive woman.

'Fire away. You've got twenty minutes.'

'Do you think there's any link between the inquiry into adoptions and the bombing of your office?'

'Who knows? Mental illness and substance abuse are sometimes linked to early childhood trauma. There's certainly evidence that forced adoptions were traumatic for the natural mothers and often the children too. That doesn't mean the inquiry *caused* the bombing.'

'But you can't rule it out, can you?'

'Nothing can be ruled in or out at this stage.'

'What do you know about Albert Steptoe?'

'It wasn't his real name. We just called him that. He was a harmless vagrant. Sometimes he'd wander in and we'd give him a cup of tea. Look, I know the police are treating him as the prime suspect, and he can't speak for himself because he's dead. He was a bit simple but he wasn't dangerous.'

'What about Bertram Porter?'

Vann shook her head. 'Don't know him.'

'The morning of the bombing, was a parcel delivered to the office?'

'I wouldn't know. My staff would have attended to it.'

'A delivery man was seen leaving your office just before the explosion.'

'Is that so?' She leaned forward, her elbows on the desk. The colour of her eyes was an alluring hue, halfway between green and blue.

He dropped his gaze, examined the screen of his phone as if it would provide the answers. 'Well, that's what I heard.'

'Wait, I'd almost forgotten. When the bomb went off I was talking to Freya on the phone. She said a package had come in.' She gasped, rolled back her chair and began to pace the room. 'I knew they were barking up the wrong tree with Steptoe. Someone out there is after me.'

Seth abandoned his phone and focused all his attention on her. 'Do you have any idea who or why?'

She chewed the corner of her mouth. Twice she took a breath as if to speak and let it out again. Her expression proclaimed that she was guilty as hell. But of what?

He summoned all his powers of persuasion and patted the seat of her swivel chair. 'Sit down and stop worrying. We'll talk off the record.'

She did as she was told. 'This is definitely off the record?'

Solemnly Seth drew a cross on his heart.

Her face relaxed. 'I don't know why I trust you, Seth VerBeek, but I do. Lord knows my judgement in men hasn't always been the best. Please don't let me down.'

'I've been around long enough to know if you burn your bridges, you can kiss your sweet journalistic arse goodbye.' He'd also been around long enough to smell a blockbuster. This one had his nostrils flaring.

Vann drained the coffee. 'I know a place about an hour west of here. It was a home for teenage girls who were in trouble. All the babies were given up for adoption and the girls were sworn to secrecy. I'm talking the nineteen-seventies, when being unmarried and pregnant was shameful and wrong. Anyway, it seems there was more to it than appeared on the surface. A former inmate had a stillborn child who was buried in a cemetery on the grounds. But two years ago, a woman claiming to be her daughter turned up. I suspect the place was involved in some sort of illegal trade in babies.'

'So, the adoptions inquiry might have rattled the branches?'

'I've been mulling it over all night. There's simply no evidence.'

'There's one way to get it.' He leaned back in the chair and cracked his knuckles. 'What appointments can you get out of today?'

'You're not suggesting …'

'My car's outside. You can run your office by mobile phone. It's seven o'clock now. We could be back here by noon. And, unless you decide otherwise, it's entirely off the record. What's there to lose?'

Her mouth was half open. 'I must be mad. Let's do it!'

18

Wednesday 15th March 1972

All night Miffy's pains came and went in waves. Soft, persistent. Like wide bands of elastic gripping and loosening at the base of her bulge. Sometimes they were close together, sometimes far apart. As each set began, she'd grit her teeth and count down the seconds until it was over.

Days before, the baby had stopped using her as a human trampoline. It lay motionless and heavy in her pelvis. A relief at first, now she missed the constant reminder of the life she'd created.

Throughout the quiet night hours, she chewed her fingernails to the quick. If Claire died, it would be her fault. She'd been told to stay in bed, yet she'd chosen to ignore the advice. Tears seeped between her eyelids and rolled onto the pillow. The night seemed interminable.

She slept.

Later the first pang of true pain jolted her. Sunlight filtered through the curtain, its warm fingers massaged her aching body. Despite the exhaustion, her spirits soared. This would be the day she'd meet her beloved Claire. Even the date was auspicious. The fifteenth of March, the Ides. What a gorgeous autumn day to be born!

Somehow she'd convince them she'd make a good mother. Whatever they offered or threatened her with, she'd stick with her decision to keep the baby.

Ma Doyle herself brought in the breakfast tray. Two slabs of white toast, a dollop of strawberry jam and a glass of milk. One glance and it was a frown.

'How long have you been like this?'

Halfway through a contraction, Miffy responded with a grunt.

'Running away was pure madness, girl. It put the child at terrible risk.

It'll be a miracle if there's no permanent damage. Selfish trollop, you ought to be ashamed!'

The contraction passed. Sweating, Miffy stretched out her legs and released her breath. She was hungry, for the previous night she'd eaten only a bowl of cold soup. She reached for the toast. Her hand was slapped away.

'No food for you. Feet up in the stirrups.' Ma Doyle tied on a white apron and washed her hands at the basin.

Before Miffy could object, her knickers were off and cold fingers plunged into the cavern between her legs.

'Good. Three inches dilated. Won't be much longer.'

'I'm going to keep the baby so don't try and talk me out of it.'

'You aren't old enough to make that decision. Anyway, it was signed away months ago.'

'Who by?'

'Why, your father of course. He did what was best for you.'

'I know what's best for me … and for my baby.'

'Don't make this any harder than it has to be, girl.'

'I'm not giving it up –.' Suddenly her body seized up. All she could do was groan and surf the tidal wave.

Ma Doyle stood calmly by the bed until the worst of it had passed, then she poured water on a flannel and folded it across Miffy's mouth. 'Bite on this next time.'

Miffy sucked the moisture from the cloth. It was comforting in a childish way. A dim corner of her memory stirred. Her mother's all-encompassing embrace, a pink threadbare blanket she called *Bunny,* the taste of her own saliva percolating through the brushed cotton. She was about to have a baby of her own and all she could think about was this snapshot in time when her world was new and wonderful.

'I'd better get the midwife.' Ma Doyle swept out of the room, locking the door behind her. She needn't have bothered for the prisoner was in no fit state to abscond.

Kathleen O'Brien and the next wave of pain arrived at the same moment. But before the cramp took a proper hold, she felt a sharp jab to the right arm. She bit into the flannel and steeled herself for the onslaught. But instead of intense pain, a warm release surged through her veins.

She floated about in a haze of comfortable confusion. Time seemed to expand and contract with the rhythm of her womb. A flurry of voices, a blur of colours. She couldn't comprehend a word that was said. She was caught in a surreal dream where she was able to see through closed eyes and speak without using her voice.

Once, she became aware of hands busy beneath her nightdress. She sucked water from the flannel and kept her eyes shut. Then came an irresistible urge to push, push, push. A thin cry, not her own. Was it Claire? Muffled conversations hovered above and around her. The door opened and shut again.

She must have slept.

'Mary, wake up! You need to sign this form.' The man's voice was harsh and insistent.

Miffy squinted through heavy lids. On the ceiling a single light-bulb glowed. His face was obscured by shadow, but his voice she'd heard before. Through the muddle inside her head she tried to put order to her thoughts. Where did she know him from?

He helped her sit, propped up on pillows, folded a biro into the claw of her hand, thrust a clip-board of papers onto her lap.

She pushed it away. 'Where's my baby?' Her words came out fuzzy even to her own ears. She tried again. Her tongue was practically stuck to the roof of her mouth.

He gave her a glass of water.

She guzzled it, spilling more than she drank. Spent, she collapsed on the pillow and her mind whirled into a distant and peaceful place.

Undeterred he raised her up and again manoeuvred the pen into position. 'Sign it!' he commanded.

'My baby?' At last she could speak coherently.

'A difficult birth, unfortunately the child didn't survive.' He slid the clipboard folder beneath her hand. 'You must sign this now.'

Without fully comprehending what he'd said, Miffy gazed at the papers. Random print scurried about on the page. It made no sense, held no meaning. She looked up at the man's face. Green like spring pasture after rain, his eyes were focused on the forms. There was no hint of sympathy for the life that had been lost. For him this was a mere business transaction, no more significant than paying a bill or posting a letter.

He guided the pen to the signature lines. 'This is the death certificate and this is the release form so we can bury the child.' He spoke more gently than before.

The door opened. Ma Doyle appeared at the other side of the bed and patted Miffy's hand. 'We did the best we could under the circumstances, dear. Remember, you brought this on with your selfishness. Running away when you should have been resting. Now, Mary, be a good girl and sign the papers for the doctor.'

The room was awash with tears. She might as well have smothered her child with a pillow, poor kitten. What sort of monster was she?

Obediently she signed where she was shown.

He took the clip-board. Almost as an afterthought he said, 'What name should I give the deceased?'

'Was it a boy or a girl?'

'Girl,' said Ma Doyle.

'Her name is Claire.' Somehow she'd known it would end like this. And that made it all the worse. As the weight of the awful news bore down on her, she covered her face with her hands and wept.

The doctor said, 'Come on, Iris. We'll leave her to have a good cry.'

Iris. It was him, the lover.

Four miserable days of grief and discomfort crawled by. The pills she'd been given to dry up her milk made her so sick that she couldn't keep food or liquid in her stomach. Her breasts were swollen and sore. To make matters worse she was bleeding profusely, as if her body were making up for all nine missed periods simultaneously.

Once, she'd asked Ma Doyle about Claire.

Pull yourself together and forget she ever existed was the response.

The following Saturday, Ma Doyle pronounced her well enough for the journey home. After breakfast, Miffy packed the few possessions she'd taken to the big house and stood with her bag at the top of the staircase. It was steep and her legs were wobbly. She held the bannister rail all the way down.

The dorm was deserted. The clatter of the treadle machines in the workroom below filtered up through the floorboards. She walked along the corridor to her bed, second from the end. Someone had kindly made it up with fresh sheets and laid a teddy on the pillow. She turned to the hanging space, pulled a t-shirt from the rack.

It was canary yellow.

She never wore that colour. With her auburn hair, she'd look like a sunflower.

She flicked through the rack. None of her clothes were there.

The drawers beneath were full of another girl's stuff. Fuming, she did a lap of the dorm, found her clothes jammed into a waxed box marked *NQ Bananas*.

With tight lips she sorted through the jumble, keeping only a few items that would not remind her of this place. She repacked the bag she'd brought from home five months earlier and zipped it up. Then she took her fat-belly clothes up to the big house, where she had been told to wait. In the kitchen she stuffed them into firebox of the slow combustion stove. With satisfaction she watched them blaze. Then she scrubbed her hands at the sink and strode out to the front veranda.

The farm ute rumbled up the driveway and stopped. The driver must have been seventy. Her skin was leather, her hair was like snow. She wore the stoic expression of a person who'd battled life in the bush and won.

Ma Doyle came out to tie up the dogs. She exchanged small talk with the driver, whom she called Missus K. For appearances, she gave Miffy an emotionless hug and whispered a morsel of advice in her ear.

'Throw your stuff in the back, kid.' Missus K revved the spluttering engine which threatened to conk out. It farted a black cloud of smoke and then renewed its erratic rhythm. 'Make sure you tie the tarp down good and tight.'

Miffy slouched in the front passenger's seat, window down, eyelashes fluttering against the breeze. Country music whined from the radio. The lyrics were about *long … sad … lonely*. As the ute bounded down the gravel track, she took one last look at the homestead, standing proud and tall on the ridge.

She was free at last, she ought to feel jubilant. Yet the sadness of her loss threatened to choke her. *Goodbye darling Claire*, she whispered to herself. *I'll never forget you, not as long as I live.*

Out on the highway she gazed across the black soil plains, at the crops and the cattle and the vast stretch of sky. If she could erase the last five months of her life, she'd be excited about going home, seeing her friends, going back to school. But in her heart, she knew that home would be a different place.

She thought about what Ma Doyle had said to her as she left.

You can't change the past, but you can learn from it.

It was probably the best piece of advice she'd ever heard. Unexpected too, coming from a sour Puss-arse.

Missus K puffed on a cigarette and steered one-handed with her elbow on the window frame. 'So, what did you think of Puss-arse?'

In amazement Miffy turned toward the driver.

The old woman wore an impish grin. 'They've called her that for years. You think she doesn't know?' She pursed her lips like Ma Doyle then cackled at her own cleverness. 'Poor pet, age hasn't treated her well.'

'How long have you known her?' said Miffy.

'Most of her life. She's a smart cookie, that one. Does a fine job of running that big place on her own.'

Miffy sniffed. 'Hardly on her own. She's got plenty of workers … us girls.'

'Maybe so. You think she's a tough old biddy, don't you?'

Miffy nodded.

'Well I can tell you,' she took a final drag of the smoke, 'that woman's got a heart of gold.' She crushed the butt into the dashboard ashtray and snapped it shut.

The subject appeared to be closed. Obviously Ma Doyle should be in line for a sainthood and Miffy was too blind to see why. She leant on her hand and tried to think of one instance, in all those months, when she'd seen kindness. She shook her head and fiddled with the air-vent to stop it from blowing hot air into her lap.

'How far to town?'

'Be on the outskirts in half an hour,' said Missus K. 'I was told to take you to Doctor Grice's in New Farm, but I can take you home if you'd rather.'

Miffy shrank into the seat and gnawed a fingernail. 'Home, I guess.'

'Where do you live?'

She gave her address in Riverdale. 'I don't know if anyone will be there but they leave a spare key outside.'

'You worried?'

'Yeah, a bit.'

'Here's some advice from an old woman. Look your troubles in the face. If you run away, you'll have to keep on running.'

'Easy to say. You don't know my mum.'

Missus K shrugged. 'Take it or leave it. Nothing in this world's easy.'

They drove the rest of the way in silence. Miffy had run out of fingernails to chew. She hadn't spoken to or heard from her parents since that day last October when she'd been bundled off in the car. As per the rules of *Maidenhead,* there'd been no card at Christmas and no letters either. At times she'd wondered if they were still alive. Perhaps they'd disowned her, or forgotten she ever existed.

When they turned off the main road into Riverdale, Miffy gave directions to the house. From the outside it looked exactly the same. Trimmed hedges, mown lawn, miniature tin flag flying above the letterbox to show if there was mail. She opened the door of the ute and swung her bag over her shoulder.

Missus K said, 'Remember my advice, kid. Good luck.'

19

Tuesday 11 March

As the Jeep sped westward along the highway, Seth quizzed Vann about the girls' home she called *Maidenhead*. She was remarkably knowledgeable, especially since she claimed never to have been there. Google, she explained. He knew this to be lie, because he and Cate had Googled every word they could think of in their search for unmarried mothers' homes of the nineteen-sixties and seventies.

Twenty minutes west of Ipswich, Vann directed him to turn right onto a disused dirt track, which was overgrown with lantana and redtop grass. The track was steep and furrowed with washouts but the four-wheel drive negotiated it with ease.

At the crest were two massive camphor laurel trees, beyond which was the silhouette of a vast iron roof with several redbrick chimneys. A hundred metres short of the two-storey mansion the track stopped at an imposing gate. There was no way around, for a three-metre-high electrified fence on either side made the place as secure as a prison.

Seth stopped the vehicle. 'Wow! You sure this is the right address?'

Vann didn't answer. She was out of the car, straining to get a look at the house through the vegetation.

He stood a short distance behind her. As if the fence wasn't barrier enough, the boundary line was covered with prickly bougainvillea vines and masses of impenetrable lantana.

'Have you got a shovel?' Vann said suddenly.

'If it's not urgent, there's a servo with toilets ten minutes back.'

She grinned. 'I don't mean for *that*.'

He opened the Jeep's hatch and rummaged between tool-boxes and canvas chairs, his computer bag, and the odd empty beer bottle. The folding shovel was still in its plastic. On impulse he'd bought months ago after toying with the idea of a weekend camping on the beach at Moreton Island.

'Follow me.' Vann took the shovel and set off at a cracking pace along a goat track through the scrub.

They skirted to the south of the old house, which in its heyday must have been a trophy. Built on the highest point it overlooked pastures and orchards. The mansion's iron-lace, lattice and French doors epitomised old world grace and high-class arrogance. He would have given his back teeth to take a look inside. But there'd be little chance of that. The electrified fence made it clear visitors were not welcome.

Inside the compound were two barnlike structures separated by a stretch of grass. The corrugated iron rooves shimmered in the sun. The hum of machinery and the sound of female voices drifted towards them.

They ducked behind a tangle of red-and-yellow lantana where the collective chirp of a thousand cicadas was deafening. For five minutes they squatted in the dust and prickles, peering through the puzzle of twisted vines. No-one appeared.

Under cover of the vegetation, Vann continued along the goat track. Beyond the southernmost barn she veered away from the fence and launched fearlessly into the long grass. It was all he could do to keep up. Ahead was a grove of lofty eucalypt trees.

'You're obviously not worried about snakes,' he said by way of a caution.

She ignored him and swung the shovel from side to side to clear a path through the undergrowth.

His foot caught in a bandicoot hole and he twisted his ankle. An old football injury, he winced in pain. She was already twenty metres ahead, so he gave the ankle a quick massage, tested his weight, decided nothing was damaged and pushed on.

Up ahead she'd stopped in a clearing where several boulders formed a circle reminiscent of Stonehenge. She was in the centre, hands on her hips, auburn hair flowing like a high priestess. A smirk of self-satisfaction danced on her lips.

'This is the spot. I knew I'd find it.'

The space inside the boulder formation wasn't as overgrown as the rest of the property. All the same, it hadn't been visited by humans in a very long time. Vann moved the shovel gently, as if searching for lost treasure.

'Can I help?' He limped into the circle.

'Don't stand on the graves.' She peered intently at the ground, then fell to her knees. Jubilantly she pulled two pieces of wood, flaky with white paint, from the tangle of grass and held them together to form a cross.

On the horizontal piece one faint word was written. *Hope.*

Without a minute's hesitation, the point of the shovel was down in the dirt. The ground was dry and hard, her smart city shoes were red with dust.

'Let me.' Seth stood on the shovel with his full weight. 'I seem to recall that grave-robbing is a crime. Now you've made me an accomplice. Just as well this is off the record.'

About thirty centimetres below the surface he broke into a cavity. He knelt and pulled away the baked-earth clods with his bare hands.

Instantly she was beside him, clawing at rotted pieces of pine that might once have been a coffin. She shut her eyes and reached inside. A slick of sweat gleamed on her forehead. From deep in the hole she drew out a bundle in a white shroud. It was as long as her forearm, round and stiff.

She placed it on ground, looked up at him. Tears rolled down her cheeks.

Carefully she unpicked the fragile cloth. It fell away to reveal the 'corpse', a large Coca-Cola bottle part-filled with sand.

'Now I know,' she whispered.

In silence they sat on the trampled grass. Midmorning sunlight dappled across the granite boulders, a breeze lifted the gum leaves. Magpies warbled.

Seth lit a cigarette and clamped his arms around his knees. She cradled the bottle, caressing the smooth ridges with her fingers. She was in a distant place, lost in emotions he could only guess at. That fluted glass bottle was the key that unlocked a vault in her mind. Now, if he was patient and played his cards right, her secrets would be released.

She laid the bottle on the ground and eyed the cigarette. 'Mind if I have one?'

'Didn't know you smoked.' He offered her the pack. It was his all-time favourite, green teeth and bleeding gums. Oh, for the classy gold packs of the old days.

The disturbing picture on the pack unnerved her. 'Maybe not. I could sure do with a drink.'

'That makes two of us.'

She rewrapped the bottle in its swaddling cloth and replaced it in the hole. He scraped the earth over it and they retraced the goat track to the Jeep.

They slapped dust and grass seeds from their clothes and rinsed their hands in water from the jerry-can he kept in the back for emergencies. According to the satnav, the nearest township was Mundingo, ten kilometres to the west. Out here a township was likely to consist of the pub, the post office cum corner store, and not much else. It was worth a shot. Ten kilometres was scarcely off course.

The Plains Hotel was an old-style establishment with two storeys. A public bar and liquor store were downstairs, and accommodation was above. Guest accommodation was mandatory for all country pubs in order to keep the liquor licence. These days only backpackers, desperados, and the occasional prostitute ever took it up. The wide veranda on the ground floor was furnished with aluminium tables and chairs. At the entrance were two Alexander palms standing as erect as military guards.

They walked up three timber steps into the shade. Vann's phone was ringing.

'It's James,' she whispered. 'This will take a while to sort out.' She turned her back and strayed along the deserted veranda to the far end, where she settled on a cane sofa and immediately engaged in a heavy-duty discussion.

Seth left her there and went inside to buy the drinks.

The public bar was empty apart from a white-haired woman who was watching TV from a stool behind the bar. She looked the same vintage as the pub and seemed to be part of the furniture.

'G'day. What's yer poison?' she drawled.

He ordered a Scotch and soda for Vann and a XXXX draught for himself.

She pulled the beer tap with the hand of experience. Not too fast and with exactly the right angle to the glass. The result was a masterpiece, a neat frothy head and a nice glossy finish to the glass. As she hunted for the Scotch bottle he ventured, 'We're researching family history. I'm looking for a property called *Maidenhead* but it's not on the map. Do you know anything about it?'

'Ah, the naughty girls' home. If you want directions, it's about five minutes south, up on the ridge.'

'Is it still operating?'

'Not the way it used to. After old Dr Doyle passed away, it went to wrack and ruin. But now his son's fixed it up. Be warned, they don't take visitors.'

'Is Mr Doyle Junior the owner?'

'Yeah, but Barry doesn't live there. He's got an office in the city and a flash apartment on the river. His mother, Iris, is still alive.'

'Does she live far away?'

'The silly old biddy lives next door. She'd be ninety if she's a day.' Talk about the pot calling the kettle black. The geriatric barmaid slid the glasses across the counter. 'That'll be nine dollars eighty.'

He took the drinks outside. Vann had finished her phone call and was sitting at an aluminium table on the veranda. Her eyes followed him as he set down the glasses on coasters, a feat he completed without spilling a drop.

'You look rather pleased with yourself,' she observed.

'Ask and ye shall get,' he said flippantly. 'Does the name *Doyle* ring a bell?'

She blanched and looked away.

He'd hit a raw nerve, which meant he'd struck a seam of gold.

'Cheers.' He swallowed a long cool mouthful. Hot day, nice woman, draught beer off the wood. Perfect.

'I'll get some food.' Vann abruptly disappeared inside.

Seth heard an exchange of voices but couldn't make out what was said. When she returned she seemed more composed. Or had she reapplied her pollie's poker face?

'I ordered us ham and cheese toasted sandwiches. Okay?' Without waiting for an answer, she resumed her place at the table and took a sip of Scotch. 'Right after lunch, I'm going to pay Mrs Doyle a visit.'

'Want me to come?' he offered.

'Nope. This, I have to do alone.'

On the table he put the tin of Eclipse mints and the cigarette pack side by side. Which one to choose? The sleek green tin or the slimy green teeth? He already knew which he *should* have. His doctor had warned him off the latter. But he was about to take a mighty personal risk. If he blew it, he'd miss out on a story and be banished from her circle of trust. He'd have to tread lightly, for he was skating on extremely thin ice.

'This isn't the first time you've been there,' he said. This was a statement, not a question.

Vann twisted the paper serviette.

'In fact, you seem to know your way around the property pretty well.'

Her sigh was deep and tremulous. 'I haven't told another living soul, not even Lance. It was more than forty years ago, for Chrissakes.'

She picked up his cigarette pack and slotted one between her lips.

He struck a match, cupped his hand around the flame and they lit up together. For several minutes they smoked in silence. 'Look Vann, I can see this is difficult. Why did you agree to come here with me?'

'I'm not proud of my past, but it's done and gone. I want to understand what went on at *Maidenhead*. That grave in the forest was where my friend's baby was supposed to be buried. But here's the crunch, I was spun the same heap of bullshit. All these years I believed my own child had died but seeing that fake coffin out there makes me think she might be still alive.'

Seth fingered the hard edge of the Polaroid in his pocket. 'We've all got secrets, we've all got regrets. When our past comes back to bite us, sometimes we need a bit of help.' He reached across the table and gave her hand a squeeze.

20

Saturday 25ᵗʰ March 1972

Miffy ambled down the path to the front door of her parents' house. It was locked. She had no idea whether they expected her or not. Ma Doyle hadn't said if she'd phoned ahead and she hadn't thought to ask.

She lifted the terracotta pot of geraniums and retrieved the spare key from the saucer. Opening the door, she stepped into the familiar surroundings of her former life. The musty odour of stale tobacco mingled with last night's fried fish. A religious ritual she'd never understood dictated that Merle must cook fish on Fridays. There was absolutely no point to fish, especially the oily creatures her mother bought. It took hours to pick through the hair-thin bones in search of titbits of brown meat.

As usual the kitchen was clean and tidy. The diamond pattern on the lino danced a tango right up the hall. The living room was smaller than she recalled and woefully over-furnished. Arthur's smoker's stand stood sentry over his favourite armchair, the cocktail cabinet, and the black-and-white TV set.

She dumped her bag on her bed. Her room was exactly as she'd left it, right down to the text book open on the desk. She remembered the night before she went, cramming for exams she'd never be able to sit. What now?

One name sprang to mind. Michelle. How she'd missed her best friend all those lonely days and nights. Last time they'd spoken Michelle was in a terrible state when her mother ...

Remembering that disturbing call, she ran to the phone and dialled the number straight off by heart.

A young female voice answered.

'It's me,' said Miffy. 'I'm back!'

'Who's this?' said girl on the other end.

'It's Miffy, you dumb-bum.'

'I'm sorry. You must have the wrong number.' The phone clicked.

Miffy redialled, making sure she got the number right this time. 'May I speak with Michelle please?'

'Did you call a minute ago?'

'Yes. Sorry I was rude. Is Michelle there?'

'There's no-one here by that name. We've had this number since January.'

'Oh,' said Miffy, speechless. This was news that she least expected.

'Perhaps you should try directory assistance. Bye.'

Miffy hung up and immediately phoned Gaye.

'Did you get my letter?' were Gaye's first words.

'No. It was like I was on another planet.'

'So, you haven't heard about Michelle?' There was an edge to her voice.

'You're going to have to tell me.'

Several shaky breaths hissed through the earpiece. The response that came was like a lightning strike out of a clear blue sky.

'She killed herself.'

'She *what*? Please tell me you're joking!' There was no way it could be true.

'Oh Miffy, it was so, so horrible.' Gaye was sobbing out of control.

'When?' The room was beginning to spin, slowly like start of the Chair-o-plane ride at the Ekka. The lime-green swirls of her mother's carpet swam into one and a wave of nausea crashed over her.

'The last day of term. We were going to celebrate. She never made it to school.'

Miffy slid down the wall and sat in a numb heap on that hideous carpet. Stunned beyond comprehension, she pressed the receiver against her chest. The pain of childbirth was mild in comparison to this ache in her heart.

Of course it was her fault. She wasn't there when Shelley needed her most.

That last breathless call from the phone booth in Byron Bay should have given her a clue. She could hear the anguish in Michelle's voice when she said *it's gone*. Yet she was so full of her own selfish problems that she didn't think to help her friend. Her *best* friend.

Gaye spoke through her tears. 'I tried to let you know. In the end I wrote a letter and gave it to your folks. They said they'd get it to you. For some reason they didn't want me to know your address. It was awful. She cut her wrists in the downstairs bathroom. Her little sister found her and—'

'I'll call you back.' Miffy slammed down phone and ran to the bathroom to be sick. Afterwards, she sat on the toilet seat with her chin in her hands and stared at her father's cut-throat razor near the basin. Michelle had taken a blade just like it and—

The very thought of it … she spun around and threw up again.

When she'd recovered she searched the house for Gaye's letter. It wasn't on the clip in the kitchen where the shopping list and reminders and supermarket coupons lived. Nor was it in the lounge room.

Arthur's so-called den was a garbage tip with newspapers, empty cups, and overflowing ashtrays. It was the one room he had to himself, and it proved his housekeeping skills were non-existent. She sifted through two piles of likely-looking papers before leaving the place to the dust mites.

She returned to her bedroom, slid out the bedside drawer. There it was, on top of her tissues and creams. Blue stationery, scented, unopened. A handwritten instruction at the bottom of the envelope read, *Please forward.*

She ripped it open and took out a close-written sheet. As she read, bands of sorrow squeezed her chest. By the time she got to the place and time of the funeral, she could scarcely breathe.

Please come, Gaye had written. *If you can, wear her favourite colour. Pink.*

It was too painful. She screwed the paper into a ball and flung it at the wall. If only she'd have been here, she could have comforted her, talked her out of it, set things right. Something must have pushed her over the brink. Perhaps Gaye knew the answer.

On the phone again Gaye said, 'That Monday when you didn't show up at school, I called your mum and she told me about your nan's accident.'

'What did she tell you?' Miffy sat with her legs tucked up and her back against the tongue-in-groove wall. Merle would stop at nothing to protect her precious reputation.

'That you'd gone up to Dalby to look after your nan's farm while she was in hospital. That was gutsy, Miffy. Missing the exams and all. When you didn't write, I phoned again and Merle said you were staying on until your nan was off crutches. I asked how long and she said four more months. Geez Miffy, you've missed a lot of school. How will you ever catch up?'

'Actually, it's only six weeks. That's not important. Tell me about Michelle.'

'You know that flu she had … the time she pulled out of the musical? Well, when she came back to school she was really different. It was like she didn't want me as a friend anymore.'

'Do you know why she …'

'No idea.'

They both fell quiet. Tears rolled down Miffy's cheeks. The black Bakelite receiver was as wet and slippery as an eel.

At length she said, 'Where did they bury her?'

'Pinnaroo Lawn Cemetery. It's nice and new, lots of gardens. Maybe we could go out there together and see her.'

'I'd like that.'

'I'm so glad you're home, Miffy.'

'Me too.'

Two sets of footsteps plodded up the back stairs.

'Arthur! Did you leave the door open?' Merle's voice was shriller than usual.

'Of course not,' he grumbled.

'I have to go.' Miffy hung up the phone and scrambled to her feet.

'Shhhh! Did you hear that? Someone's inside,' said Merle.

Two fat brown-paper grocery bags appeared through the doorway and a stern face between. 'Who's there?' Arthur's voice resonated like a drill sergeant's (he'd had plenty of practice during the war). Any self-respecting burglar would have fled rather than meet the wrath of the man behind the sonic boom.

Miffy squeaked, 'It's only me.'

Merle jumped in fright. A packet of Iced VoVo toppled from her grocery bag and smashed on the floor. 'Myfanwy! When did you get here?'

'About an hour ago.' Miffy squatted to pick up the broken biscuits.

Arthur discarded the shopping bags and bundled her into his arms. 'We missed you, honey.'

Merle said, 'Thank goodness we can put all that *unpleasantness* behind us.'

She started to unpack the groceries onto the bench-top. Tins of spaghetti, beetroot, pineapple pieces, apricot halves, fresh fruit and veg.

'That stupid girl always puts the potatoes on top of the fruit,' said Merle. 'Just look at these tomatoes! They're ruined! I'll have to use them for cooking.'

'So, how've you been?' said Miffy.

'Can't complain,' said Arthur. He undid the butcher's paper, took out lamb chops and sausages and put them in the meat-keeper. 'Did they look after you at that place?'

'Yeah, I suppose. We had to work on the farm but we didn't go hungry.'

Arthur said, 'So the little problem you had. That's all been taken care of?'

Miffy's eyes brimmed with tears and she quickly turned away. She picked up three cans from the bench and stowed them in the cupboard. She wiped her nose and steeled her voice. 'Yeah. All done and dusted.'

'So, you're fit and well?' He made it sound like she'd had a sinus infection.

'Yep.'

'That's good, because Monday morning it's off to the Commonwealth Employment Service to get a job.' Merle rattled a box of corn flakes for Miffy to put away.

She grabbed the box and filed it next to the All-Bran. 'I'd rather go back to school. I haven't missed much. If I study hard, I'll soon catch up.'

'Well you'd better think again, my girl,' said Merle. 'You've had your chance and you blew it. Your father and I aren't getting any younger. We can't spend the rest of our lives supporting you while you swan around having a lovely time. We already paid a pretty penny for your farm holiday. It's about time you showed some appreciation.'

'I thought it was for free.'

'Whatever gave you that idea? Doesn't matter what it is, someone has to pay.'

'But school is only until November. I could get a job over the holidays and—'

'And what if you don't get your precious scholarship? What then?'

'She could go to teachers' college, Merle. Or business school and learn shorthand and typing.'

'Yes, Dad. That's exactly what I could do.' An ally, she could have kissed him.

'Arthur! We've already discussed this and made up our minds. Don't go soft on her. What she did to this family's reputation deserves punishment. The fibs I had to tell, the shame I had to endure! I'd never be able to show my face at tuckshop again.'

'I never asked you to cover up for me.'

'No, I did it to protect you. If people knew what you'd really been up to! The only place you're qualified to work is a massage parlour down the Valley.'

Miffy slammed a packet of crackers on the bench and stormed to her room. She banged the door behind her and launched herself onto the bed. How could they be so cruel? She shouldn't have come back. She'd already made up her mind to leave. But without any money it would have been impossible.

As she lay there fuming, her parents' angry voices filtered through the VJs. They were engaged in a slamming match. It was World War Three, thumps and bumps and curses. Merle never used to swear. Glass objects smashed against the wall.

She'd never known her parents to have an all-out fight before. It sounded ugly. She pressed her pillow over her ears. Gaye's folks sometimes hit each other. The thought of physical violence made Miffy squirm.

Arthur and Merle weren't like that. Were they?

After what seemed an age, the house fell quiet. She waited another ten minutes before slowly opening the door.

Bits of broken china were all over the floor. Barefoot she tiptoed between them to the kitchen. Splotches of tomato pulp oozed down the walls, egg slime dripped from the benches.

Apart from the amazing mess, the kitchen was empty. She walked down the hallway to the lounge room. A pall of smoke hovered over Arthur's armchair. He was puffing on his pipe so hard she could hear the fizz of the tobacco. Further down the hallway, the door of the main bedroom was shut.

Miffy sidled onto the sofa. She twisted a lock of hair into her mouth—a *filthy habit* Merle often nagged her about—and sat there quiet and watchful as an owl.

Furrows crisscrossed Arthur's brow, his cheeks were flushed. With his arms folded across his paunch, he stared straight ahead at the TV set. The screen was blank.

For a good ten minutes neither spoke.

Eventually Arthur sniffed. 'Your mother and I have had a few *problems* lately.'

'Oh?'

'Mostly because of you. She wants to punish you, but I reckon you've suffered enough. What do you think?'

He'd never spoken to her that way before, as an adult rather than a child.

'The baby died. It's been tough for me.'

'Sorry. The woman who phoned—Mrs Doyle—didn't say.'

'Dad, I want to finish school. There's only eight months until the Senior exams. I'll work hard to get that uni scholarship. I promise. Then I'll move out.'

'Do you still want to do science?'

'I've been thinking about it. I want to work with people, help them get through rough patches like I've been through.'

'You want to be a counsellor?'

'Yeah, maybe. I owe it to the girls at the baby farm. And I owe it to Michelle. You knew what happened, why didn't you contact me?'

Arthur nodded. 'Yes, Gaye told us. I phoned Julia Grice for advice. She said it would be too distressing for you to deal with. We only tried to do what was best.'

'If you wouldn't have sent me to *Maidenhead* in the first place, I would have talked her out of it.' Her voice was trembling. 'I could have *saved* her.'

Arthur sat on the sofa beside her and put his arms around her. 'It's not your fault, honey. Seems she didn't talk to anyone and she didn't leave a note. No-one will ever know what was going on inside her head.'

'I knew.' Miffy pressed her lips together. How easy it would be to let slip the guilty secret.

'What did she tell you?' Arthur was quick to pounce.

She swallowed a gigantic lump in her throat. 'Only that I was her best friend.'

He stroked her gently. She leant into him and inhaled the comforting dad-odour of tobacco and mothballs.

'Leave Merle to me. A couple of weeks and she'll get over it. But be warned, it'll be like Antarctica until she does.'

Living at home that year was not easy. Merle could scarcely look her in the eye and picked her up on the slightest fault or misdemeanour. Although Miffy tried to be compliant and help out around the house, she couldn't do anything right. As soon as the school year was over she was determined to move out into a place of her own.

November came, along with the dreaded Senior exams that would determine her future. Two years of study were distilled into twelve three-hour exams, two per subject. A total of thirty-six hours of misery. In the final weeks, there were last-minute cram sessions, all-nighters, dreams dominated by formulae and impossible calculations, a useless claw of a writing hand, frozen through overuse.

Then an agonising wait for the results.

In the meantime, Miffy lived up to her promise and went to the Commonwealth Employment Service to look for a job. Scores of people, young and old, queued at the counter. She filled out a card and saw an interviewer, a mousy man in a cheap brown shirt.

'Are you going to uni next year?' That was the first question.

'If I get in. I need money to move out of home.'

'So, you're only available for the vacation?'

'That's nearly three months. I can definitely work until the end of February.'

'Our employers want permanent staff, not students. Perhaps you could try the shops. They take casuals for Christmas and the January sales. You seem like a bright enough girl. I'm sure you'll land yourself a position.' And with that he tore up her card.

Miffy plodded down the steps. She tried Myer, McDonnell and East, Coles, Woolworths, and Waltons but everyone said their books were closed and suggested she try again next year. Dejected, she caught the bus home.

Every day she scanned the Job Vacancies column of the newspaper. Most of the ads demanded several years of experience and the office junior jobs required typing, a skill she didn't have.

Weeks of job hunting slipped by without a single interview. Unlike Merle, she wasn't perturbed. Her heart wasn't in finding a job, but rather in winning that uni scholarship. Finally, the day in December came when the Senior results would be published. She'd arranged to meet Gaye at six in the morning at *The Morning Post's* distribution centre at Bowen Hills.

She left home at five. Too early for the buses, she walked a mile to the station and caught the train. A crowd had already gathered on the lawn outside Newspaper House. On the wall sat dozens of teenagers chattering like noisy lorikeets. She found a space and climbed up. Her legs dangled into a hedge of pink azaleas. From her vantage point she could watch the comings and goings of the place. Her intention was to be first in line when the newspapers came on sale.

On the other side of the lawn, Gaye was walking hand in hand with her latest boyfriend. Miffy waved and the pair trotted over.

'This is Dean. He was at Riverdale High until Grade Ten. Remember?'

Miffy smiled, 'Of course.'

Then he'd been a pimple-faced dimwit who'd only excelled at sport. Now he was tall and muscular. Not bad looking either in denim and a tight-fitting t-shirt.

'Churchie pinched him to play fullback.' Gaye hugged his hulking great arm.

'Yeah, we won the A-grade premiership.' His lips had a curl of arrogance.

'You should've been there. Dean was *amazing*. Ooooh, the thought makes me go all goosy.' Gaye stood on tiptoe and planted a kiss on his cheek.

Miffy rolled her eyes.

The crowd was on the move towards the entrance of the building. Inside, two men carried wire-bound bundles of papers. The doors opened and the teenagers surged.

'Let's go!' Miffy slid down onto the grass and ran.

She paid the man twenty cents and grabbed a paper, scrambled to the middle section where the results were listed. Her finger zoomed down the columns to 406612, her student number. Three sevens, one six, and two fives. A seven was the best score, a high distinction. Scholarships would be awarded to the top performers over five subjects. She'd done well, but was it good enough?

Unexpectedly she burst into tears. What if she missed out by one point? She should have studied harder. She should have put her grief into a steel box and focused on the task. So many nights she'd lain awake, weeping for what might have been. She couldn't go through another year of that. Whatever had happened, she must move on. She must find a way.

Gaye and Dean lay side-by-side on the lawn with the paper spread between them like a picnic blanket.

'How'd you go?' Gaye's expression was noncommittal.

'Okay. You?'

Gaye lowered her eyes and pointed to the line. Only two subjects were shown, English and Art. Both were graded three, pass conceded. They didn't show the subjects you'd failed. 'Dad's going to absolutely murder me.'

The day before Christmas the long-awaited letter with the Commonwealth crest arrived. With trembling hands, she ripped it open.

> *Congratulations, your application for a scholarship for undergraduate study at the University of Queensland has been successful.*

She whooped with joy and danced around the house. 'I got it! I got it!'

Merle said, 'That's nice, dear. When you've finished gloating, you can hang out the washing.'

Two weeks later Miffy landed a part-time job as a junior in a suburban law firm. The pay was meagre but combined with her scholarship living allowance it was enough to move into a room in a rambling boarding house. There was a share kitchen, a share bathroom, and a share laundry downstairs. It was cheap and handy to transport, and most of the other tenants were young.

Arthur, for all his lecturing about single girls being targets for good-time Charlies and rapists, seemed relieved to see her go. Merle was positively delighted.

For Miffy it was a dream come true. Freedom to do what she wanted at last.

21

Vann left Seth to drink his beer alone on the veranda of the Plains Hotel. She was thankful the old dear at the bar had assumed they were a long-married couple, the one partner substituting seamlessly for the other. The antique barmaid continued to make disparaging comments about Ma Doyle as if Vann had been present for the entire conversation.

Before her courage evaporated, she hurried to the neighbouring house and rapped on the door. The woman who answered had a size-fourteen skin shrivelled onto a size-eight frame. Even her false teeth were too big for her mouth. Although she looked a hundred years old, her eyes were sharp and lucid. Undoubtedly the woman was Puss-arse.

'Do you know who I am?' Vann said.

'I never forget a face Mary,' she snapped. 'What do you want?'

Frail as she was, she was still capable of evoking the flight or fight reflex. One question and Vann was trembling. 'I've just been out to *Maidenhead* ...' she stammered.

'That's private property. You had no right to go there.'

Vann took a breath and pushed on. If she didn't get it out now, she'd lose her nerve and never say what she intended. 'I found the babies' cemetery in the forest.'

'There's no graveyard at *Maidenhead*.'

'I went there to pay my respects to an infant who died.' She managed to keep a lid on the toxic emotions percolating inside her body. The grief and horror she'd felt the first time she'd seen those crosses in the stone circle came flooding back. Sheer willpower stopped her from strangling the woman who'd wrecked so many lives. This evil woman, this walking corpse.

Ma Doyle sniffed. 'Oh, the *pet* cemetery. There's nothing human there.'

153

'I know that now.' Blood hammered inside her head.

With narrow eyes Iris Doyle gave her the once-over. 'What do you mean, girl?'

'I want to know what happened to the babies who died.'

'They were given proper Christian burials.'

'What about Fiona's baby?'

The answer came too fast to be convincing. 'I can't remember.'

'How convenient, forgetful when it suits. What about my child?'

Was there hesitation, a flicker of guilt? The old bat rubbed her jaw. The skin of her hand was the colour of salami. 'If you're so interested, you should check the parish records.'

'I'll check more than the parish records, Mrs Doyle. I know for a fact that Fiona's baby survived, and I suspect mine did too. There's more to this than you're letting on and I intend to the bottom of it.' She pulled herself up to full height, which was not much over 160 centimetres, but nevertheless she towered over her foe. 'When I do find the truth, I'll expose you as the scheming liar you are.'

Vann turned and stormed down the path, leaving the witch to stew.

When she returned to the pub, her face was burning.

'Get me a double Scotch.' She flung herself into the chair.

'You serious?' Seth pushed himself up, about to go to the bar.

'No,' she growled. 'Rat poison would be better ... to give to *her*.'

'Want to talk about it?'

'No. We'd better go.'

They drove back to town without speaking. He turned up the radio and sang out-of-tune to the music. She leant her elbow on the windowsill and gazed at the rolling hills. Not much had changed. Patchwork crops, irrigated pasture, scrubland, all fenced in by the blue wall of the mighty Great Divide.

Her mobile phone rang several times but she made no attempt to answer it. For once in her life she couldn't care less if she was sacked from the ministry, or the Premier resigned, or Parliament House was blown up by a latter-day Guy Fawkes.

There were too many important matters to think about. She was onto something big. What it looked like and smelt like, she was yet to discover. But discover it, she would. She owed it to Claire.

At the turnoff to Riverdale she broke the silence. 'Thanks for taking me. I couldn't have done it alone.'

He shrugged. 'All in a day's work.'

As the Jeep turned into Station Road, the one o'clock news came on. Murders and car smashes and job losses. The usual assortment of joy. The footpath outside her office was full of high-school kids, cocooned from the nasty world by ear-buds. In her day, they had transistor radios called *trannies*. Earplugs were the size of gran's hearing aid and no-one left school until the stroke of three. She was showing her age.

Suddenly and for no reason, she felt flighty. 'Drop me off in the basement?'

Seth swung the Jeep down the driveway into the tunnel beneath the building. Beyond the line of cars were the elevator and the fire stairs. At the yellow-striped loading zone he stopped and left the engine idling.

In the twilight, a surge of warmth flushed her body. Gratitude, appreciation, and another sensation she hadn't felt in a while. She was tingling with forbidden desire. She felt alive, invigorated. Not wanting their secret escapade to end, she took an extra-long time to gather her things.

Without thinking, she took his hand. 'Off the record, remember?'

He held on longer than was polite. 'You betcha.'

On impulse she leant across the console and pecked his cheek. In an eye-blink, she opened the door and ran up the fire stairs to her sanctuary.

In the office, she asked James to do a search of the official records for Claire Jones, born and deceased at *Maidenhead* on the fifteenth of March 1972. She didn't say why she was interested, and he took it on as if it were another piece of research.

The next day he came to her with what he'd found.

'In the Register of Births there's a Claire Jones, born on the date in question. The birth was registered in Ipswich, not the place you said. The mother's name was Mary Jones, aged sixteen. The father was unknown.'

Vann heaved an involuntary sigh. 'That's her. What else did you find?'

'The Register of Deaths drew a blank and there's no parish record. Either the death wasn't recorded or she's still alive.'

'So, she didn't die at birth after all. Did you check the adoption records?'

'Sure did. Zilch.' He watched her like a cat, feigning indifference when his curiosity had been roused. Young he might have been, but he was no fool.

'Thanks, you've done well.' Now she regretted giving him the leg-work.

He put the photocopied document—the record of birth—on the desk and left the office. He'd probably put the pieces together already. But she trusted him implicitly and he'd never betrayed her. All she needed was a few more days.

22

Tuesday 11 March

In his cubicle at Newspaper House, Seth rubbed his boots, dull with Mundingo dust. The paper towel he used ground the grit into the leather, making them look old and uncared for. His trousers prickled with cobblers' pegs. Sticky red dough—a mixture of bulldust and sweat—was moulded into the folds of his skin. What he needed was a long hot shower, but that'd have to wait until he went home sometime after six.

The fridge-like draught of the air conditioning made his nose run. When he dived in his pocket for a hanky, his fingers snagged on the sharp edge of the Polaroid he'd 'borrowed' from Vann's office earlier.

He tilted the photo to the natural light from the window. The young man had a wispy moustache and lusty grin, his identity was unmistakable.

Holding the evidence in his left hand, Seth scrolled through the contacts on his phone for the number and hit the call button.

The syrupy baritone that answered was as familiar as his own voice.

'Hey, it's me. Want a blast from the past?' Seth clamped the phone under his chin and examined the happy-snap through a magnifying glass. Beneath the youth's brocade waistcoat was the Black Sabbath t-shirt.

'Whose past, yours or mine?' In the background the final riffs of *Stairway to Heaven* were pumping. 'Wait on a sec. Gotta change tracks.'

The phone clinked against a hard surface and that smooth-as-caramel voice was at work. 'You're on *Retro FM*. It's one-fifteen on this glorious afternoon in Perth. Stay tuned. Plenty of hits still to come in this super-seventies lunchbox special.'

With silken vocal chords, no wonder he'd carved a career in radio.

'Okay, bro. I'm back,' said the DJ.

Seth said, 'Good to hear classic rock. Very appropriate, in fact.'

'What are you crapping on about?'

'In my hot little hand, I have a rather amorous photograph of you and the Minister for Communities, Vann Willis.'

'Impossible. I don't even know the woman.'

'At a guess it was taken in the early seventies. She looks quite delectable in a white cheesecloth top. You're wearing that Sabbath t-shirt I sold my soul to get for your eighteenth birthday.'

'God, how can you remember that stuff? The entire decade draws a blank with me. Too much Bundy and weed, I guess.'

'I'll scan the photo and email it to you. Might give you a laugh.'

'Thanks, bro. Talk soon.'

Seth hung up the phone and slipped the Polaroid into the scanner.

Later, an email pinged into his inbox. The subject line was *Party Chick*. He clicked it open and found the usual two-liner. That bastard was the all-time master of minimalist communication.

Hey bro. Ta for the pic. Now I remember. The chick's name wasn't Vann at all, it was Miffy. Good time was had by all, if you know what I mean.

Vann was called Miffy? Sounded like the sort of name you'd give a cat.

He reread the last part—good time had by all—and laughed out loud. If he was looking for dirt, he'd have enough to grow potatoes. The dropout and the over-achiever. He couldn't think of a less likely pair.

He blue-tacked the Polaroid to the edge of his computer screen. From that angle, the long-haired lad looked directly at him as if to say *chill bro*. He leant back in the chair, staring at the photo and wondering. He'd bought that t-shirt in early 1971.

After a quick Google search, he had everything he needed.

Vann Willis, Minister for Communities, Member of Parliament for Riverdale since 1989. Born Myfanwy Willis Jones, 20 July 1955. Secondary education, Riverdale State High. Bachelor of Arts (Majors: Government and Political Science), University of Queensland 1976.

Vann would have been about sixteen on the party night, when a *good time was had by all*. Suddenly his mouth was as dry as an empty bourbon bottle. His mind was doing somersaults. Pieces were falling into place. Could it be?

He picked up the phone and rang her office.

James answered. 'Ms Willis is otherwise engaged.'

Seth spun a bit of palaver and got an appointment for Thursday morning, the only time available for an emergency meeting. It would buy him time to consider his approach, for there was more at stake now than a mere newspaper article.

23

Thursday 13 March

At eight o'clock Thursday morning Vann, loaded with a box of untouched overnight reading material, pushed open the office door with her derriere. This time in March was always difficult and this year promised to be no different. She'd had almost no sleep. All night long she'd puzzled over the alleged baby trade and how it was linked to the bombing.

The glass door was stuck half open. She squatted and pulled out a wad of paper concertinaed beneath.

It was a plain envelope, addressed *Vann Willis, Personal.* The three words were type-written with no return address.

She used her key to rip it open. One page. A message of cut-out letters, each from a different headline of a newspaper or magazine. It looked like a ransom note in a Hollywood thriller.

ThiS is your FIRst and FiNAl wARnING.

SToP MEDdling with adOPtiONs NOW

or ELSE.

Hurriedly she snibbed the lock and rushed into her office. In her desk drawer she scrabbled for the business card he'd given her the day after the bombing.

Detective Sergeant Dave Frame, Criminal Investigations Branch.

On the reverse side was his direct phone number. *Call me immediately if you receive any threats,* he'd said. She couldn't press the numbers fast enough.

As if he'd been waiting for her call, Dave Frame answered the phone after just one ring. When she told him about the note he said, 'Where is it now?'

'In my hand.'

'Put it down and don't touch it again. There might be fingerprints.'

'Should I take it seriously?' she said.

'Absolutely. I'm on my way. Lock the doors and don't leave the office.'

'But I've got back-to-back meetings all day.'

'Ms Willis, whoever is behind this might make another attempt on your life. Treat everyone with suspicion. Write down names and numbers of anyone who calls. And don't open that door until I get there.'

The phone clicked. With the election looming, this was not what she needed. But it seemed proof that a potential assassin was still at large. She'd never believed Steptoe had it in him to conceal explosives in his overcoat. Admittedly she didn't know any suicide bombers, but Steptoe wasn't the type.

A shiver thrilled through her body. In her floor-to-ceiling-glass office she spun around to check that all was secure.

Outside was the usual ebb and flow of people between the station and the shopping centre. School kids, men in suits, youths in jeans. The culprit could be any one of them. Perhaps he was watching her now as she moved about her goldfish bowl. She had no idea of who or what to expect.

The warning note glared at her. The odd-sized letters ran higgledy-piggledy along the three lines as if stuck there by a toddler.

She trawled her memory for people who'd contacted her, angry or upset about adoptions. The birth mothers, whose babies had been taken without consent, snatched as callously as the children of the *Stolen Generation*. The adoptees, now adults, who'd suffered physically or emotionally as a result. All victims of a paternalistic system of government that afforded no rights to the vulnerable.

She too had spent a lifetime trying to forget yet wanting to remember. Every March she wrote a letter to a precious angel who'd never stood a chance. On the top shelf of her closet, beneath the winter jumpers she never wore, was the box. Blue with love hearts. She'd never told a soul, not even Lance. Even if she could explain, he wouldn't understand.

She made herself a cup of coffee, drew the blinds around the glass, and sank into the faux-leather swivel chair. Calmly and critically she reread the patchwork message from its position on the desk.

Or else what? Vague and nonspecific, it wasn't necessarily a death threat. It could be just a bit of mischief, or a protest, or a practical joke.

She checked her watch: twenty past eight.

Outside, the roar of the rush hour was waning. Gutter-language filtered in from the street. A mob of scruffy Riverdale High boys scrapped over a football while showcasing their fine command of the Australian vernacular. On the other side walked the St Brigit's girls, prim in navy skirts and white blouses. Opposites attract, so they say. Clearly intrigued by the *bad boys*, they giggled and whispered behind their hands.

Not much had changed.

A knock at the door. Her heart leapt into her mouth. She flattened her body against the filing cabinet. From that angle she couldn't see who was there and her imagination ran wild. She snatched up her mobile phone, poised her finger to hit 000, and edged along the wall to the corridor.

Through the frosted glass she saw the shape of a man of average build, average height. It wasn't tall Dave Frame and it wasn't James who would've used his key.

The man knocked again.

On the far side of the room was a narrow window with a view to the door. Scarcely breathing, Vann crept toward it. The man had his back toward her. He fumbled a small black object from his pocket. A gun? Her heart pounded.

Suddenly her phone flashed and the *Doctor Who* theme began to wail. She ducked behind the reception desk and hit the answer button.

'Are you okay?'

The chocolaty voice was familiar, but she was in no mood for guessing games.

'Who is this?' she rasped.

'Seth VerBeek. I'm outside. You're acting kind of strange.'

She opened the door and relocked it behind him. 'You gave me an awful fright.'

'Do I look that bad?'

The tension dissolved. Unexpectedly she began to laugh. With him, she always felt safe and protected. She took him into the inner office and pointed to the cut-and-paste note on her desk. 'Don't touch. Fingerprints.'

'So, there's another nutter on the loose,' he said. 'Any idea who sent it?'

Tears prickled her eyes. 'I'd hoped all this nonsense was over. Guess it confirms my suspicion that Steptoe wasn't the mastermind behind the bombing.' The dam wall burst and the tears rolled freely down her cheeks.

Without a word he handed her a hanky, white and monogrammed. What was it that sent her into a hormonal meltdown every time she saw him?

She unfolded the cloth square and blew her nose. 'For the first time in my life I'm really, really scared.'

His arms wrapped around her and she sobbed into his shoulder. Being held by a man other than Lance was an odd sensation. The shape of his body, the scent of his skin, how he stroked her hair were completely different from her long-time partner. A dangerous energy that was both thrilling and hypnotic passed between them. She was sixteen again, balancing on a precipice between common sense and forbidden pleasure. Which should she choose?

She sighed, stepped away, cleared her throat. 'Thanks, I'm okay now.' Businesslike she moved around the desk and sank into her swivel chair.

The phone in reception began to ring. She picked up the call from her desk. It was James, late due to heavy traffic on Coro Drive. That stretch of road was a nightmare.

As she was telling James about the note, there was another knock at the door. The blood drained from her face.

Seth motioned for her to stay seated. 'I'll get it.'

Through the doorway, she could hear them talking like old mates.

Detective Sergeant Frame's long shadow preceded him into her office.

Vann rose to shake his hand. To Seth she said, 'I'm sorry, Mr VerBeek, but I need to get this sorted out. Can we catch up another time?'

Like a cheeky schoolboy too smart for his own good, he stood with his feet apart, hands behind his back, and rocked back and forth on his heels. 'Sure. When?'

She checked her electronic diary and sucked air through her teeth. 'Schedule's pretty tight.'

'I've got something that will interest you.' He arched an eyebrow suggestively.

From the visitor's chair Dave Frame watched the exchange with amusement.

Flustered, she scrolled through the appointments screen. 'Got an hour between the community centre opening and the Streetkidz Choir. Six-thirty Monday night. Okay?' Heat rushed to her cheeks and she could feel her face growing pink. Menopause, it made you look guilty even when you weren't.

'Meet me here,' she said. 'I'll shout you take-away.'

'Perfect,' he said.

The front door flew open and James burst in. 'Sorry, sorry, sorry.' He was puffing so hard he must've sprinted the entire length of Coro Drive.

'James Fuller, this is Detective Sergeant Frame of the CIB.'

The two shook hands.

'Mr VerBeek is just leaving,' prompted Vann.

'I can take a hint.' Seth moved toward the door and gave the detective a friendly slap on the shoulder. 'Catch you later, mate.'

The meeting with Dave Frame didn't go as well as Vann had hoped. The detective wanted to know everything about her movements and engagements since the bombing.

She'd been so caught up in the maelstrom that it all blurred together. Even with her diary notes, she could scarcely separate one day from the next.

James fired up his computer and printed off a list of her engagements, copies of the speeches she'd made, and the press releases he'd written on her behalf. As the interview progressed he'd interrupt to add a remark. He gave information about constituents who'd contacted the office, in particular those he politely referred to as *difficult customers*.

Vann knew who he meant, the sort who'd whinge about the cold until you gave them the coat off your back, and then they'd whinge about the colour.

Dave Frame listened and leafed through the printouts. From time to time his finger came to rest on a name and he asked follow-up questions. By the end of an hour they were no closer to the identity of a person who'd make death threats about adoption.

Finally, Dave Frame put on cotton gloves and sealed the letter and its envelope into a zip-lock bag. 'I'll send these to forensics. I'll let you know the outcome.'

'What should I do in the meantime?' said Vann. 'You must appreciate how disruptive this is to my work.'

'Do whatever you have to do. But keep your wits about you and don't go out alone. Call me at once if you see or hear anything suspicious.'

Vann forced a smile. 'Thanks for your help.'

As soon as he was gone, she sent James out to Café Nero for espressos and double-choc muffins. *Sweet solace when all else fails.* Full of home-spun advice, Merle might have once said this. The excuse had served her well over the years of struggling to make her mark in politics. The head-on battles, the double-crosses, the unfulfilled promises of others to take action, the stubborn lazy power-hungry misogynistic bastards she'd had to deal with. Coffee and cake healed all.

She began to make a list of all the people she'd crossed swords with. Politicians, some from her own Party, most from the Opposition. The PPP and Jake Stone (though she doubted a twelve-year-old wannabe politician would have the balls). She examined the list, shook her head and crossed them all out again. Disputes were at the heart of politics, a part and parcel of the job. She wasn't particularly proud of some of her so-called *debates*. She enjoyed the point-scoring, as did others of her profession. It was part of the theatre of Parliament. True, sledging and name-calling were frequent, but there was little real malice in their wars of words.

She screwed up the page, got out a fresh sheet and poised the biro. She started writing the names of people associated with *Maidenhead*. In the nineteen seventies, they'd clearly been operating outside the law. Dr Rowland Doyle, his wife Iris, and Kathleen O'Brien the midwife were either in their eighties now or pushing up daisies.

Who else had been involved?

She had a few ideas, but no evidence. This vendetta was personal and she was determined to bring it to a head. But how could she proceed without them finding out?

One name sprang to mind. Seth. He was an investigative journalist and he had *something that would interest her.* It came at high personal risk, for although he'd promised to keep their discussions off the record, she couldn't expect that to continue. But he was good at what he did and he had access to researchers and material she couldn't get.

Yes, she'd plant the idea and see what eventuated. Shouldn't be hard for a smooth-talking politician.

24

Monday 17 March

Outside Vann's electorate office Monday evening, Seth leant casually against a concrete planter box full of sad-looking palms and smoked. When he'd arrived five minutes earlier, the door was locked but the lights inside were ablaze, an indication that she wasn't far away.

He looked up, spotted her darting across the road with a bulging plastic bag. He waved and stubbed out the cigarette in the dirt.

She apologised for being late and opened the door. The mouth-watering aroma of hot spicy food escaped from the bag. 'Hope you like Thai.'

'Absolutely my favourite.' Seth followed her to a tiny lunchroom, furnished with a metal table, two chairs, mini-fridge, and Zip heater.

While she located the plates, he opened the take-away containers, releasing a cloud of jasmine-scented steam. He closed his eyes and breathed it in, so hungry he could have eaten the lot.

'Chopsticks okay?' she said as she dished up.

'No probs. I lived in South-east Asia for three years.'

'You never told me. Where?'

'Vietnam, in the seventies. Nasho. I don't talk about it much.'

'Sorry ... I shouldn't have ... '

'It's fine. It was a long time ago. I learnt a lot about love and war and human nature. Learnt a lot about myself too.'

'The trials of youth. What we survive makes us stronger.' With chopsticks she mixed rice and sauce, deftly scooped up mouthfuls and sighed with satisfaction. 'Have you ever tasted better Thai?'

'Don't believe I have. Where'd you get it?'

'Little place round the corner. *Thai me up.*'

'Was that an offer?' he said straight-faced.

She laughed. A real laugh right from her belly.

'You should do that more often. It suits you.'

Suddenly she became serious. 'I've almost forgotten how.'

'All work and no play … so they say.' He sensed she was listening, even though she neither agreed with nor contradicted him.

'Green tea?'

'Sure. Mind if I finished this off?' Without waiting for an answer, he tipped the remainder of the red curry onto his plate.

She flipped teabags into two blue mugs and filled them with boiling water from the Zip heater. 'Now, Mr VerBeek, you didn't make this appointment because you wanted my company and a free feed.'

He smiled. 'I *do* like your company and I *really* enjoyed the food. But you're right, there's an important matter I want to discuss.'

'Fire away.' Immediately she blushed. 'Oh God, I'm sorry.'

Puzzled, he frowned.

'Bad choice of words. The war …' She bit her lip. 'I'm making it worse, aren't I?' She seemed to be close to tears.

'What's gotten into you tonight? Do I have to give you *another* one of my hankies? On my meagre journalist's salary, I can't afford to keep buying them.'

She leant her elbows on the table and raised her face. 'I don't mean to rush you, but I have to leave in ten minutes.'

He cleared his throat. 'Right, here it is. I've done some more research and come up with a surprising result.'

'About with me, or the bomb, or that bizarre letter last week?'

'Maybe all three.' He told her about the visit to Mrs Wilson at the old people's home and then the reconnaissance mission to the house in New Farm. 'It was exactly as she'd described it. Spanish mission, palms on either side of the gate.'

The blood drained from Vann's cheeks. She set down the mug and pressed her hands to her forehead. 'Oh my God,' she moaned. 'Did you see Julia Grice?'

'You *know* her?'

'She convinced my folks to send me to *Maidenhead*. She drove me and Fiona there in a clapped-out Kombi van. Fiona's the one who told me about her baby Hope.'

'Of course. The grave in the forest.' He'd have to play this cool.

'What did Julia Grice say?'

'Nothing. She slammed the door in my face.' It was best to keep Mrs Grice senior out of the equation. Despite the allegation that she'd neatly ripped off one now-elderly customer, it appeared she'd had her heart in the right place when it came to errant girls. Besides, she was long gone. He also wished to avoid any accidental mention of his 'interrogation' of Maureen the hairdresser. In this city where everyone still knew everyone, he didn't fancy some brute of a cuckold husband wielding a cricket bat on his doorstep at midnight.

'I've started making a list of suspects.' Vann rummaged in her handbag and brought out a folded sheet of paper. 'I only thought of Julia Grice this morning. At the time she seemed to be on our side, but she had to be in on it. This is like a jigsaw puzzle with a twist. We've all got all the pieces but we're missing the picture on the box.'

'Speaking of puzzle pieces …' He put the Polaroid photo on the table.

Her eyebrows knitted. 'Did you take that from my office?'

In a gesture of surrender, he held up his hands. 'Guilty as charged, your Honour.'

She glowered at him, which made her hair redder and her eyes greener. As a mature woman she was like a full-blown rose, far more alluring than the tight-furled bud she'd been at sixteen.

'*Borrowed*,' he corrected. 'Unlike *some*, I return what I borrow.' A playful shot, but he couldn't resist.

'Okay, smart-arse.' She flipped open her handbag and slammed his two laundered hankies on the table. 'Thanks for the loan. You have no idea the trouble they caused. Who, in this day and age, gets their hankies monogrammed?'

'Let's call it a draw.' He grinned and pocketed the hankies. 'Now, the photo. Two young people, circa 1971. You—and I must say you looked ravishing—and your boyfriend. I happen to be acquainted with both.'

'He *wasn't* my boyfriend.'

'No? Never mind …'

'He was at the party with a friend of a friend. We sort of hit it off.'

'And his name?'

'Dirk.' She flushed slightly, fiddled with a paper clip she'd plucked from a bowl of assorted clips, pins and thumb-tacks.

'To be perfectly accurate, he is Dirk Johannes VerBeek. My brother.'

For a moment Vann looked as if she might faint.

He put out a hand to steady her but she pushed him away.

There'd been no other way to say it, no way of breaking the news gently. Her reaction, as big and bold as a flashing neon sign, confirmed what he'd suspected.

'Geez Vann, I thought you'd put two and two together. VerBeek isn't exactly your garden-variety surname.'

Weakly she smiled. 'I never knew his last name. Actually, I didn't know much about him at all. It was Michelle's sixteenth birthday and her boyfriend brought along the members of his band. They played heavy metal. Dirk was the lead guitarist. I'm trying to remember what it was called. It was to do with fire … or was it a bird … *Phoenix*. Yes, that's it. He said the name was a tribute to his dad … your dad.'

'Pa was a tram driver. He died in 1962, shortly after the fire that destroyed the tram depot in Paddington. Dirk never got over it. He was close to the old man.'

'Sorry, I'm saying everything wrong tonight.' A tear fell on the table.

'Shit happens.'

'Did you show Dirk the photo?'

'I scanned it and emailed him. He lives in Perth.'

'And?'

'He remembers you.' It wasn't an actual lie and he wasn't about to rub salt in the wounds by repeating his brother's arrogant response.

'Did you tell him about *Maidenhead* and the baby?'

Seth lowered his eyelids.

'Did you tell him he was the father?' she continued.

'He doesn't know and I'm not the one who should tell him.'

'I was so young and naïve. I'd never been with a boy before. Afterwards I only saw him once again at the Ekka. He was with another girl. Anyway, it doesn't matter now. The baby died … or so I thought.'

'What did you call her?'

'Claire,' she said.

'Claire,' he repeated. His luscious voice made the name sound like a French pastry.

Vann continued. 'I've searched and there's no record of her death. It isn't conclusive, but it's promising. If she was adopted, she'd have a different name entirely.'

Seth held the photo between his hands and flicked his eyes from the image of his brother to the image of the young Vann, trying to imagine how Claire might look as a mature woman. 'We must find her.'

'It's kind of you to offer, but this is my problem.'

'We're in this together. She's your daughter, but she's my niece.'

Vann gave him a grateful smile. For a moment he thought she might kiss him. But just then her phone tinged. Instead she put on her glasses and read the text message.

'Gosh, I'm late for Streetkidz!'

'Is it always like this? You hardly get a minute to yourself.'

'It'll be better after the election.' She rushed to her desk, stuffed papers into her bag, slicked on lipstick, pulled a brush through her hair.

'Do you have a car or can I offer you a lift?'

'I'd do anything for a lift.' She said it lightly, playfully.

'*Anything?*' He raised his eyebrows and grinned.

In the Jeep, she spoke on the phone to rearrange the time for the presentations. They were midway down Coro Drive heading for the city centre. The traffic was surprisingly thin. Ahead was the familiar wall of illuminated office towers and blue-striped cranes in spaces where more buildings would soon appear. To the right, navigational beacons blinked on the dark river.

At the corner of Park Road, the traffic lights went red. He braked and watched her from the corner of his eye. 'All good?'

'Yeah.' She ended the call and slid the phone into her handbag.

His hand rested loosely on the centre console. Palm up, a subtle invitation.

She took the hint and knitted her fingers into his.

The lights changed. He needed to manoeuvre the gearstick and had to let her go. They drove through the bright lights of the CBD, then through China Town and past the Valley Pool. He turned right, right, left through a maze of narrow streets that should never have been a main thoroughfare. Into the trendy precinct of James Street where café tables spilled across the footpath. Waiters served fancy cocktails to early diners.

The Powerhouse theatre was directly ahead, beyond a treed stretch of concrete flanked by unaffordable luxury townhouses. It had been a dream run. Nights when an accident or some other catastrophe gridlocked the streets, the same drive could take upward of an hour.

'How long until you're on?' he asked.

'Twenty minutes.'

He swerved into a parking bay between two jacaranda trees. The dense foliage screened them from the blaze of the streetlight. The engine purred like a sleek black cat.

She fidgeted with the strap of her handbag, as if debating whether she should demand that he drive on, or jump out and run the final two hundred metres to the venue.

'Before you go, I want to say something.' His pulse was racing. He hadn't felt like this in years. As soon as he opened his mouth, he knew it was too soon to declare his hand. He didn't want to scare her off. Perhaps he'd misread the signals. Perhaps she was using him to resolve a personal crisis or win an election. But she was an intriguing woman and he wanted nothing more than to be part of her mixed-up world.

She scrutinised his face. 'Go on.'

'I'm not like my brother.' He leant in close and pressed his lips to her forehead. 'Through all of this, I'm on your side.'

'I know.' In the dim light her eyes were as soft as moss.

Straightening, he shifted gears and let out the clutch. The Jeep rolled forward along the avenue. A few minutes later he dropped her off in the car park, close to the main entrance of the converted industrial building. Its stark brick walls towered like battlements over a hard landscape of concrete and bitumen. Some would describe the architectural feat of a disused power station transformed into a performance venue as *edgy*, but in his opinion it was just plain ugly.

She opened the car door and walked up a steep unforgiving staircase. At the top she turned, waggled her fingers, and vanished into the jaws of the monolith.

25

Monday 17 March

Seth reversed out of the parking bay. On the street he lit a smoke, turned up the radio and revved the Jeep through the chicanes of Lamington Street. Straight home, or to his favourite bar? Whichever he chose, he needed to do plenty of thinking.

He took the scenic route, east along Kingsford Smith Drive to the old airport, back on the Gateway tailgated by a snarling B-double, left at the flyover to Sandgate, and left again into a quiet tree-lined street.

He pulled on the handbrake, cut the engine and lit another smoke. Without realising it, his homing instincts had guided him to his own apartment block in Clayfield.

Once inside, he rummaged in the fridge for a Corona. He snapped off the lid, pressed its frothing mouth to his lips and drank in the malty comfort.

The apartment was stuffy. The lingering odour of last night's fry-up had been heightened by the hot day. He opened the balcony door and settled in a deckchair. The stars were pale specks, muted by light-sheen emitted by a city of more than a million inhabitants.

In the bush, the spangle of stars was dazzling. On a cloudless night each constellation was visible and clearly defined. When he was on bivouac with the army in the weeks before his youth was stolen by the Vietnam War, he'd marvelled at the vast expanse of night sky unblemished by pollution. Lying on his back in the dust he'd pick out Orion and the Seven Sisters and the Southern Cross while the other conscripts played poker or smoked weed or did other unmentionable things that would have brought them before a court martial.

What would he have done, had he known about his brother's transgressions? As the head of the household would he have made Dirk pay for an abortion or insisted that he take responsibility for his child? Would he have gone the coward's route and turned a blind eye?

When Dirk said he'd lost an entire decade, he wasn't joking. He'd walked the knife-edge between being employed and stoned, and being unemployed and stoned. At the end of 1972 he skidded to the bottom of a ravine. Off his face on drugs, he'd gone on a crazed rampage through the Valley with a crow-bar, smashed about a hundred panes of glass. As he neared the end of the super-hero phase, a glimmer of common sense or a guardian angel transported him to a phone booth and he'd called the only person who cared.

Seth's battalion was camped at the Enoggera army barracks, marking time before being shipped to Vietnam. His sergeant was kind enough to give him two days' leave. He caught the train to the Valley and searched for his brother in every abandoned building and squat. There were plenty to choose from.

A tipoff from a wino led him to a laneway at the back of Romeo's Nightclub. There, he found Dirk lying in a pool of blood. The assault weapon, his trusty crow-bar, was in an industrial bin nearby. The paramedics who attended did their best and for a while it was touch and go. He was taken to the Royal Hospital where his battered body was patched up. But hospital beds were scarce. One week later when Seth's ship departed—not to a fanfare but a sea of anti-conscription protesters—Dirk was already back on the streets.

In Vietnam, Seth didn't hear from his brother in months.

Later he learnt that Dirk had admitted himself to the Wolston Park Hospital to dry out. This time the treatment stuck.

Music had been his downfall, but it was also his salvation. He moved to Perth and formed a band with another recovering addict. They made a pact to keep each other clean. Ever since he'd worked in the radio station by day and done the pub circuit by night. He took up with a woman who had her head screwed on right, and they'd lived together ever since like an average suburban couple with one kid, two dogs, and a mortgage. The sort of life a younger Dirk had been determined to avoid.

It was astounding his brother had survived the fucked-up years. Seth didn't have it in his heart to blame him entirely. Hot-blooded young men would always be hot-blooded young men. And, from the photos he'd seen, Vann in her youth had been deliciously hot herself.

She still was.

He finished the beer and ambled to the kitchen for a second. On the way back, he brought his laptop. He set it up on the wobbly outdoor table and sat down on a matching chair. The metal was cold and uncomfortable and he'd paid way too much for the set. He remembered buying it from a long-legged beauty in the design shop. She'd given him such a spectacular sales pitch that he'd caved without even asking for a discount.

The computer screen lit up at his home page. *Google*. The search box beckoned. Where should a person begin to unravel the secrets of a lifetime?

He typed in a name, Barry Doyle. A bit obvious perhaps, but the obvious often bore fruit. There were lots of Barry Doyles. They were in the US, South Africa, Canada, Great Britain, Italy and Iceland. Facebook was full of them.

Scrolling down the list, he located a Dr Barry Doyle at Newstead. He had a website. Seth clicked on the link. When the page opened, his heart missed a beat.

Dr Doyle ran a fertility clinic.

He offered a plethora of services from IVF and sperm donation to genetic screening and cryopreservation of human eggs. But his specialty, according to the advertisement, was *innovative alternate interventions for infertile couples*. Of the last, no details were provided and there was no mention of the price.

Intrigued, Seth took a chug from the Corona bottle. Sticking with his plan to pursue the obvious, he clicked *Contact Us*. In the template that appeared, he typed his snooping email address, bvs51@hottie.com. In the comments section he wrote:

> *My wife and I have been trying for a child for ten years, and have just found your website. We have already undertaken fertility testing and had several rounds of IVF, unfortunately to no avail. We feel we are running out of options. We are most interested in your advertised 'innovative alternate interventions for infertile couples'. Would you kindly provide us with information?*

He hit the Send button, wondering how long it would take to get a reply. Idly he browsed the other search results and gave up after four pages of crap.

As an afterthought he logged into the employee section of *The Morning Post*. Dr Doyle was a city-based doctor, for heaven's sake. Doctors did research, made submissions, attended conferences. There was bound to be material in the newspaper's archives.

Most of what came up was paid advertising for the clinic. Not very illuminating. But when he searched the collection of images, he struck a glittering seam of diamond.

The photo was dated 2002. Taken at the opening cocktails of the Australian Fertility Conference on the Gold Coast, a man and a woman were captured on film as they clinked glasses of champagne. The man was young. His hair was black, his eyes were dark, and his skin was the colour of coffee.

In contrast the older woman's white hair was drawn up and back from her face. Slender and elegantly dressed in a blue beaded gown, she looked remarkably familiar.

The caption beneath read, Dr Barry Doyle and Dr Julia Grice get bubbly about babies.

Double whammy. What a find!

Before the file corrupted, or gremlins hacked the archive, or a freak of nature caused the picture to vanish forever, he copied it into his personal computer folder and clicked print. On paper the image was large and clear. With a magnifying glass he examined the two faces. Julia Grice was exactly as he remembered her from that brief, rude encounter at her home. In the photo, surrounded by like-minded professionals, she looked relaxed and confident.

Barry Doyle was not what he expected. First there was his obvious youth. At the time the man wouldn't have been older than thirty. And second, from his berry-brown complexion, flattened nose and dark eyes, Barry Doyle was certainly not Caucasian. He'd not actually seen Rowland or Iris Doyle— the parents—but from all accounts they were both as white as the Queen of England. Yet another complication.

Seth glanced at his wristwatch. It was going on nine. Vann would be on her way home from the concert. The discovery was too good to wait.

On the second ring, she answered. 'What's up?'

'I've got a pic of Barry Doyle and let's say he's not what you'd expect. I'll email it to you. Call me back?'

He sent her the file, then rummaged in the fridge for something to eat. He was polishing off the corn chips and a tub of baba ganoush when she phoned.

'Holy Dooley!' she said. 'There's no way he's their natural son. Is he adopted too?'

'Is that a possibility?' Seth munched on a corn chip.

'I'm sure they didn't have any kids in 1972. If he's thirty in the photo, he would've been born around then. I always thought Mrs Doyle was ancient. Fifty at least. God, I've got to do the maths. If she's ninety now, that'd be about right. Fifty would be a bit beyond having babies, don't you think?'

'Do I have the right man?' he said through a mouthful of corn chips.

'We know their son is Barry, you found that out from the barmaid at the Plains Hotel. The woman in the photo is definitely Julia Grice. Has the name of the man in the photo been correctly published? Papers sometimes make mistakes.'

'Mistakes? No chance!' Seth took a sip of beer and began to chuckle. 'Anyway, I'll find out soon enough. I'm going to see him about having a baby.'

'You're what?'

'Check out his website. I've sent him an email about their special deal for childless couples. Can't wait to hear what's on offer.'

'I'm absolutely fascinated.'

'I'll call you after the appointment,' he said. 'You might be interested yourself.'

She laughed. 'Talk to you soon.'

He pictured her in her smart blue suit. On the way home to her live-in lover, the lucky man.

After a night of troubled dreams, Seth woke at six-thirty with a kink in his neck and a mouth like a sewer. Rolling to one side, he lit a breakfast cigarette. The health warning on today's pack, gangrene. How better to start the day than a revolting image of decaying oozing flesh?

One day he'd quit. He knew the risks. Only six months before he'd had a scare. It's you or the smokes, his doctor had told him.

Yeah, one day soon he'd throw them away for good. But not this day.

In the kitchen he packed finely-ground coffee into the Italian percolator and set it on the stove. He turned on the TV for the news and half-listened while he made toast with cumquat marmalade fresh from the farmers' markets last Saturday.

The reporter's voice was too shrill for the wake-up timeslot. He was close to turning it off when he heard, 'The overnight attack comes on the back of a bomb that destroyed the minister's former office, killing two and seriously injuring others.'

Seth snapped around to the screen. The reporter was standing outside the electorate office where he and Vann had shared Thai take-away just twelve hours earlier. He pumped up the volume. The segment was almost done.

'Police are appealing for any witnesses to come forward.'

The final shot showed an entire glass wall smashed to smithereens and a zoom-in of house-bricks found inside the building.

He shoved the toast into his mouth and abandoned the too-hot coffee. In less than ten minutes he'd showered and dressed. At this hour the traffic was light and the Jeep made Riverdale in record time. He parked in a side street away from the mayhem of Station Road and clear of the Council's draconian parking patrol.

The section around Vann's office was crawling with police and television crews. It seemed the plate-glass bore the brunt of the attack and no-one was hurt.

He pushed through a mob of bystanders and sticky-beaks to get a look at the damage. The police had cordoned off the footpath and access to the office. From where he stood he could see that the panels on either side of the door had been smashed. He tried to picture the dapper Dr Doyle hurling bricks through a politician's window at midnight. It was not an image that easily came to mind. If the Doyles were involved, they'd have engaged a hit man to do the dirty work. Despite Vann Willis's vivid imagination, he doubted that a respected medical family would be behind it at all.

With his phone he took a few shots, which he immediately emailed through to his office. They'd do for *The Morning Post* website until a professional photographer arrived. In fact they weren't half-bad, for they captured the overkill reaction of the crowd. The panicked expressions of the onlookers contrasted with the calmness of the police investigators. It was only a couple of bricks, for God's sake.

At the centre of the action was Detective Sergeant Dave Frame, in charge and in control as usual. He was interrogating a man in a white cap and overalls, a pest controller judging by the Krush-a-Roach logo across his back.

When he'd finished, Seth called out. 'Hey Davo! Got a minute?'

Dave Frame acknowledged him with a flash of the eyebrows. He took three strides towards the blue-and-white checked tape and extended his hand to shake.

'What's news?' said Seth, notebook out and ready.

'Classic break and enter. Two house bricks were found inside.'

'Much stolen?'

'Nothing it seems.'

'Any link to the cryptic note?'

'Can't rule it in, can't rule it out. What have you found out, my supersleuth friend?' In a light-hearted warning Frame added, 'Remember, there are laws about withholding information.'

'All hunches and no proof, I'm afraid.' Seth shut the notebook.

'Try me.'

'I need to talk to Vann Willis first.' He patted his top pocket for cigarettes, remembered his doctor's advice and popped an Eclipse mint instead.

'You can do that in a few minutes. She's on her way.' The Detective Sergeant's mobile phone began to ring. 'Sorry mate, duty calls.'

The morning traffic was starting to build. From all directions pedestrians swarmed to and from the busy railway station. Businessmen and women headed to the CBD; retail workers headed up the hill to the Riverdale Mall; students lugging sports equipment or musical instruments headed to the various schools. Down the road Café Nero was pumping out crinkle-cardboard take-away cups by the score.

The aroma of coffee lured him like a love potion. He succumbed.

With a steaming cup of macchiato and a cigarette (he'd give up tomorrow), he loitered outside the electorate office, waiting for Vann to arrive.

Minutes later a taxi turned through the queue of traffic onto the apron of the car park. The police opened the cordon to let it through. Dave Frame spoke briefly to Vann before they disappeared together into the damaged office.

Seth took a last look at the scene. The police were going about their business, the residents and workers were going about theirs. The morning TV crew had packed up and gone. He didn't have hours to waste on the slim chance of a development so he returned to Café Nero for a second heart-starter and walked along the strip of shopfronts towards his car.

Outside the hairdresser's salon he stopped. An important piece of information had slipped his mind. Maureen had made a comment that he'd never resolved. Two minutes before the blast, a package was delivered to Vann's office. All his focus had been on Julia Grice and her mother. Had he been barking up the wrong tree? With more questions than answers, he felt an important piece of information was missing. Who was the courier?

In the Jeep, he switched the radio off. The breakfast-show drivel was getting on his nerves. He needed time to think.

At his office in Bowen Hills he opened his snooping email account. Amongst the myriad of spam selling Viagra and hot chicks from Russia was a response from Dr Doyle's fertility clinic. If nothing else, they were prompt.

Thank you for your inquiry. Because each client is unique, we prefer to discuss our alternative intervention options in person. This ensures our service is tailored to meet your specific needs. If you would like to make an appointment, please phone Anne.

Nothing ventured, nothing gained. He lifted the receiver and punched in the number.

A bright young voice answered. 'Angels from Blue Heaven. This is Anne.'

Not the business name he expected. Quickly he checked the number to make sure he hadn't rung a brothel by mistake.

'Hi, Anne. I just got your email. Can I make an appointment?'

'Sure. You're in luck, there's a cancellation this afternoon. Would two o'clock suit?' She sounded doubtful.

'Perfect.'

'May I have both your names?'

'Brian Smith. My wife's Janine. I'd like to come alone if it's all the same to you. Janine's been through the mill with IVF and so forth. I'd like to understand what's possible before getting her hopes up again.'

'I understand completely, Mr Smith. Do you have our address?'

'The one on the website?'

'Yes. You can park at the back of the building.'

At the appointed time, Seth entered the uber-modern premises of *Angels from Blue Heaven*. The décor was white on white with lots of bling. Glass, chrome, and crystal.

The young woman at reception raised an eyebrow. 'Mr Smith?'

He smiled. 'That's me.'

'I'm Anne. Please take a seat. Dr Doyle will be with you directly.'

He almost choked. Never did he expect to score an appointment with Barry Doyle straight up. He'd imagined an initial meeting with a spruiker who'd try and convince him to hand over his hard-earned cash for various fertility treatments. He expected to undergo an interrogation about his medical history—he'd prepared one earlier—and a bureaucratic obstacle course before even coming close to the good doctor.

He'd have to think on his feet to pull off the role of Brian Smith, loving husband and desperate father-to-be. He could have done with a smoke, but it wouldn't be allowed inside a fertility clinic. Besides, he wanted to make a good impression. These days, smoking was on par with having leprosy. He slipped two Eclipse mints into his cheek.

In less than five minutes Anne called his name. He followed her into a spacious office, which was decorated in the same modern minimalist style. A picture window overlooked the treetops to the river beyond. Behind the vast desk was a well-built man in an impossibly white shirt. Perhaps the fabric appeared whiter than it actually was, due to the contrast with his dark skin.

The doctor stood, extended a hand. 'Hello Mr Smith. I'm Barry Doyle.'

Seth returned the handshake. 'Thanks for seeing me at short notice.'

'What can I do for you, sir?'

Seth adjusted his posture and began his fabricated story. It was full of longing, grief, anticipation, and frustration. He so perfectly depicted the desperation of being unable to make a baby that by the end, he'd almost convinced himself his sole aim in life was to procreate.

'Ah yes, many of my clients have been through similar woes. While it's admirable that you wish to shoulder the burden yourself, is it true that you haven't yet mentioned our services to your wife?'

'I want to know what's involved first. Another failure would destroy her.'

'There are several options, some more expensive than others. Is money a problem, Mr Smith?' The doctor opened his hands expansively and leant back in his overstuffed leather chair. His shirtsleeve lifted a few centimetres, revealing a gold Rolex watch beneath. Seth had seen a dazzling array of cheap Asian copies in his time, and this definitely was not one.

Seth dragged his eyes from the timepiece and looked Barry Doyle in the eye. 'We've already spent a fortune on IVF and we're not wealthy people. Can you give me an indication of the costs?'

'Sure. Before we start I need to know your ages and state of health.'

How much of an age reduction could he get away with? He took a breath. 'I'm fifty-four and my wife is thirty-eight. Neither of us has any health issues.'

'Excellent. Of course, if you choose to engage our services, you'll need to provide evidence in support.' He smiled and tapped his fingertips together.

'Naturally.'

'The least expensive option is adoption. Is your wife also Caucasian?'

'Yes.'

'Would you have any objection to a child of another race or country?'

'Wait on. We want to have our own child. Adoption isn't on our radar, certainly not overseas adoption.'

'Perhaps you should consider it. It's difficult to source healthy Caucasian babies. These days there's a whole raft of support for mothers who are on their own. Baby bonuses, supporting parent's benefit, government assistance for childcare. Most of the infants up for adoption in Australia have an impediment.'

'Meaning?'

'A disability or behavioural problems. They might have been born to a drug-addicted mother or come from a situation of neglect or domestic violence.'

'Hmm. Sounds like more than we could handle. What else you can suggest?'

'Have you tried donor eggs or sperm?'

'Yeah, just the eggs. No luck. By the way, it's not me that's the problem.' Hell, he was as virile as ever. There was no way he was going to lose face, even if this was a complete fiction.

'Then surrogacy might suit. Your sperm, together with eggs harvested from a healthy young woman, and a contracted hothouse until birth. It's guaranteed, but let me warn you, it's top of the range and comes at considerable cost.'

'Isn't there a law against that?'

'Not how we do it. I can assure you our operation is beyond reproach.'

'What sort of amount are we talking?'

'Depends on what you want. This is where we can really get into customisation.' His eyes glistened. It was obviously where he got his jollies.

'Such as …?'

'We maintain a catalogue. You can pick whoever you want. We can match the physical characteristics of your wife, or we can go all out.'

'All out?'

'Our egg-women are amazing! Brains, talent, physical prowess, or simply drop-dead gorgeous. You can browse our catalogue on-line. All you need is a password. And remember, you get what you pay for.'

'Whoa, I had no idea!'

'Most people don't. The way we package it will astound you. Having the perfect child has never been so easy. Think it over, talk to your wife. Here's my number if you have any questions.' He slid a business card across the desk. 'Before you go, Anne can make an appointment for you both to come in and discuss details.'

Dr Barry Doyle rose to shake hands. 'I'm pleased we've met, Mr Smith. Have a lovely afternoon and I look forward to your call.'

At the reception desk Seth took the earliest available appointment. He practically sprinted to the Jeep, dropping the keys in his haste. He ground the gears, over-revved the engine and stalled it. In a cloud of smoke, the vehicle roared out of the car park and onto the main road.

After that performance he needed a drink and fast.

One kilometre down the road was a tavern. He pulled in, lit a smoke and sucked on it as if it were life support. By the time he'd reached the public bar he was inhaling the fumes of the smouldering filter tip.

He ordered a double Johnny Walker Black on the rocks. In a couple of gulps it was gone. A gush of wellbeing flowed into his veins. He sat on a stool at the bar, elbows on the polished counter, and ordered another.

'Rough day?' said the barman.

'You got it, mate.' Out came his phone. The screen was black and dead. He was about to start cursing when he realised he'd turned it off earlier. He pressed the button, the inbox tinged with messages.

Three in a row were from Cate. *The boss is looking for you.*

Seth groaned. What now? He hadn't missed a deadline in weeks.

Another was from Vann. *I've been grounded. Detective Sergeant Frame told me to cancel everything and go home. I feel like a kid wagging school. Call me.*

The afternoon clientele at the tavern was rowdy. Most were tradies in shorts and steel-capped boots who seemed to have been mates for years. Their territory was the table in the corner near the windows. Their beer came by the jug, their rum by the bottle. Their jokes were seamy enough to curl the wallpaper.

Begrudgingly Seth phoned the office.

The boss quizzed him about the articles on adoptions he'd been promising. 'Where's this heading, man? I want hard-hitting, I want gutsy. I don't want mushy human interest shit.'

'I'm almost there. Had a breakthrough today.'

'How much longer? I want that feature article ASAP.'

'Another week. Maximum.'

'Okay. What's all that noise in the background?'

'Ummm … I popped into Macca's to take a leak.'

'Must be the booziest Macca's in Australia.'

How to make a person feel guilty, his boss was a master at it. Geez, he hadn't done this during work time in ages. And he'd been caught out. He'd have to write a brilliant article to make it up. If there was ever a way to an editor's heart, it was a fabulous piece of journalism.

One thing was certain, the Barry Doyle story was about to become more interesting. All he needed in order to complete the research was a plausible wife.

When Seth returned to the office it was nearly five. The whisky had done its job and his nerves were under control. His desk looked like a rubbish tip, his computer hummed accusingly, and the message light on his phone was flashing.

In the next cubicle, Cate was noisily packing food containers into carry bags.

Why hadn't he thought of her sooner? He slapped his forehead and poked his head over the partition. 'Cate, got a minute?'

'One minute, that's it. I'll miss my train.'

'Give me ten and I'll drive you home.'

'I live at Darra. It's a long way.'

'No matter. This baby story is about to explode. I need your help.'

'Okay, but I've got to be home by six.' She came around the low divider with her notepad—he'd taught her well—and sat in the chair by his desk.

After a dramatic pause he said, 'Cate, I want you to be my wife.'

She jumped up and glared at him. 'I thought you were serious about the story. I'm off.'

'Wait. Hear me out.' He stood between her and the exit route.

She hesitated then eased back into the chair. 'This had better be good.'

'I've got an appointment at a fertility clinic tomorrow. I've been posing as a client but I can't get the info I need unless I bring my wife. Would you, in a strictly professional sense, accompany me? If you agree, the article will have a joint by-line. Seth VerBeek and Cate Bradshaw. Has a nice ring to it, don't you think?'

A wicked smile spread across her face. 'My name goes first.'

'Sweetheart, you're dreaming.'

'A girl's got to try. Okay, I'll do it.'

He briefed her about the day's meeting and the information he'd already provided to the clinic about Mrs Janine Smith.

She glanced at her watch. 'We've really got to go. Family celebration. Surprise birthday party for my mother. By the way, I've had a bit of a breakthrough myself. Tell you in the car.'

The Inner City Bypass was clear of the usual peak-hour crawl. The Jeep glided easily through the spaghetti of overpasses, underpasses and loops. Soon they were speeding westward on the motorway past the tombstones and spires of the Toowong Cemetery.

Cate said, 'You told me that the Doyle family once ran a home for unmarried mothers near Mundingo. The farm was called *Maidenhead*, right?'

'Correct.'

'I spent the afternoon trawling the internet, looking for references.'

'And?'

'Not a lot there, so I searched the satellite images. I found a place that matches your description, but now it's called Double Happy Language Farm.'

'Are you sure it's the right place? I was there last week. There weren't any signs, just a ginormous electrified fence that shouted KEEP OUT.'

'The images are so clear you can see people dotted between the trees.'

'That doesn't prove much.'

'Did you know I speak Mandarin?'

'I'm impressed. What's that got to do with the price of eggs?'

'The business name on the satellite image is written in Chinese characters. I Googled it and you won't believe what I found!' Her eyes were snapping with excitement.

'You'd better tell me before you burst.'

She grinned. 'Sure boss.' It was part of the game.

He winced and pulled a sour face, exactly as she would've expected.

In a mother-superior lilt she said, 'The Double Happy Language Farm offers a complete package for young Chinese women. They get a year in a rural Australian setting, return air fares, full board, skills training, and English language tuition.'

'How much does all that cost?'

'It's absolutely free. According to the ad, all expenses are covered by a philanthropic society called Robair International. I don't get it. What's the catch?'

'That, my dear Watson, we are about to find out.'

The Darra turnoff was up ahead. Cate gave him directions. Take the underpass at the station, second exit at the roundabout, and straight ahead along a flat stretch of road bordered by drab fibro cottages.

The lights outside number seventy-one were blazing. Cate gathered her carry bags and slid from the passenger's seat onto the footpath.

'See you tomorrow, Mrs Smith,' he said.

'Night-night, dear.' She blew him a kiss and disappeared up the path.

26

Tuesday 18 March

The series of threats and incidents was taking its toll on Vann. After the stern talking-to by Detective Sergeant Dave Frame about personal safety and taking Hollywood-style warning letters seriously, she began to question her decision to stand for re-election. Tuesday was a sitting day in Parliament. Normally she'd be out there, psyched up and ready to bat away criticisms from a hostile Opposition. Instead, she'd given herself a premeditated sickie, her first unofficial day off in fifteen years.

To her frustration, her body clock—set for six-thirty a.m.—was as punctual as ever. Even an eye mask and earplugs didn't help. At seven-fifteen she got up, leaving Lance to serenade the bedroom with rasping noises like a crosscut saw. Even in the kitchen she could hear him.

She read the morning papers then put on an egg to boil but forgot to set the eggtimer for three minutes. While she jiggled a teabag in a mug of hot water, she counted the seconds out loud. A soft-boiled egg was an art of perfect balance. Too hard, and it was like chalk. Too runny, and it tasted like snot. At one hundred and seventeen seconds, her phone began to ring.

It was James. There was a problem at the office.

'I found another envelope under the door this morning,' he said. 'Handwritten. It says, *To be opened by Ms Vann Willis herself.*'

'Not again,' she groaned. 'What did you do with it?'

'It's unopened on your desk.'

She tapped her nails against the plastic phone case and tried to think. Years ago, there'd been cases of hate mail laced with anthrax powder. There'd also been letter-bombs and poison ink and kidnappings with ransom notes. The Riverdale bomber had already claimed two lives and was still at large. What he might do next was anyone's guess.

'Call Detective Sergeant Frame and get his advice.'

'Okay. I'll ring you back.'

She left the phone close on the bench. The saucepan was bubbling cheerfully on the stove. Who knew how many minutes had elapsed. She drained the water and broke the top off the egg. Inside looked like a greyish superball, yet another culinary failure. Not being one to waste food—Merle had often told her *the poor people of Africa would kill for a meal like that*—she picked off the shell and mashed it onto a slice of bread with mayo. As she was about to sink in her teeth, the phone began to flash.

Detective Sergeant Frame sounded as if he were at the bottom of a well. Cursing the sporadic mobile reception in her apartment block, she walked onto the balcony so she could hear.

'Were you expecting any mail of a confidential nature?' he said.

'Not really.'

'Because of what's happened, the envelope should be opened under controlled conditions. Just as a precaution you understand. Because it's marked *personal*, it'd be best if you could come to the police station.'

'Am I'm allowed out? Last time I got a weirdo letter, you made me sit in the naughty corner.'

He chuckled beneath his breath. 'Yes, you're allowed out but don't draw attention to yourself. If you intend to drive, I'll reserve a car park under the building.'

'Is a white Mazda nondescript enough for you?'

'Perfect. See you soon.'

She put down the phone and poked her head into the bedroom. Lance was on his back. His snoring hadn't missed a beat. On the side table were the car keys. She kneeled on the bed and reached across his body.

Without warning his hand snapped around her wrist.

'Oww! You're hurting me.' She tried to twist out of his grip.

He tightened his hold. 'Why do you want my car?'

'That was the CIB. They have a suspicious letter that's addressed to me.'

'And you want my car for …?'

'I'm keeping a low profile until this is sorted out.'

'*What* needs to be sorted out? You're not making any sense.' He pulled her down onto his chest, wrapped his arms around her. She caught a whiff of cologne on his stubble. Citrus with cinnamon undertones. Typical of a restaurateur to use a fragrance that smelt like dessert.

She pushed him back. 'Lance, this is serious.'

He frowned. 'So am I.' He turned away, swung his legs over the bed and pulled on a pair of shorts. The hedge of hair across his shoulder blades bristled. Not a good sign. When he turned around again, his face was like a thunderstorm.

They stood apart glaring, the bed a no-man's-land between them.

'When is this rubbish going stop?' he said. 'We don't need the money and we don't need the stress.'

Her earlier notion of quitting politics immediately went out the window. She'd fight him until Christmas if she had to. She crossed her arms. 'A couple more weeks. Then it'll settle down.'

'A couple more weeks and then another term. That, in my calculation, is more than *three years*. Are you going to keep up this pace for another three years? Vann, you're at an age when most people retire.'

'Like *you* can talk!'

'Do I have bombs exploding in my restaurant? Do I get crazy-person letters? I love what I do and it makes me happy. It brings in more than enough income for us to live on.' His voice had softened to that persuasive tone she usually found hard to resist.

But not today. Today, she wanted answers. The whole catastrophe was about to come to a head: the adoption inquiry, the bomber, the extortionist, the unanswered questions about Claire, her own secret past, and quite possibly the future of their relationship. 'I know you want me to quit before the election, but I can't. Not now. It's gone too far. I'd let down my Party and my constituents. And my friend Freya, who would have lost her life for nothing. I'm not going to give up on the inquiry either. I'll get to the bottom of it if it kills me.'

'It just might.'

Reluctantly he tossed her the car keys. 'Don't take any risks.'

She gave him a tight-lipped smile. 'If it makes any difference, there's a strong possibility I won't retain the seat. Everyone's enchanted by the PPP's pretty-boy, Jake Stone. The polls aren't looking too flash. '

'That, my dear, would be a blessing.'

For the second time in a month, Vann was in police headquarters. This time Detective Sergeant Frame took her not to an interview room, but to his own tiny office. Battlements of manila folders were strategically placed around the desk. His second line of defence was a wall of office hardware: two computer screens, phone, scanner, printer.

He offered her a visitors' chair then took up his position behind the barrier in a swivel chair squashed against the wall. Even seated he towered over her. She wondered how his praying-mantis body could fold itself into such a tight space.

Apologising for the mess, he dropped a stack of folders onto the floor. In its place he laid out a pair of disposable gloves, a letter opener, and the mystery envelope. The address was in blue biro. The script was rounded, the downstrokes strong and confident. It was not a hand that she recognised.

'Go ahead,' he said. 'We've x-rayed it and run it by the sniffer dog. It's clear of noxious substances. All the same take care as you open it.'

'I know the drill, there might be fingerprints.' She put on the gloves, positioned the steel opener and slit the flap.

Inside was a greeting card, a picture of red roses on blue. When she opened it, a folded square of notepaper fell onto her lap.

The card was completely blank, no printed messages to get well or of best wishes for the future. The note inside was set out formally, the way a teacher or a maiden aunt would write, except no return address was given at the top.

The name at the end was astonishing. No, it was a miracle. Vann pressed her hand against her heart and read.

Dear Ms Willis

Please forgive me if I'm mistaken.

I've been trying to discover my natural mother because I believe I was adopted. Recently, a friend from Toogoolawah helped me go through my family's documents. One gave the following details: Baby Claire Jones, born 15th March 1972, Maidenhead.

My friend burst into tears. She explained she'd been sent to Maidenhead in the seventies because she was single and pregnant. It was a secret she'd kept all this time. She'd never told anyone, not even her husband.

She remembered the names of others in her dorm. One was Mary (she didn't know the surname), who called her unborn baby Claire.

Your picture was in The Morning Post *that day, together with an article about the adoption inquiry. She said the resemblance between you and Mary was remarkable.*

Are you Mary? Am I your Claire?

If I'm right, please email claire1972@frogslider.com.

If I'm wrong, I apologise and won't bother you again.

Yours sincerely

Claire Jones.

Vann shut her eyes and let out a little groan. Fearing she might faint, she gripped the edge of the table.

The detective rushed to steady her. 'Can I get you a glass of water?'

She nodded and pinched the bridge of her nose. The hospital odour of the rubber glove reminded her of blood, which made the room spin even faster.

A teacup of water appeared. She peeled off the gloves, gulped down the water. It was chilled to just above freezing, a good temperature to bring her back to her senses.

The card and note lay on the desk.

'No more death threats?' said Dave Frame.

'No, quite the opposite,' she croaked. 'A shock all the same.'

'Something I can do to help?'

She smiled. 'You've done heaps already. This, I must handle on my own. If any other suspicious items appear under my door, I'll call you straight away.'

'Before you go, I have some information about the bombing. The deceased male person was positively identified by his father as Bertram Porter. He had a criminal record, but nothing too sinister. And remember the CCTV footage that showed the odd shape at the back of his overcoat?'

'Yes, we thought it might be explosives.'

'Forensics identified it as a garden variety backpack with aluminium cans inside. He must've put the coat on over it. The supermarket bag he was carrying was also full of cans. It seems he was going door to door, collecting them to recycle.'

'I'm sad that he died, but I'm glad he was innocent.'

'This means you must be especially vigilant. Until the perpetrator is found you should consider cancelling public appearances and hiring security staff. Don't forget the threat the other day and the bricks through your window.'

'I'm not afraid.'

'For the next week I'll have a police car drive by your office every few hours.'

'Thanks, but I'll be fine.'

He walked her to the door. 'Take care. I *mean* that.'

Alone in the car Vann rested her head on the steering wheel and debated what to do. Claire's letter changed everything. Although there was an assassin out there who wanted to kill her, this was a more important. Her daughter was alive. Alive! Not only that, she'd tracked her down and wanted to make contact.

Vann reread the letter. It seemed sincere. She desperately wanted to believe every word. Was it another cruel trick?

Claire Jones had given no information about herself, apart from a date of birth (which was correct) and an email address. Was she married? Did she have children?

Children! That would make her a grandmother. Suddenly Vann felt old.

Her phone was cradled in her palm.

One short email to *claire1972@frogslider.com* had the potential to turn her life around. She'd gain a daughter, but she'd likely lose Lance and possibly her political career. Should she wait until after the election? Should she respond at all?

There was no proof other than the say-so of a woman who called herself Claire Jones and her unnamed friend from Toogoolawah who'd helped her join the dots. It could be a ploy. She'd already had three warnings her life was on the line. The person who tried to sabotage her adoption inquiry might have the same information. The letter was plausible enough for a mother to believe it was from her long-lost child.

She typed in the email address. Her hands were trembling. To send or not to send?

What about Lance? She had no idea how he'd react to the news. Worse, by remaining silent on the matter for the past ten years, she'd as good as lied to him. That wouldn't go down well.

She wrote a brief response and hit *save message*. She turned the ignition key and shoved the gearstick into first. Time to think was what she needed. Time and a friend to talk it through with.

Before she knew it, she'd located the number and hit *call*.

'Can I see you? It's urgent,' she said.

The voice that answered was like refrigerated chocolate, brittle at the start and melting into dreamy smoothness. 'What's happened?'

'Nothing … yet.' She turned off the ignition and pushed back the seat. The car felt like a cattle crush. The steering wheel, the dashboard, the drab grey upholstery was pressing into her. She could scarcely breathe.

In the car park, marked police cars came and went. Men and women in blue uniforms scrutinised her as they walked past on the way to the stairs.

'Can we meet? Somewhere quiet,' she whispered.

'I'd kill for a decent cup of coffee.'

'Do you know the park off River Esplanade? I'll wait for you on the seat beside the Moreton Bay fig tree.'

'Okay. See you in twenty.'

27

Tuesday 18 March

Seth arrived at the isolated park off River Esplanade not knowing what to expect. On the phone Vann had sounded agitated and reluctant to talk. Her elected meeting place was both surprising and puzzling. That end of the Esplanade wound past a private golf course and ended in a disused dirt track. Apart from the willy-wagtails and swallows that inhabited the river bank, they were guaranteed to be alone.

A white Mazda was parked beneath a giant Moreton Bay fig tree. Vann was sitting on a bench seat overlooking the river. The autumn sun made her hair look as if it were ablaze.

She turned and smiled. 'Thanks for coming. You're the only one I can talk to.' She handed him a crinkle-cardboard cup with the Café Nero logo down the side.

He sat close beside her. Waited for her to speak.

Instead she took an envelope from her bag and passed it to him.

He opened the paper and read. 'Whoa! That's what I call a leap of faith.'

'It's all true, every word. I was called Mary and she was called Claire.'

He didn't know what to say so he folded the letter and gave it back.

For several minutes they sat in silence, watching the lazy flow of the river. The carcass of a tree drifted by, its naked arms stretched skywards in a plea for mercy.

'Have you emailed her?' said Seth.

'I wanted to think about it first. It might be a trick to bring down my career or get extortion money.'

'Who else knows about your past?'

'Fiona, the other girls at *Maidenhead*, Julia Grice, the midwife. Iris Doyle and her husband, Rowland, who made me sign her away.' Vann dropped her eyes and examined the card. Red roses on a sky-blue background. 'You know, this card reminds me of something.'

'What about the son, Barry? Would he know?'

'It's possible. After all these years, Iris Doyle recognised me straight off. She might have told him I'd been there asking questions.' She fingered the edge of the card. 'That photo you sent of Barry … that was a real shock.'

Seth drained the coffee and immediately wished there was more. His eyeballs weren't holding up too well in the glare, he'd left his sunglasses at home. Much as he yearned to stay there with her, an appointment at the fertility clinic loomed and he needed to brief his young accomplice.

'Unless …' She dropped her gaze and disappeared inside her thoughts.

A few seconds later she said, 'When I was taken up to the big house, I overheard the Doyles arguing about a *permanent solution* for an unwanted child. At night I'd heard the poor mite crying in another room and wondered whose it was. In the end I pieced it together. The baby must have been Daphne's. She was a rebel of a girl, who'd apparently had a fling with an African-American basketball player. I remember the old woman who drove me home to Riverdale made the oddest comment. She was talking about Mrs Doyle. *That woman's got a heart of gold,* she said. I've never forgotten it. If you'd have asked me, her heart was made of granite.'

Seth lit a cigarette and offered her one from the pack. Today's feature picture, tongue cancer. She declined. He said, 'Yesterday I met Barry Doyle in person. He's tall, dark and about forty. If you're right and the Doyles did adopt him, they've treated him well. Six years studying medicine at university doesn't come cheap. Perhaps you misjudged Mrs Doyle after all.'

The morning was balmy yet Vann shivered. 'There's more to it. There has to be.'

'What you do intend to do about Claire Jones?' said Seth.

She sucked air through her teeth and shrugged.

'Think of it this way, what's to lose and what's to gain?'

She fidgeted with her phone, turning it over and over in her hand. The plastic protective cover, as black and sleek as polished onyx, caught the sun. Its alarm went off, she checked the time.

'I'll work it out. Thanks for listening.' She pressed her lips to his cheek.

He closed his eyes and smelled the scent of her skin, as warm and alluring as the froth on a full-cream cappuccino. He folded his arms around her and hugged her briefly.

'I'd better get on,' she said, pulling away.

Seth's appointment with *Angels from Blue Heaven* was at eleven and he hadn't yet been to the office. When he'd taken Vann's phone call earlier, he'd been naked and dripping from the shower. He'd thrown on an unironed shirt from the chair by the bed and hot-footed the Jeep to their secluded meeting place.

When he finally walked into his cubicle at Bowen Hills, Cate danced in behind him. A smile played on her lips. She wore a calf-length frock with a white lace collar. It was the frumpiest dress he'd ever seen. She must have borrowed it from her grandmother or picked it out of a St Vinnie's bin.

'How do I look, dear?' She swirled around and the skirt billowed out like a floral parachute.

He pulled a face.

'If I'm old enough to be your wife, I have to look the part. You're looking a bit wrinkled yourself.'

'Thanks for the compliment.'

'I meant your shirt.'

'Oh.' He smoothed it with his hands. 'Mrs Smith is meant to be thirty-eight. That dress makes you look seventy. No wonder you can't get pregnant!'

She laughed. 'If you think it's too much, I've brought another outfit.' She dashed to the other side of the partition and held up black trousers and a green silk shirt.

'That's more like it. You'd better change. We're on in half an hour.'

In the car park outside *Angels from Blue Heaven*, Seth looked squarely at Cate. 'You sure you're up for this?'

'Try stopping me!'

'Okay, *honey*. Shall we hold hands and go inside?'

'You've got to be kidding. We've been married fifteen years!'

Side by side, they walked across the bitumen and up the stairs. The waiting room was devoid of clients. Seth wondered if the baby business, along with many other local businesses, had fallen victim to a slowing economy. The receptionist called Anne greeted them by name. On a two-seater sofa they sat as far apart as possible and flipped silently through baby magazines.

Seth was halfway through an enlightening article about spa-bath birthing when Barry Doyle called them in. In a black suit with red-and-white striped shirt, he looked every bit the successful professional, brimming with self-confidence down to the buckles of his expensive chisel-toe shoes.

From his throne behind the massive desk, Dr Doyle outlined the options he'd spoken about the day before. At the end of the sales spiel, he looked directly at Cate. 'Do you have any questions, Mrs Smith?'

'Can you tell me more about surrogacy. We had our hearts set on a child of our own. You said we could use Brian's sperm and another woman's egg. How does that work?'

'Before we get into specifics, I want to be very clear about the costs. This is our most expensive option, but we guarantee a healthy child.'

'What sort of money are we looking at?' said Seth.

'Upward of one hundred thousand.'

Seth whistled. He grasped Cate's hand and gave it a convincing squeeze. On her ring finger was a band that was not there earlier. He glanced down and caught a glint of fake gold.

'Whatever it takes, we'll do it,' he said.

Cate nodded vigorously.

Barry Doyle reached into a drawer and produced a photo album. Inside were numbered pictures of young women. Lots of them. Under each photo were dot-points of their attributes. It read like the menu of a Chinese restaurant.

Seth flicked through the first ten pages. All the women there were Asian. In the centre were blondes and brunettes and redheads like you'd see on any Australian beach in summer. 'Wow! These women are gorgeous!'

'Let me see.' Cate took the album and leafed through. 'What about this one, honey? Number one fifty-three.' She pointed to a girl who was practically her mirror image.

'Perfect. Do we use artificial insemination or the *natural* method?'

Cate kicked him beneath the desk.

Barry Doyle frowned disapprovingly. 'Mr Smith, the woman supplies an egg which is fertilized *in vitro*. The embryo is implanted in a surrogate who carries the foetus until full term.'

'Do we get to meet her?' said Cate.

'Absolutely not! Privacy and discretion are of utmost importance.'

'What happens when the baby is born?' she said.

'We give it a comprehensive check-up before you take delivery.'

Seth shifted uncomfortably in his chair. Doyle sounded like a man selling inanimate objects like vacuum cleaners or used cars. These were *human babies*, for Chrissakes.

'What if there's an issue with their health?' said Cate.

'Genetic defects are screened out early in the piece. Congenital abnormalities are rare, but if there is a problem we'll make other arrangements. As I said before, you are absolutely guaranteed a healthy baby. No exceptions.'

Cate seemed shaken by Doyle's response. To her credit she took a breath and persisted with the interrogation. 'So, is the child born in Australia?'

'Of course.'

'Where?'

'We have our own private facility.'

'Can we see it? I don't like the idea of a baby factory,' said Cate.

Seth squeezed her hand. 'Steady on, sweetheart.'

A storm was forming on Barry Doyle's face. 'Mrs Smith, I can assure you that our antenatal centre is world class.'

'I want your assurance that this is strictly legal and above board.'

Barry Doyle gave Cate a stiff smile. 'My family has been in this business for three generations. We know what we're doing. I personally oversee each and every confinement.'

'That's good enough for me.' Seth was itching to leave. 'What happens next?'

'In a nutshell, there's paperwork to sign and we'll need a deposit. Instalments are staged. Thirty percent on successful implantation and twenty percent after six months incubation. The remainder is due when you take delivery of your child. If you agree to proceed today, I can give you a ten percent discount.'

'Can we read through the documents first?' said Cate.

'Naturally. Our placement advisor has already prepared them. I'll introduce you. Call me if you have any other questions.'

They followed Dr Doyle through the reception area and down a short corridor to a frosted-glass door. He gave two short knocks and pushed it open without waiting for a response.

Inside was a wooden desk the size of a billiard table. It completely dwarfed the slender white-haired woman seated behind it.

Seth's stomach took a dive.

The white-haired woman stood to greet them. A frown crossed her brow. Laser-sharp eyes bored into him. 'We've met somewhere before, haven't we?'

For once he was lost for an answer. After an awkward handshake he mumbled, 'You must be mistaken, ma'am.'

'I never forget a face,' she barked.

'I'll leave you and Dr Grice to discuss business.' Barry Doyle backed out of there faster than a mongrel mutt escaping the wrath of a rolled-up newspaper.

Cate said, 'I'm Janine and this is my husband Brian.'

The older woman's face relaxed slightly, but she continued to glare at Seth.

An official-looking document was open on the desk, tagged with little coloured flags where names and signatures should go.

'Can we take the contract home and return it tomorrow?' said Cate.

'I'm afraid not. Commercial in confidence. You may read it here. Take all the time you need.' As she slid the six-page document across the desk, her phone began to ring.

Into the receiver she hissed, 'I'm busy … Can't this wait? … Fine … Yes.'

'Please excuse me.' Julia Grice pushed back the chair and stormed out.

The instant she was gone, Seth whipped out his phone and positioned it above the document.

Snap.

Cate sprinted to the door and put her eye to the crack. 'Quick, she's coming!'

Snap. Snap.

Seth heard the door click and Cate's voice outside. 'Dr Grice, I need to use the bathroom urgently. Can you show me where it is?'

Their footsteps retreated.

Snap. Snap. Snap.

There, it was done.

The door opened. The phone was safe in his pocket and he was hunched over the document if he'd been reading it the entire time.

Julia Grice narrowed her eyes. 'You're the reporter who came to my house.'

Seth looked directly at her. 'You know, I must have a *doppelganger*. A lot of people think they've met me before.'

'What *do* you do for a living, Mr Smith?'

'We're both public servants.' He'd used that one before, many times. In his experience it was a sure-fire way to shut down further questions. Quite simply, it was the most boring occupation he could think of. On other occasions he'd been more specific and fibbed he was a tax office auditor. Conversation-stopper guaranteed.

Cate returned, white-faced and clutching her stomach. 'Honey, we need to go. It must have been something I ate.'

'Sorry Dr Grice, I'll call and make another appointment,' he said rising.

In the Jeep he said to Cate, 'You're good. You're very good indeed. In fact, that performance was magnificent.'

'Did you get the photos?'

He patted his pocket. 'Right here. Fancy a drive, Mrs Smith?'

'Where to?'

'*Maidenhead*, aka the *Double Happy Language Farm*.'

'Might as well. We're on a roll.'

It was early afternoon when the Jeep turned off the main highway on the western plains. The track was as overgrown as before, an indication of the infrequency of its use. The chimney spires of the old house loomed dark against the smoky hue of the sky. The wires of the electrified fence that separated the homestead from the rest of the world hummed in the breeze. The gate was bound with chains and fastened with a heavy padlock. The grounds were deserted.

He slid the gearstick into reverse, put his head out the window, and eased the Jeep backwards to where the weathered wheel-ruts disappeared into lantana scrub. He manoeuvred into the thick of the vegetation and cut the engine. There the car would be screened from the track, as well as the house and the main road.

'I hope you aren't wearing stilettos,' he said to Cate.

'Nope, middle-aged women like me wear ballet flats.'

He sniffed. *Middle-aged* indeed! 'Follow me.'

He pushed into the red-and-yellow lantana and opened the scratchy branches for Cate to climb through. Beyond the tangle of vegetation, they took the overgrown track that skirted around the hill.

'Won't there be snakes?' she said.

'Probably.'

'I'm scared of snakes.' Her nervous eyes darted across the ground.

'They're more scared of you.' He never knew he was capable of such bravado.

She made a little whining sound that reminded him of a terrier he'd once owned. Every time that white dog he called Lily cornered a skink or a mouse or the neighbour's cat, she'd whimper in that same agitated manner. He winced. Poor little pet was just two years old when she died after being bitten by ...

He gulped and found a good-sized stick. One end was pointy and the other thick like a club. 'I'll take this along just in case.'

They began to climb up and around the knoll, via the same route Vann had shown him to the cemetery. On the far side of the rise were the two barnlike buildings constructed of timber and corrugated iron. Metal whirly-birds whizzed on the roof.

The electrified fence, it seemed, ran the entire perimeter of the compound. No easy entry and no escape.

Through the vegetation drifted voices, high-pitched and tinkling with laughter.

Seth motioned for Cate to get down low.

They squatted in the tall Guinea grass and peered between its rustling spears. Inside the fence, not two metres from their hiding place, were two diminutive women walking arm in arm. Both had straight black hair and both were unmistakeably pregnant. Seth cocked an ear to the conversation, but it was not in English.

He glanced at Cate beside him. The expression on her face was intense. She seemed to be following every word. As if in meditation she fingered the grass fronds, let them slip through her fingers. Suddenly she stood up and walked to the fence.

She greeted the girls with a bow. They began a whispered conversation in a language he presumed was Mandarin. Several tones higher than usual, Cate's voice flowed in the lilt of an Oriental opera. The exchange went on for maybe ten minutes, then Cate bowed again and backed away.

When she returned to the nest of Guinea grass, her face was flushed. She grabbed his hand and practically dragged him along the path to the lantana hide where the Jeep was parked.

'Go, go, go!' she said as soon they were inside.

It wasn't until they were on the highway that she regained her composure. 'That's the place all right. The girls are recruited from poor rural districts of China and come out here for a year. Yes, it's free of charge. And yes, they learn new skills. But not what they were promised. They're taught to use industrial sewing machines and they make high-end fashion. I'll bet it's sold as *Made in Australia* for an outrageous premium.' She snorted.

'So, it's a labour and immigration scam?'

'Yes ... I mean no ... it's more than that.' She was jumping out of her skin.

Seth pulled the Jeep to the side of the road and turned to her. 'Are you going to tell me or do I have to learn Mandarin and ask them myself?'

'Those girls haven't received one minute of English tuition since they arrived seven months ago. This isn't a *language* farm, it's a *baby* farm. They are our surrogates. The girls are paid for producing healthy babies. Afterwards they fly home to China with a pocketful of cash. A pittance to us, but to them it's enough to support their families for a year. It's all advertised on the Internet. There's a network of spotters in Beijing and Shanghai who go out to the countryside to recruit. The girls come in on student visas. And, because it's all in Mandarin, no-one in authority in Australia has the slightest inkling about what's really going on.'

'Until now. What a story! Cate, you're a marvel! Shame there's no pix.'

'Who says there aren't?' she said slyly.

She lifted a tiny digital camera from beneath her blouse and scrolled through the photos. There were at least two dozen taken at various points of their surveillance. Images of the old house, the dormitories, the electrified fence, and the two Chinese surrogates in captivity inside.

'Now we must confirm who's behind the scheme,' said Seth.

'Don't we already know?'

'We've got a big problem if we're wrong. There's also the matter of a bomb and death-threats to the Minister.'

He shoved the gearstick into first, clicked on the indicator and tramped on the accelerator. In seconds he was up to one hundred and twenty on the smooth flat highway.

'I'll do some research on this tonight,' she offered. 'Maybe I'll start with a search of the companies register. If Robair International is a legitimate corporation, there'll be records of the directors.'

'Tonight, I hope to get some answers myself,' he said cryptically.

28

Tuesday 18 March

Half an hour after she'd emailed the reply to Claire Jones, Vann parked the Mazda outside a modest three-storey walk-up about two kilometres from her electorate office. The building would have been constructed in the mid-seventies, a pale brick six-pack with a depressing line of tilt-door garages down one side. It was the sort of place you'd see on the news for all the wrong reasons. Drug labs, neighbours from hell, bikie gangs.

She locked the car and walked along the concrete driveway, checking the numbers. Unit 5 was upstairs at the rear. The staircase was imprisoned in wrought-iron bars. She gritted her teeth and climbed the stairs to the catwalk on the first floor.

The fall of her shoes on the concrete treads rebounded off the architecture. Eerie, empty, intimidating. At Unit 5, she knocked.

No-one came.

Vann pressed her spine against the steel bars and rechecked the address given in Claire's reply email. Had she'd mixed up the numbers or the time? She was so close, so very close. Minutes ticked by. Each one was agony.

Torn by conflicting emotions, she buried her face in her hands and wept. The course of both their lives had been cruelly altered by the one calculated deception.

The lies she'd been told! She flushed with rage as she remembered Puss-arse's smug expression the day she inadvertently signed away her one and only child.

She fumbled in her bag for the envelope Claire had left beneath her door. *Ms Vann Willis*, it read. Even her name was a lie.

Myfanwy Willis Jones was what it should have been. At university she'd adjusted her name and adopted a new persona to escape her parents and her past. She was nothing but a fake and a fraud.

Her hands, resting on the steel balustrades, were no longer the velvet hands of youth. Like the roots of a strangler fig, purple veins crisscrossed her skin. Lance was right, she was too old to keep this up. But she was too pigheaded to resign.

Once she was reunited with Claire, she might ...

Wait, you don't know this woman from a bar of soap. She could hear Merle's voice messing with her head.

Could she trust a so-called daughter she'd never met? Shouldn't she consider her faithful partner, the man she'd loved and lived with for a decade?

The hopes and dreams of a lifetime, pinned on this one moment, might turn out to be yet another swindle.

With slumped shoulders, she turned to leave when she noticed a woman walking along the driveway downstairs. A clingy green top and skinny jeans showed off her over-endowed curves. On her shoulder was a yellow bag. She disappeared momentarily beneath the building. Her footsteps clanged up the stairs.

'Lara!' said Vann astonished.

Lara blushed then burst into tears. In a tiny voice she said, 'Mary, it's me. I'm Claire.'

For a moment they stared awkwardly at one another. Then Vann threw her arms around Claire and they both sobbed with joy.

'Why didn't you just call me?' said Vann when she'd recovered enough to speak.

'I wasn't sure. I didn't want you to hate me if I'd got it wrong.' Claire unlocked the door to her apartment. 'Come inside, we don't want the whole world to hear.'

Vann followed her into a compact but functional living room with retro TV chairs and a low glass coffee table covered in food magazines.

'Champagne?' said Claire.

'Absolutely!' Vann put her bag down on the sofa and followed her daughter into the kitchen. 'You knew, didn't you? The day of the bomb.'

'Not then, but shortly after.'

The galley kitchen was fragrant with the aroma of fresh-ground coffee. Taking up half the bench was an enormous contraption with dual chrome spouts that looked like a Dalek turned barista.

Claire opened the fridge and took out a bottle of Moet. 'I bought this last week, after I came to see you. That's when I knew in my heart. I didn't dare say a word until I'd talked it over with Belle.'

'Who?'

'Belle Morgan, my friend from Toogoolawah. We used to work together. Last year she took a redundancy and went bush. She thought you were in the same dorm at *Maidenhead*. Don't you remember her?'

'I kind of kept to myself.' Vann cast her mind back to that dreadful place. 'Belle. Hmm. What does she look like?'

Claire thought. 'I wasn't around when she was sixteen of course, but I've seen photos. Long chestnut hair, slim, great tan. She told me her job was to cut out patches for hospital sheets.'

'Oh Isabelle. I used to call her *scissor-girl*.' Vann laughed. 'We weren't allowed to use surnames. On the first day there was a misunderstanding that put us at odds. Later we made it up.'

'I keep on pinching myself, hoping this isn't a dream.'

Vann gave her a hug. 'Me too.'

'Thank God for that tin my mother kept. Sorry, my *adoptive* mother.'

'Do you still have it?'

'In my room.' Claire disappeared through an archway and returned with a biscuit tin, sky-blue with red roses.

'That card you sent! Blue with roses, it was a hint.' Vann began to chuckle. 'This is going to sound creepy, but I've got a tin almost the same. Know what I keep in it?'

Claire, hanging on every word, shook her head.

'Letters to my baby girl. There's one for each year of her life. This time I can say it in person. Happy birthday!'

'Oh, that's sweet!' Claire poured more champagne and they clinked glasses. 'To us.'

The alcohol loosened their tongues. An hour passed in a whirlwind of revelations and stories about their lives and families. The rose biscuit tin lay unopened on the pile of magazines on the glass table.

Suddenly Claire grew serious. She took up the tin, levered off the lid and lifted out a bundle of old papers.

On top were Lara Dainford's birth certificate, the receipt made out to her father for an extraordinary amount, and some black-and-white photos. These Vann had seen before. Beneath, were newspaper clippings of weddings, births, funerals. Next was the title deed of the Dainford family home and mortgage documents showing a top-up of the loan in 1972. The final payment was made two decades later.

At the bottom of the tin was a document, brittle with age. *Agreement between the Parties* was printed across the top. Vann had been *Minister for Adoptions*—as Lance called her—for so long, she could recognise a genuine department adoption agreement when she saw one. This, most definitely, was not.

She skimmed the two pages. Some sections were typed; some were handwritten in blue biro in a style that was heavy and masculine. The baby was referred to as 'female issue'. There were no names apart from the receiving parents, the Dainfords.

Vann flipped it over. At the end was a section of fine print, followed by an unsteady autograph she recognised too well. Her jaw dropped. 'That bastard! He told me it was a death certificate. He made me sign. If he were alive, I'd cut off his balls and hang them out to dry.'

Claire squeezed her hand. 'Don't punish yourself. It's okay.'

For a few minutes they sat in silence, mulling over what had happened and what might have been. At length Claire said, 'You said something about the Doyles having a son. What if the scam's still going on?'

A kaleidoscope of emotions and champagne bubbles swirled about inside Vann's brain. 'It might explain ... '

'It might explain *this*!' Claire pointed to the scarring on her face. 'That bomb was no random act. If anyone's going to get busted over this, it sure as hell is not going to be us. We must track him down and stop him.' She banged her fist into the couch.

The theme from *Dr Who* wailed from Vann's handbag. The tension was broken. She dived for her phone before the call went to message bank.

It was Seth. 'Call me Sherlock. You won't believe what I've found.'

'Neither will you. I'm sitting on the couch with your niece.'

Claire's eyeballs were popping. 'I've got an *uncle*?'

Vann whispered to her, 'Do you want to meet him?'

'Of course! But you said you were an only child. That makes him?'

'Your *father's* brother. I haven't told you that story yet.'

Vann returned to Seth's call, trying to winkle out of him what he'd discovered, but he played it coy and said he wanted to tell her in person.

While she was talking, Claire's weight shifted from the couch. In the kitchen, plates clattered. The duel aromas of hot coffee and buttered toast wafted into the room. Soon after, Claire placed a lunch tray on the glass table and sat in the armchair opposite.

'Now,' she said settling back. 'Tell me about my father.'

29

Friday 4 April

Minister Vann Willis's last public appearance before the government switched into election mode was at the Riverdale Rovers Leagues Club. After the pre-season match there'd be a barbeque, presentations to players, and the opportunity to put in a plug for her Party. With free entry and an open invitation to all, there'd be high exposure but also high risk to her personal safety.

Ever vigilant Detective Sergeant Frame advised, 'Cancel or get someone else to do it. What about your understudy, James?'

But she'd have none of it. To cave in to an extortionist would be weak, an insult to the victims of the bombing. Whatever it took, she was determined to be a true representative of her constituents, right to the bitter end.

Tonight, she planned to make an announcement. A make or break statement that would change the course of her life. She'd pondered on it for days and had prepared two different versions. She was yet to decide which one to use.

Lance, she expected, would be hard to extract from his restaurant. *The joys of small business*, he usually said as an apology for not going to her engagements. He detested being *the Minister's handbag*. With animosity mounting between them, Vann had expected a battle. But he'd surprised her by volunteering to go without even being asked. He said he'd rearrange the shifts at work. In order to get away early he'd do the prep and entrees. Myra—the temporary chef—would stay for the mains and desserts.

Perhaps he was glad the whole debacle was coming to a head. Perhaps he was simply pleased to have a night off work.

Alone in her apartment, Vann pondered over her costume. This was a performance as much as any concert or play. As a female public figure, she'd learnt the hard way that her appearance always overshadowed the message she delivered. Early in her career, one newspaper reporter routinely dedicated her column to a critique of Vann's fashion sense. Her biggest *faux pas* in the nineties was to succumb to a cutting-edge maroon-and-gold balloon dress, which turned her then-slender body into the shape of a Christmas cracker.

She decided on black trousers and a classic silk blouse flecked with the red and green colours of the Riverdale Rovers.

After doing her make-up, she phoned her limo driver. Government cost-cutting measures meant she could arrive in style only on special occasions such as this. For all other travel, it was plain old taxis. If the budget situation got any worse, they'd find themselves having to catch the bus.

The notes for her two alternative speeches were safely in her folder. She checked the certificates for presentation to this year's players.

First division seniors, check.

Second division seniors, check.

Juniors …

They weren't there. She swore beneath her breath. That temp worker James had hired as Freya's replacement was totally useless! Monday she'd have to go.

The beep of a text message advised the limo was outside.

A youngish man in chauffeur's uniform held open the rear door. On his hands were white driving gloves. His face was partially hidden by the peak of his cap and a pair of dark-framed glasses. He wasn't the usual driver.

'Where's Frank?' she asked, breezing past.

'He's sick, ma'am. I'm from the Agency.' His voice was as stiff as his manner. 'I understand you're going to the Rovers Leagues Club.'

'Yes, but first I have to go to my office.'

He tapped a message into his phone and hit the car's ignition.

On the way he made a wrong turn, which necessitated a long detour on the motorway and a five-minute wait in traffic at the railway crossing. Then he was in the wrong lane to turn right and they had to do a lap of the back streets. His incompetence was so complete, it would have been funny had she not been running late.

The fleeting sub-tropical twilight evaporated as the car dived down the ramp beside her office. The basement car park was empty and in total darkness, save for the sweep of the headlights on the concrete walls.

He stopped near the stairwell, left the engine idling and the lights on while he skirted around the car and opened her door.

'Would you like me to accompany you, ma'am?' he said.

'No, I'm fine.' She punched the security code into the keypad and used the flashlight app on her phone to illuminate the way up two flights of stairs.

The upstairs sensor light didn't come on. She fumbled in her bag for the keys to the back door.

Inside the office she flicked the light switches to no avail. Outside, unlit power poles stood like fire-charred tree trunks in the dim glow of the western sky. Their shadows fell through the plate glass windows and inched eerily across the floor. Although she wouldn't admit it, she'd never overcome her childhood fear of the dark. When the kitchenette fridge rattled as the motor kicked in, she leapt in fright, then immediately laughed at her own silliness.

The beam from the phone panned her private office. On one corner of her desk were the missing certificates. Hastily she scooped them up, slid them into her bag.

Next to them was the commission of inquiry's *Report into Possible Corruption and Illegal Activities Relating to Forced Adoption.* Her pièce de résistance. Proudly she ran her fingers over its glossy cover. She'd prepared the government's response and had obtained the Premier's approval. A lot of thought and much soul searching had gone into it. An option she'd previously been adamant about—compensation for past victims—had hit the shredder. Tomorrow, one day before the pre-election caretaker period began, she'd announce the details at a press conference in the city.

She was confident her solution would meet with public approval, for she'd decided not to make the usual kneejerk response of indiscriminately throwing money at the problem. What she proposed would make a *real* difference.

She turned to leave.

In the door at the far end of the hall, a key clicked in the lock. She froze and listened. The only sound was the hum of the fridge compressor. She shook her head, berated herself for being such a scaredy cat.

Then came the squeak of leather. Her ears weren't playing up after all.

Footsteps.

Soft. Persistent.

Coming down the hall.

'Who's there?' she whispered. Her mouth was as dry as sawdust. She shut off the flashlight. No-one answered.

Gingerly she peeped out the door, into the tunnel to the rear exit. The vision of a barn owl wouldn't penetrate the blackness. Whatever had made the noises had stopped. Perhaps it was an overactive imagination, combined with four weeks of disturbed sleep and distress.

She sidled around her desk to the window that overlooked the street. In the process she stubbed her big toe on a metal stand, one of a set stored there. It hurt like hell, but she dared not make a whimper. Headlights flashed around the corner. The footpath was deserted. The businesses along the strip—the hairdresser, the coffee shop, the accountant on the corner—were shut for the weekend. If by day her office was a bright goldfish bowl, by night it was a cod hole in a dark and brooding river.

Suddenly her desk phone began to ring. Automatically she reached for it. Her hand hovered over the receiver. If she answered she'd give away her whereabouts. The ring-tone was shrill, insistent. Whoever was on the other end didn't give up easily. After eight rings, her nerves could stand no more. She picked it up.

A muffled voice said, 'I know where you are and I know you're alone.'

'Who are you?' she breathed.

'You've had three warnings and you took no heed. Now you will pay.'

The line went dead.

She punched in triple-0, but the phone was as silent as a block of wood.

Panicking, she pressed the pre-set number on her mobile phone for the police. A lame *blip-blip* advised she was out of battery.

She scrambled beneath the desk and hugged her knees to her chest. She must think up an escape plan.

The footsteps resumed. Slow, deliberate.

Shoe leather creaked.

Closer. Closer.

Through the window, headlights flashed.

Two black shoes stood close to her desk. Men's shoes. Chisel toes with a silver buckle.

Her heart was pounding so hard he'd surely hear it. She willed her body to stone, breathed like a butterfly. Papers rustled on the desk above.

'I know you're here,' he said quietly. His accent was clipped and precise. 'There's no point in hiding.'

She held her tongue.

'I can wait all night,' he said. The shoes stepped back. The cushion of the visitor's chair hissed. One shoe crossed over the other. He was toying with a mechanical device that made the metallic *ker-chink* of a precision instrument.

Vann shut her eyes, prayed it was not a gun. Her jaws ached, her elbows were stiff, her legs had gone to sleep. But be damned if she'd give up.

A piece of hard plastic—the telephone handset—dug into her thigh. With all her might she pegged it across the room. It sailed into the reception area and clattered against the tiles near the front door.

The shoes disappeared. 'Stop or I'll shoot!'

Her split-second chance. She grabbed the metal stand, heaved it against the window. The laminated glass crumbled with one blow.

Pushing her way out, she scrambled across the planter box and jumped to the footpath. Across the road she sprinted.

A car horn blasted, the screech of brakes. 'Stupid fuckin' bitch!'

She ducked into the laneway beside Café Nero.

Behind her, footsteps pounded on the concrete.

At the end was a courtyard with tables and chairs, potted palms, and a hedge of bougainvillea. She made a dash for the hedge, nicked in behind, flattened her body against the wall. Her lungs were bursting, she couldn't breathe.

He was almost upon her.

She had no strength left to fight.

30

Friday 4 April

Seth sprinted down the laneway beside Café Nero. 'Vann!' he puffed. 'It's me.'

The sound she made was little more than a squeak.

He sidestepped through the bougainvillea and snatched her up. 'Quick, through here.' He bundled her through a gap in the hedge, over a chain-wire fence and into the car park behind the cinema.

In a few minutes he had her safe inside the Jeep. He manoeuvred the vehicle around chicanes formed by dozens of potholes. On the main road he turned right, then right again onto a single-lane carriageway that wound along the riverbank. Around and down, past ritzy houses that hung off the cliff face, vying for a view of the boxy iron bridge and the murky waters beneath.

Beyond the playing fields he slowed to a crawl. Ahead was a driveway, partly hidden by trees. He turned in. The tyres made crackly noises on the gravel.

'Where are we?' she said.

'Home of an old mate.'

Through the bushes, houselights flickered. He cut the engine, unlocked her seatbelt and drew her to him. She flung her arms around his neck.

'How did you know where I was?' She clutched him so tight that her fingernails dug through his shirt.

'When I phoned your mobile and you didn't answer, I rang James. He was in a flap because you were late and he couldn't raise you either. I guessed there might be trouble so I swung by your office.' Reassuringly he stroked her hair.

'Thank you,' she said in a quivery voice.

He cupped her face and pressed his lips to hers.

She relaxed and surrendered into the embrace. Her lips were firm but gentle. Her delicious curves were soft against his chest. Crazy with desire, he moved his hand across the silk of her shirt to the cleft between her breasts.

'Don't ... we can't ... it's not right.' Her inner politician struggled for control.

Undeterred he clasped her hands, caressed her fingers with his lips. 'I can't let you go, Vann. Not now, not ever.' He sighed and shut his eyes.

She leant in and kissed him again, tender and deep. It was all he could do to stop himself from having her, there on the front seat of the Jeep.

'We should go in,' she said at length. 'Do I know this friend of yours?' She straightened her blouse and patted her hair into place.

'Indeed you do.'

In the doorway of the house stood a tall silhouette. 'Great news, we got him!'

'Well done, Detective Sergeant.' Seth shook Dave Frame's outstretched hand.

'Ms Willis, welcome to my humble abode. Would you like a cup of tea?'

'A Scotch would be better.'

They sat on a wide veranda overlooking the river and the city lights beyond. It was calm and quiet, save for the rustle of leaves, the grunt of possums and the devil's screech of overhead flying foxes.

Dave Frame said, 'It was lucky you phoned when you did, mate. The police car was there in minutes. They captured the suspect in a laneway beside a coffee shop. Seems he tripped in the dark and did his ankle in.'

'Oh God! He must have been right behind us,' said Vann shivering. 'Do you know his name?'

'Doyle. Barrington Doyle.'

Seth put his head in his hands and groaned. 'It's all my fault. I should have told you sooner, Davo. I've been on his trail for weeks.'

Vann arched an eyebrow at Seth.

'Bloody journos! You should leave investigations to the professionals. The man had a firearm. I could've lost my oldest mate.' Dave Frame frowned benevolently as he delivered his little lecture.

Vann explained the Doyle family's connection with *Maidenhead*, the deceptions that were employed, and the enormous sums of money that had changed hands.

'So why didn't *you* come to us, Ms Willis?'

'I'm trying to run a complex portfolio with many stakeholders. The commissioner's report is on my desk. Tomorrow I'm calling a press conference about the government's response to the adoption inquiry. That's when I could have told you.'

For his part, Seth bit his tongue. There was so much more he could have added. But it would blow the epic story awaiting a final edit. The baby scam had been going on for so long that another day wouldn't make much difference. Especially now that Barry Doyle had made a stupid move and had been taken into custody.

'Lordy, is that the time?' said Vann, checking her watch. 'I'm meant to be at the Leagues Club!'

'Cancel,' said Dave Frame. 'I told you that before.'

'I can't and the bad guy's locked up anyway.'

'I'll drive you,' said Seth.

'Can I get into my office to get the players' certificates?'

'I'll arrange for the boys to let you in. Take care, both of you.'

They piled into the Jeep and in less than five minutes were back at Vann's office. A young constable accompanied Vann into the building where she retrieved her handbag, the certificates, and the commissioner's report.

The fulltime whistle sounded as the Jeep entered the packed Leagues Club car park. Vann asked to be dropped at the entrance and insisted that he come in and listen.

As she gathered her things, Seth caught her hand. 'Good luck, gorgeous.'

She pecked his cheek, slid out of the passenger's seat and ran up the steps. As he drove around the car park, he could hear the boom of the loudspeakers. The chairman of the Rovers had begun his opening address.

He took the only vacant car space a long way from the entrance and trotted back between lines of parked vehicles. At the gate he stopped to catch his breath, another reminder he should give up the smokes. Maybe next month.

Inside the stand, he picked his way along the back row. At the foot of the podium James was a human coat rack, loaded with football jerseys, papers, and a ladies handbag.

To the right of the stage the footy players were grouped according to their teams. Although barely out of primary school, their bodies were strong and well-developed.

The stand was packed with parents and supporters. Everyone wore the colours of the Rovers, red and green.

Vann was introduced and the crowd gave her a hearty cheer as she walked to the microphone. For a politician she certainly seemed popular. But then again, she'd supported the Rovers since the club was founded in the nineteen-eighties. Thanks to her, they'd received government funding to build the clubhouse and do an upgrade of the grounds.

'Football,' she said, 'is not just a great sport. It is living proof that organised physical activity for young men boosts self-esteem, lowers crime rates and improves civic pride.'

Wise words and true.

On the podium she presented participation certificates to the players, introducing each one by name. Midway through, she faltered and glanced at the front row of the stand. A faint smile crossed her lips but she quickly regained her rhythm. Whoever was there was a mystery, for their identity was concealed by the bobbing heads of the crowd.

After the presentations, she said a few words of encouragement to the players then began what appeared to be an *ad lib* speech.

'Fellow Rovers supporters, I promise this will not be a long and boring speech. As we head towards an election you must be heartily sick of politicians.'

A ripple of polite laughter. Seth admired her ability to speak to a massive crowd with confidence and without prompts. It was a skill he'd never had much desire to develop. The very thought scared him witless. For him the printed word was what mattered, the rest was just hot air.

'Tonight, I want you to be the first to hear my news. My decision to stand for re-election was not easily made. I decided to go ahead because of unfinished business that has been swept under the carpet for too long.

'What I am referring to is the issue of forced adoptions and certain illegal activities that have been uncovered. The commission of inquiry established by the government has been a turning point in more ways than one. As you recall, it triggered a terrible tragedy that claimed the lives of two innocent people. One was a dear friend and staff member, and the other was a local man who added colour and diversity to our neighbourhood. This evening, thanks to the excellent efforts of the police and my good friend Seth VerBeek, a suspect has been apprehended and is now in custody.

'As well, the adoption inquiry has brought me personal joy. I was recently reunited with someone very important to me. You see, at sixteen, I too was a victim of an adoption scandal. My daughter, Claire, is here tonight.' Vann raised her arm to the grandstand.

Claire stood and waved, a natural public persona.

Vann positioned herself so she was speaking to the person in the front row. 'I've served the community faithfully and honestly for twenty-four years, but for me it's not enough. There should be more to life than duty. Tonight, I make this pledge to Lance, my faithful supporter and long-suffering partner. If I'm not fortunate enough to be re-elected, I hereby promise that I'll retire from politics immediately.'

She descended the stairs and made a grab for Lance's hands.

Impassive, his hands remained by his side, as limp as day-old lettuce leaves. They stood eye to eye. He spoke and she replied. Neither looked particularly pleased. Then he gave a lopsided smile and kissed her on the mouth. The crowd went wild as if he'd scored the first try of the season.

Seth's spirits drained away, down through the slats in the timber seats and onto the ground below. In all his years of news reporting he'd witnessed births and massacres, experienced famines and fires and storms. Once he'd been held hostage by a madman wielding a machete. But never—never in his life—had he learnt to understand women.

Defeated and destroyed, he turned on his heel and left.

31

When the polling booths closed at six o'clock, Vann was barely able to stand. An overwhelming feeling of exhaustion hit her like a two-ton truck. Yet to come was an endless night of watching and waiting with her supporters as the votes were counted. The hard work was over. She'd done everything she could do. The people of Riverdale had made their decision. Soon enough the outcome would become known.

In the function room of the Rovers Leagues Club, she positioned herself as far from the TV screen as possible. Preliminary results began to roll in. If the early booths went against her, she'd be in for a long night of fingernail biting. From a tall glass she sipped lemon, lime and bitters. It lacked the necessary punch. What she craved most was a nice strong Scotch and soda. But, win or lose, she'd have to make a speech at the end and it wouldn't do to sound pissed.

Much was riding on the outcome. She promised Lance that a loss would end her political career. In some respects, she wished it were already over. She could put up her feet and enjoy the freedom her retired friends bragged about. Lazy lunches, globe-trotting on low-season fares, reading entire series of novels, playing day-long tournaments of golf. All the pursuits she'd never had time for.

Was that what she *really* wanted from life?

Perhaps she could help at *Due Fratelli* until Lance's brother recovered from his broken wrist. From all impressions that temporary chef—Marlie or Mariette or whatever—hadn't turned out as well as they'd hoped. Lately Lance had said little about her, apart from grumbling about the extra time he'd had to put in at work, presumably to finish what she hadn't done. Yes, she could take the role of *maître d'* and leave Lance to concentrate on cooking.

The leagues club function room, with its own bar and servery, was like a vast industrial shed. Unapologetically masculine, the structural hardware was upfront and in your face. Steel girders straddled the walls. An oversized screen broadcast live coverage from the central tally room. The election post-mortems had already begun. A panel of commentators and political experts, including academics from two sandstone universities, took turns giving their predictions. In all, they made a formidable line-up of opinionated old men. Some criticised right-wing politicians like Vann for promoting left-wing policies. She didn't care what they said. Her hide had become as thick as a crocodile's.

Keeping her back to the screen, Vann drifted between guests. A perpetual smile was painted on like makeup. No matter what the result, that smile would remain throughout the night. In the morning her facial muscles would be stiff and immobile, as if they'd been injected with Botox. That was her way. Whether she won or lost, she'd keep on going as if the one result were as good as the other. Unforgiveable was when grown men blubbered like spoilt brats on losing a seat to a rival.

On the far side of the room James was working the crowd. Head and shoulders above the rest and trailed by several female admirers, he looked the part of an upcoming political representative. Her choice of understudy had been a good one. She might even pass him the baton mid-term.

She'd reconsider her position after the recommendations of the Inquiry were in place, for she didn't believe James would follow through. His heart wasn't in it. More than once he'd tried to persuade her to let it go.

'What's past is past,' he'd said to her. 'You should be forward looking. That's what the electorate expects. Issues like climate change, education reform, medical research, those are the way of the future. People don't want hangovers from the 1970s. They don't want governments to throw money away on ageing survivors who were screwed decades ago.'

Before she bowed out she was determined to get criminal convictions for those who'd profited from or swindled or abused vulnerable young women. As for compensation for the victims, for once she'd listened. Her *Pathways to Healing* program would celebrate families of all types and configurations. Funding would help parents and children reunite and deal with the issues that tore them apart. She was proud of her revitalised solution and excited at the prospect of launching it.

Tallies of the votes scrolled down the TV screen. The announcer worked his way alphabetically through the electorates. Riverdale was towards the end, right after Redlands. Although very few polling booths had sent in results, the commentators were already predicting a significant swing away from the government in favour of the PPP.

It was nothing more than an attention grab, as accurate as forecasting a cyclone when there was a low-pressure system halfway across the Pacific. Anything was possible, everything could change. Yet the self-assured commentator didn't hesitate to say *landslide defeat* and *annihilation* about the government's chances of re-election.

'Now for Riverdale. With two percent of the votes counted, sitting member Vann Willis looks to be in trouble. In the primary vote she's trailing newcomer Jake Stone of the PPP. This will be one to watch.'

Her blood pressure shot through the steel girders. *Jake bloody Stone!* How could anyone in their right mind have voted for a schoolboy? Throughout the campaign he'd scarcely strung together one intelligent sentence. He was all slogans and promises, with not one ounce of analysis or funding behind them.

Carrying two glasses of red wine, Lance brushed against her arm. He whispered in her ear, 'Does the ex-Member for Riverdale intend to keep her promise?'

'I'm not conceding defeat on two percent of the vote if that's what you mean.'

He grinned and continued walking to the corner table where his restaurant cronies were gathered. Out of respect for her, or for some other mysterious reason of his own, Lance had declared *Due Fratelli* closed for the evening. An unusual move, since boozy election post-mortems were popular sport and he could have made a killing.

Of course, his colleagues were ACP supporters but Vann couldn't help thinking they were mainly there for free grog and food they didn't have to prepare themselves. Looking particularly comfortable in her surroundings was the temporary chef. Myra was her name. Myra in the low-cut crimson top. Her jeans were so tight they could have been spray-painted on. She sat on a stool, legs slightly apart, stilettos hooked on the crossbars. When Lance offered her a glass of wine she reached forward. Her full boobs rolled into the V of the bodice, barely secured by a wisp of lace. If he noticed her obscene pose, he didn't show it. He plumped himself down on a stool and took up a conversation with his smallgoods supplier.

Vann was in demand herself. Everyone wanted to shake her hand or give her air kisses as if she were a celebrity. More small talk, more greetings. More glasses of soft-drink. Her stomach sloshed with syrupy fizz. The two people she wanted to see most hadn't yet arrived. One eye was on the door.

At last Claire appeared, the younger and darker version of herself, looking spectacular in a rich maroon blouse. Her hair was swept up and back from her face, her war wounds now completely healed.

She threaded between the guests to reach Vann's side. 'How's it going?'

'Too early to call, but that doesn't stop them from saying I'm gone.'

'When I came in, your mates were laying bets on Jake Stone.'

'Bastards! I hope they choke on the chorizo.'

Claire laughed and the world seemed right. Suddenly her expression turned serious and she brought a newspaper clipping out of her yellow Mimco bag. 'Did you see this morning's *Post*?'

'No. I've been a bit busy today.'

Claire laughed again. 'You've got a wicked wit, mother dear.'

Vann grinned. 'Please enlighten me about the latest journalistic triumph.'

'Tomorrow there's a lift-out report about forced adoptions, including revelations about a fraudster and a baby trade racket.'

Vann knitted her brows. She knew it was coming. She would have been a fool to believe her secret would remain buried, along with heartache and Coke bottles, in the cemetery at *Maidenhead*. She should have been relieved that Seth delayed until after the election. She couldn't hold it against him. Reporting was his livelihood just as politics was hers. All the same, she felt betrayed and disappointed that all she'd meant to him was an exclusive scoop and a means of progressing his career.

She gave Claire a one-armed hug. 'Thanks for the heads up. How about a proper drink? I'd love a Scotch.'

Three hours later the counting was all but over. As predicted the PPP had indeed enjoyed a massive swing, in particular in the city seats. The overall result was not entirely clear-cut, but with the distribution of preferences in the eight undecided electorates, the ACP was likely to retain government by a slim margin.

In Riverdale the result was too close to call. It would take several days for the outcome to be known and the postal vote could be the decider.

At the end of the night, Vann's victory speech morphed into a roll-call of *thankyous* to supporters who'd helped in the campaign. Despite her protestations that a celebration might be premature and jinx her chances, James cracked the champagne for toasts.

Sore-footed, weary and a little bleary-eyed at the end of a marathon night, Vann rang for a taxi to go home. Earlier she'd noticed that Lance had devoted an entire twenty minutes getting to know Claire. It was the first time they'd conversed since Vann had dropped the bombshell. Shortly afterwards, he made excuses about being on Sunday breakfast shift and promptly left without her.

All in all, it was a disappointing event. No definitive result, no certainty about her future, and now a big expose in the Sunday press to worry about.

When the taxi arrived, it was almost two o'clock in the morning. The *Post* would already be out. Instead of going home, she told the cabbie to take her to the central business district, to a vendor who'd sold early morning newspapers for as long as she could remember.

In the inner city young people roamed the streets in rowdy packs, bumping into each other, giggling, swearing, arguing. *Doof doof* music boomed from a brute of a ute that thrummed at the lights near the GPO. The driver looked like a refugee from the eighties with a porn-star moustache and hair in a ponytail. A drunken girl in platform shoes flashed him her tits and veered away laughing.

As Vann rummaged for coins for the newspaper, the phone inside her handbag beeped with an incoming text message.

Are you still awake?

She pushed the phone back in its slot and grabbed a paper from the stand. By the light of the streetlamp she flicked through the pages to a centre lift-out section entitled *Baby Farm*.

On the cover was a picture of two pregnant Asian girls, whose faces were purposely obscured. They stood behind a high wire fence with a gothic homestead in the background. Vann knew the place only too well.

She glanced at the by-line, expecting to see Seth's name. Instead, the article was accredited to Cate Bradshaw. Vann had never heard of her. Perhaps she was new. Certainly with an expose of this magnitude—the report and accompanying photographs ran to four pages—she'd soon be a household name.

The taxi's cabin light wasn't strong enough for reading, so she scanned the pictures. An office building in a riverside suburb, a Spanish mission bungalow in New Farm, an elderly woman in silhouette with a caged canary, pregnant women carrying heavy rolls of cloth.

'Have you made up yer mind where you wanna go?' said the cabbie. The engine was idling. They were stopped in a loading zone. Not that it mattered at two-thirty in the morning. The only vehicles around were other taxis.

'Riverdale. I'll give you directions when we get close.'

The taxi swung onto the road and roared down Queen Street, narrowly missing a straggle of skateboarders playing chicken at the lights.

The cabbie shook his head. 'Damn kids need a good kick up the arse. What're they doin' out this time o' night anyway? They should be home in bed.'

In the front seat Vann pushed the call button on her phone. It rang twice before a deep velvet voice said, 'Hey, gorgeous.'

'Why didn't you come?'

'It was your night. I'd hoped for your sake it would have been a victory celebration.' In the background ice clinked against glass.

'I just picked up a copy of the *Sunday Post*. What happened to your feature article?'

'Usurped by a wily colleague.' He laughed. 'All good. She deserves it.'

'I haven't read it properly. Does she reveal my misspent youth?'

'You're in the clear, I made sure of that. Once she gets her pilot's wings Cate's going to be a top journo. My word she is. Now, no more or I'll spoil the story for you. Go home and read. I'll call you.'

Vann settled into the vinyl seat of the cab. She released her breath. It fanned the downy hairs of her forearm. For the first time in weeks her jaw muscle loosened and her shoulder muscles relaxed. If she wasn't careful she'd be asleep before they reached Coro Drive.

Too weary to read, Vann dumped the newspaper on the sideboard and headed to the bedroom. Lance lay like a starfish on the bed. The noise he made was like a tractor grinding up a hill. In darkness she stripped off her suit and pulled on the daggy t-shirt she slept in. Pushing his left leg away, she wriggled beneath the covers. He didn't stir. She lifted his arm from her pillow and it left a trace of perfume. Floral. She fell asleep and dreamt of roses.

When she woke, the sun was high and his side of the bed was empty. For a few minutes she luxuriated in the warmth and softness of her nest. Then she remembered the newspaper lift-out and her trek across town in the wee hours to get it.

With a pink pashmina around her shoulders and a mug of tea in her hand, she spread out the paper on the coffee table and leant in to read.

The story was written in several sections. The first was about an elderly woman who, in the nineteen-sixties, had purchased a baby from a maternity nurse by the name of Sister Grice.

In the second Cate Bradshaw had tracked down the daughter of that nurse, who'd taken over the reins of the baby business and who now sold bespoke babies using illegal surrogacy arrangements. Photos taken at the establishment run by Julia Grice and her business partner, Barry Doyle, showed a typical sales contract. The babies were produced locally, taking advantage of an immigration loophole which allowed Asian students to work as fashion industry machinists throughout their confinement.

The journo interviewed two of the Asian women. They'd been duped into coming to Australia to learn English. They'd unwittingly become pregnant after an 'internal examination' which, they were told, was part of a health check. They had no money and no means of escape from a place on the western plains called the *Double Happy Language Farm*. The only redeeming features of the scheme were a ticket home to China and an envelope of cash after the baby was handed over.

The third section was about the Doyle dynasty and its stronghold on a baby trade that had gone on for decades. Deception and lies had played a major role. In the days before reliable contraception and support for unmarried mothers, pregnant teenage girls were recruited through Julia Grice's clinic in New Farm. Often the unfortunate girls' parents were the instigators who paid for them to be cared for at a 'rest home' in the countryside. It turned out they did everything but rest.

Maidenhead was run by Dr Rowland Doyle and his wife, Iris. Later Dr Barrington Doyle, their son, modernised the business and refocused on providing designer babies from surrogates. But there was the crux, neither Rowland Doyle nor Barry Doyle had ever been a registered medical practitioner, yet their con-man tactics had fooled three generations of desperate couples and thousands of young girls.

The entire operation had slipped under the radar of the authorities. The report went on to cover the circumstances surrounding Barry Doyle's arrest and his extortion activities involving several high-profile identities.

By the time Vann reached the end, her tea was stone cold.

What a shock!

She was breathless from the ride. Her hands were shaking. Outrage, but also relief that her dirty washing was still in the laundry. Could all those allegations be substantiated? She hoped for Cate Bradshaw's sake the facts were right, otherwise her career would be over before it began.

Her first impulse was to call Seth. She got as far as her handbag on the floor by the bed before having second thoughts. He'd said he'd call her. He would when he was ready. Perhaps he had plans. She didn't want to be a clinging vine. She had plans herself, a nice long soak in the tub with a good book and a bottle of wine. The last time she'd done absolutely nothing was so long ago she couldn't remember.

An hour later she was bored. The novel was so poorly written she'd binned it in disgust. Instead she cleaned out her wardrobe and filled a garbage bag with give-aways for St Vinnies. Sorting through her stuff and clearing out the crap was therapeutic. It marked an end and a new beginning. Tomorrow, or the day after, she'd learn if she was still a Member of Parliament. Now, as she tied the neck of the garbage bag, she couldn't have cared less.

Her main purpose in standing for re-election had been achieved by the Cate Bradshaw report. No-one, neither the police nor the government nor the opposition, could deny the culprits must be brought to justice and it must never be allowed to happen again.

At last it was out in the open. Just as the 1980s *Moonlight State* report lifted the lid on police corruption and prompted an inquiry that changed the system, so would *Baby Farm* be the catalyst for reform in the field of surrogacy and adoption.

On the Thursday after the election, the seat of Riverdale was declared. Only fifty-two votes separated the two leading candidates. Vann had expected it to be close, the wait had been agonising.

In those five long days, a staggering number of victims of the baby farm scam had come forward. The Premier-elect had announced he would have the legislation tightened to prevent further baby trafficking and the police had swooped on both the *Angels from Blue Heaven* agency and the *Double Happy Language Farm*. The young Chinese surrogates had been given temporary accommodation in a motel, pending a decision by the Immigration Department about whether they'd face deportation or be allowed to stay until their student visas expired.

When Vann got the call from the Electoral Commission on Thursday afternoon, it was the anticlimax of the week. At the time she was home, rearranging the pantry and listening to a debate about wild rivers on Radio National.

The voice of the senior public servant who informed her was as dry and brittle as a stick. 'Congratulations,' he said in a deadpan tone. She could tell he didn't mean it.

When Lance came in after his lunch-time shift at the restaurant, she told him the news. Instead of cracking the bottle of Moet she'd chilled in the fridge, he put on the electric jug and made tea.

'So, are you happy?' he said.

'It's what I wanted.'

'Good then.' He spooned honey into the tea and stirred.

'Look, I know it's not what you'd hoped for …'

'To be honest, Vann, you have no idea what I hope for.'

'What are you saying?'

He played with the rim of the mug, tracing circles with his fingertips.

'I asked you a question.' Heat rose up her body, her cheeks were burning, her head was full of steam.

'It's over, Vann. I'm leaving you.'

Suddenly her skin turned to ice and her throat was frozen. A single word cracked through. 'Why?'

'Our lives don't fit together any more. What you want and what I want are at the opposite ends of the universe. And while you've had your head up your own arse, I've been seeing someone who appreciates me.'

'Do I know the lady?' Her voice snapped like frost.

'You've met her, but I expect you didn't take much notice. Her name is Myra.'

She sniffed with distain. 'The chef with the boobs. I should've known you'd go for another foodie. Do you love her?'

He ignored her question. 'Don't play the innocent with me, Vann. You must think I'm blind as well as stupid.'

His face loomed close, his breath was putrid with garlic.

She turned away, which he seemed to interpret as an admission of guilt.

With renewed vigour he snarled, 'I've seen you flashing your bedroom eyes at a certain reporter who's been following you around like a lovesick pup. So, my dear, you are free to pursue whatever you wish. Your career, your daughter, your lover. Congratulations, Vann. You've got it all.'

Tears welled. In her heart she'd known their relationship was hopeless. In fact, it had been doomed from the start, an attraction of opposites with little in common. He loved food, she ate to survive. She wanted to save the world, he was happy to sit back and watch. Worse. He stuck his head in the sand and pretended nothing was worth saving. They'd rubbed up against each other so often that the thin layer of glue that once held them together had eroded away.

'Just for the record,' she said, 'unlike you, I *don't* have a lover. For what it's worth, I was faithful to you the whole time we were together.'

'I stand corrected. Your sense of duty before self is truly inspirational. As for me, I don't give a shit about duty. I want to live my life before I'm too old to enjoy it.'

'When will you go?'

Her nerves were quivering. This wasn't how she imagined it would play out. This wasn't how it was supposed to end.

'I'll pack an overnight bag and get the rest of my stuff tomorrow.'

He finished his tea, put the cup in the dishwasher, went to the bedroom and returned five minutes later with a bulging gym bag.

'Tomorrow I'll leave the key on the sideboard. That way you won't even need to take a day off work.'

Lost for words she chewed her bottom lip. On the bench her phone began to buzz. She glanced at the screen. *Seth.* What timing!

Lance had seen it too. He shrugged. 'You're a free woman, Vann.'

Before she could reply, he swung the gym bag over his shoulder and strode out the door.

His footsteps echoed along the corridor, the elevator took them away.

The phone call went to message bank. Numb, she sat on the stool and stared out the sliding glass doors at the horizon. Suddenly her life was a vacuum, a vast empty space between one sleep and the next.

Did she still love Lance? It was hard to say. He'd been there through her highs and lows, suffered her when she was insufferable and picked up the pieces when she broke. In her tumultuous public world, he'd always been the safe warm cave she'd escaped to.

Was that love?

She picked up the phone, pressed the button to replay the messages.

A rich chocolaty voice said, 'Hey gorgeous, just heard the news of your victory. Congratulations! Call me. Call me soon.'

Her heart skipped a few beats. Like a teenager again, she smiled in anticipation. She was about to go on her first real date with the *brother* of the boy who'd started it all.

Brushing the tears from her cheeks, she took a deep breath then hit the call button before she could change her mind.

* * *

Thank you for reading *Baby Farm*.
For indie authors like me, reviews are like gold.

If you enjoyed the read, please take a minute to leave a review on the website of your favourite bookseller or a reader review site such as Goodreads.

Thank you again and happy reading
Debbie Terranova

ACKNOWLEDGMENTS

Dr Venero Armanno. Inspirational, knowledgeable and entertaining tutor of *Year of the Novel 2012*, the Queensland Writers Centre course where this project began.

The ladies from *Year of the Novel 2012* in particular Marianna, Lucretia, Sarah, Zina, Kate, and Margie. Thanks for your honest critiques, kind words and reassurance.

My intrepid writing buddy Ruth Bonetti. You must have read this manuscript twenty times and never once complained.

My husband Sam for putting up with me during the long silent hours of self-imposed solitary confinement, and for holding my hand through the highs and lows of this frustrating and exciting creative process.

My daughter Elise and son Adam for listening and giving me encouragement.

Rosetta Lake Mills for the delightful cover design.

ABOUT THE AUTHOR

Debbie Terranova is a prize-winning author of historical fiction and crime mysteries with a conscience. She has been writing creatively for more than ten years and has published novels, novellas, and short stories.

The Scarlet Key, her second novel, is the companion to *Baby Farm*. The journalistic superheros, Seth VerBeek and Cate Bradshaw, are thrust into a gripping new crime adventure. Their challenge is to identify the body of a tattooed corpse. Why and how did she die? What secret life did she lead?

Debbie's latest release is *Enemies within these Shores*, historical fiction based on an untold true story. The novel is about life, love, and the internment of enemy civilians in Australia during World War Two.

Mowbray Brothers, a heart-warming short fiction about coming of age and brotherly love, was a winner of *One Book Many Brisbanes* in 2011.

Connect with Debbie Terranova

Website: terranovapublications.com
Email: terranovapublications@gmail.com
Facebook: Terranova Books

www.ingramcontent.com/pod-product-compliance
Lightning Source LLC
Chambersburg PA
CBHW021012120726
47905CB00009B/2970